The Editor

NICHOLAS CRONK is Director of the Voltaire Foundation and Professor of French Literature at the University of Oxford. He is General Editor of the *Complete Works of Voltaire*, the first scholarly edition of the entirety of Voltaire's writings, and also President of the *Société des études voltairiennes*. He has published widely on French literature of the Ancien Régime, and in particular on Voltaire.

For a complete list of Norton Critical Editions, visit
wwnorton.com/nortoncriticals

A NORTON CRITICAL EDITION

Voltaire

CANDIDE,
OR OPTIMISM

THE ROBERT M. ADAMS TRANSLATION

BACKGROUNDS

CRITICISM

THIRD EDITION

Edited by

NICHOLAS CRONK
UNIVERSITY OF OXFORD

W · W · NORTON & COMPANY · *New York* · *London*

W. W. Norton & Company has been independent since its founding in 1923, when William Warder Norton and Mary D. Herter Norton first published lectures delivered at the People's Institute, the adult education division of New York City's Cooper Union. The firm soon expanded its program beyond the Institute, publishing books by celebrated academics from America and abroad. By midcentury, the two major pillars of Norton's publishing program—trade books and college texts—were firmly established. In the 1950s, the Norton family transferred control of the company to its employees, and today—with a staff of four hundred and a comparable number of trade, college, and professional titles published each year—W. W. Norton & Company stands as the largest and oldest publishing house owned wholly by its employees.

Manufacturing by Maple Press
Book design by Antonina Krass
Production manager: Steven Cestaro

Library of Congress Cataloging-in-Publication Data

Names: Voltaire, 1694–1778 author. | Adams, Robert M. (Robert Martin),
    1915–1996 translator. | Cronk, Nicholas, editor.
Title: Candide or, Optimism : the Robert M. Adams translation, backgrounds,
    criticism / Voltaire; edited by Nicholas Cronk.
Other titles: Candide. English | Optimism
Description: Third edition. | New York: W. W. Norton & Company, 2016. |
    Series: A Norton critical edition | Includes bibliographical references.
Identifiers: LCCN 2015050883 | ISBN 9780393932522 (pbk.)
Subjects: LCSH: Voltaire, 1694–1778. Candide.
Classification: LCC PQ2082.C3 E5 2016 | DDC 843/.5—dc23
    LC record available at http://lccn.loc.gov/2015050883

ISBN: 978-0-393-93252-2 (pbk.)

W. W. Norton & Company, Inc., 500 Fifth Avenue, New York, NY 10110
wwnorton.com

W. W. Norton & Company Ltd., 15 Carlisle Street, London W1D 3BS

7 8 9 0

Contents

Introduction

Candide has been delighting readers continuously for over 250 years. The work was an instant hit when it first appeared in early 1759, and that same year no fewer than three English translations were published in London. Never since out of print, the novel has been translated into every conceivable language and continues to feed our imaginations by being repeatedly illustrated, imitated, adapted. For the first book under its new imprint, Random House in 1928 commissioned Rockwell Kent to illustrate *Candide* (and his image of Candide's house remains to this day the company's logo). Leonard Bernstein's "comic operetta" *Candide*, a collaboration with the author Lillian Hellman, premiered on Broadway in 1956 and continues to enjoy frequent revivals. In the 1950s the work was widely seen as a satirical response to the show trials of the McCarthy era, while 50 years on, Robert Carsen's 2006 production, perfomed on both sides of the Atlantic, contained an explicit satire of the leaders of the invasion of Iraq: it seems that whenever we are faced by dogmatism and absurdity, it is to Voltaire's *Candide* that we turn.

One reason, of course, is that this short novel is accessible—or seems to be. The sentences are mostly short, the story is funny, there are some good jokes, and the action moves fast. All this makes the book enjoyable and easy to read. But while it makes us laugh, it makes us laugh uneasily: this is also a book that sets out to provoke us, even to make us think. The subtitle of the novel warns us that this is a novel of ideas (*Optimism* is a philosophical term newly coined in the period), but what precisely those ideas are, and what we are to make of them, is by no means obvious. The background and critical writings collected in this edition cover a wide range of different approaches that will help deepen your response to this work. But first, here are some questions to consider as you read, and reread, this remarkable novel.

Do We Learn from Experience?

Candide tells the story of a young man setting out on a journey: this is an archetypal template much favored in the eighteenth century. Typically the hero (and it is usually a hero rather than a heroine)

vii

goes on a journey that is metaphorical as much as real, undergoing experiences that form him as a man. Behind this fictional model is the English philosopher Locke, whose *Essay Concerning Human Understanding* (1689) taught empiricism, the idea that truth is discovered through experience and experiment rather than being something innate. This is perhaps the key concept in the eighteenth-century movement of ideas that we call the Enlightenment, the moment, as Kant put it, of man's emergence from self-imposed immaturity: henceforth, he said, man should "dare to know!" In this perspective, Candide, whose name means "white" in Latin (*candidus*), recalls Locke's blank slate (*tabula rasa*) on which experiences are notched up. But how much does Candide really learn from his experiences? Does he ever really understand what happens to him? There is one moment in the novel, only one, when he sheds tears, which might suggest a glimmer of understanding or at least empathy with another. And what of the other characters, in particular Pangloss? He endlessly, comically, parrots the idea that "all is for the best," but how does this relate to his experience of the world? Or is it rather the case that we as readers can learn from experience because the characters in the novel cannot?

How Do We Achieve Happiness?

The eighteenth century was much preoccupied with the idea and pursuit of happiness. After many centuries during which the tenets of Christian belief had shaped absolutely all areas of knowledge in European culture, there was now a growing move to put man at the center of intellectual endeavor. This does not necessarily mean that religious belief suddenly disappeared, far from it; but religious teaching was now subject to public scrutiny in a way it had not been before and, equally important, man was put more squarely at the center of human enquiry. It is this strand of Enlightenment thought that culminates in the U.S. Declaration of Independence: the "unalienable rights" given to all human beings by their Creator, which governments are created to protect, are there described, in a famous phrase, as "life, liberty and the pursuit of happiness."

The question of human happiness is therefore a new one in this century, and the chapters set in Eldorado at the heart of the novel pose a direct challenge to the reader: is the life described there really the height of human happiness? Or is it rather a spoof on eighteenth-century notions of luxury? It is at least surprising that Candide and his companions discover this place of ultimate luxury, only then to escape from it.

The existence of evil is the most obvious threat to human happiness, and the eighteenth century came up with a new solution to the age-old philosophical question of why a beneficent God allowed evil to exist on earth. What seems evil to human beings, so the argument goes, appears so only because of our limited perspective; from God's point of view, the world we inhabit is actually the "best of all possible worlds"—in other words, evil doesn't really exist when viewed in the larger context. This response to the problem of evil, which in the eighteenth century goes under the misleading name of Optimism, derives from the German philosopher Leibniz, and a somewhat simplified version of this idea is associated with the English poet Alexander Pope, whose *Essay on Man* (1734) was widely read across Europe.

Leibnizian Optimism assumes a static worldview that has no place for any notion of change or evolution; at its heart lies a Providential sense of order in the universe, where God is in his place. It was common in the eighteenth century to suggest that this underlying sense of structure was proof of God's existence, the so-called argument from design. Voltaire liked to refer to "God the watchmaker": when you look inside a watch, you know that the machinery was designed and assembled by a superior intelligence, the watchmaker. Thus the design or harmonious shape of the universe is proof of a divine designer or creator. This idea (refuted robustly by David Hume in the mid-eighteenth century) is akin to the notion of "intelligent design," a concept much discussed since a key U.S. Supreme Court ruling of 1987 concerning the teaching of creationism in American schools.

Candide clearly plays with all these ideas. The character Pangloss is a mouthpiece for Optimism (albeit in a rather simplified version), and as he becomes increasingly a figure of fun, not least because of his spectacular inability to learn from experience, so the ideas of Optimism seem to be discredited. But is Voltaire's main purpose to discredit Optimism? Or to make fun of Pangloss's unthinking dogmatism? The question is not easy to answer because, even if it seems evident that Voltaire finds the Leibnizian solution to happiness rather doubtful, he does elsewhere seem to be in basic agreement with the notion of an underlying providential order in the world. The novel poses clearly the problem of evil; it is not so obvious that it posits a clear answer.

Where Is Voltaire's Voice?

In the first paragraph of Chapter 1, an "I" intervenes to offer an opinion: the presence of such a first-person narrator in a novel is a standard technique, but what is odd here is that this "I" then disappears for the rest of the novel, leaving the reader to ponder the somewhat slippery nature of Voltaire's voice. If there is one term forever associated with Voltaire's style, it is *irony*. The traditional definition of irony is that it involves saying one thing while meaning another. This sounds simple enough, though in practice it is anything but simple. In his *A Rhetoric of Irony*, Wayne Booth considers the complexities of reading a single sentence from *Candide*:

> Our best evidence of the intentions behind any sentence in *Candide* will be the whole of *Candide*, and for some critical purposes it thus makes sense to talk only of the *work's* intentions, not the author's. But dealing with irony shows us the sense in which our court of final appeal is still a conception of the author: when we are pushed about any 'obvious interpretation' we finally want to be able to say, 'It is inconceivable that the author could have put those words together in this order without having intended this precise ironic stroke.[1]

In other words, readers have to work hard at every stage to try to make sense of what precisely Voltaire might mean and to consider how we are being manipulated by the text. Does the irony create distance, as when the bayonet is described as the "sufficient reason" for the death of thousands, or generate empathy, as when war is described as "heroic butchery"? These two examples are both drawn from the opening paragraph of Chapter 3: the satire of war here is clear and devastating, but the complex and shifting ironies that underpin that satire are difficult to unravel. Faced by the multiple ambiguities of this novel, critics have often been tempted to take refuge in the final catchphrase about cultivating the garden: this, surely, must be the ultimate encapsulation of the work's wisdom? But is it? Or is even the title of Chapter 30, "Conclusion," to be treated with scepticism?

What Sort of Book Is This?

How we read a book depends very much on our understanding of what sort of book we want to read. The point is well made by James Thurber in his story *The Macbeth Murder Mystery*: a woman who only ever reads murder mysteries is given by mistake Shakespeare's historical tragedy *Macbeth*; blissfully unaware of this generic blunder, she has no difficulty in reading *Macbeth* as a whodunit, and even finds the clues to work out who the real murderer is (not the person we suspected . . .). Similarly with *Candide*: if we are told at the start that this is a novel of ideas, then we read it as such (even though readers have never quite agreed on what those ideas are). If, on the other hand, we are told that this is a comic novel in the tradition of *Don Quixote*, then it is equally possible to read the work as

---

1. Wayne C. Booth, *A Rhetoric of Irony* (University of Chicago Press, 1974), pp. 11–12.

an antinovel that draws attention to its own fictional devices. Modern fiction is born out of the parody of medieval chivalric epic, as practiced by the poet Ariosto (whose *Orlando furioso* was a particular favorite of Voltaire's) and later, in prose, by Cervantes (*Don Quixote*); so when Candide, driven mad by love, starts carving on the bark of trees the name of his beloved Cunégonde (Chapter 19), he is mimicking precisely the crazed lovers in Cervantes and Ariosto. *Candide* brims with allusions to what we might call narrative prototypes, and the shipwrecks, chance meetings, and amazing coincidences are all, at one level, spoofs of earlier adventure novels: this is a novel of ideas, certainly, but it is also a novel about novels.

One constant in these different approaches to the novel is the tension between order and disorder. The disruptive comedy of *Candide* is radically subversive, and it gives the lie to the Leibnizian world view that presupposes order and harmony. As readers of *Candide*, we try to make meaning out of chaos and to find order in disorder: we laugh at the end of Chapter 1 when the Baron kicks Candide out of the castle, not so much because the scene is comic in itself but because it parodies the Fall of Man and Adam's expulsion from the Garden of Eden. We use our knowledge of earlier fictions (and these include, in Voltaire's view, the Bible) to impose order on the chaos of the narrative, in much the same way that Pangloss strives to impose philosophical order on the world that surrounds him. This is a novel that makes demands on the reader because it forces us to reflect on how we make sense of the world. And it is because the world seems always in chaos that the novel remains always ripe for rereading. The words of the English novelist Aldous Huxley, written a century ago, still ring true:

> But read the book today; you feel yourself entirely at home in its pages. It is like reading a record of the facts and opinions of 1922; nothing was ever more applicable, more completely to the point. The world in which we live is recognizably the world of Candide and Cunégonde.[2]

NICHOLAS CRONK

2. Aldous Huxley, "On Re-Reading *Candide*," in *On the Margin* (London, Chatto & Windus, 1923), pp. 12–17.

Preface to the Second Edition

When Candide first set forth into the world, in January 1759, he did not do so under the aegis of M. de Voltaire, the well-known poet, tragedian, historian, philosopher, and friend of Frederick the Great. As illegitimale as its hero, the book *Candide* proposed itself as the work of "Dr. Ralph"; and if it had not been signed extravagantly between the lines with another and better-known autograph, would doubtless figure today only in Barbier and Billard's labyrinthine listing of anonymous literature.

The little book made its way, in other words, on its own—was read because it was amusing, and for that reason alone, and has only lately started to appear on assigned-reading lists and enumerations of "the world's great books." Now that it is a classic, I suppose the first thing the startled student must be told is that it is still funny.

The other things about the story, and there are a good many of them, come a long way after this first article.

Candide is a cruel and destructive book as well as a funny one. Funny and cruel: the qualities go together more easily perhaps than we like to think. But they would not suffice for the peculiar vitality of *Candide*, unless something else were added. If all it did was demolish a long-outdated system of German philosophy, its fun might feel as antiquated and its cruelty as gratuitous as Shakespeare's puns or Pope's malignant hounding after dunces. But *Candide*'s cruelty is not sour, and its fun remains modern and relevant. Dozens of heroes in modern fiction are Candides under one disguise or another,[1] as our standard heroine is a reworked Madame Bovary—who herself has more than a touch of Candide in her complexion. Why Voltaire's little book feels so modern clearly has something to do with the things it destroys and the way in which it carries out that work of destruction. But it is neither necessary nor possible to be peremptory in defining its targets, for satire generally works more widely than even its creator realizes. There's something in it for everyone.

---

1. For example, all the Evelyn Waugh and Aldous Huxley heroes, as well as Augie March, Holden Caulfield, Huckleberry Finn and all his multitudinous descendants, not to mention the "étranger" of Camus, good soldier Schweik, and an infinity of other battered innocents.

So the book's exact import is evidently up to the decision of the duly informed and sensitive reader—for whose individual responses to the actual work of art there neither is nor can be any substitute.

Though its action scampers dizzily around the perimeter of the civilized world, Candide is an essentially European book in its passionate addiction to, and scepticism of, the reasonable life. It could easily have a number of subtitles other than "Optimism"; one good one would be "Civilization and Its Discontents."

The present translation has aimed to be neither literal nor loose, but to preserve a decent respect for English idiom while rendering a French intent. It was made from the old standard Morize edition, still a classic despite its age, and especially useful for the dry, neat erudition of its notes. But in its late stages, the English text was read against, and modified to conform with, M. René Pomeau's 1959 edition, which introduces a few recent textual modifications. The text of Candide contains little that is problematic; it is clean and clear with only a couple of unimportant and relatively unsuccessful afterthoughts. When and where exactly the first printing of the first edition appeared is still doubtful; Voltaire was both a master of publicity and a past master at covering his tracks. But these fine points are for the difficult determinations of textual scholars.

As for Voltaire's prose, it is late in the day to pronounce in its favor; a translator, however, may speak with special feeling of its lucidity, lightness, and swiftness of tonal variation. It is a joy to experience.

ROBERT M. ADAMS

The Text of
CANDIDE,
or Optimism

translated from the German of Doctor Ralph
with the additions which were found in the Doctor's pocket
when he died at Minden in the Year of Our Lord 1759

Translated and annotated by Robert M. Adams

Candide

CHAPTER I

How Candide Was Brought up in a Fine Castle and How He Was Driven Out of It

There lived in Westphalia,[1] in the castle of the Baron of Thunder-Ten-Tronckh, a young man on whom nature had bestowed the perfection of gentle manners. His features admirably expressed his soul, he combined an honest mind with great simplicity of heart; and I think it was for this reason that they called him Candide. The old servants of the house suspected that he was the son of the Baron's sister by a respectable, honest gentleman of the neighborhood, whom she had refused to marry because he could prove only seventy-one quarterings,[2] the rest of his family tree having been lost in the passage of time.

The Baron was one of the most mighty lords of Westphalia, for his castle had a door and windows. His great hall was even hung with a tapestry. The dogs of his courtyard made up a hunting pack on occasion, with the stableboys as huntsmen; the village priest was his grand almoner. They all called him "My Lord," and laughed at his stories.

The Baroness, who weighed in the neighborhood of three hundred and fifty pounds, was greatly respected for that reason, and did the honors of the house with a dignity which rendered her even more imposing. Her daughter Cunégonde, aged seventeen, was a ruddy-cheeked girl, fresh, plump, and desirable. The Baron's son seemed in every way worthy of his father. The tutor Pangloss was the oracle of the household, and little Candide listened to his lectures with all the good faith of his age and character.

---

1. A province of western Germany, near Holland and the lower Rhineland. Flat, boggy, and drab, it is noted chiefly for its excellent ham. In a letter to his niece, written during his German expedition of 1750, Voltaire described the "vast, sad, sterile, detestable countryside of Westphalia."
2. Genealogical divisions of one's family tree. Seventy-one of them is a grotesque number to have, representing something over 2,000 years of uninterrupted aristocracy. Cunégonde, who is of flawless nobility, has seventy-two quarterings.

Pangloss gave instruction in metaphysico-theologico-cosmolo-onigology.[3] He proved admirably that there cannot possibly be an effect without a cause and that in this best of all possible worlds[4] the Baron's castle was the most beautiful of all castles and his wife the best of all possible Baronesses.

—It is clear, said he, that things cannot be otherwise than they are, for since everything is made to serve an end, everything necessarily serves the best end. Observe: noses were made to support spectacles, hence we have spectacles. Legs, as anyone can plainly see, were made to be breeched, and so we have breeches. Stones were made to be shaped and to build castles with; thus My Lord has a fine castle, for the greatest Baron in the province should have the finest house; and since pigs were made to be eaten, we eat pork all year round.[5] Consequently, those who say everything is well are uttering mere stupidities; they should say everything is for the best.

Candide listened attentively and believed implicitly; for he found Miss Cunégonde exceedingly pretty, though he never had the courage to tell her so. He decided that after the happiness of being born Baron of Thunder-Ten-Tronckh, the second order of happiness was to be Miss Cunégonde; the third was seeing her every day; and the fourth was listening to Master Pangloss, the greatest philosopher in the province and consequently in the entire world.

One day, while Cunégonde was walking near the castle in the little woods that they called a park, she saw Dr. Pangloss in the underbrush; he was giving a lesson in experimental physics to her mother's maid, a very attractive and obedient brunette. As Miss Cunégonde had a natural bent for the sciences, she watched breathlessly the repeated experiments which were going on; she saw clearly the doctor's sufficient reason, observed both cause and effect, and returned to the house in a distracted and pensive frame of mind, yearning for knowledge and dreaming that she might be the sufficient reason of young Candide—who might also be hers.

As she was returning to the castle, she met Candide, and blushed; Candide blushed too. She greeted him in a faltering tone of voice; and Candide talked to her without knowing what he was saying. Next

---

3. The "looney" I have buried in this burlesque word corresponds to a buried *nigaud— booby* in the French. Christian Wolff, disciple of Leibniz, invented and popularized the word *cosmology*.
4. These catchphrases, echoed by popularizers of Leibniz, make reference to the determinism of his system, its linking of cause with effect, and its optimism. As his correspondence indicates, Voltaire habitually thought of Leibniz's philosophy (which, having been published in definitive form as early as 1710, had been in the air for a long time) in terms of these catchphrases.
5. The argument from design supposes that everything in this world exists for a specific reason; Voltaire objects not to the argument as a whole, but to the abuse of it. Noses, he would say, were not designed to support spectacles, but spectacles were adapted to the preexisting fact of noses. His full view finds expression in the article on "causes finales" in the *Philosophical Dictionary*.

day, as everyone was rising from the dinner table, Cunégonde and Candide found themselves behind a screen; Cunégonde dropped her handkerchief, Candide picked it up; she held his hand quite innocently, he kissed her hand quite innocently with remarkable vivacity, grace, and emotion; their lips met, their eyes lit up, their knees trembled, their hands wandered. The Baron of Thunder-Ten-Tronckh passed by the screen and, taking note of this cause and this effect, drove Candide out of the castle by kicking him vigorously on the backside. Cunégonde fainted; as soon as she recovered, the Baroness slapped her face; and everything was confusion in the most beautiful and agreeable of all possible castles.

CHAPTER 2

What Happened to Candide among the Bulgars[6]

Candide, ejected from the earthly paradise, wandered for a long time without knowing where he was going, weeping, raising his eyes to heaven, and gazing back frequently on the most beautiful of castles which contained the most beautiful of Baron's daughters. He slept without eating, in a furrow of a plowed field, while the snow drifted over him; next morning, numb with cold, he dragged himself into the neighboring village, which was called Waldberghofftrarbk-dikdorff; he was penniless, famished, and exhausted. At the door of a tavern he paused forlornly. Two men dressed in blue[7] took note of him:

—Look, chum, said one of them, there's a likely young fellow of just about the right size.

They approached Candide and invited him very politely to dine with them.

—Gentlemen, Candide replied with charming modesty, I'm honored by your invitation, but I really don't have enough money to pay my share.

—My dear sir, said one of the blues, people of your appearance and your merit don't have to pay; aren't you five feet five inches tall?

—Yes, gentlemen, that is indeed my stature, said he, making a bow.

—Then, sir, you must be seated at once; not only will we pay your bill this time, we will never allow a man like you to be short of money; for men were made only to render one another mutual aid.

---

6. Voltaire chose this name to represent the Prussian troops of Frederick the Great because he wanted to make an insinuation of pederasty against both the soldiers and their master. Cf. French *bougre*, English "bugger."
7. The recruiting officers of Frederick the Great, much feared in 18th-century Europe, wore blue uniforms. Frederick had a passion for sorting out his soldiers by size; several of his regiments would accept only six-footers.

—You are quite right, said Candide; it is just as Dr. Pangloss always told me, and I see clearly that everything is for the best.

They beg him to accept a couple of crowns, he takes them, and offers an I.O.U.; they won't hear of it, and all sit down at table together.

—Don't you love dearly . . . ?

—I do indeed, says he, I dearly love Miss Cunégonde.

—No, no, says one of the gentlemen, we are asking if you don't love dearly the King of the Bulgars.

—Not in the least, says he, I never laid eyes on him.

—What's that you say? He's the most charming of kings, and we must drink his health.

—Oh, gladly, gentlemen; and he drinks.

—That will do, they tell him; you are now the bulwark, the support, the defender, the hero of the Bulgars; your fortune is made and your future assured.

Promptly they slip irons on his legs and lead him to the regiment. There they cause him to right face, left face, present arms, order arms, aim, fire, doubletime, and they give him thirty strokes of the rod. Next day he does the drill a little less awkwardly and gets only twenty strokes; the third day, they give him only ten, and he is regarded by his comrades as a prodigy.

Candide, quite thunderstruck, did not yet understand very clearly how he was a hero. One fine spring morning he took it into his head to go for a walk, stepping straight out as if it were a privilege of the human race, as of animals in general, to use his legs as he chose.[8] He had scarcely covered two leagues when four other heroes, each six feet tall, overtook him, bound him, and threw him into a dungeon. At the court-martial they asked which he preferred, to be flogged thirty-six times by the entire regiment or to receive summarily a dozen bullets in the brain. In vain did he argue that the human will is free and insist that he preferred neither alternative; he had to choose; by virtue of the divine gift called "liberty" he decided to run the gauntlet thirty-six times, and actually endured two floggings. The regiment was composed of two thousand men. That made four thousand strokes, which laid open every muscle and nerve from his nape to his butt. As they were preparing for the third beating, Candide, who could endure no more, begged as a special favor that they

---

8. This episode was suggested by the experience of a Frenchman named Courtilz, who had deserted from the Prussian army and been bastinadoed for it. Voltaire intervened with Frederick to gain his release. But it also reflects the story that Wolff, Leibniz's disciple, got into trouble with Fredrick's father when someone reported that his doctrine denying free will had encouraged several soldiers to desert. "The argument of the grenadier," who was said to have pleaded preestablished harmony to justify his desertion, so infuriated the king that he had Wolff expelled from the country.

would have the goodness to smash his head. His plea was granted; they bandaged his eyes and made him kneel down. The King of the Bulgars, passing by at this moment, was told of the culprit's crime; and as this king had a rare genius, he understood, from everything they told him of Candide, that this was a young metaphysician, extremely ignorant of the ways of the world, so he granted his royal pardon, with a generosity which will be praised in every newspaper in every age. A worthy surgeon cured Candide in three weeks with the ointments described by Dioscorides.[9] He already had a bit of skin back and was able to walk when the King of the Bulgars went to war with the King of the Abares.[1]

CHAPTER 3

*How Candide Escaped from the Bulgars,
and What Became of Him*

Nothing could have been so fine, so brisk, so brilliant, so well-drilled as the two armies. The trumpets, the fifes, the oboes, the drums, and the cannon produced such a harmony as was never heard in hell. First the cannons battered down about six thousand men on each side; then volleys of musket fire removed from the best of worlds about nine or ten thousand rascals who were cluttering up its surface. The bayonet was a sufficient reason for the demise of several thousand others. Total casualties might well amount to thirty thousand men or so. Candide, who was trembling like a philosopher, hid himself as best he could while this heroic butchery was going on.

Finally, while the two kings in their respective camps celebrated the victory by having *Te Deums*[2] sung, Candide undertook to do his reasoning of cause and effect somewhere else. Passing by mounds of the dead and dying, he came to a nearby village which had been burnt to the ground. It was an Abare village, which the Bulgars had burned, in strict accordance with the laws of war. Here old men, stunned from beatings, watched the last agonies of their butchered wives, who still clutched their infants to their bleeding breasts; there, disemboweled girls, who had first satisfied the natural needs of various heroes, breathed their last; others, half-scorched in the

9. Dioscorides's treatise on *materia medica*, dating from the 1st century c.e., was not the most up to date.
1. The name actually designates a tribe of semicivilized Scythians, who might be supposed at war with the Bulgars. Allegorically, the Abares are the French, who opposed the Prussians in the conflict known to hindsight history as the Seven Years' War (1756–63). For Voltaire, at the moment of writing *Candide*, it was simply the current war. One notes that according to the title page of 1761, "Doctor Ralph," the dummy author of *Candide*, himself perished at the battle of Minden (Westphalia) in 1759.
2. Hymns sung to give thanks for a victory; having both sides sing at the same time is obviously ridiculous. After hideous casualties, the war actually ended in stalemate, so neither side was entitled to a triumph.

flames, begged for their death stroke. Scattered brains and severed limbs littered the ground.

Candide fled as fast as he could to another village; this one belonged to the Bulgars, and the heroes of the Abare cause had given it the same treatment. Climbing over ruins and stumbling over twitching torsos, Candide finally made his way out of the war area, carrying a little food in his knapsack and never ceasing to dream of Miss Cunégonde. His supplies gave out when he reached Holland; but having heard that everyone in that country was rich and a Christian, he felt confident of being treated as well as he had been in the castle of the Baron before he was kicked out for the love of Miss Cunégonde.

He asked alms of several grave personages, who all told him that if he continued to beg, he would be shut up in a house of correction and set to hard labor.

Finally he approached a man who had just been talking to a large crowd for an hour on end; the topic was charity. Looking doubtfully at him, the orator demanded:

—What are you doing here? Are you here to serve the good cause?

—There is no effect without a cause, said Candide modestly; all events are linked by the chain of necessity and arranged for the best. I had to be driven away from Miss Cunégonde, I had to run the gauntlet, I have to beg my bread until I can earn it; none of this could have happened otherwise.

—Look here, friend, said the orator, do you think the Pope is Antichrist.[3]

—I haven't considered the matter, said Candide; but whether he is or not, I'm in need of bread.

—You don't deserve any, said the other; away with you, you rascal, you rogue, never come near me as long as you live.

Meanwhile, the orator's wife had put her head out of the window, and, seeing a man who was not sure the Pope was Antichrist, emptied over his head a pot full of —— Scandalous! The excesses into which women are led by religious zeal!

A man who had never been baptized, a good Anabaptist named Jacques, saw this cruel and heartless treatment being inflicted on one of his fellow creatures, a featherless biped possessing a soul;[4] he

---

3. Voltaire is satirizing extreme Protestant sects that have sometimes seemed to make hatred of Rome the sum and substance of their creed. Holland, as the home of religious liberty, had offered asylum to the Anabaptists, whose radical views on property and religious discipline had made them unpopular during the 16th century. Granted tolerance, they settled down into respectable burghers. Since this behavior confirmed some of Voltaire's major prejudices, he had a high opinion of contemporary Anabaptists.

4. Plato's famous minimal definition of a man, which he corrected by the addition of a soul to distinguish man from a plucked chicken. The point is that the Anabaptist sympathizes with men simply because they are human.

took Candide home with him, washed him off, gave him bread and beer, presented him with two florins, and even undertook to give him a job in his Persian-rug factory—for these items are widely manufactured in Holland. Candide, in an ecstasy of gratitude, cried out:

—Master Pangloss was right indeed when he told me everything is for the best in this world; for I am touched by your kindness far more than by the harshness of that black-coated gentleman and his wife.

Next day, while taking a stroll about town, he met a beggar who was covered with pustules, his eyes were sunken, the end of his nose rotted off, his mouth twisted, his teeth black, he had a croaking voice and a hacking cough, and spat a tooth every time he tried to speak.

CHAPTER 4

How Candide Met His Old Philosophy Tutor, Doctor Pangloss, and What Came of It

Candide, more touched by compassion even than by horror, gave this ghastly beggar the two florins that he himself had received from his honest Anabaptist friend Jacques. The phantom stared at him, burst into tears, and fell on his neck. Candide drew back in terror.

—Alas, said one wretch to the other, don't you recognize your dear Pangloss any more?

—What are you saying? You, my dear master! you, in this horrible condition? What misfortune has befallen you? Why are you no longer in the most beautiful of castles? What has happened to Miss Cunégonde, that pearl among young ladies, that masterpiece of Nature?

—I am perishing, said Pangloss.

Candide promptly led him into the Anabaptist's stable, where he gave him a crust of bread, and when he had recovered: —Well, said he, Cunégonde?

—Dead, said the other.

Candide fainted. His friend brought him around with a bit of sour vinegar which happened to be in the stable. Candide opened his eyes.

—Cunégonde, dead! Ah, best of worlds, what's become of you now? But how did she die? It wasn't of grief at seeing me kicked out of her noble father's elegant castle?

—Not at all, said Pangloss; she was disemboweled by the Bulgar soldiers, after having been raped to the absolute limit of human endurance; they smashed the Baron's head when he tried to defend her, cut the Baroness to bits, and treated my poor pupil exactly like his sister.[5] As for the castle, not one stone was left on another, not a shed, not a sheep, not a duck, not a tree; but we had the satisfaction of revenge, for the Abares did exactly the same thing to a nearby barony belonging to a Bulgar nobleman.

At this tale Candide fainted again; but having returned to his senses and said everything appropriate to the occasion, he asked about the cause and effect, the sufficient reason, which had reduced Pangloss to his present pitiful state.

—Alas, said he, it was love; love, the consolation of the human race, the preservative of the universe, the soul of all sensitive beings, love, gentle love.

—Unhappy man, said Candide, I too have had some experience of this love, the sovereign of hearts, the soul of our souls; and it never got me anything but a single kiss and twenty kicks in the rear. How could this lovely cause produce in you such a disgusting effect?

Pangloss replied as follows: —My dear Candide! you knew Paquette, that pretty maidservant to our august Baroness. In her arms I tasted the delights of paradise, which directly caused these torments of hell, from which I am now suffering. She was infected with the disease, and has perhaps died of it. Paquette received this present from an erudite Franciscan, who took the pains to trace it back to its source; for he had it from an elderly countess, who picked it up from a captain of cavalry, who acquired it from a marquise, who caught it from a page, who had received it from a Jesuit, who during his novitiate got it directly from one of the companions of Christopher Columbus.[6] As for me, I shall not give it to anyone, for I am a dying man.

—Oh, Pangloss, cried Candide, that's a very strange genealogy. Isn't the devil at the root of the whole thing?

—Not at all, replied that great man; it's an indispensable part of the best of worlds, a necessary ingredient; if Columbus had not caught, on an American island, this sickness which attacks the source of generation and sometimes prevents generation entirely—which thus strikes at and defeats the greatest end of Nature herself—we should have neither chocolate nor cochineal.[7] It must also be noted that until the present time this malady, like religious

---

5. The theme of homosexuality that attaches to Cunégonde's brother seems to have no general satiric point, but its presence is unmistakable. See Chapters 14, 15, and 28. Note also that the sides in this lunatic war are scrambled; though Candide is fighting for the Bulgars, they loot his home; but he gets "revenge" when the Abares also loot a Bulgar castle.
6. Syphilis was the first contribution of the New World to the happiness of the Old. Voltaire's information comes from Astruc, *Traité des maladies vénériennes* (1734).
7. A scarlet dye prepared from insects living exclusively in Mexico and Peru. "Chocolate": prepared from the cacao bean, perhaps a greater gift from the Americas to the world.

controversy, has been wholly confined to the continent of Europe. Turks, Indians, Persians, Chinese, Siamese, and Japanese know nothing of it as yet; but there is a sufficient reason for which they in turn will make its acquaintance in a couple of centuries. Meanwhile, it has made splendid progress among us, especially among those big armies of honest, well-trained mercenaries who decide the destinies of nations. You can be sure that when thirty thousand men fight a pitched battle against the same number of the enemy, there will be about twenty thousand with the pox on either side.

—Remarkable indeed, said Candide, but we must see about curing you.

—And how can I do that, said Pangloss, seeing I don't have a cent to my name? There's not a doctor in the whole world who will let your blood or give you an enema without demanding a fee. If you can't pay yourself, you must find someone to pay for you.

These last words decided Candide; he hastened to implore the help of his charitable Anabaptist, Jacques, and painted such a moving picture of his friend's wretched state that the good man did not hesitate to take in Pangloss and have him cured at his own expense. In the course of the cure, Pangloss lost only an eye and an ear. Since he wrote a fine hand and knew arithmetic, the Anabaptist made him his bookkeeper. At the end of two months, being obliged to go to Lisbon on business, he took his two philosophers on the boat with him. Pangloss still maintained that everything was for the best, but Jacques didn't agree with him.

—It must be, said he, that men have somehow corrupted Nature, for they are not born wolves, yet that is what they become. God gave them neither twenty-four-pound cannon nor bayonets, yet they have manufactured both in order to destroy themselves. Bankruptcies have the same effect, and so does the justice which seizes the goods of bankrupts in order to prevent the creditors from getting them.[8]

—It was all indispensable, replied the one-eyed doctor, since private misfortunes make for public welfare, and therefore the more private misfortunes there are, the better everything is.

While he was reasoning, the air grew dark, the winds blew from all directions, and the vessel was attacked by a horrible tempest within sight of Lisbon harbor.

---

8. Voltaire had suffered losses from various bankruptcy proceedings, which lend a personal edge to his satire here, besides diverting its point a bit.

CHAPTER 5

Tempest, Shipwreck, Earthquake, and What Happened to Doctor Pangloss, Candide, and the Anabaptist, Jacques

Half of the passengers, weakened by the frightful anguish of sea-sickness and the distress of tossing about on stormy waters, were incapable of noticing their danger. The other half shrieked aloud and fell to their prayers, the sails were ripped to shreds, the masts snapped, the vessel opened at the seams. Everyone worked who could stir, nobody listened for orders or issued them. The Anabaptist was lending a hand in the after part of the ship when a frantic sailor struck him and knocked him to the deck; but just at that moment, the sailor lurched so violently that he fell head first over the side, where he hung, clutching a fragment of the broken mast. The good Jacques ran to his aid, and helped him to climb back on board, but in the process was himself thrown into the sea under the very eyes of the sailor, who allowed him to drown without even glancing at him. Candide rushed to the rail, and saw his benefactor rise for a moment to the surface, then sink forever. He wanted to dive to his rescue; but the philosopher Pangloss prevented him by proving that the bay of Lisbon had been formed expressly for this Anabaptist to drown in. While he was proving the point *a priori*,[9] the vessel opened up and everyone perished except for Pangloss, Candide, and the brutal sailor who had caused the virtuous Anabaptist to drown; this rascal swam easily to shore, while Pangloss and Candide drifted there on a plank.

When they had recovered a bit of energy, they set out for Lisbon; they still had a little money with which they hoped to stave off hunger after escaping the storm.

Scarcely had they set foot in the town, still bewailing the loss of their benefactor, when they felt the earth quake underfoot; the sea was lashed to a froth, burst into the port, and smashed all the vessels lying at anchor there. Whirlwinds of fire and ash swirled through the streets and public squares; houses crumbled, roofs came crashing down on foundations, foundations split; thirty thousand inhabitants of every age and either sex were crushed in the ruins.[1] The sailor whistled through his teeth, and said with an oath: —There'll be something to pick up here.

—What can be the sufficient reason of this phenomenon? asked Pangloss.

---

9. By deduction from general principles.
1. The great Lisbon earthquake and fire occurred on November 1, 1755; between 30,000 and 40,000 deaths resulted.

—The Last Judgment is here, cried Candide.

But the sailor ran directly into the middle of the ruins, heedless of danger in his eagerness for gain; he found some money, laid violent hands on it, got drunk, and, having slept off his wine, bought the favors of the first streetwalker he could find amid the ruins of smashed houses, amid corpses and suffering victims on every hand. Pangloss however tugged at his sleeve.

—My friend, said he, this is not good form at all; your behavior falls short of that required by the universal reason; it's untimely, to say the least.

—Bloody hell, said the other, I'm a sailor, born in Batavia; I've been four times to Japan and stamped four times on the crucifix;[2] get out of here with your universal reason.

Some falling stonework had struck Candide; he lay prostrate in the street, covered with rubble, and calling to Pangloss: —For pity's sake bring me a little wine and oil; I'm dying.

—This earthquake is nothing novel, Pangloss replied; the city of Lima, in South America, underwent much the same sort of tremor, last year; same causes, same effects; there is surely a vein of sulphur under the earth's surface reaching from Lima to Lisbon.

—Nothing is more probable, said Candide; but, for God's sake, a little oil and wine.

—What do you mean, probable? replied the philosopher; I regard the case as proved.

Candide fainted and Pangloss brought him some water from a nearby fountain.

Next day, as they wandered amid the ruins, they found a little food which restored some of their strength. Then they fell to work like the others, bringing relief to those of the inhabitants who had escaped death. Some of the citizens whom they rescued gave them a dinner as good as was possible under the circumstances; it is true that the meal was a melancholy one, and the guests watered their bread with tears; but Pangloss consoled them by proving that things could not possibly be otherwise.

—For, said he, all this is for the best, since if there is a volcano at Lisbon, it cannot be somewhere else, since it is unthinkable that things should not be where they are, since everything is well.

A little man in black, an officer of the Inquisition,[3] who was sitting beside him, politely took up the question, and said: —It would

---

2. The Japanese, originally receptive to foreign visitors, grew fearful that priests and proselytizers were merely advance agents of empire and expelled both the Portuguese and the Spanish early in the 17th century. Only the Dutch were allowed to retain a small foothold, under humiliating conditions, of which the notion of stamping on the crucifix is symbolic. It was never what Voltaire suggests here, an actual requirement for entering the country.
3. Specifically, a *familier* or *poursuivant*, an undercover agent with powers of arrest.

seem that the gentleman does not believe in original sin, since if everything is for the best, man has not fallen and is not liable to eternal punishment.

—I most humbly beg pardon of your excellency, Pangloss answered, even more politely, but the fall of man and the curse of original sin entered necessarily into the best of all possible worlds.

—Then you do not believe in free will? said the officer.

—Your excellency must excuse me, said Pangloss; free will agrees very well with absolute necessity, for it was necessary that we should be free, since a will which is determined . . .

Pangloss was in the middle of his sentence, when the officer nodded significantly to the attendant who was pouring him a glass of port, or Oporto, wine.

CHAPTER 6

*How They Made a Fine Auto-da-Fé to Prevent Earthquakes,
and How Candide Was Whipped*

After the earthquake had wiped out three quarters of Lisbon, the learned men of the land could find no more effective way of averting total destruction than to give the people a fine auto-da-fé;[4] the University of Coimbra had established that the spectacle of several persons being roasted over a slow fire with full ceremonial rites is an infallible specific against earthquakes.

In consequence, the authorities had rounded up a Biscayan convicted of marrying a woman who had stood godmother to his child, and two Portuguese who while eating a chicken had set aside a bit of bacon used for seasoning.[5] After dinner, men came with ropes to tie up Doctor Pangloss and his disciple Candide, one for talking and the other for listening with an air of approval; both were taken separately to a set of remarkably cool apartments, where the glare of the sun is never bothersome; eight days later they were both dressed in *san-benitos* and crowned with paper mitres;[6] Candide's mitre and *san-benito* were decorated with inverted flames and with devils who had neither tails nor claws; but Pangloss's devils had both tails and claws, and his flames stood upright. Wearing these costumes, they marched in a procession, and listened to a very touching sermon,

---

4. Literally, "act of faith," a public ceremony of repentance and humiliation. Such an auto-da-fé was actually held in Lisbon, June 20, 1756.
5. The Biscayan's fault lay in marrying someone within the forbidden bounds of relationship, an act of spiritual incest. The men who declined pork or bacon were understood to be crypto-Jews.
6. The cone-shaped paper cap (intended to resemble a bishop's miter) and flowing yellow cape were customary garb for those pleading before the Inquisition.

followed by a beautiful concert of plainsong. Candide was flogged in cadence to the music; the Biscayan and the two men who had avoided bacon were burned, and Pangloss was hanged, though hanging is not customary. On the same day there was another earthquake, causing frightful damage.[7]

Candide, stunned, stupefied, despairing, bleeding, trembling, said to himself: —If this is the best of all possible worlds, what are the others like? The flogging is not so bad, I was flogged by the Bulgars. But oh my dear Pangloss, greatest of philosophers, was it necessary for me to watch you being hanged, for no reason that I can see? Oh my dear Anabaptist, best of men, was it necessary that you should be drowned in the port? Oh Miss Cunégonde, pearl of young ladies, was it necessary that you should have your belly slit open?

He was being led away, barely able to stand, lectured, lashed, absolved, and blessed, when an old woman approached and said, —My son, be of good cheer and follow me.

CHAPTER 7

*How an Old Woman Took Care of Candide,
and How He Regained What He Loved*

Candide was of very bad cheer, but he followed the old woman to a shanty; she gave him a jar of ointment to rub himself, left him food and drink; she showed him a tidy little bed; next to it was a suit of clothing.

—Eat, drink, sleep, she said; and may Our Lady of Atocha, Our Lord St. Anthony of Padua, and Our Lord St. James of Compostela watch over you. I will be back tomorrow.

Candide, still completely astonished by everything he had seen and suffered, and even more by the old woman's kindness, offered to kiss her hand.

—It's not *my* hand you should be kissing, said she. I'll be back tomorrow; rub yourself with the ointment, eat and sleep.

In spite of his many sufferings, Candide ate and slept. Next day the old woman returned bringing breakfast; she looked at his back and rubbed it herself with another ointment; she came back with lunch; and then she returned in the evening, bringing supper. Next day she repeated the same routine.

—Who are you? Candide asked continually. Who told you to be so kind to me? How can I ever repay you?

7. In fact, the second quake occurred December 21, 1755.

The good woman answered not a word; she returned in the evening, and without food.

—Come with me, says she, and don't speak a word.

Taking him by the hand, she walks out into the countryside with him for about a quarter of a mile; they reach an isolated house, quite surrounded by gardens and ditches. The old woman knocks at a little gate, it opens. She takes Candide up a secret stairway to a gilded room furnished with a fine brocaded sofa; there she leaves him, closes the door, disappears. Candide stood as if entranced; his life, which had seemed like a nightmare so far, was now starting to look like a delightful dream.

Soon the old woman returned; on her feeble shoulder leaned a trembling woman, of a splendid figure, glittering in diamonds, and veiled.

—Remove the veil, said the old woman to Candide.

The young man stepped timidly forward, and lifted the veil. What an event! What a surprise! Could it be Miss Cunégonde? Yes, it really was! She herself! His knees give way, speech fails him, he falls at her feet, Cunégonde collapses on the sofa. The old woman plies them with brandy, they return to their senses, they exchange words. At first they could utter only broken phrases, questions and answers at cross purposes, sighs, tears, exclamations. The old woman warned them not to make too much noise, and left them alone.

—Then it's really you, said Candide, you're alive, I've found you again in Portugal. Then you never were raped? You never had your belly ripped open, as the philosopher Pangloss assured me?

—Oh yes, said the lovely Cunégonde, but one doesn't always die of these two accidents.

—But your father and mother were murdered then?

—All too true, said Cunégonde, in tears.

—And your brother?

—Killed too.

—And why are you in Portugal? and how did you know I was here? and by what device did you have me brought to this house?

—I shall tell you everything, the lady replied; but first you must tell me what has happened to you since that first innocent kiss we exchanged and the kicking you got because of it.

Candide obeyed her with profound respect; and though he was overcome, though his voice was weak and hesitant, though he still had twinges of pain from his beating, he described as simply as possible everything that had happened to him since the time of their separation. Cunégonde lifted her eyes to heaven; she wept at the death of the good Anabaptist and at that of Pangloss; after which she told the following story to Candide, who listened to every word while he gazed on her with hungry eyes.

CHAPTER 8

Cunégonde's Story

—I was in my bed and fast asleep when heaven chose to send the Bulgars into our castle of Thunder-Ten-Tronckh. They butchered my father and brother, and hacked my mother to bits. An enormous Bulgar, six feet tall, seeing that I had swooned from horror at the scene, set about raping me; at that I recovered my senses, I screamed and scratched, bit and fought, I tried to tear the eyes out of that big Bulgar—not realizing that everything which had happened in my father's castle was a mere matter of routine. The brute then stabbed me with a knife on my left thigh, where I still bear the scar.

—What a pity! I should very much like to see it, said the simple Candide.

—You shall, said Cunégonde; but shall I go on?

—Please do, said Candide.

So she look up the thread of her tale: —A Bulgar captain appeared, he saw me covered with blood and the soldier too intent to get up. Shocked by the monster's failure to come to attention, the captain killed him on my body. He then had my wound dressed, and took me off to his quarters, as a prisoner of war. I laundered his few shirts and did his cooking; he found me attractive, I confess it, and I won't deny that he was a handsome fellow, with a smooth, white skin; apart from that, however, little wit, little philosophical training; it was evident that he had not been brought up by Doctor Pangloss. After three months, he had lost all his money and grown sick of me; so he sold me to a jew named Don Issachar, who traded in Holland and Portugal, and who was mad after women. This jew developed a mighty passion for my person, but he got nowhere with it; I held him off better than I had done with the Bulgar soldier; for though a person of honor may be raped once, her virtue is only strengthened by the experience. In order to keep me hidden, the jew brought me to his country house, which you see here. Till then I had thought there was nothing on earth so beautiful as the castle of Thunder-Ten-Tronckh; I was now undeceived.

—One day the Grand Inquisitor took notice of me at mass; he ogled me a good deal, and made known that he must talk to me on a matter of secret business. I was taken to his palace; I told him of my rank; he pointed out that it was beneath my dignity to belong to an Israelite. A suggestion was then conveyed to Don Issachar that he should turn me over to My Lord the Inquisitor. Don Issachar, who is court banker and a man of standing, refused out of hand. The inquisitor threatened him with an auto-da-fé. Finally my jew, fearing for his life, struck a bargain by which the house and I would belong to both of them as joint tenants; the jew would get Mondays, Wednesdays, and the Sabbath, the inquisitor would get the other days of the week. That has been the arrangement for six months now. There have been quarrels; sometimes it has not been clear whether the night from Saturday to Sunday belonged to the old or the new dispensation. For my part, I have so far been able to hold both of them off; and that, I think, is why they are both still in love with me.

—Finally, in order to avert further divine punishment by earthquake, and to terrify Don Issachar, My Lord the Inquisitor chose to celebrate an auto-da-fé. He did me the honor of inviting me to attend. I had an excellent seat; the ladies were served with refreshments between the mass and the execution. To tell you the truth, I was horrified to see them burn alive those two jews and that decent Biscayan who had married his child's godmother; but what was my surprise, my terror, my grief, when I saw, huddled in a *san-benito* and wearing a mitre, someone who looked like Pangloss! I rubbed my eyes, I watched his every move, I saw him hanged; and I fell back in a swoon. Scarcely had I come to my senses again, when I saw you stripped for the lash; that was the peak of my horror, consternation, grief, and despair. I may tell you, by the way, that your skin is even whiter and more delicate than that of my Bulgar captain. Seeing you, then, redoubled the torments which were already overwhelming me. I shrieked aloud, I wanted to call out, 'Let him go, you brutes!' but my voice died within me, and my cries would have been useless. When you had been thoroughly thrashed: 'How can it be,' I asked myself, 'that agreeable Candide and wise Pangloss have come to Lisbon, one to receive a hundred whiplashes, the other to be hanged by order of My Lord the Inquisitor, whose mistress I am? Pangloss must have deceived me cruelly when he told me that all is for the best in this world.'

—Frantic, exhausted, half out of my senses, and ready to die of weakness, I felt as if my mind were choked with the massacre of my father, my mother, my brother, with the arrogance of that ugly Bulgar soldier, with the knife slash he inflicted on me, my slavery, my kitchen-drudgery, my Bulgar captain, my nasty Don Issachar, my abominable inquisitor, with the hanging of Doctor Pangloss, with that great plainsong *miserere*[8] which they sang while they flogged you—and above all, my mind was full of the kiss which I gave you

---

8. The fiftieth Psalm in the Vulgate (Latin) Bible begins with the word *Miserere* (have mercy); it is fittingly included among the penitential psalms. "Plainsong": a particularly unadorned form of medieval music.

behind the screen, on the day I saw you for the last time. I praised God, who had brought you back to me after so many trials. I asked my old woman to look out for you, and to bring you here as soon as she could. She did just as I asked; I have had the indescribable joy of seeing you again, hearing you and talking with you once more. But you must be frightfully hungry, I am, myself; let us begin with a dinner.

So then and there they sat down to table; and after dinner, they adjourned to that fine brocaded sofa, which has already been mentioned; and there they were when the eminent Don Issachar, one of the masters of the house, appeared. It was the day of the Sabbath; he was arriving to assert his rights and express his tender passion.

CHAPTER 9

What Happened to Cunégonde, Candide, the Grand Inquisitor, and a Jew

This Issachar was the most choleric Hebrew seen in Israel since the Babylonian captivity.

—What's this, says he, you bitch of a Christian, you're not satisfied with the Grand Inquisitor? Do I have to share you with this rascal, too?

So saying, he drew a long dagger, with which he always went armed, and, supposing his opponent defenseless, flung himself on Candide. But our good Westphalian had received from the old woman, along with his suit of clothes, a fine sword. Out it came, and though his manners were of the gentlest, in short order he laid the Israelite stiff and cold on the floor, at the feet of the lovely Cunégonde.

—Holy Virgin! she cried. What will become of me now? A man killed in my house! If the police find out, we're done for.

—If Pangloss had not been hanged, said Candide, he would give us good advice in this hour of need, for he was a great philosopher. Lacking him, let's ask the old woman.

She was a sensible body, and was just starting to give her opinion of the situation, when another little door opened. It was just one o'clock in the morning, Sunday morning. This day belonged to the inquisitor. In he came, and found the whipped Candide with a sword in his hand, a corpse at his feet, Cunégonde in terror, and an old woman giving them both good advice.

Here now is what passed through Candide's mind in this instant of time; this is how he reasoned: —If this holy man calls for help, he will certainly have me burned, and perhaps Cunégonde as well; he has already had me whipped without mercy; he is my rival; I have already killed once; why hesitate?

It was a quick, clear chain of reasoning; without giving the inquisitor time to recover from his surprise, he ran him through, and laid him beside the jew.

—Here you've done it again, said Cunégonde; there's no hope for us now. We'll be excommunicated, our last hour has come. How is it that you, who were born so gentle, could kill in two minutes a jew and a prelate?

—My dear girl, replied Candide, when a man is in love, jealous, and just whipped by the Inquisition, he is no longer himself.

The old woman now spoke up and said: —There are three Andalusian steeds[9] in the stable, with their saddles and bridles; our brave Candide must get them ready: my lady has some gold coin and diamonds; let's take to horse at once, though I can only ride on one buttock; we will go to Cadiz. The weather is as fine as can be, and it is pleasant to travel in the cool of the evening.

Promptly, Candide saddled the three horses. Cunégonde, the old woman, and he covered thirty miles without a stop. While they were fleeing, the Holy Brotherhood[1] came to investigate the house; they buried the inquisitor in a fine church and threw Issachar on the dunghill.

Candide, Cunégonde, and the old woman were already in the little town of Avacena, in the middle of the Sierra Morena; and there, as they sat in a country inn, they had this conversation.

CHAPTER 10

In Deep Distress, Candide, Cunégonde, and the Old Woman Reach Cadiz; They Put to Sea

—Who then could have robbed me of my gold and diamonds? said Cunégonde, in tears. How shall we live? what shall we do? where shall I find other inquisitors and jews to give me some more?

—Ah, said the old woman, I strongly suspect that reverend Franciscan friar who shared the inn with us yesterday at Badajoz. God save me from judging him unfairly! But he came into our room twice, and he left long before us.

—Alas, said Candide, the good Pangloss often proved to me that the fruits of the earth are a common heritage of all, to which each man has equal right. On these principles, the Franciscan should at least have left us enough to finish our journey. You have nothing at all, my dear Cunégonde?

—Not a maravedi, said she.

—What to do? said Candide.

---

9. Spanish horses, proverbially swift and strong.
1. A semireligious order with police powers, very active in 18th-century Spain.

—We'll sell one of the horses, said the old woman; I'll ride on the croup behind my mistress, though only on one buttock, and so we will get to Cadiz.

There was in the same inn a Benedictine prior; he bought the horse cheap. Candide, Cunégonde, and the old woman passed through Lucena, Chillas, and Lebrixa, and finally reached Cadiz. There a fleet was being fitted out and an army assembled, to reason with the Jesuit fathers in Paraguay, who were accused of fomenting among their flock a revolt against the kings of Spain and Portugal near the town of St. Sacrement.[2] Candide, having served in the Bulgar army, performed the Bulgar manual of arms before the general of the little army with such grace, swiftness, dexterity, fire, and agility, that they gave him a company of infantry to command. So here he is, a captain; and off he sails with Miss Cunégonde, the old woman, two valets, and the two Andalusian steeds which had belonged to My Lord the Grand Inquisitor of Portugal.

Throughout the crossing, they spent a great deal of time reasoning about the philosophy of poor Pangloss.

—We are destined, in the end, for another universe, said Candide; no doubt that is the one where everything is well. For in this one, it must be admitted, there is some reason to grieve over our physical and moral state.

—I love you with all my heart, said Cunégonde; but my soul is still harrowed by thoughts of what I have seen and suffered.

—All will be well, replied Candide; the sea of this new world is already better than those of Europe, calmer and with steadier winds. Surely it is the New World which is the best of all possible worlds.

—God grant it, said Cunégonde; but I have been so horribly unhappy in the world so far, that my heart is almost dead to hope.

—You pity yourselves, the old woman told them; but you have had no such misfortunes as mine.

Cunégonde nearly broke out laughing; she found the old woman comic in pretending to be more unhappy than she.

—Ah, you poor old thing, said she, unless you've been raped by two Bulgars, been stabbed twice in the belly, seen two of your castles destroyed, witnessed the murder of two of your mothers and two of your fathers, and watched two of your lovers being whipped in an auto-da-fé, I do not see how you can have had it worse than me. Besides, I was born a baroness, with seventy-two quarterings, and I have worked in a scullery.

---

2. Actually, Colonia del Sacramento. Voltaire took great interest in the Jesuit role in Paraguay, which he has much oversimplified and largely misrepresented here in the interests of his satire. In 1750 they did, however, offer armed resistance to an agreement made between Spain and Portugal. They were subdued and expelled in 1769.

—My lady, replied the old woman, you do not know my birth and rank; and if I showed you my rear end, you would not talk as you do, you might even speak with less assurance.

These words inspired great curiosity in Candide and Cunégonde, which the old woman satisfied with this story.

CHAPTER II

The Old Woman's Story

—My eyes were not always bloodshot and red-rimmed, my nose did not always touch my chin, and I was not born a servant. I am in fact the daughter of Pope Urban the Tenth and the Princess of Palestrina.[3] Till the age of fourteen, I lived in a palace so splendid that all the castles of all your German barons would not have served it as a stable; a single one of my dresses was worth more than all the assembled magnificence of Westphalia. I grew in beauty, in charm, in talent, surrounded by pleasures, dignities, and glowing visions of the future. Already I was inspiring the young men to love; my breast was formed—and what a breast! white, firm, with the shape of the Venus de Medici; and what eyes! what lashes, what black brows! What fire flashed from my glances and outshone the glitter of the stars, as the local poets used to tell me! The women who helped me dress and undress fell into ecstasies, whether they looked at me from in front or behind; and all the men wanted to be in their place.

—I was engaged to the ruling prince of Massa-Carrara; and what a prince he was! as handsome as I, softness and charm compounded, brilliantly witty, and madly in love with me. I loved him in return as one loves for the first time, with a devotion approaching idolatry. The wedding preparations had been made, with a splendor and magnificence never heard of before; nothing but celebrations, masks, and comic operas, uninterruptedly; and all Italy composed in my honor sonnets of which not one was even passable. I had almost attained the very peak of bliss, when an old marquise who had been the mistress of my prince invited him to her house for a cup of chocolate. He died in less than two hours, amid horrifying convulsions. But that was only a trifle. My mother, in complete despair (though less afflicted than I), wished to escape for a while the oppressive atmosphere of grief. She owned a handsome property near Gaeta.[4] We embarked on a papal galley gilded like the altar of St. Peter's in

---

3. Voltaire left behind a comment on this passage, a note first published in 1829: "Note the extreme discretion of the author: hitherto there has never been a pope named Urban X; he avoided attributing a bastard to a known pope. What circumspection! what an exquisite conscience!"

4. About halfway between Rome and Naples.

Rome. Suddenly a pirate ship from Salé[5] swept down and boarded us. Our soldiers defended themselves as papal troops usually do; falling on their knees and throwing down their arms, they begged of the corsair absolution *in articulo mortis*.[6]

—They were promptly stripped as naked as monkeys, and so was my mother, and so were our maids of honor, and so was I too. It's a very remarkable thing, the energy these gentlemen put into stripping people. But what surprised me even more was that they stuck their fingers in a place where we women usually admit only a syringe. This ceremony seemed a bit odd to me, as foreign usages always do when one hasn't traveled. They only wanted to see if we didn't have some diamonds hidden there; and I soon learned that it's a custom of long standing among the genteel folk who swarm the seas. I learned that my lords the very religious knights of Malta never overlook this ceremony when they capture Turks, whether male or female; it's one of those international laws which have never been questioned.

—I won't try to explain how painful it is for a young princess to be carried off into slavery in Morocco with her mother. You can imagine everything we had to suffer on the pirate ship. My mother was still very beautiful; our maids of honor, our mere chambermaids, were more charming than anything one could find in all Africa. As for myself, I was ravishing, I was loveliness and grace supreme, and I was a virgin. I did not remain so for long; the flower which had been kept for the handsome prince of Massa-Carrara was plucked by the corsair captain; he was an abominable negro, who thought he was doing me a great favor. My Lady the Princess of Palestrina and I must have been strong indeed to bear what we did during our journey to Morocco. But on with my story; these are such common matters that they are not worth describing.

—Morocco was knee deep in blood when we arrived. Of the fifty sons of the emperor Muley-Ismael,[7] each had his faction, which produced in effect fifty civil wars, of blacks against blacks, of blacks against browns, halfbreeds against halfbreeds; throughout the length and breadth of the empire, nothing but one continual carnage.

—Scarcely had we stepped ashore, when some negroes of a faction hostile to my captor arrived to take charge of his plunder. After the diamonds and gold, we women were the most prized possessions. I was now witness of a struggle such as you never see in the

5. A seaport town in Morocco.
6. Literally, when at the point of death. Absolution from a corsair in the act of murdering one is of very dubious validity.
7. Having reigned for more than 50 years, a potent and ruthless sultan of Morocco, he died in 1727 and left his kingdom in much the condition described.

temperate climate of Europe. Northern people don't have hot blood; they don't feel the absolute fury for women which is common in Africa. Europeans seem to have milk in their veins; it is vitriol or liquid fire that pulses through these people around Mount Atlas. The fight for possession of us raged with the fury of the lions, tigers, and poisonous vipers of that land. A Moor snatched my mother by the right arm, the first mate held her by the left; a Moorish soldier grabbed one leg, one of our pirates the other. In a moment's time almost all our girls were being dragged four different ways. My captain held me behind him while with his scimitar he killed everyone who braved his fury. At last I saw all our Italian women, including my mother, torn to pieces, cut to bits, murdered by the monsters who were fighting over them. My captive companions, their captors, soldiers, sailors, blacks, browns, whites, mulattoes, and at last my captain, all were killed, and I remained half dead on a mountain of corpses. Similar scenes were occurring, as is well known, for more than three hundred leagues around, without anyone skimping on the five prayers a day decreed by Mohammed.

—With great pain, I untangled myself from this vast heap of bleeding bodies, and dragged myself under a great orange tree by a neighboring brook, where I collapsed, from terror, exhaustion, horror, despair, and hunger. Shortly, my weary mind surrendered to a sleep which was more of a swoon than a rest. I was in this state of weakness and languor, between life and death, when I felt myself touched by something which moved over my body. Opening my eyes, I saw a white man, rather attractive, who was groaning and saying under his breath: 'O che sciagura d'essere senza coglioni!'[8]

CHAPTER 12

The Old Woman's Story Continued

—Amazed and delighted to hear my native tongue, and no less surprised by what this man was saying, I told him that there were worse evils than those he was complaining of. In a few words, I described to him the horrors I had undergone, and then fainted again. He carried me to a nearby house, put me to bed, gave me something to eat, served me, flattered me, comforted me, told me he had never seen anyone so lovely, and added that he had never before regretted so much the loss of what nobody could give him back.

'I was born at Naples, he told me, where they caponize two or three thousand children every year; some die of it, others acquire a voice more beautiful than any woman's, still others go on to become

---

8. "Oh what a misfortune to have no testicles!"

governors of kingdoms.[9] The operation was a great success with me, and I became court musician to the Princess of Palestrina . . .

'Of my mother,' I exclaimed.

'Of your mother,' cried he, bursting into tears; 'then you must be the princess whom I raised till she was six, and who already gave promise of becoming as beautiful as you are now!'

'I am that very princess; my mother lies dead, not a hundred yards from here, cut into quarters and buried under a pile of corpses.'

—I told him my adventures, he told me his: that he had been sent by a Christian power to the King of Morocco, to conclude a treaty granting him gunpowder, cannon, and ships with which to liquidate the traders of the other Christian powers.

'My mission is concluded,' said this honest eunuch; 'I shall take ship at Ceuta and bring you back to Italy. *Ma che sciagura d'essere senza coglioni!'*

—I thanked him with tears of gratitude, and instead of returning me to Italy, he took me to Algiers and sold me to the dey of that country. Hardly had the sale taken place, when that plague which has made the rounds of Africa, Asia, and Europe broke out in full fury at Algiers. You have seen earthquakes; but tell me, young lady, have you ever had the plague?

—Never, replied the baroness.

—If you had had it, said the old woman, you would agree that it is far worse than an earthquake. It is very frequent in Africa, and I had it. Imagine, if you will, the situation of a pope's daughter, fifteen years old, who in three months' time had experienced poverty, slavery, had been raped almost every day, had seen her mother quartered, had suffered from famine and war, and who now was dying of pestilence in Algiers. As a matter of fact, I did not die; but the eunuch and the dey and nearly the entire seraglio of Algiers perished.

—When the first horrors of this ghastly plague had passed, the slaves of the dey were sold. A merchant bought me and took me to Tunis; there he sold me to another merchant, who resold me at Tripoli; from Tripoli I was sold to Alexandria, from Alexandria resold to Smyrna, from Smyrna to Constantinople. I ended by belonging to an aga of janizaries, who was shortly ordered to defend Azov against the besieging Russians.[1]

9. The castrato Farinelli (1705–82), originally a singer, came to exercise considerable political influence on the kings of Spain, Philip V and Ferdinand VI.
1. Azov, near the mouth of the Don, was besieged by the Russians under Peter the Great in 1695–96. "Aga": or agha; in Muslim countries, a military commander about equivalent to a major. "Janizaries": slaves, prisoners, or captured Christians who served the sultan as an elite group of mercenary soldiers.

—The aga, who was a gallant soldier, took his whole seraglio with him, and established us in a little fort amid the Maeotian marshes,[2] guarded by two black eunuchs and twenty soldiers. Our side killed a prodigious number of Russians, but they paid us back nicely. Azov was put to fire and sword without respect for age or sex; only our little fort continued to resist, and the enemy determined to starve us out. The twenty janizaries had sworn never to surrender. Reduced to the last extremities of hunger, they were forced to eat our two eunuchs, lest they violate their oaths. After several more days, they decided to eat the women too.

—We had an imam,[3] very pious and sympathetic, who delivered an excellent sermon, persuading them not to kill us altogether.

'Just cut off a single rumpsteak from each of these ladies,' he said, 'and you'll have a fine meal. Then if you should need another, you can come back in a few days and have as much again; heaven will bless your charitable action, and you will be saved.'

—His eloquence was splendid, and he persuaded them. We underwent this horrible operation. The imam treated us all with the ointment that they use on newly circumcised children. We were at the point of death.

—Scarcely had the janizaries finished the meal for which we furnished the materials, when the Russians appeared in flat-bottomed boats; not a janizary escaped. The Russians paid no attention to the state we were in; but there are French physicians everywhere, and one of them, who knew his trade, took care of us. He cured us, and I shall remember all my life that when my wounds were healed, he made me a proposition. For the rest, he counselled us simply to have patience, assuring us that the same thing had happened in several other sieges, and that it was according to the laws of war.

—As soon as my companions could walk, we were herded off to Moscow. In the division of booty, I fell to a boyar who made me work in his garden, and gave me twenty whiplashes a day; but when he was broken on the wheel after about two years, with thirty other boyars, over some little court intrigue,[4] I seized the occasion; I ran away; I crossed all Russia; I was for a long time a chambermaid in Riga, then at Rostock, Wismar, Leipzig. Cassel, Utrecht, Leyden. The Hague, Rotterdam; I grew old in misery and shame, having only half a backside and remembering always that I was the daughter of a Pope. A hundred times I wanted to kill myself, but always I

---

2. The Roman name of the so-called Sea of Azov, a shallow swampy lake near the town.
3. In effect, a chaplain.
4. What Voltaire has in mind here was an ineffectual conspiracy against Peter the Great known as the "revolt of the strelitz" or musketeers, which took place in 1698. Though easily put down, it provoked from the emperor a massive and atrocious program of reprisals. "Boyar": a class of petty Russian nobility.

loved life more. This ridiculous weakness is perhaps one of our worst instincts; is anything more stupid than choosing to carry a burden that really one wants to cast on the ground? to hold existence in horror, and yet to cling to it? to fondle the serpent which devours us till it has eaten out our heart?

—In the countries through which I have been forced to wander, in the taverns where I have had to work, I have seen a vast number of people who hated their existence; but I never saw more than a dozen who deliberately put an end to their own misery: three negroes, four Englishmen, four Genevans, and a German professor named Robeck.[5] My last post was as servant to the jew Don Issachar; he attached me to your service, my lovely one; and I attached myself to your destiny, till I have become more concerned with your fate than with my own. I would not even have mentioned my own misfortunes, if you had not irked me a bit, and if it weren't the custom, on shipboard, to pass the time with stories. In a word, my lady, I have had some experience of the world, I know it; why not try this diversion? Ask every passenger on this ship to tell you his story, and if you find a single one who has not often cursed the day of his birth, who has not often told himself that he is the most miserable of men, then you may throw me overboard head first.

CHAPTER 13

How Candide Was Forced to Leave the Lovely Cunégonde and the Old Woman

Having heard out the old woman's story, the lovely Cunégonde paid her the respects which were appropriate to a person of her rank and merit. She took up the wager as well, and got all the passengers, one after another, to tell her their adventures. She and Candide had to agree that the old woman had been right.

—It's certainly too bad, said Candide, that the wise Pangloss was hanged, contrary to the custom of autos-da-fé; he would have admirable things to say of the physical evil and moral evil which cover land and sea, and I might feel within me the impulse to dare to raise several polite objections.

As the passengers recited their stories, the boat made steady progress, and presently landed at Buenos Aires. Cunégonde, Captain Candide, and the old woman went to call on the governor, Don Fernando d'Ibaraa y Figueroa y Mascarenes y Lampourdos y Souza. This

---

5. Johann Robeck (1672–1739) published a treatise advocating suicide and showed his conviction by drowning himself. But he waited till he was 67 before putting his theory to the test. For a larger view of the issue, see L. C. Crocker, "The Discussion of Suicide in the 18th Century," *Journal of the History of Ideas* 13 (1952): 47–72.

nobleman had the pride appropriate to a man with so many names. He addressed everyone with the most aristocratic disdain, pointing his nose so loftily, raising his voice so mercilessly, lording it so splendidly, and assuming so arrogant a pose, that everyone who met him wanted to kick him. He loved women to the point of fury; and Cunégonde seemed to him the most beautiful creature he had ever seen. The first thing he did was to ask directly if she were the captain's wife. His manner of asking this question disturbed Candide; he did not dare say she was his wife, because in fact she was not; he did not dare say she was his sister, because she wasn't that either; and though this polite lie was once common enough among the ancients,[6] and sometimes serves moderns very well, he was too pure of heart to tell a lie.

—Miss Cunégonde, said he, is betrothed to me, and we humbly beg your excellency to perform the ceremony for us.

Don Fernando d'Ibaraa y Figueroa y Mascarenes y Lampourdos y Souza twirled his moustache, smiled sardonically, and ordered Captain Candide to go drill his company. Candide obeyed. Left alone with my lady Cunégonde, the governor declared his passion, and protested that he would marry her tomorrow, in church or in any other manner, as it pleased her charming self. Cunégonde asked for a quarter-hour to collect herself, consult the old woman, and make up her mind.

The old woman said to Cunégonde: —My lady, you have seventy-two quarterings and not one penny; if you wish, you may be the wife of the greatest lord in South America, who has a really handsome moustache; are you going to insist on your absolute fidelity? You have already been raped by the Bulgars; a jew and an inquisitor have enjoyed your favors; miseries entitle one to privileges. I assure you that in your position I would make no scruple of marrying my lord the Governor, and making the fortune of Captain Candide.

While the old woman was talking with all the prudence of age and experience, there came into the harbor a small ship bearing an alcalde and some alguazils.[7] This is what had happened.

As the old woman had very shrewdly guessed, it was a long-sleeved Franciscan who stole Cunégonde's gold and jewels in the town of Badajoz, when she and Candide were in flight. The monk tried to sell some of the gems to a jeweler, who recognized them as belonging to the Grand Inquisitor. Before he was hanged, the Franciscan confessed that he had stolen them, indicating who his victims were

---

6. Voltaire has in mind Abraham's adventures with Sarah (Genesis 12) and Isaac's with Rebecca (Genesis 26).
7. Police officers accompanying a mayor, or royal official.

and where they were going. The flight of Cunégonde and Candide was already known. They were traced to Cadiz, and a vessel was hastily dispatched in pursuit of them. This vessel was now in the port of Buenos Aires. The rumor spread that an alcalde was aboard, in pursuit of the murderers of my lord the Grand Inquisitor. The shrewd old woman saw at once what was to be done.

—You cannot escape, she told Cunégonde, and you have nothing to fear. You are not the one who killed my lord, and, besides, the governor, who is in love with you, won't let you be mistreated. Sit tight.

And then she ran straight to Candide: —Get out of town, she said, or you'll be burned within the hour.

There was not a moment to lose; but how to leave Cunégonde, and where to go?

CHAPTER 14

How Candide and Cacambo Were Received
by the Jesuits of Paraguay

Candide had brought from Cadiz a valet of the type one often finds in the provinces of Spain and in the colonies. He was one quarter Spanish, son of a halfbreed in the Tucuman;[8] he had been choir-boy, sacristan, sailor, monk, merchant, soldier, and lackey. His name was Cacambo, and he was very fond of his master because his master was a very good man. In hot haste he saddled the two Andalusian steeds.

—Hurry, master, do as the old woman says; let's get going and leave this town without a backward look.

Candide wept: —O my beloved Cunégonde! must I leave you now, just when the governor is about to marry us! Cunégonde, brought from so far, what will ever become of you?

—She'll become what she can, said Cacambo; women can always find something to do with themselves; God sees to it; let's get going.

—Where are you taking me? where are we going? what will we do without Cunégonde? said Candide.

—By Saint James of Compostela, said Cacambo, you were going to make war against the Jesuits, now we'll go make war for them. I know the roads pretty well, I'll bring you to their country, they will be delighted to have a captain who knows the Bulgar drill; you'll make a prodigious fortune. If you don't get your rights in one world,

---

8. A city and province of Argentina, to the northwest of Buenos Aires, just at the juncture of the Andes and the Grand Chaco.

you will find them in another. And isn't it pleasant to see new things and do new things?

—Then you've already been in Paraguay? said Candide.

—Indeed I have, replied Cacambo; I was cook in the College of the Assumption, and I know the government of Los Padres[9] as I know the streets of Cadiz. It's an admirable thing, this government. The kingdom is more than three hundred leagues across; it is divided into thirty provinces. Los Padres own everything in it, and the people nothing; it's a masterpiece of reason and justice. I myself know nothing so divine as Los Padres, who in this hemisphere make war on the kings of Spain and Portugal, but in Europe hear their confessions; who kill Spaniards here, and in Madrid send them to heaven; that really tickles me; let's get moving, you're going to be the happiest of men. Won't Los Padres be delighted when they learn they have a captain who knows the Bulgar drill!

As soon as they reached the first barricade, Cacambo told the frontier guard that a captain wished to speak with my lord the Commander. A Paraguayan officer ran to inform headquarters by laying the news at the feet of the commander. Candide and Cacambo were first disarmed and deprived of their Andalusian horses. They were then placed between two files of soldiers; the commander was at the end, his three-cornered hat on his head, his cassock drawn up, a sword at his side, and a pike in his hand. He nods, and twenty-four soldiers surround the newcomers. A sergeant then informs them that they must wait, that the commander cannot talk to them, since the reverend father provincial has forbidden all Spaniards from speaking, except in his presence, and from remaining more than three hours in the country.[1]

—And where is the reverend father provincial? says Cacambo.

—He is reviewing his troops after having said mass, the sergeant replies, and you'll only be able to kiss his spurs in three hours.

—But, says Cacambo, my master the captain, who, like me, is dying from hunger, is not Spanish at all, he is German; can't we have some breakfast while waiting for his reverence?

The sergeant promptly went off to report this speech to the commander.

—God be praised, said this worthy; since he is German, I can talk to him; bring him into my bower.

Candide was immediately led into a leafy nook surrounded by a handsome colonnade of green and gold marble and trellises amid

---

9. The Jesuit fathers. R. B. Cunningham-Grahame has written an account of the Jesuits in Paraguay 1607–1767, under the title *A Vanished Arcadia*.
1. In fact, the Jesuits, who had organized their Indian parishes into villages under a system of tribal communism, did their best to discourage contact with the outside world.

which sported parrots, birds of paradise,[2] humming birds, guinea fowl, and all the rarest species of birds. An excellent breakfast was prepared in golden vessels; and while the Paraguayans ate corn out of wooden bowls in the open fields under the glare of the sun, the reverend father commander entered into his bower.

He was a very handsome young man, with an open face, rather blonde in coloring, with ruddy complexion, arched eyebrows, liquid eyes, pink ears, bright red lips, and an air of pride, but a pride somehow different from that of a Spaniard or a Jesuit. Their confiscated weapons were restored to Candide and Cacambo, as well as their Andalusian horses; Cacambo fed them oats alongside the bower, always keeping an eye on them for fear of an ambush.

First Candide kissed the hem of the commander's cassock, then they sat down at the table.

—So you are German? said the Jesuit, speaking in that language.

—Yes, your reverence, said Candide.

As they spoke these words, both men looked at one another with great surprise, and another emotion which they could not control.

—From what part of Germany do you come? said the Jesuit.

—From the nasty province of Westphalia, said Candide; I was born in the castle of Thunder-Ten-Tronckh.

—Merciful heavens! cries the commander. Is it possible?

—What a miracle! exclaims Candide.

—Can it be you? asks the commander.

—It's impossible, says Candide.

They both fall back in their chairs, they embrace, they shed streams of tears.

—What, can it be you, reverend father! you, the brother of the lovely Cunégonde! you, who were killed by the Bulgars! you, the son of my lord the Baron! you, a Jesuit in Paraguay! It's a mad world, indeed it is. Oh, Pangloss! Pangloss! how happy you would be, if you hadn't been hanged.

The commander dismissed his negro slaves and the Paraguayans who served his drink in crystal goblets. He thanked God and Saint Ignatius a thousand times, he clasped Candide in his arms, their faces were bathed in tears.

—You would be even more astonished, even more delighted, even more beside yourself, said Candide, if I told you that my lady

2. In this passage and several later ones, Voltaire uses in conjunction two words, both of which mean humming bird. The French system of classifying humming birds, based on the work of the celebrated Buffon, distinguishes *oiseaux-mouches* with straight bills from *colibris* with curved bills. This distinction is wholly fallacious. Humming birds have all manner of shaped bills, and the division of species must be made on other grounds entirely. At the expense of ornithological accuracy, I have therefore introduced birds of paradise to get the requisite sense of glitter and sheen.

Cunégonde, your sister, who you thought was disemboweled, is enjoying good health.

—Where?

—Not far from here, in the house of the governor of Buenos Aires; and to think that I came to make war on you!

Each word they spoke in this long conversation added another miracle. Their souls danced on their tongues, hung eagerly at their eats, glittered in their eyes. As they were Germans, they sat a long time at table, waiting for the reverend father provincial; and the commander spoke in these terms to his dear Candide.

CHAPTER 15

How Candide Killed the Brother of His Dear Cunégonde

—All my life long I shall remember the horrible day when I saw my father and mother murdered and my sister raped. When the Bulgars left, that adorable sister of mine was nowhere to be found; so they loaded a cart with my mother, my father, myself, two serving girls, and three little butchered boys, to carry us all off for burial in a Jesuit chapel some two leagues from our ancestral castle. A Jesuit sprinkled us with holy water; it was horribly salty, and a few drops got into my eyes; the father noticed that my lid made a little tremor; putting his hand on my heart, he felt it beat; I was rescued, and at the end of three weeks was as good as new. You know, my dear Candide, that I was a very pretty boy; I became even more so; the reverend father Croust,[3] superior of the abbey, conceived a most tender friendship for me; he accepted me as a novice, and shortly after, I was sent to Rome. The Father General had need of a resupply of young German Jesuits. The rulers of Paraguay accept as few Spanish Jesuits as they can; they prefer foreigners, whom they think they can control better. I was judged fit, by the Father General, to labor in this vineyard. So we set off, a Pole, a Tyrolean, and myself. Upon our arrival, I was honored with the posts of subdeacon and lieutenant; today I am a colonel and a priest. We will be giving a vigorous reception to the King of Spain's men; I assure you they will be excommunicated as well as trounced on the battlefield. Providence has sent you to help us. But is it really true that my dear sister, Cunégonde, is in the neighborhood, with the governor of Buenos Aires?

Candide reassured him with a solemn oath that nothing could be more true. Their tears began to flow again.

The baron could not weary of embracing Candide; he called him his brother, his savior.

---

3. It is the name of a Jesuit rector at Colmar with whom Voltaire had quarreled in 1754.

—Ah, my dear Candide, said he, maybe together we will be able to enter the town as conquerors, and be united with my sister Cunégonde.

—That is all I desire, said Candide; I was expecting to marry her, and I still hope to.

—You insolent dog, replied the baron, you would have the effrontery to marry my sister, who has seventy-two quarterings! It's a piece of presumption for you even to mention such a crazy project in my presence.

Candide, terrified by this speech, answered: —Most reverend father, all the quarterings in the world don't affect this case; I have rescued your sister out of the arms of a jew and an inquisitor; she has many obligations to me, she wants to marry me. Master Pangloss always taught me that men are equal; and I shall certainly marry her.

—We'll see about that, you scoundrel, said the Jesuit baron of Thunder-Ten-Tronckh; and so saying, he gave him a blow across the face with the flat of his sword. Candide immediately drew his own sword and thrust it up to the hilt in the baron's belly; but as he drew it forth all dripping, he began to weep.

—Alas, dear God! said he, I have killed my old master, my friend, my brother-in-law; I am the best man in the world, and here are three men I've killed already, and two of the three were priests.

Cacambo, who was standing guard at the entry of the bower, came running.

—We can do nothing but sell our lives dearly, said his master; someone will certainly come; we must die fighting.

Cacambo, who had been in similar scrapes before, did not lose his head; he took the Jesuit's cassock, which the commander had been wearing, and put it on Candide; he stuck the dead man's square hat on Candide's head, and forced him onto horseback. Everything was done in the wink of an eye.

—Let's ride, master; everyone will take you for a Jesuit on his way to deliver orders; and we will have passed the frontier before anyone can come after us.

Even as he was pronouncing these words, he charged off, crying in Spanish: —Way, make way for the reverend father colonel!

CHAPTER 16

What Happened to the Two Travelers with Two Girls, Two Monkeys, and the Savages Named Biglugs

Candide and his valet were over the frontier before anyone in the camp knew of the death of the German Jesuit. Foresighted Cacambo had taken care to fill his satchel with bread, chocolate, ham, fruit, and several bottles of wine. They pushed their Andalusian horses

forward into unknown country, where there were no roads. Finally
a broad prairie divided by several streams opened before them. Our
two travelers turned their horses loose to graze; Cacambo suggested
that they eat too, and promptly set the example. But Candide said:
—How can you expect me to eat ham when I have killed the son of
my lord the Baron, and am now condemned never to see the lovely
Cunégonde for the rest of my life? Why should I drag out my miserable days, since I must exist far from her in the depths of despair
and remorse? And what will the *Journal de Trévoux* say of all this?[4]

Though he talked this way, he did not neglect the food. Night fell.
The two wanderers heard a few weak cries which seemed to be
voiced by women. They could not tell whether the cries expressed
grief or joy; but they leaped at once to their feet, with that uneasy
suspicion which one always feels in an unknown country. The out-
cry arose from two girls, completely naked, who were running swiftly
along the edge of the meadow, pursued by two monkeys who snapped
at their buttocks. Candide was moved to pity; he had learned marks-
manship with the Bulgars, and could have knocked a nut off a bush
without touching the leaves. He raised his Spanish rifle, fired twice,
and killed the two monkeys.

—God be praised, my dear Cacambo! I've saved these two poor
creatures from great danger. Though I committed a sin in killing
an inquisitor and a Jesuit, I've redeemed myself by saving the lives
of two girls. Perhaps they are two ladies of rank, and this good deed
may gain us special advantages in the country.

He had more to say, but his mouth shut suddenly when he saw the
girls embracing the monkeys tenderly, weeping over their bodies, and
filling the air with lamentations.

—I wasn't looking for quite so much generosity of spirit, said he
to Cacambo; the latter replied: —You've really fixed things this time,
master; you've killed the two lovers of these young ladies.

—Their lovers! Impossible! You must be joking, Cacambo; how can
I believe you?

—My dear master, Cacambo replied, you're always astonished by
everything. Why do you think it so strange that in some countries
monkeys succeed in obtaining the good graces of women? They are
one quarter human, just as I am one quarter Spanish.

—Alas, Candide replied, I do remember now hearing Master Pangloss say that such things used to happen, and that from these mix-
tures there arose pans, fauns, and satyrs,[5] and that these creatures

---

4. A journal published by the Jesuit order, founded in 1701 and consistently hostile to
   Voltaire.
5. Hybrid creatures of mythology, half-animal, half-human.

had appeared to various grand figures of antiquity; but I took all that for fables.

—You should be convinced now, said Cacambo; it's true, and you see how people make mistakes who haven't received a measure of education. But what I fear is that these girls may get us into real trouble.

These sensible reflections led Candide to leave the field and to hide in a wood. There he dined with Cacambo; and there both of them, having duly cursed the inquisitor of Portugal, the governor of Buenos Aires, and the baron, went to sleep on a bed of moss. When they woke up, they found themselves unable to move; the reason was that during the night the Biglugs,[6] natives of the country, to whom the girls had complained of them, had tied them down with cords of bark. They were surrounded by fifty naked Biglugs, armed with arrows, clubs, and stone axes. Some were boiling a caldron of water, others were preparing spits, and all cried out: —It's a Jesuit, a Jesuit! We'll be revenged and have a good meal; let's eat some Jesuit, eat some Jesuit!

—I told you, my dear master, said Cacambo sadly, I said those two girls would play us a dirty trick.

Candide, noting the caldron and spits, cried out: —We are surely going to be roasted or boiled. Ah, what would Master Pangloss say if he could see these men in a state of nature? All is for the best, I agree; but I must say it seems hard to have lost Miss Cunégonde and to be stuck on a spit by the Biglugs.

Cacambo did not lose his head.

—Don't give up hope, said he to the disconsolate Candide; I understand a little of the jargon these people speak, and I'm going to talk to them.

—Don't forget to remind them, said Candide, of the frightful inhumanity of eating their fellow men, and that Christian ethics forbid it.

—Gentlemen, said Cacambo, you have a mind to eat a Jesuit today? An excellent idea; nothing is more proper than to treat one's enemies so. Indeed, the law of nature teaches us to kill our neighbor, and that's how men behave the whole world over. Though we Europeans don't exercise our right to eat our neighbors, the reason is simply that we find it easy to get a good meal elsewhere; but you don't have our resources, and we certainly agree that it's better to eat your enemies than to let the crows and vultures have the fruit of your victory. But, gentlemen, you wouldn't want to eat your friends.

6. Voltaire's name is "Oreillons" from Spanish "Orejones," a name mentioned in Garcilaso de Vega's *Historia General del Perú* (1609), on which Voltaire drew for many of the details in his picture of South America. See Richard A. Brooks, "Voltaire and Garcilaso de Vega," *Studies in Voltaire and the 18th Century* 30:189–204.

You think you will be spitting a Jesuit, and it's your defender, the enemy of your enemies, whom you will be roasting. For my part, I was born in your country; the gentleman whom you see is my master, and far from being a Jesuit, he has just killed a Jesuit, the robe he is wearing was stripped from him; that's why you have taken a dislike to him. To prove that I am telling the truth, take his robe and bring it to the nearest frontier of the kingdom of Los Padres; find out for yourselves if my master didn't kill a Jesuit officer. It won't take long; if you find that I have lied, you can still eat us. But if I've told the truth, you know too well the principles of public justice, customs, and laws, not to spare our lives.

The Biglugs found this discourse perfectly reasonable; they appointed chiefs to go posthaste and find out the truth; the two messengers performed their task like men of sense, and quickly returned bringing good news. The Biglugs untied their two prisoners, treated them with great politeness, offered them girls, gave them refreshments, and led them back to the border of their state, crying joyously: —He isn't a Jesuit, he isn't a Jesuit!

Candide could not weary of exclaiming over his preservation.

—What a people! he said. What men! what customs! If I had not had the good luck to run a sword through the body of Miss Cunégonde's brother, I would have been eaten on the spot! But, after all, it seems that uncorrupted nature is good, since these folk, instead of eating me, showed me a thousand kindnesses as soon as they knew I was not a Jesuit.

CHAPTER 17

Arrival of Candide and His Servant at the Country of Eldorado,[7] and What They Saw There

When they were out of the land of the Biglugs, Cacambo said to Candide: —You see that this hemisphere is no better than the other; take my advice, and let's get back to Europe as soon as possible.

—How to get back, asked Candide, and where to go? If I go to my own land, the Bulgars and Abares are murdering everyone in sight; if I go to Portugal, they'll burn me alive; if we stay here, we risk being skewered any day. But how can I ever leave this part of the world where Miss Cunégonde lives?

—Let's go toward Cayenne, said Cacambo, we shall find some Frenchmen there, for they go all over the world; they can help us; perhaps God will take pity on us.

---

7. The myth of this land of gold somewhere in Central or South America had been widespread since the 16th century.

To get to Cayenne was not easy; they knew more or less which way to go, but mountains, rivers, cliffs, robbers, and savages obstructed the way everywhere. Their horses died of weariness; their food was eaten; they subsisted for one whole month on wild fruits, and at last they found themselves by a little river fringed with coconut trees, which gave them both life and hope.

Cacambo, who was as full of good advice as the old woman, said to Candide: —We can go no further, we've walked ourselves out; I see an abandoned canoe on the bank, let's fill it with coconuts, get into the boat, and float with the current; a river always leads to some inhabited spot or other. If we don't find anything pleasant, at least we may find something new.

—Let's go, said Candide, and let Providence be our guide.

They floated some leagues between banks sometimes flowery, sometimes sandy, now steep, now level. The river widened steadily; finally it disappeared into a chasm of frightful rocks that rose high into the heavens. The two travelers had the audacity to float with the current into this chasm.[8] The river, narrowly confined, drove them onward with horrible speed and a fearful roar. After twenty-four hours, they saw daylight once more; but their canoe was smashed on the snags. They had to drag themselves from rock to rock for an entire league; at last they emerged to an immense horizon, ringed with remote mountains. The countryside was tended for pleasure as well as profit; everywhere the useful was joined to the agreeable.[9] The roads were covered, or rather decorated, with elegantly shaped carriages made of a glittering material, carrying men and women of singular beauty, and drawn by great red sheep which were faster than the finest horses of Andalusia, Tetuan, and Mequinez.[1]

—Here now, said Candide, is a country that's better than Westphalia.

Along with Cacambo, he climbed out of the river at the first village he could see. Some children of the town, dressed in rags of gold brocade, were playing quoits at the village gate; our two men from the other world paused to watch them; their quoits were rather large, yellow, red, and green, and they glittered with a singular luster. On a whim, the travelers picked up several; they were of gold, emeralds, and rubies, and the least of them would have been the greatest ornament of the Grand Mogul's throne.

---

8. This journey down an underground river is probably adapted from a similar episode in the story of Sinbad the Sailor.
9. Echoes a famous tag from Horace's *Art of Poetry* 343, "miscere utile dulci." The Eldoradan landscape is like a well-composed humanist poem.
1. Or Meknes, in North Africa. Its horses are Berber steeds, swift as or even swifter than Spanish stallions. The sheep of Eldorado come from Voltaire's reading of travelers' tales; we know them now as llamas and alpacas.

—Surely, said Cacambo, these quoit players are the children of the king of the country.

The village schoolmaster appeared at that moment, to call them back to school.

—And there, said Candide, is the tutor of the royal household.

The little rascals quickly gave up their game, leaving on the ground their quoits and playthings. Candide picked them up, ran to the schoolmaster, and presented them to him humbly, giving him to understand by sign language that their royal highnesses had forgotten their gold and jewels. With a smile, the schoolmaster tossed them to the ground, glanced quickly but with great surprise at Candide's face, and went his way.

The travelers did not fail to pick up the gold, rubies, and emeralds.

—Where in the world are we? cried Candide. The children of this land must be well trained, since they are taught contempt for gold and jewels.[2]

Cacambo was as much surprised as Candide. At last they came to the finest house of the village; it was built like a European palace. A crowd of people surrounded the door, and even more were in the entry; delightful music was heard, and a delicious aroma of cooking filled the air. Cacambo went up to the door, listened, and reported that they were talking Peruvian; that was his native language, for every reader must know that Cacambo was born in Tucuman, in a village where they talk that language exclusively.[3]

—I'll act as interpreter, he told Candide; it's an hotel, let's go in.

Promptly two boys and two girls of the staff, dressed in cloth of gold, and wearing ribbons in their hair, invited them to sit at the host's table. The meal consisted of four soups, each one garnished with a brace of parakeets, a boiled condor which weighed two hundred pounds, two roast monkeys of an excellent flavor, three hundred birds of paradise in one dish and six hundred humming birds in another, exquisite stews, delicious pastries, the whole thing served up in plates of what looked like rock crystal. The boys and girls of the staff poured them various beverages made from sugar cane.

The diners were for the most part merchants and travelers, all extremely polite, who questioned Cacambo with the most discreet circumspection, and answered his questions very directly.

When the meal was over, Cacambo as well as Candide supposed he could settle his bill handsomely by tossing onto the table two of

---

2. Training in contempt for precious metals and gemstones was a conspicuous feature of the Utopian society imagined by Sir Thomas More (1516).
3. Cacambo's linguistic skills are an obvious joke: even in Peru there is no Peruvian language, and in Tucuman, which is a province of Argentina, they speak Spanish predominantly.

those big pieces of gold which they had picked up; but the host and hostess burst out laughing, and for a long time nearly split their sides. Finally they subsided.

—Gentlemen, said the host, we see clearly that you're foreigners; we don't meet many of you here. Please excuse our laughing when you offered us in payment a couple of pebbles from the roadside. No doubt you don't have any of our local currency, but you don't need it to eat here. All the hotels established for the promotion of commerce are maintained by the state. You have had meager entertainment here, for we are only a poor town; but everywhere else you will be given the sort of welcome you deserve.[4]

Cacambo translated for Candide all the host's explanations, and Candide listened to them with the same admiration and astonishment that his friend Cacambo showed in reporting them.

—What is this country, then, said they to one another, unknown to the rest of the world, and where nature itself is so different from our own? This probably is the country where everything is for the best; for it's absolutely necessary that such a country should exist somewhere. And whatever Master Pangloss said of the matter, I often had occasion to notice that things went pretty badly in Westphalia.

CHAPTER 18

What They Saw in the Land of Eldorado

Cacambo revealed his curiosity to the host, and the host told him:—I am an ignorant man and content to remain so; but we have here an old man, retired from the court, who is the most knowing person in the kingdom, and the most talkative.

Thereupon he brought Cacambo to the old man's house. Candide now played second fiddle, and acted as servant to his own valet. They entered an austere little house, for the door was merely of silver and the paneling of the rooms was only gold, though so tastefully wrought that the finest paneling would not surpass it. If the truth must be told, the lobby was only decorated with rubies and emeralds; but the patterns in which they were arranged atoned for the extreme simplicity.

The old man received the two strangers on a sofa stuffed with bird-of-paradise feathers, and offered them several drinks in diamond carafes; then he satisfied their curiosity in these terms.

---

4. Voltaire's imaginary South America owes this special feature partly to his anticlericalism, partly to his readings about Quaker customs in Pennsylvania. Without a Catholic hierarchy, he supposed, people would be more natural in their feelings, hence more generous toward visitors.

—I am a hundred and seventy-two years old, and I heard from my late father, who was liveryman to the king, about the astonishing revolutions in Peru which he had seen. Our land here was formerly the native land of the Incas, who rashly left it in order to conquer another part of the world, and who were ultimately destroyed by the Spaniards. The wisest princes of their house were those who never left their native valley; they decreed, with the consent of the nation, that henceforth no inhabitant of our little kingdom should ever leave it; and this rule is what has preserved our innocence and our happiness. The Spaniards heard vague rumors about this land, they called it El Dorado; and an English knight named Raleigh[5] even came somewhere close to it about a hundred years ago; but as we are surrounded by unscalable mountains and precipices, we have managed so far to remain hidden from the rapacity of the European nations, who have an inconceivable rage for the pebbles and mud of our land, and who, in order to get some, would butcher us all to the last man.

The conversation was a long one; it turned on the form of the government, the national customs, on women, public shows, the arts. At last Candide, whose taste always ran to metaphysics, told Cacambo to ask if the country had any religion.

The old man grew a bit red.

—How's that? he said. Can you have any doubt of it? Do you suppose we are altogether thankless scoundrels?

Cacambo asked meekly what was the religion of Eldorado. The old man flushed again.

—Can there be two religions? he asked. I suppose our religion is the same as everyone's, we worship God from morning to evening.

—Then you worship a single deity? said Cacambo, who acted throughout as interpreter of the questions of Candide.

—It's obvious, said the old man, that there aren't two or three or four of them. I must say the people of your world ask very remarkable questions.

Candide could not weary of putting questions to this good old man; he wanted to know how the people of Eldorado prayed to God.

—We don't pray to him at all, said the good and respectable sage; we have nothing to ask him for, since everything we need has already been granted; we thank God continually.

Candide was interested in seeing the priests; he had Cacambo ask where they were. The old gentleman smiled.

---

5. *The Discovery of Guiana*, published in 1595, described Sir Walter Raleigh's infatuation with the myth of Eldorado and served to spread the story across Europe.

—My friends, said he, we are all priests; the king and all the heads of household sing formal psalms of thanksgiving every morning, and five or six thousand voices accompany them.

—What! you have no monks to teach, argue, govern, intrigue, and burn at the stake everyone who disagrees with them?

—We should have to be mad, said the old man; here we are all of the same mind, and we don't understand what you're up to with your monks.

Candide was overjoyed at all these speeches, and said to himself: —This is very different from Westphalia and the castle of My Lord the Baron; if our friend Pangloss had seen Eldorado, he wouldn't have called the castle of Thunder-Ten-Tronckh the finest thing on earth; to know the world one must travel.

After this long conversation, the old gentleman ordered a carriage with six sheep made ready, and gave the two travelers twelve of his servants for their journey to the court.

—Excuse me, said he, if old age deprives me of the honor of accompanying you. The king will receive you after a style which will not altogether displease you, and you will doubtless make allowance for the customs of the country if there are any you do not like.

Candide and Cacambo climbed into the coach; the six sheep trotted off like the wind, and in less than four hours they reached the king's palace at the edge of the capital. The entryway was two hundred and twenty feet high and a hundred wide; it is impossible to describe all the materials of which it was made. But you can imagine how much finer it was than those pebbles and sand which we call gold and jewels.

Twenty beautiful girls of the guard detail welcomed Candide and Cacambo as they stepped from the carriage, took them to the baths, and dressed them in robes woven of humming-bird feathers; then the high officials of the crown, both male and female, led them to the royal chamber between two long lines, each of a thousand musicians, as is customary. As they approached the throne room, Cacambo asked an officer what was the proper method of greeting his majesty: if one fell to one's knees or on one's belly; if one put one's hands on one's head or on one's rear; if one licked up the dust of the earth—in a word, what was the proper form?[6]

—The ceremony, said the officer, is to embrace the king and kiss him on both cheeks.

Candide and Cacambo warmly embraced his majesty, who received them with all the dignity imaginable, and asked them politely to dine.

6. Candide's questions may be related to those of Gulliver on a somewhat similar occasion; see *Gulliver's Travels*, book 4.

In the interim, they were taken about to see the city, the public buildings rising to the clouds, the public markets and arcades, the fountains of pure water and of rose water, those of sugar cane liquors which flowed perpetually in the great plazas paved with a sort of stone which gave off odors of gillyflower and rose petals. Candide asked to see the supreme court and the hall of parliament; they told him there was no such thing, that lawsuits were unknown. He asked if there were prisons, and was told there were not. What surprised him more, and gave him most pleasure, was the palace of sciences, in which he saw a gallery two thousand paces long, entirely filled with mathematical and physical instruments.

Having passed the whole afternoon seeing only a thousandth part of the city, they returned to the king's palace. Candide sat down to dinner with his majesty, his own valet Cacambo, and several ladies. Never was better food served, and never did a host preside more jovially than his majesty. Cacambo explained the king's witty sayings to Candide, and even when translated they still seemed witty. Of all the things which astonished Candide, this was not, in his eyes, the least astonishing.

They passed a month in this refuge. Candide never tired of saying to Cacambo:—It's true, my friend, I'll say it again, the castle where I was born does not compare with the land where we now are; but Miss Cunégonde is not here, and you doubtless have a mistress somewhere in Europe. If we stay here, we shall be just like everybody else, whereas if we go back to our own world, taking with us just a dozen sheep loaded with Eldorado pebbles, we shall be richer than all the kings put together, we shall have no more inquisitors to fear, and we shall easily be able to retake Miss Cunégonde.

This harangue pleased Cacambo; wandering is such pleasure, it gives a man such prestige at home to be able to talk of what he has seen abroad, that the two happy men resolved to be so no longer, but to take their leave of his majesty.

—You are making a foolish mistake, the king told them; I know very well that my kingdom is nothing much; but when you are pretty comfortable somewhere, you had better stay there. Of course I have no right to keep strangers against their will, that sort of tyranny is not in keeping with our laws or our customs; all men are free; depart when you will, but the way out is very difficult. You cannot possibly go up the river by which you miraculously came; it runs too swiftly through its underground caves. The mountains which surround my land are ten thousand feet high, and steep as walls; each one is more than ten leagues across; the only way down is over precipices. But since you really must go, I shall order my engineers to make a machine which can carry you conveniently. When we take you over the mountains, nobody will be able to go with you, for my subjects have sworn never to leave their refuge, and they are too sensible to break their vows. Other than that, ask of me what you please.

—We only request of your majesty, Cacambo said, a few sheep loaded with provisions, some pebbles, and some of the mud of your country.

The king laughed.

—I simply can't understand, said he, the passion you Europeans have for our yellow mud; but take all you want, and much good may it do you.

He promptly gave orders to his technicians to make a machine for lifting these two extraordinary men out of his kingdom. Three thousand good physicists worked at the problem; the machine was ready in two weeks' time, and cost no more than twenty million pounds sterling, in the money of the country. Cacambo and Candide were placed in the machine; there were two great sheep, saddled and bridled to serve them as steeds when they had cleared the mountains, twenty pack sheep with provisions, thirty which carried presents consisting of the rarities of the country, and fifty loaded with gold, jewels, and diamonds. The king bade tender farewell to the two vagabonds.

It made a fine spectacle, their departure, and the ingenious way in which they were hoisted with their sheep up to the top of the mountains. The technicians bade them good-bye after bringing them to safety, and Candide had now no other desire and no other object than to go and present his sheep to Miss Cunégonde.

—We have, said he, enough to pay off the governor of Buenos Aires—if, indeed, a price can be placed on Miss Cunégonde. Let us go to Cayenne, take ship there, and then see what kingdom we can find to buy up.

CHAPTER 19

What Happened to Them at Surinam, and How Candide Got to Know Martin

The first day was pleasant enough for our travelers. They were encouraged by the idea of possessing more treasures than Asia, Europe, and Africa could bring together. Candide, in transports, carved the name of Cunégonde on the trees. On the second day two of their sheep bogged down in a swamp and were lost with their loads; two other sheep died of fatigue a few days later; seven or eight others starved to death in a desert; still others fell, a little after, from precipices. Finally, after a hundred days' march, they had only two sheep left. Candide told Cacambo:—My friend, you see how the riches of this world are fleeting; the only solid things are virtue and the joy of seeing Miss Cunégonde again.

—I agree, said Cacambo, but we still have two sheep, laden with
more treasure than the king of Spain will ever have; and I see in the
distance a town which I suspect is Surinam; it belongs to the Dutch.
We are at the end of our trials and on the threshold of our
happiness.

As they drew near the town, they discovered a negro stretched on
the ground with only half his clothes left, that is, a pair of blue drawers; the poor fellow was also missing his left leg and his right hand.

—Good Lord, said Candide in Dutch, what are you doing in that
horrible condition, my friend?

—I am waiting for my master, Mr. Vanderdendur,[7] the famous
merchant, answered the negro.

—Is Mr. Vanderdendur, Candide asked, the man who treated you
this way?

—Yes, sir, said the negro, that's how things are around here. Twice
a year we get a pair of linen drawers to wear. If we catch a finger in
the sugar mill where we work, they cut off our hand; if we try to run
away, they cut off our leg: I have undergone both these experiences.
This is the price of the sugar you eat in Europe. And yet, when my
mother sold me for ten Patagonian crowns on the coast of Guinea,
she said to me: 'My dear child, bless our witch doctors, reverence
them always, they will make your life happy; you have the honor of
being a slave to our white masters, and in this way you are making
the fortune of your father and mother.' Alas! I don't know if I made
their fortunes, but they certainly did not make mine. The dogs, monkeys, and parrots are a thousand times less unhappy than we are.
The Dutch witch doctors who converted me tell me every Sunday
that we are all sons of Adam, black and white alike. I am no gene-
alogist; but if these preachers are right, we must all be remote cous-
ins; and you must admit no one could treat his own flesh and blood
in a more horrible fashion.

—Oh Pangloss! cried Candide, you had no notion of these abom-
inations! I'm through, I must give up your optimism after all.

—What's optimism? said Cacambo.

—Alas, said Candide, it is a mania for saying things are well when
one is in hell.[8]

And he shed bitter tears as he looked at his negro, and he was still
weeping as he entered Surinam.

The first thing they asked was if there was not some vessel in
port which could be sent to Buenos Aires. The man they asked

---

7. A name intended to suggest Van Duren, a Dutch bookseller with whom Voltaire had
   quarreled.
8. The story of European mistreatment of slaves on the sugar plantations—apart from
   being basically true—reached Voltaire through the treatise *De L'Esprit* by Helvetius
   (1758).

was a Spanish merchant who undertook to make an honest bargain with them. They arranged to meet in a cafe; Candide and
the faithful Cacambo, with their two sheep, went there to meet
with him.

Candide, who always said exactly what was in his heart, told the
Spaniard of his adventures, and confessed that he wanted to recap-
ture Miss Cunégonde.

—I shall take good care *not* to send you to Buenos Aires, said the
merchant; I should be hanged, and so would you. The lovely Cunégonde is his lordship's favorite mistress.

This was a thunderstroke for Candide; he wept for a long time;
finally he drew Cacambo aside.

—Here, my friend, said he, is what you must do. Each one of us
has in his pockets five or six millions' worth of diamonds; you are
cleverer than I; go get Miss Cunégonde in Buenos Aires. If the governor makes a fuss, give him a million; if that doesn't convince him,
give him two millions; you never killed an inquisitor, nobody will
suspect you. I'll fit out another boat and go wait for you in Venice.
That is a free country, where one need have no fear either of Bulgars or Abares or jews or inquisitors.

Cacambo approved of this wise decision. He was in despair at
leaving a good master who had become a bosom friend: but the
pleasure of serving him overcame the grief of leaving him. They
embraced, and shed a few tears; Candide urged him not to forget
the good old woman. Cacambo departed that very same day; he was
a very good fellow, that Cacambo.

Candide remained for some time in Surinam, waiting for another
merchant to take him to Italy, along with the two sheep which were
left him. He hired servants and bought everything necessary for
the long voyage; finally Mr. Vanderdendur, master of a big ship,
came calling.

—How much will you charge, Candide asked this man, to take
me to Venice—myself, my servants, my luggage, and those two sheep
over there?

The merchant set a price of ten thousand piastres; Candide did
not blink an eye.

—Oh ho, said the prudent Vanderdendur to himself, this stranger
pays out ten thousand piastres at once, he must be pretty well fixed.

Then, returning a moment later, he made known that he could
not set sail under twenty thousand.

—All right, you shall have them, said Candide.

—Whew, said the merchant softly to himself, this man gives
twenty thousand piastres as easily as ten.

He came back again to say he could not go to Venice for less than
thirty thousand piastres.

—All right, thirty then, said Candide.[9]

—Ah ha, said the Dutch merchant, again speaking to himself; so thirty thousand piastres mean nothing to this man; no doubt the two sheep are loaded with immense treasures; let's say no more; we'll pick up the thirty thousand piastres first, and then we'll see.

Candide sold two little diamonds, the least of which was worth more than all the money demanded by the merchant. He paid him in advance. The two sheep were taken aboard. Candide followed in a little boat, to board the vessel at its anchorage. The merchant bides his time, sets sail, and makes his escape with a favoring wind. Candide, aghast and stupefied, soon loses him from view.

—Alas, he cries, now there is a trick worthy of the old world!

He returns to shore sunk in misery; for he had lost riches enough to make the fortunes of twenty monarchs.

Now he rushes to the house of the Dutch magistrate, and, being a bit disturbed, he knocks loudly at the door, goes in, tells the story of what happened, and shouts a bit louder than is customary. The judge begins by fining him ten thousand piastres for making such a racket; then he listens patiently to the story, promises to look into the matter as soon as the merchant comes back, and charges another ten thousand piastres as the costs of the hearing.

This legal proceeding completed the despair of Candide. In fact he had experienced miseries a thousand times more painful, but the coldness of the judge, and that of the merchant who had robbed him, roused his bile and plunged him into a black melancholy. The malice of men rose up before his spirit in all its ugliness, and his mind dwelt only on gloomy thoughts. Finally, when a French vessel was ready to leave for Bordeaux, since he had no more diamond-laden sheep to transport, he took a cabin at a fair price, and made it known in the town that he would pay passage and keep, plus two thousand piastres, to any honest man who wanted to make the journey with him, on condition that this man must be the most disgusted with his own condition and the most unhappy man in the province.

This drew such a crowd of applicants as a fleet could not have held. Candide wanted to choose among the leading candidates, so he picked out about twenty who seemed companionable enough, and of whom each pretended to be more miserable than all the others. He brought them together at his inn and gave them a dinner, on condition that each would swear to tell truthfully his entire history. He would select as his companion the most truly miserable and rightly

---

9. The business of jacking up one's price in the middle of a bargain points directly at the bookseller Van Duren, to whom Voltaire had successively offered 1,000, 1,500, 2,000, and 3,000 florins for the return of the manuscript of Frederick the Great's *Anti-Machiavel*.

discontented man, and among the others he would distribute various gifts.

The meeting lasted till four in the morning. Candide, as he listened to all the stories, remembered what the old woman had told him on the trip to Buenos Aires, and of the wager she had made, that there was nobody on the boat who had not undergone great misfortunes. At every story that was told him, he thought of Pangloss.

—That Pangloss, he said, would be hard put to prove his system. I wish he was here. Certainly if everything goes well, it is in Eldorado and not in the rest of the world.

At last he decided in favor of a poor scholar who had worked ten years for the booksellers of Amsterdam. He decided that there was no trade in the world with which one should be more disgusted.

This scholar, who was in fact a good man, had been robbed by his wife, beaten by his son, and deserted by his daughter, who had got herself abducted by a Portuguese. He had just been fired from the little job on which he existed; and the preachers of Surinam were persecuting him because they took him for a Socinian.[1] The others, it is true, were at least as unhappy as he, but Candide hoped the scholar would prove more amusing on the voyage. All his rivals declared that Candide was doing them a great injustice, but he pacified them with a hundred piastres apiece.

CHAPTER 20

What Happened to Candide and Martin at Sea

The old scholar, whose name was Martin, now set sail with Candide for Bordeaux. Both men had seen and suffered much; and even if the vessel had been sailing from Surinam to Japan via the Cape of Good Hope, they would have been able to keep themselves amused during the entire trip with instances of moral and physical evil.

However, Candide had one great advantage over Martin, that he still hoped to see Miss Cunégonde again, while Martin had nothing to hope for; besides, he had gold and diamonds, and though he had lost a hundred big red sheep loaded with the greatest treasures of the earth, though he had always at his heart a memory of the Dutch merchant's villainy, yet, when he thought of the wealth that remained in his hands, and when he talked of Cunégonde, especially just after a good dinner, he still inclined to the system of Pangloss.

---

1. A follower of Faustus and Laelius Socinus, 16th-century Polish theologians, who proposed a form of "rational" Christianity that exalted the rational conscience and minimized such mysteries as the trinity. The Socinians, by a special irony, were vigorous optimists. But in Voltaire's day, "Socinian" was used mostly as a loose term of theological abuse.

—But what about you, Monsieur Martin, he asked the scholar, what do you think of all that? What is your idea of moral evil and physical evil?

—Sir, answered Martin, those priests accused me of being a Socinian, but the truth is that I am a Manichee.[2]

—You're joking, said Candide; there aren't any more Manichees in the world.

—There's me, said Martin; I don't know what to do about it, but I can't think otherwise.

—You must be possessed of the devil, said Candide.

—He's mixed up with so many things of this world, said Martin, that he may be in me as well as elsewhere; but I assure you, as I survey this globe, or globule rather, I think that God has abandoned it to some evil spirit—all of it except Eldorado. I have scarcely seen one town that did not wish to destroy its neighboring town, no family that did not wish to exterminate some other family. Everywhere the weak loathe the powerful, before whom they cringe, and the powerful treat them like brute cattle, to be sold for their meat and fleece. A million regimented assassins roam Europe from one end to the other, plying the trades of murder and robbery in an organized way for a living, because there is no more honest form of work for them; and in the cities which seem to enjoy peace and where the arts are flourishing, men are devoured by more envy, cares, and anxieties than a whole town experiences when it's under siege. Private griefs are worse even than public trials. In a word, I have seen so much and suffered so much, that I am a Manichee.

—Still there is some good, said Candide.

—That may be, said Martin, but I don't know it.

In the middle of this discussion, the rumble of cannon was heard. From minute to minute the noise grew louder. Everyone reached for his spyglass. At a distance of some three miles they saw two vessels fighting; the wind brought both of them so close to the French vessel that they had a pleasantly comfortable seat to watch the fight. Presently one of the vessels caught the other with a broadside so low and so square as to send it to the bottom. Candide and Martin saw clearly a hundred men on the deck of the sinking ship; they all raised their hands to heaven, uttering fearful shrieks; and in a moment everything was swallowed up.

—Well, said Martin, that is how men treat one another.

2. Mani, a Persian mage and philosopher of the 3rd century C.E., taught (probably under the influence of traditions stemming from Zoroaster and the worshipers of the sun god Mithra) that the earth is a field of dispute between two almost equal powers, one of light and one of darkness, both of which must be propitiated. Saint Augustine was much exercised by the heresy, to which he was at one time himself addicted, and Voltaire came to some knowledge of it through the encyclopedic learning of the 17th-century scholar Pierre Bayle.

—It is true, said Candide, there's something devilish in this business.

As they chatted, he noticed something of a striking red color floating near the sunken vessel. They sent out a boat to investigate; it was one of his sheep. Candide was more joyful to recover this one sheep than he had been afflicted to lose a hundred of them, all loaded with big Eldorado diamonds.

The French captain soon learned that the captain of the victorious vessel was Spanish and that of the sunken vessel was a Dutch pirate. It was the same man who had robbed Candide. The enormous riches which this rascal had stolen were sunk beside him in the sea, and nothing was saved but a single sheep.

—You see, said Candide to Martin, crime is punished sometimes; this scoundrel of a Dutch merchant has met the fate he deserved.

—Yes, said Martin; but did the passengers aboard his ship have to perish too? God punished the scoundrel, the devil drowned the others.[3]

Meanwhile the French and Spanish vessels continued on their journey, and Candide continued his talks with Martin. They disputed for fifteen days in a row, and at the end of that time were just as much in agreement as at the beginning. But at least they were talking, they exchanged ideas, they consoled one another. Candide caressed his sheep.

—Since I have found you again, said he, I may well rediscover Miss Cunégonde.

CHAPTER 21

Candide and Martin Approach the Coast of France: They Reason Together

At last the coast of France came in view.

—Have you ever been in France, Monsieur Martin? asked Candide.

—Yes, said Martin, I have visited several provinces. There are some where half the inhabitants are crazy, others where they are too sly, still others where they are quite gentle and stupid, some where they venture on wit; in all of them the principal occupation is lovemaking, the second is slander, and the third stupid talk.

—But, Monsieur Martin, were you ever in Paris?

—Yes, I've been in Paris; it contains specimens of all these types; it is a chaos, a mob, in which everyone is seeking pleasure and where hardly anyone finds it, at least from what I have seen. I did not live

---

3. Martin claims to be a Manichee, but this snappy formula closely parallels a dictum of Cicero's, *De Natura Deorum* 3.37.

there for long; as I arrived, I was robbed of everything I possessed by thieves at the fair of St. Germain; I myself was taken for a thief, and spent eight days in jail, after which I took a proofreader's job to earn enough money to return on foot to Holland. I knew the writing gang, the intriguing gang, the gang with fits and convulsions.[4] They say there are some very civilized people in that town; I'd like to think so.

—I myself have no desire to visit France, said Candide; you no doubt realize that when one has spent a month in Eldorado, there is nothing else on earth one wants to see, except Miss Cunégonde. I am going to wait for her at Venice; we will cross France simply to get to Italy; wouldn't you like to come with me?

—Gladly, said Martin; they say Venice is good only for the Venetian nobles, but that on the other hand they treat foreigners very well when they have plenty of money. I don't have any; you do, so I'll follow you anywhere.

—By the way, said Candide, do you believe the earth was originally all ocean, as they assure us in that big book[5] belonging to the ship's captain?

—I don't believe any of that stuff, said Martin, nor any of the dreams which people have been peddling for some time now.

—But why, then, was this world formed at all? asked Candide.

—To drive us mad, answered Martin.

—Aren't you astonished, Candide went on, at the love which those two girls showed for the monkeys in the land of the Biglugs that I told you about?

—Not at all, said Martin, I see nothing strange in these sentiments; I have seen so many extraordinary things that nothing seems extraordinary any more.

—Do you believe, asked Candide, that men have always massacred one another as they do today? That they have always been liars, traitors, ingrates, thieves, weaklings, sneaks, cowards, backbiters, gluttons, drunkards, misers, climbers, killers, calumniators, sensualists, fanatics, hypocrites, and fools?

—Do you believe, said Martin, that hawks have always eaten pigeons when they could get them?

—Of course, said Candide.

—Well, said Martin, if hawks have always had the same character, why do you suppose that men have changed?

4. The Jansenists, a sect of strict Catholics, became notorious for spiritual ecstasies. Their public displays reached a height during the 1720s, and Voltaire described them in *Le Siècle de Louis XIV* (chap. 37), as well as in the article on "Convulsions" in the *Philosophical Dictionary*. Voltaire's older brother, Armand Arouet, was for a while an associate of the convulsionaries.
5. The Bible. Voltaire is straining at a dark passage in Genesis 1.

—Oh, said Candide, there's a great deal of difference, because freedom of the will . . .

As they were disputing in this manner, they reached Bordeaux.

CHAPTER 22

What Happened in France to Candide and Martin

Candide paused in Bordeaux only long enough to sell a couple of Dorado pebbles and to fit himself out with a fine two-seater carriage, for he could no longer do without his philosopher Martin; only he was very unhappy to part with his sheep, which he left to the academy of science in Bordeaux. They proposed, as the theme of that year's prize contest, the discovery of why the wool of the sheep was red; and the prize was awarded to a northern scholar who demonstrated by A plus B minus C divided by Z that the sheep ought to be red and die of sheep rot.[6]

But all the travelers with whom Candide talked in the roadside inns told him:—We are going to Paris.

This general consensus finally inspired in him too a desire to see the capital; it was not much out of his road to Venice.

He entered through the Faubourg Saint-Marceau,[7] and thought he was in the meanest village of Westphalia.

Scarcely was Candide in his hotel, when he came down with a mild illness caused by exhaustion. As he was wearing an enormous diamond ring, and people had noticed among his luggage a tremendously heavy safe, he soon found at his bedside two doctors whom he had not called, several intimate friends who never left him alone, and two pious ladies who helped to warm his broth. Martin said: —I remember that I too was ill on my first trip to Paris; I was very poor; and as I had neither friends, pious ladies, nor doctors, I got well.

However, as a result of medicines and bleedings, Candide's illness became serious. A resident of the neighborhood came to ask him politely to fill out a ticket, to be delivered to the porter of the other world.[8] Candide wanted nothing to do with it. The pious ladies assured him it was a new fashion; Candide replied that he wasn't a

---

6. The satire is pointed at Maupertuis Le Lapon, philosopher and mathematician, whom Voltaire had accused of trying to adduce mathematical proofs of the existence of God and whose algebraic formulae were easily ridiculed.
7. A district on the left bank, notably grubby in the 18th century, "'As I entered [Paris] through the Faubourg Saint Marceau, I saw nothing but dirty stinking little streets, ugly black houses, a general air of squalor and poverty, beggars, carters, menders of clothes, sellers of herb-drinks and old hats.' Rousseau, *Confessions*, Book IV."
8. In the middle of the 18th century, it became customary to require persons who were grievously ill to sign *billets de confession*, without which they could not be given absolution, admitted to the last sacraments, or buried in consecrated ground.

man of fashion. Martin wanted to throw the resident out the window. The cleric swore that without the ticket they wouldn't bury Candide. Martin swore that he would bury the cleric if he continued to be a nuisance. The quarrel grew heated; Martin took him by the shoulders and threw him bodily out the door; all of which caused a great scandal, from which developed a legal case.

Candide got better; and during his convalescence he had very good company in to dine. They played cards for money; and Candide was quite surprised that none of the aces were ever dealt to him, and Martin was not surprised at all.

Among those who did the honors of the town for Candide there was a little abbé from Perigord, one of those busy fellows, always bright, always useful, assured, obsequious, and obliging, who waylay passing strangers, tell them the scandal of the town, and offer them pleasures at any price they want to pay. This fellow first took Candide and Martin to the theatre. A new tragedy was being played. Candide found himself seated next to a group of wits. That did not keep him from shedding a few tears in the course of some perfectly played scenes. One of the commentators beside him remarked during the intermission: —You are quite mistaken to weep, this actress is very bad indeed; the actor who plays with her is even worse; and the play is even worse than the actors in it. The author knows not a word of Arabic, though the action takes place in Arabia; and besides, he is a man who doesn't believe in innate ideas.[9] Tomorrow I will show you twenty pamphlets written against him.[1]

—Tell me, sir, said Candide to the abbé, how many plays are there for performance in France?

—Five or six thousand, replied the other.

—That's a lot, said Candide; how many of them are any good?

—Fifteen or sixteen, was the answer.

—That's a lot, said Martin.

Candide was very pleased with an actress who took the part of Queen Elizabeth in a rather dull tragedy[2] that still gets played from time to time.

—I like this actress very much, he said to Martin, she bears a slight resemblance to Miss Cunégonde; I should like to meet her.

The abbé from Perigord offered to introduce him. Candide, raised in Germany, asked what was the protocol, how one behaved in France with queens of England.

---

9. Descartes proposed certain ideas as innate; Voltaire followed Locke in categorically denying innate ideas. The point is simply that in faction fights all the issues get muddled together.
1. Here begins a long passage interpolated by Voltaire in 1761; it ends on p. 57.
2. *Le Comte d'Essex* by Thomas Corneille.

—You must distinguish, said the abbé; in the provinces, you take them to an inn; at Paris they are respected while still attractive, and thrown on the dunghill when they are dead.[3]

—Queens on the dunghill! said Candide.

—Yes indeed, said Martin, the abbé is right; I was in Paris when Miss Monime herself passed, as they say, from this life to the other; she was refused what these folk call 'the honors of burial,' that is, the right to rot with all the beggars of the district in a dirty cemetery; she was buried all alone by her troupe at the corner of the Rue de Bourgogne; this must have been very disagreeable to her, for she had a noble character.[4]

—That was extremely rude, said Candide.

—What do you expect? said Martin; that is how these folk are. Imagine all the contradictions, all the incompatibilities you can, and you will see them in the government, the courts, the churches, and the plays of this crazy nation.

—Is it true that they are always laughing in Paris? asked Candide.

—Yes, said the abbé, but with a kind of rage too; when people complain of things, they do so amid explosions of laughter; they even laugh as they perform the most detestable actions.

—Who was that fat swine, said Candide, who spoke so nastily about the play over which I was weeping, and the actors who gave me so much pleasure?

—He is a living illness, answered the abbé, who makes a business of slandering all the plays and books; he hates the successful ones, as eunuchs hate successful lovers; he's one of those literary snakes who live on filth and venom; he's a folliculator . . .

—What's this word *folliculator*? asked Candide.

—It's a folio filler, said the abbé, a Fréron.[5]

It was after this fashion that Candide, Martin, and the abbé from Perigord chatted on the stairway as they watched the crowd leaving the theatre.

—Although I'm in a great hurry to see Miss Cunégonde again, said Candide, I would very much like to dine with Miss Clairon,[6] for she seemed to me admirable.

---

3. Voltaire engaged in a long and vigorous campaign against the rule that actors could not be buried in consecrated ground. The superstition probably arose from a feeling that by assuming false identities they denied their own souls.
4. Adrienne Lecouvreur (1690–1730), so called because she made her debut as Monime in Racine's *Mithridate*. Voltaire had assisted at her secret midnight funeral and wrote an indignant poem about it.
5. A successful and popular journalist, who had attacked several of Voltaire's plays, including *Tancrède*. Voltaire had a fine story that the devil attended the first night of *Tancrède* disguised as Fréron: when a lady in the balcony wept at the play's pathos, her tear dropped on the devil's nose; he thought it was holy water and shook it off—psha! psha! psha! G. Desnoiresterres, *Voltaire et Jean-Jacques Rousseau*, pp. 3–4.
6. Actually Claire Leris (1723–1803). She had played the lead role in *Tancrède* and was for many years a leading figure on the Paris stage.

The abbé was not the man to approach Miss Clairon, who saw only good company.

—She has an engagement tonight, he said; but I shall have the honor of introducing you to a lady of quality, and there you will get to know Paris as if you had lived here four years.

Candide, who was curious by nature, allowed himself to be brought to the lady's house, in the depths of the Faubourg St.-Honoré; they were playing faro;[7] twelve melancholy punters held in their hands a little sheaf of cards, blank summaries of their bad luck. Silence reigned supreme, the punters were pallid, the banker uneasy; and the lady of the house, seated beside the pitiless banker, watched with the eyes of a lynx for the various illegal redoublings and bets at long odds which the players tried to signal by folding the corners of their cards; she had them unfolded with a determination which was severe but polite, and concealed her anger lest she lose her customers. The lady caused herself to be known as the Marquise of Parolignac.[8] Her daughter, fifteen years old, sat among the punters and tipped off her mother with a wink to the sharp practices of these unhappy players when they tried to recoup their losses. The abbé from Perigord, Candide, and Martin came in; nobody arose or greeted them or looked at them; all were lost in the study of their cards.

—My Lady the Baroness of Thunder-Ten-Tronckh was more civil, thought Candide.

However, the abbé whispered in the ear of the marquise, who, half rising, honored Candide with a gracious smile and Martin with a truly noble nod; she gave a seat and dealt a hand of cards to Candide, who lost fifty thousand francs in two turns; after which they had a very merry supper. Everyone was amazed that Candide was not upset over his losses; the lackeys, talking together in their usual lackey language, said: —He must be some English milord.

The supper was like most Parisian suppers: first silence, then an indistinguishable rush of words; then jokes, mostly insipid, false news, bad logic, a little politics, a great deal of malice. They even talked of new books.

—Have you seen the new novel by Dr. Gauchat,[9] the theologian? asked the abbé from Perigord.

---

7. A game of cards, about which it is necessary to know only that a number of punters (bettors) play against a banker or dealer. The pack is dealt out two cards at a time, and each player may bet on any card as much as he pleases. The sharp practices of the punters consist essentially of tricks for increasing their winnings without corresponding risks.

8. A *paroli* is an illegal redoubling of one's bet; her name therefore implies a title grounded in cardsharping.

9. He had written against Voltaire, and Voltaire suspected him (wrongly) of having committed a novel, *L'Oracle des nouveaux philosophes.*

—Oh yes, answered one of the guests; but I couldn't finish it. We have a horde of impudent scribblers nowadays, but all of them put together don't match the impudence of this Gauchat, this doctor of theology. I have been so struck by the enormous number of detestable books which are swamping us that I have taken up punting at faro.

—And the *Collected Essays* of Archdeacon T[1]— asked the abbé, what do you think of them?

—Ah, said Madame de Parolignac, what a frightful bore he is! He takes such pains to tell you what everyone knows; he discourses so learnedly on matters which aren't worth a casual remark! He plunders, and not even wittily, the wit of other people! He spoils what he plunders, he's disgusting! But he'll never disgust me again; a couple of pages of the archdeacon have been enough for me.

There was at table a man of learning and taste, who supported the marquise on this point. They talked next of tragedies; the lady asked why there were tragedies which played well enough but which were wholly unreadable. The man of taste explained very clearly how a play could have a certain interest and yet little merit otherwise; he showed succinctly that it was not enough to conduct a couple of intrigues, such as one can find in any novel, and which never fail to excite the spectator's interest; but that one must be new without being grotesque, frequently touch the sublime but never depart from the natural; that one must know the human heart and give it words; that one must be a great poet without allowing any character in the play to sound like a poet; and that one must know the language perfectly, speak it purely, and maintain a continual harmony without ever sacrificing sense to mere sound.

—Whoever, he added, does not observe all these rules may write one or two tragedies which succeed in the theatre, but he will never be ranked among the good writers; there are very few good tragedies; some are idylls in well-written, well-rhymed dialogue, others are political arguments which put the audience to sleep, or revolting pomposities; still others are the fantasies of enthusiasts, barbarous in style, incoherent in logic, full of long speeches to the gods because the author does not know how to address men, full of false maxims and emphatic commonplaces.

Candide listened attentively to this speech and conceived a high opinion of the speaker; and as the marquise had placed him by her side, he turned to ask her who was this man who spoke so well.

---

1. His name was Trublet, and he had said, among other disagreeable things, that Voltaire's epic poem, the *Henriade*, made him yawn and that Voltaire's genius was "the perfection of mediocrity."

—He is a scholar, said the lady, who never plays cards and whom the abbé sometimes brings to my house for supper; he knows all about tragedies and books, and has himself written a tragedy that was hissed from the stage and a book, the only copy of which ever seen outside his publisher's office was dedicated to me.

—What a great man, said Candide, he's Pangloss all over.

Then, turning to him, he said: —Sir, you doubtless think everything is for the best in the physical as well as the moral universe, and that nothing could be otherwise than as it is?

—Not at all, sir, replied the scholar, I believe nothing of the sort. I find that everything goes wrong in our world; that nobody knows his place in society or his duty, what he's doing or what he ought to be doing, and that outside of mealtimes, which are cheerful and congenial enough, all the rest of the day is spent in useless quarrels, as of Jansenists against Molinists,[2] parliament-men against churchmen, literary men against literary men, courtiers against courtiers, financiers against the plebs, wives against husbands, relatives against relatives—it's one unending warfare.

Candide answered: —I have seen worse; but a wise man, who has since had the misfortune to be hanged, taught me that everything was marvelously well arranged. Troubles are just the shadows in a beautiful picture.

—Your hanged philosopher was joking, said Martin; the shadows are horrible ugly blots.

—It is human beings who make the blots, said Candide, and they can't do otherwise.

—Then it isn't their fault, said Martin.

Most of the faro players, who understood this sort of talk not at all, kept on drinking; Martin disputed with the scholar, and Candide told part of his story to the lady of the house.

After supper, the marquise brought Candide into her room and sat him down on a divan.

—Well, she said to him, are you still madly in love with Miss Cunégonde of Thunder-Ten-Tronckh?

—Yes, ma'am, replied Candide. The marquise turned upon him a tender smile.

—You answer like a young man of Westphalia, said she; a Frenchman would have told me: 'It is true that I have been in love with Miss Cunégonde; but since seeing you, madame, I fear that I love her no longer.'

—Alas, ma'am, said Candide, I will answer any way you want.

2. The party of the Jesuits (from Luis Molina). Their central issue of controversy was the relative importance of divine grace and human will to the salvation of man. "Jansenists": a relatively strict party of religious reformers (from Corneille Jansen, 1585–1638).

—Your passion for her, said the marquise, began when you picked up her handkerchief; I prefer that you should pick up my garter.

—Gladly, said Candide, and picked it up.

—But I also want you to put it back on, said the lady; and Candide put it on again.

—Look you now, said the lady, you are a foreigner; my Paris lovers I sometimes cause to languish for two weeks or so, but to you I surrender the very first night, because we must render the honors of the country to a young man from Westphalia.

The beauty, who had seen two enormous diamonds on the two hands of her young friend, praised them so sincerely that from the fingers of Candide they passed over to the fingers of the marquise.

As he returned home with his Perigord abbé, Candide felt some remorse at having been unfaithful to Miss Cunégonde; the abbé sympathized with his grief; he had only a small share in the fifty thousand francs which Candide lost at cards, and in the proceeds of the two diamonds which had been half-given, half-extorted. His scheme was to profit, as much as he could, from the advantage of knowing Candide. He spoke at length of Cunégonde, and Candide told him that he would beg forgiveness from his beloved for his infidelity when he met her at Venice.

The Perigordian overflowed with politeness and unction, taking a tender interest in everything Candide said, everything he did, and everything he wanted to do.[3]

—Well, sir, said he, so you have an assignation at Venice?

—Yes indeed, sir, I do, said Candide; it is absolutely imperative that I go there to find Miss Cunégonde.

And then, carried away by the pleasure of talking about his love, he recounted, as he often did, a part of his adventures with that illustrious lady of Westphalia.

—I suppose, said the abbé, that Miss Cunégonde has a fine wit and writes charming letters.

—I never received a single letter from her, said Candide; for, as you can imagine, after being driven out of the castle for love of her, I couldn't write; shortly I learned that she was dead; then I rediscovered her; then I lost her again, and I have now sent, to a place

---

3. Here ends the long passage interpolated by Voltaire in 1761, which began on p. 52. In the original version the transition was managed as follows. After the "commentator's" speech, ending: —Tomorrow I will show you twenty pamphlets written against him.

—Sir, said the abbé from Perigord, do you notice that young person over there with the attractive face and the delicate figure? She would only cost you ten thousand francs a month, and for fifty thousand crowns of diamonds . . .

—I could spare her only a day or two, replied Candide, because I have an urgent appointment at Venice.

Next night after supper, the sly Perigordian overflowed with politeness and assiduity.

—Well, sir, said he, so you have an assignation at Venice?

more than twenty-five hundred leagues from here, a special agent whose return I am expecting.

The abbé listened carefully, and looked a bit dreamy. He soon took his leave of the two strangers, after embracing them tenderly. Next day Candide, when he woke up, received a letter, to the following effect:

—Dear sir, my very dear lover, I have been lying sick in this town for a week, I have just learned that you are here. I would fly to your arms if I could move. I heard that you had passed through Bordeaux; that was where I left the faithful Cacambo and the old woman, who are soon to follow me here. The governor of Buenos Aires took everything, but left me your heart. Come; your presence will either return me to life or cause me to die of joy.

This charming letter, coming so unexpectedly, filled Candide with inexpressible delight, while the illness of his dear Cunégonde covered him with grief. Torn between these two feelings, he took gold and diamonds, and had himself brought, with Martin, to the hotel where Miss Cunégonde was lodging. Trembling with emotion, he enters the room; his heart thumps, his voice breaks. He tries to open the curtains of the bed, he asks to have some lights.

—Absolutely forbidden, says the serving girl; light will be the death of her.

And abruptly she pulls shut the curtain.

—My dear Cunégonde, says Candide in tears, how are you feeling? If you can't see me, won't you at least speak to me?

—She can't talk, says the servant.

But then she draws forth from the bed a plump hand, over which Candide weeps a long time, and which he fills with diamonds, meanwhile leaving a bag of gold on the chair.

Amid his transports, there arrives a bailiff followed by the abbé from Perigord and a strong-arm squad.

—These here are the suspicious foreigners? says the officer; and he has them seized and orders his bullies to drag them off to jail.

—They don't treat visitors like this in Eldorado, says Candide.

—I am more a Manichee than ever, says Martin.

—But, please sir, where are you taking us? says Candide.

—To the lowest hole in the dungeons, says the bailiff.

Martin, having regained his self-possession, decided that the lady who pretended to be Cunégonde was a cheat, the abbé from Perigord was another cheat who had imposed on Candide's innocence, and the bailiff still another cheat, of whom it would be easy to get rid.

Rather than submit to the forms of justice, Candide, enlightened by Martin's advice and eager for his own part to see the real

Cunégonde again, offered the bailiff three little diamonds worth about three thousand pistoles apiece.

—Ah, my dear sir! cried the man with the ivory staff, even if you have committed every crime imaginable, you are the most honest man in the world. Three diamonds! each one worth three thousand pistoles! My dear sir! I would gladly die for you, rather than take you to jail. All foreigners get arrested here; but let me manage it; I have a brother at Dieppe in Normandy; I'll take you to him; and if you have a bit of a diamond to give him, he'll take care of you, just like me.

—And why do they arrest all foreigners? asked Candide.

The abbé from Perigord spoke up and said: —It's because a beggar from Atrebatum listened to some stupidities; that made him commit a parricide, not like the one of May, 1610, but like the one of December, 1594, much on the order of several other crimes committed in other years and other months by other beggars who had listened to stupidities.[4]

The bailiff then explained what it was all about.[5]

—Foh! what beasts! cried Candide. What! monstrous behavior of this sort from a people who sing and dance? As soon as I can, let me get out of this country, where the monkeys provoke the tigers. In my own country I've lived with bears; only in Eldorado are there proper men. In the name of God, sir bailiff, get me to Venice where I can wait for Miss Cunégonde.

—I can only get you to Lower Normandy, said the guardsman.

He had the irons removed at once, said there had been a mistake, dismissed his gang, and took Candide and Martin to Dieppe, where he left them with his brother. There was a little Dutch ship at anchor. The Norman, changed by three more diamonds into the most helpful of men, put Candide and his people aboard the vessel, which was bound for Portsmouth in England. It wasn't on the way to Venice, but Candide felt like a man just let out of hell; and he hoped to get back on the road to Venice at the first possible occasion.

---

4. Atrebatum is the Latin name for the district of Artois, from which came Robert François Damiens, who tried to stab Louis XV in 1757. The assassination failed, like that of Châtel, who tried to kill Henri IV in 1594, but unlike that of Ravaillac, who succeeded in killing him in 1610.

5. The point, in fact, is not too clear since arresting foreigners is an indirect way at best to guard against homegrown fanatics, and the position of the abbé from Perigord in the whole transaction remains confused. Has he called in the officer just to get rid of Candide? If so, why is he sardonic about the very suspicions he is trying to foster? Candide's reaction is to the notion that Frenchmen should be capable of political assassination at all; it seems excessive.

CHAPTER 23

Candide and Martin Pass the Shores of England; What They See There

—Ah, Pangloss! Pangloss! Ah, Martin! Martin! Ah, my darling Cuné-gonde! What is this world of ours? sighed Candide on the Dutch vessel.

—Something crazy, something abominable, Martin replied.

—You have been in England; are people as crazy there as in France?

—It's a different sort of crazy, said Martin. You know that these two nations have been at war over a few acres of snow near Canada, and that they are spending on this fine struggle more than Canada itself is worth.[6] As for telling you if there are more people in one country or the other who need a strait jacket, that is a judgment too fine for my understanding; I know only that the people we are going to visit are eaten up with melancholy.

As they chatted thus, the vessel touched at Portsmouth. A multi-tude of people covered the shore, watching closely a rather bulky man who was kneeling, his eyes blindfolded, on the deck of a man-of-war. Four soldiers, stationed directly in front of this man, fired three bullets apiece into his brain, as peaceably as you would want; and the whole assemblage went home, in great satisfaction.[7]

—What's all this about? asked Candide. What devil is everywhere at work?

He asked who was that big man who had just been killed with so much ceremony.

—It was an admiral, they told him.

—And why kill this admiral?

—The reason, they told him, is that he didn't kill enough people; he gave battle to a French admiral, and it was found that he didn't get close enough to him.

—But, said Candide, the French admiral was just as far from the English admiral as the English admiral was from the French admiral.

—That's perfectly true, came the answer; but in this country it is useful from time to time to kill one admiral in order to encourage the others.

6. The wars of the French and English over Canada dragged intermittently through the 18th century till the peace of Paris sealed England's conquest (1763). Voltaire thought the French should concentrate on developing Louisiana, where the Jesuit influence was less marked.
7. Candide has witnessed the execution of Admiral John Byng, defeated off Minorca by the French fleet under Galisonnière and executed by firing squad on March 14, 1757. Voltaire had intervened to avert the execution.

Candide was so stunned and shocked at what he saw and heard, that he would not even set foot ashore; he arranged with the Dutch merchant (without even caring if he was robbed, as at Surinam) to be taken forthwith to Venice.

The merchant was ready in two days; they coasted along France, they passed within sight of Lisbon, and Candide quivered. They entered the straits, crossed the Mediterranean, and finally landed at Venice.

—God be praised, said Candide, embracing Martin; here I shall recover the lovely Cunégonde. I trust Cacambo as I would myself. All is well, all goes well, all goes as well as possible.

CHAPTER 24

About Paquette and Brother Giroflée

As soon as he was in Venice, he had a search made for Cacambo in all the inns, all the cafés, all the stews—and found no trace of him. Every day he sent to investigate the vessels and coastal traders; no news of Cacambo.

—How's this? said he to Martin. I have had time to go from Surinam to Bordeaux, from Bordeaux to Paris, from Paris to Dieppe, from Dieppe to Portsmouth, to skirt Portugal and Spain, cross the Mediterranean, and spend several months at Venice—and the lovely Cunégonde has not come yet! In her place, I have met only that female pretender and that abbé from Perigord. Cunégonde is dead, without a doubt; and nothing remains for me too but death. Oh, it would have been better to stay in the earthly paradise of Eldorado than to return to this accursed Europe. How right you are, my dear Martin; all is but illusion and disaster.

He fell into a black melancholy, and refused to attend the fashionable operas or take part in the other diversions of the carnival season; not a single lady tempted him in the slightest. Martin told him: —You're a real simpleton if you think a half-breed valet with five or six millions in his pockets will go to the end of the world to get your mistress and bring her to Venice for you. If he finds her, he'll take her for himself; if he doesn't, he'll take another. I advise you to forget about your servant Cacambo and your mistress Cunégonde.

Martin was not very comforting. Candide's melancholy increased, and Martin never wearied of showing him that there is little virtue and little happiness on this earth, except perhaps in Eldorado, where nobody can go.

While they were discussing this important matter and still waiting for Cunégonde, Candide noticed in St. Mark's Square a young

Theatine monk[8] who had given his arm to a girl. The Theatine seemed fresh, plump, and flourishing; his eyes were bright, his manner cocky, his glance brilliant, his step proud. The girl was very pretty, and singing aloud; she glanced lovingly at her Theatine, and from time to time pinched his plump cheeks.

—At least you must admit, said Candide to Martin, that these people are happy. Until now I have not found in the whole inhabited earth, except Eldorado, anything but miserable people. But this girl and this monk, I'd be willing to bet, are very happy creatures.

—I'll bet they aren't, said Martin.

—We have only to ask them to dinner, said Candide, and we'll find out if I'm wrong.

Promptly he approached them, made his compliments, and invited them to his inn for a meal of macaroni, Lombardy partridges, and caviar, washed down with wine from Montepulciano, Cyprus, and Sarnos, and some Lacrima Christi. The girl blushed but the Theatine accepted gladly, and the girl followed him, watching Candide with an expression of surprise and confusion, darkened by several tears. Scarcely had she entered the room when she said to Candide: —What, can it be that Master Candide no longer knows Paquette?

At these words Candide, who had not yet looked carefully at her because he was preoccupied with Cunégonde, said to her: —Ah, my poor child! so you are the one who put Doctor Pangloss in the fine fix where I last saw him.

—Alas, sir, I was the one, said Paquette; I see you know all about it. I heard of the horrible misfortunes which befell the whole household of my lady the Baroness and the lovely Cunégonde. I swear to you that my own fate has been just as unhappy. I was perfectly innocent when you knew me. A Franciscan, who was my confessor, easily seduced me. The consequences were frightful; shortly after my lord the Baron had driven you out with great kicks on the backside, I too was forced to leave the castle. If a famous doctor had not taken pity on me, I would have died. Out of gratitude, I became for some time the mistress of this doctor. His wife, who was jealous to the point of frenzy, beat me mercilessly every day; she was a gorgon. The doctor was the ugliest of men, and I the most miserable creature on earth, being continually beaten for a man I did not love. You will understand, sir, how dangerous it is for a nagging woman to be married to a doctor. This man, enraged by his wife's ways, one day gave her as a cold cure a medicine so potent that in two hours' time she died amid horrible convulsions. Her relatives brought suit

---

8. Member of a Catholic order founded in 1524 by Cardinal Cajetan and G. P. Caraffa, later Pope Paul IV.

against the bereaved husband; he fled the country, and I was put in prison. My innocence would never have saved me if I had not been rather pretty. The judge set me free on condition that he should become the doctor's successor. I was shortly replaced in this post by another girl, dismissed without any payment, and obliged to continue this abominable business which you men find so pleasant and which for us is nothing but a bottomless pit of misery. I went to ply the trade in Venice. Ah, my dear sir, if you could imagine what it is like to have to caress indiscriminately an old merchant, a lawyer, a monk, a gondolier, an abbé; to be subjected to every sort of insult and outrage; to be reduced, time and again, to borrowing a skirt in order to go have it lifted by some disgusting man; to be robbed by this fellow of what one has gained from that; to be shaken down by the police, and to have before one only the prospect of a hideous old age, a hospital, and a dunghill, you will conclude that I am one of the most miserable creatures in the world.

Thus Paquette poured forth her heart to the good Candide in a hotel room, while Martin sat listening nearby. At last he said to Candide: —You see, I've already won half my bet.

Brother Giroflée[9] had remained in the dining room, and was having a drink before dinner.

—But how's this? said Candide to Paquette. You looked so happy, so joyous, when I met you; you were singing, you caressed the Theatine with such a natural air of delight; you seemed to me just as happy as you now say you are miserable.

—Ah, sir, replied Paquette, that's another one of the miseries of this business; yesterday I was robbed and beaten by an officer, and today I have to seem in good humor in order to please a monk.

Candide wanted no more; he conceded that Martin was right. They sat down to table with Paquette and the Theatine; the meal was agreeable enough, and when it was over, the company spoke out among themselves with some frankness.

—Father, said Candide to the monk, you seem to me a man whom all the world might envy; the flower of health glows in your cheek, your features radiate pleasure; you have a pretty girl for your diversion, and you seem very happy with your life as a Theatine.

—Upon my word, sir, said Brother Giroflée, I wish that all the Theatines were at the bottom of the sea. A hundred times I have been tempted to set fire to my convent, and go turn Turk. My parents forced me, when I was fifteen years old, to put on this detestable robe, so they could leave more money to a cursed older brother of mine, may God confound him! Jealousy, faction, and fury spring

---

9. His name means "gillyflower." Paquette (above) means "daisy." They are lilies of the field who spin not, neither do they reap.

up, by natural law, within the walls of convents. It is true, I have preached a few bad sermons which earned me a little money, half of which the prior stole from me; the remainder serves to keep me in girls. But when I have to go back to the monastery at night, I'm ready to smash my head against the walls of my cell; and all my fellow monks are in the same fix.

Martin turned to Candide and said with his customary coolness:
—Well, haven't I won the whole bet?

Candide gave two thousand piastres to Paquette and a thousand to Brother Giroflée.

—I assure you, said he, that with that they will be happy.

—I don't believe so, said Martin; your piastres may make them even more unhappy than they were before.

—That may be, said Candide; but one thing comforts me, I note that people often turn up whom one never expected to see again; it may well be that, having rediscovered my red sheep and Paquette, I will also rediscover Cunégonde.

—I hope, said Martin, that she will some day make you happy; but I very much doubt it.

—You're a hard man, said Candide.

—I've lived, said Martin.

—But look at these gondoliers, said Candide; aren't they always singing?

—You don't see them at home, said Martin, with their wives and squalling children. The doge[1] has his troubles, the gondoliers theirs. It's true that on the whole one is better off as a gondolier than as a doge; but the difference is so slight, I don't suppose it's worth the trouble of discussing.

—There's a lot of talk here, said Candide, of this Senator Pococurante,[2] who has a fine palace on the Brenta and is hospitable to foreigners. They say he is a man who has never known a moment's grief.

—I'd like to see such a rare specimen, said Martin.

Candide promptly sent to Lord Pococurante, asking permission to call on him tomorrow.

CHAPTER 25

Visit to Lord Pococurante, Venetian Nobleman

Candide and Martin took a gondola on the Brenta, and soon reached the palace of the noble Pococurante. The gardens were large and filled with beautiful marble statues; the palace was handsomely

1. I.e., supreme magistrate of Venice.
2. His name means "small care" or "Carelittle."

designed. The master of the house, sixty years old and very rich, received his two inquisitive visitors perfectly politely, but with very little warmth; Candide was disconcerted and Martin not at all displeased.

First two pretty and neatly dressed girls served chocolate, which they whipped to a froth. Candide could not forbear praising their beauty, their grace, their skill.

—They are pretty good creatures, said Pococurante; I sometimes have them into my bed, for I'm tired of the ladies of the town, with their stupid tricks, quarrels, jealousies, fits of ill humor and petty pride, and all the sonnets one has to make or order for them; but, after all, these two girls are starting to bore me too.

After lunch, Candide strolled through a long gallery, and was amazed at the beauty of the pictures. He asked who was the painter of the two finest.

—They are by Raphael,[3] said the senator; I bought them for a lot of money, out of vanity, some years ago; people say they're the finest in Italy, but they don't please me at all; the colors have all turned brown, the figures aren't well modeled and don't stand out enough, the draperies bear no resemblance to real cloth. In a word, whatever people may say, I don't find in them a real imitation of nature. I like a picture only when I can see in it a touch of nature itself, and there are none of this sort. I have many paintings, but I no longer look at them.

As they waited for dinner, Pococurante ordered a concerto performed. Candide found the music delightful.

—That noise? said Pococurante. It may amuse you for half an hour, but if it goes on any longer, it tires everybody though no one dares to admit it. Music today is only the art of performing difficult pieces, and what is merely difficult cannot please for long. Perhaps I should prefer the opera, if they had not found ways to make it revolting and monstrous. Anyone who likes bad tragedies set to music is welcome to them; in these performances the scenes serve only to introduce, inappropriately, two or three ridiculous songs designed to show off the actress's sound box. Anyone who wants to, or who can, is welcome to swoon with pleasure at the sight of a castrate wriggling through the role of Caesar or Cato, and strutting awkwardly about the stage. For my part, I have long since given up these paltry trifles which are called the glory of modern Italy, and for which monarchs pay such ruinous prices.

Candide argued a bit, but timidly; Martin was entirely of a mind with the senator.

3. Widely reputed to be the supreme painter of the Italian Renaissance.

They sat down to dinner, and after an excellent meal adjourned to the library. Candide, seeing a copy of Homer[4] in a splendid binding, complimented the noble lord on his good taste.

—That is an author, said he, who was the special delight of great Pangloss, the best philosopher in all Germany.

—He's no special delight of mine, said Pococurante coldly. I was once made to believe that I took pleasure in reading him; but that constant recital of fights which are all alike, those gods who are always interfering but never decisively, that Helen who is the cause of the war and then scarcely takes any part in the story, that Troy which is always under siege and never taken—all that bores me to tears. I have sometimes asked scholars if reading it bored them as much as it bores me; everyone who answered frankly told me the book dropped from his hands like lead, but that they had to have it in their libraries as a monument of antiquity, like those old rusty coins which can't be used in real trade.

—Your Excellence doesn't hold the same opinion of Virgil? said Candide.

—I concede, said Pococurante, that the second, fourth, and sixth books of his *Aeneid* are fine; but as for his pious Aeneas, and strong Cloanthes, and faithful Achates, and little Ascanius, and that imbecile King Latinus, and middle-class Amata, and insipid Lavinia, I don't suppose there was ever anything so cold and unpleasant.[5] I prefer Tasso and those sleepwalkers' stories of Ariosto.[6]

—Dare I ask, sir, said Candide, if you don't get great enjoyment from reading Horace?

—There are some maxims there, said Pococurante, from which a man of the world can profit, and which, because they are formed into vigorous couplets, are more easily remembered; but I care very little for his trip to Brindisi, his description of a bad dinner, or his account of a quibblers' squabble between some fellow Pupilus, whose words he says *were full of pus*, and another whose words *were full of vinegar.*[7] I feel nothing but extreme disgust at his verses against old women and witches; and I can't see what's so great in his telling his friend Maecenas that if he is raised by him to the ranks of lyric poets, he will strike the stars with his lofty forehead. Fools admire

---

4. Since the mid-16th century, when Julius Caesar Scaliger established the dogma, it had been customary to prefer Virgil to Homer. Voltaire's youthful judgments, as delivered in the *Essai sur la poésie épique* (1728), are here summarized with minor revisions— upward for Ariosto, downward for Milton.
5. Pococurante mentions a lot of the minor characters in Virgil's *Aeneid*, to make clear that he is perfectly familiar with the book he despises.
6. Tasso and Ariosto (16th century) wrote "romantic," i.e., fantastic, epic poems often compared with those of their classical predecessors.
7. The reference is to Horace, *Satires* 1.7. Pococurante, with gentlemanly negligence, has corrupted Rupilius to Pupilus. Horace's poems against witches are *Epodes* 5, 8, 12; the one about striking the stars with his lofty forehead is *Odes* 1.1.

everything in a well-known author. I read only for my own pleasure; I like only what is in my style.

Candide, who had been trained never to judge for himself, was much astonished by what he heard; and Martin found Pococurante's way of thinking quite rational.

—Oh, here is a copy of Cicero,[8] said Candide. Now this great man I suppose you're never tired of reading.

—I never read him at all, replied the Venetian. What do I care whether he pleaded for Rabirius or Cluentius? As a judge, I have my hands full of lawsuits. I might like his philosophical works better, but when I saw that he had doubts about everything, I concluded that I knew as much as he did, and that I needed no help to be ignorant.

—Ah, here are eighty volumes of collected papers from a scientific academy, cried Martin; maybe there is something good in them.

—There would be indeed, said Pococurante, if one of these silly authors had merely discovered a new way of making pins; but in all those volumes there is nothing but empty systems, not a single useful discovery.

—What a lot of stage plays I see over there, said Candide, some in Italian, some in Spanish and French.

—Yes, said the senator, three thousand of them, and not three dozen good ones. As for those collections of sermons, which all together are not worth a page of Seneca, and all these heavy volumes of theology, you may be sure I never open them, nor does anybody else.

Martin noticed some shelves full of English books.

—I suppose, said he, that a republican must delight in most of these books written in the land of liberty.

—Yes, replied Pococurante, it's a fine thing to write as you think; it is mankind's privilege. In all our Italy, people write only what they do not think; men who inhabit the land of the Caesars and Antonines dare not have an idea without the permission of a Dominican. I would rejoice in the freedom that breathes through English genius, if partisan passions did not corrupt all that is good in that precious freedom.

Candide, noting a Milton, asked if he did not consider this author a great man.

—Who? said Pococurante. That barbarian who made a long commentary on the first chapter of Genesis in ten books of crabbed verse? That clumsy imitator of the Greeks, who disfigures creation

---

8. Roman lawyer, elocutionist, politician, and philosopher (1st century B.C.E.). Since the 16th century "advanced" opinion had often dismissed him as a windbag, so Pococurante devotes little time to him.

itself, and while Moses represents the eternal being as creating the world with a word, has the messiah take a big compass out of a heavenly cupboard in order to design his work? You expect me to admire the man who spoiled Tasso's hell and devil? who disguises Lucifer now as a toad, now as a pigmy? who makes him rehash the same arguments a hundred times over? who makes him argue theology? and who, taking seriously Ariosto's comic story of the invention of firearms, has the devils shooting off cannon in heaven? Neither I nor anyone else in Italy has been able to enjoy these gloomy extravagances.[9] The marriage of Sin and Death, and the monster that Sin gives birth to, will nauseate any man whose taste is at all refined; and his long description of a hospital is good only for a gravedigger. This obscure, extravagant, and disgusting poem was despised at its birth; I treat it today as it was treated in its own country by its contemporaries. Anyhow, I say what I think, and care very little whether other people agree with me.

Candide was a little cast down by these diatribes; he respected Homer, and had a little affection for Milton.

—Alas, he said under his breath to Martin, I'm afraid this man will have a supreme contempt for our German poets.

—No harm in that, said Martin.

—Oh what a superior man, said Candide, still speaking softly, what a great genius this Pococurante must be! Nothing can please him.

Having thus looked over all the books, they went down into the garden. Candide praised its many beauties.

—I know nothing in such bad taste, said the master of the house; we have nothing but trifles here; tomorrow I am going to have one set out on a nobler design.

When the two visitors had taken leave of his excellency: —Well now, said Candide to Martin, you must agree that this was the happiest of all men, for he is superior to everything he possesses.

—Don't you see, said Martin, that he is disgusted with everything he possesses? Plato said, a long time ago, that the best stomachs are not those which refuse all food.

—But, said Candide, isn't there pleasure in criticizing everything, in seeing faults where other people think they see beauties?

—That is to say, Martin replied, that there's pleasure in having no pleasure?

—Oh well, said Candide, then I am the only happy man . . . or will be, when I see Miss Cunégonde again.

—It's always a good thing to have hope, said Martin.

9. Voltaire, whose standards of classical correctness led him to find major flaws in Shakespeare, could not be expected to like *Paradise Lost*. But in the person of Pococurante he is satirizing the bored and superior esthete, as well as teasing respectable English taste, so he deliberately overstates his case.

But the days and the weeks slipped past; Cacambo did not come back, and Candide was so buried in his grief, that he did not even notice that Paquette and Brother Giroflée had neglected to come and thank him.

CHAPTER 26

About a Supper that Candide and Martin Had with Six Strangers, and Who They Were

One evening when Candide, accompanied by Martin, was about to sit down for dinner with the strangers staying in his hotel, a man with a soot-colored face came up behind him, took him by the arm, and said: —Be ready to leave with us, don't miss out.

He turned and saw Cacambo. Only the sight of Cunégonde could have astonished and pleased him more. He nearly went mad with joy. He embraced his dear friend.

—Cunégonde is here, no doubt? Where is she? Bring me to her, let me die of joy in her presence.

—Cunégonde is not here at all, said Cacambo, she is at Constantinople.

—Good Heavens, at Constantinople! but if she were in China, I must fly there, let's go.

—We will leave after supper, said Cacambo; I can tell you no more; I am a slave, my owner is looking for me, I must go wait on him at table; mum's the word; eat your supper and be prepared.

Candide, torn between joy and grief, delighted to have seen his faithful agent again, astonished to find him a slave, full of the idea of recovering his mistress, his heart in a turmoil, his mind in a whirl, sat down to eat with Martin, who was watching all these events coolly, and with six strangers who had come to pass the carnival season at Venice.

Cacambo, who was pouring wine for one of the strangers, leaned respectfully over his master at the end of the meal, and said to him: —Sire, Your Majesty may leave when he pleases, the vessel is ready.

Having said these words, he exited. The diners looked at one another in silent amazement, when another servant, approaching his master, said to him: —Sire, Your Majesty's litter is at Padua, and the bark awaits you.

The master nodded, and the servant vanished. All the diners looked at one another again, and the general amazement redoubled. A third servant, approaching a third stranger, said to him: —Sire, take my word for it, Your Majesty must stay here no longer; I shall get everything ready.

Then he too disappeared.

Candide and Martin had no doubt, now, that it was a carnival masquerade. A fourth servant spoke to a fourth master: —Your majesty will leave when he pleases—and went out like the others. A fifth followed suit. But the sixth servant spoke differently to the sixth stranger, who sat next to Candide. He said: —My word, sire, they'll give no more credit to Your Majesty, nor to me either; we could very well spend the night in the lockup, you and I. I've got to look out for myself, so good-bye to you.

When all the servants had left, the six strangers, Candide, and Martin remained under a pall of silence. Finally Candide broke it.

—Gentlemen, said he, here's a strange kind of joke. Why are you all royalty? I assure you that Martin and I aren't.

Cacambo's master spoke up gravely then, and said in Italian: —This is no joke, my name is Achmet the Third.[1] I was grand sultan for several years; then, as I had dethroned my brother, my nephew dethroned me. My viziers had their throats cut; I was allowed to end my days in the old seraglio. My nephew, the Grand Sultan Mahmoud, sometimes lets me travel for my health; and I have come to spend the carnival season at Venice.

A young man who sat next to Achmet spoke after him, and said: —My name is Ivan; I was once emperor of all the Russias.[2] I was dethroned while still in my cradle; my father and mother were locked up, and I was raised in prison; I sometimes have permission to travel, though always under guard, and I have come to spend the carnival season at Venice.

The third said: —I am Charles Edward, king of England;[3] my father yielded me his rights to the kingdom, and I fought to uphold them; but they tore out the hearts of eight hundred of my partisans, and flung them in their faces. I have been in prison; now I am going to Rome, to visit the king, my father, dethroned like me and my grandfather; and I have come to pass the carnival season at Venice.

The fourth king then spoke up, and said: —I am a king of the Poles;[4] the luck of war has deprived me of my hereditary estates; my father suffered the same losses; I submit to Providence like Sultan Achmet, Emperor Ivan, and King Charles Edward, to whom I hope heaven grants long lives; and I have come to pass the carnival season at Venice.

---

1. His dates are 1673–1736; he was deposed in 1730.
2. Ivan VI reigned from his birth in 1740 till 1756, then was confined in the Schlusselberg, and executed in 1764.
3. The Young Pretender (1720–88), known to his supporters as Bonnie Prince Charlie. The defeat so theatrically described took place at Culloden, April 16, 1746.
4. Augustus III (1696–1763), elector of Saxony and king of Poland, dethroned by Frederick the Great in 1756.

The fifth said: —I too am a king of the Poles;[5] I lost my kingdom twice, but Providence gave me another state, in which I have been able to do more good than all the Sarmatian kings ever managed to do on the banks of the Vistula. I too have submitted to Providence, and I have come to pass the carnival season at Venice.

It remained for the sixth monarch to speak.

—Gentlemen, said he, I am no such great lord as you, but I have in fact been a king like any other. I am Theodore; I was elected king of Corsica.[6] People used to call me *Your Majesty*, and now they barely call me *Sir*; I used to coin currency, and now I don't have a cent; I used to have two secretaries of state, and now I scarcely have a valet; I have sat on a throne, and for a long time in London I was in jail, on the straw; and I may well be treated the same way here, though I have come, like your majesties, to pass the carnival season at Venice.

The five other kings listened to his story with noble compassion. Each one of them gave twenty sequins to King Theodore, so that he might buy a suit and some shirts; Candide gave him a diamond worth two thousand sequins.

—Who in the world, said the five kings, is this private citizen who is in a position to give a hundred times as much as any of us, and who actually gives it?[7]

Just as they were rising from dinner, there arrived at the same establishment four most serene highnesses, who had also lost their kingdoms through the luck of war, and who came to spend the rest of the carnival season at Venice. But Candide never bothered even to look at these newcomers because he was only concerned to go find his dear Cunégonde at Constantinople.

---

5. Stanislas Leczinski (1677–1766), father-in-law of Louis XV, who abdicated the throne of Poland in 1736, was made duke of Lorraine and in that capacity befriended Voltaire.
6. Theodore von Neuhof (1690–1756), an authentic Westphalian, an adventurer and a soldier of fortune, who in 1736 was (for about eight months) the elected king of Corsica. He spent time in an Amsterdam as well as a London debtor's prison.
7. A late correction of Voltaire's makes this passage read: —Who is this man who is in a position to give a hundred times as much as any of us, and who actually gives it? Are you a king too, sir?
   —No, gentleman, and I have no desire to be.
   But this reading, though Voltaire's on good authority, produces a conflict with Candide's previous remark: —Why are you all royalty? I assure you that Martin and I aren't.
   Thus, it has seemed better for literary reasons to follow an earlier reading. Voltaire was very conscious of his situation as a man richer than many princes; in 1758 he had money on loan to no fewer than three highnesses: Charles Eugene, duke of Wurtemburg; Charles Theodore, elector Palatine; and the duke of Saxe-Gotha.

CHAPTER 27

Candide's Trip to Constantinople

Faithful Cacambo had already arranged with the Turkish captain who was returning Sultan Achmet to Constantinople to make room for Candide and Martin on board. Both men boarded ship after prostrating themselves before his miserable highness. On the way, Candide said to Martin: —Six dethroned kings that we had dinner with! and yet among those six there was one on whom I had to bestow charity! Perhaps there are other princes even more unfortunate. I myself have only lost a hundred sheep, and now I am flying to the arms of Cunégonde. My dear Martin, once again Pangloss is proved right, all is for the best.

—I hope so, said Martin.

—But, said Candide, that was a most unlikely experience we had at Venice. Nobody ever saw, or heard tell of, six dethroned kings eating together at an inn.

—It is no more extraordinary, said Martin, than most of the things that have happened to us. Kings are frequently dethroned; and as for the honor we had from dining with them, that's a trifle which doesn't deserve our notice.[8]

Scarcely was Candide on board than he fell on the neck of his former servant, his friend Cacambo.

—Well! said he, what is Cunégonde doing? Is she still a marvel of beauty? Does she still love me? How is her health? No doubt you have bought her a palace at Constantinople.

—My dear master, answered Cacambo, Cunégonde is washing dishes on the shores of the Propontis, in the house of a prince who has very few dishes to wash; she is a slave in the house of a onetime king named Ragotski,[9] to whom the Great Turk allows three crowns a day in his exile; but, what is worse than all this, she has lost all her beauty and become horribly ugly.

—Ah, beautiful or ugly, said Candide, I am an honest man, and my duty is to love her forever. But how can she be reduced to this wretched state with the five or six millions that you had?

—All right, said Cacambo, didn't I have to give two millions to Señor don Fernando d'Ibaraa y Figueroa y Mascarenes y Lampourdos y Souza, governor of Buenos Aires, for his permission to carry off Miss Cunégonde? And didn't a pirate cleverly strip us of

---

8. Another late change adds the following question: —What does it matter whom you dine with as long as you fare well at table?

  I have omitted it, again on literary grounds (the observation is too heavy and commonplace), despite its superior claim to a position in the text.
9. Francis Leopold Rakoczy (1676–1735), who was briefly king of Transylvania in the early 18th century. After 1720 he was interned in Turkey.

the rest? And didn't this pirate carry us off to Cape Matapan, to Melos, Nicaria, Samos, Petra, to the Dardanelles, Marmora, Scutari? Cunégonde and the old woman are working for the prince I told you about, and I am the slave of the dethroned sultan.

—What a lot of fearful calamities linked one to the other, said Candide. But after all, I still have a few diamonds, I shall easily deliver Cunégonde. What a pity that she's become so ugly!

Then, turning toward Martin, he asked: —Who in your opinion is more to be pitied, the Emperor Achmet, the Emperor Ivan, King Charles Edward, or myself?

—I have no idea, said Martin; I would have to enter men's hearts in order to tell.

—Ah, said Candide, if Pangloss were here, he would know and he would tell us.

—I can't imagine, said Martin, what scales your Pangloss would use to weigh out the miseries of men and value their griefs. All I will venture is that the earth holds millions of men who deserve our pity a hundred times more than King Charles Edward, Emperor Ivan, or Sultan Achmet.

—You may well be right, said Candide.

In a few days they arrived at the straits leading to the Black Sea. Candide began by repurchasing Cacambo at an exorbitant price; then, without losing an instant, he flung himself and his companions into a galley to go search out Cunégonde on the shores of Propontis, however ugly she might be.

There were in the chain gang two convicts who bent clumsily to the oar, and on whose bare shoulders the Levantine[1] captain delivered from time to time a few lashes with a bullwhip. Candide naturally noticed them more than the other galley slaves, and out of pity came closer to them. Certain features of their disfigured faces seemed to him to bear a slight resemblance to Pangloss and to that wretched Jesuit, that baron, that brother of Miss Cunégonde. The notion stirred and saddened him. He looked at them more closely.

—To tell you the truth, he said to Cacambo, if I hadn't seen Master Pangloss hanged, and if I hadn't been so miserable as to murder the baron. I should think they were rowing in this very galley.

At the names of 'baron' and 'Pangloss' the two convicts gave a great cry, sat still on their bench, and dropped their oars. The Levantine captain came running, and the bullwhip lashes redoubled.

—Stop, stop, captain, cried Candide. I'll give you as much money as you want.

—What, can it be Candide? cried one of the convicts.

—What, can it be Candide? cried the other.

1. From the eastern Mediterranean.

—Is this a dream? said Candide. Am I awake or asleep? Am I in this galley? Is that my lord the Baron, whom I killed? Is that Master Pangloss, whom I saw hanged?

—It is indeed, they replied.

—What, is that the great philosopher? said Martin.

—Now, sir, Mr. Levantine Captain, said Candide, how much money do you want for the ransom of my lord Thunder-Ten-Tronckh, one of the first barons of the empire, and Master Pangloss, the deepest metaphysician in all Germany?

—Dog of a Christian, replied the Levantine captain, since these two dogs of Christian convicts are barons and metaphysicians, which is no doubt a great honor in their country, you will give me fifty thousand sequins for them.

—You shall have them, sir, take me back to Constantinople and you shall be paid on the spot. Or no, take me to Miss Cunégonde.

The Levantine captain, at Candide's first word, had turned his bow toward the town, and he had them rowed there as swiftly as a bird cleaves the air.

A hundred times Candide embraced the baron and Pangloss.

—And haw does it happen I didn't kill you, my dear baron? and my dear Pangloss, how can you be alive after being hanged? and why are you both rowing in the galleys of Turkey?

—Is it really true that my dear sister is in this country? asked the baron.

—Yes, answered Cacambo.

—And do I really see again my dear Candide? cried Pangloss.

Candide introduced Martin and Cacambo. They all embraced; they all talked at once. The galley flew, already they were back in port. A jew was called, and Candide sold him for fifty thousand sequins a diamond worth a hundred thousand, while he protested by Abraham that he could not possibly give more for it. Candide immediately ransomed the baron and Pangloss. The latter threw himself at the feet of his liberator, and bathed them with tears; the former thanked him with a nod, and promised to repay this bit of money at the first opportunity.

—But is it really possible that my sister is in Turkey? said he.

—Nothing is more possible, replied Cacambo, since she is a dishwasher in the house of a prince of Transylvania.

At once two more jews were called; Candide sold some more diamonds; and they all departed in another galley to the rescue of Cunégonde.

CHAPTER 28

What Happened to Candide, Cunégonde, Pangloss, Martin, &c.

—Let me beg your pardon once more, said Candide to the baron, pardon me, reverend father, for having run you through the body with my sword.

—Don't mention it, replied the baron. I was a little too hasty myself, I confess it; but since you want to know the misfortune which brought me to the galleys, I'll tell you. After being cured of my wound by the brother who was apothecary to the college, I was attacked and abducted by a Spanish raiding party; they jailed me in Buenos Aires at the time when my sister had just left. I asked to be sent to Rome, to the father general. Instead, I was named to serve as almoner in Constantinople, under the French ambassador. I had not been a week on this job when I chanced one evening on a very handsome young ichoglan.[2] The evening was hot; the young man wanted to take a swim; I seized the occasion, and went with him. I did not know that it is a capital offense for a Christian to be found naked with a young Moslem. A cadi sentenced me to receive a hundred blows with a cane on the soles of my feet, and then to be sent to the galleys. I don't suppose there was ever such a horrible miscarriage of justice. But I would like to know why my sister is in the kitchen of a Transylvanian king exiled among Turks.

—But how about you, my dear Pangloss, said Candide; how is it possible that we have met again?

—It is true, said Pangloss, that you saw me hanged; in the normal course of things, I should have been burned, but you recall that a cloudburst occurred just as they were going to roast me. So much rain fell that they despaired of lighting the fire; thus I was hanged, for lack of anything better to do with me. A surgeon bought my body, carried me off to his house, and dissected me. First he made a cross-shaped incision in me, from the navel to the clavicle. No one could have been worse hanged than I was. In fact, the executioner of the high ceremonials of the Holy Inquisition, who was a subdeacon, burned people marvelously well, but he was not in the way of hanging them. The rope was wet, and tightened badly; it caught on a knot; in short, I was still breathing. The cross-shaped incision made me scream so loudly that the surgeon fell over backwards; he thought he was dissecting the devil, fled in an agony of fear, and fell downstairs in his flight. His wife ran in, at the noise, from a nearby room; she found me stretched out on the table with my cross-shaped incision, was even more frightened than her husband, fled, and fell over

2. A page to the sultan.

him. When they had recovered a little, I heard her say to him: 'My dear, what were you thinking of, trying to dissect a heretic? Don't you know those people are always possessed of the devil? I'm going to get a priest and have him exorcised.' At these words, I shuddered, and collected my last remaining energies to cry: 'Have mercy on me!' At last the Portuguese barber[3] took courage; he sewed me up again; his wife even nursed me; in two weeks I was up and about. The barber found me a job and made me lackey to a Knight of Malta who was going to Venice; and when this master could no longer pay me, I took service under a Venetian merchant, whom I followed to Constantinople.

—One day it occurred to me to enter a mosque; no one was there but an old imam and a very attractive young worshipper who was saying her prayers. Her bosom was completely bare; and between her two breasts she had a lovely bouquet of tulips, roses, anemones, buttercups, hyacinths, and primroses. She dropped her bouquet, I picked it up, and returned it to her with the most respectful attentions. I was so long getting it back in place that the imam grew angry, and, seeing that I was a Christian, he called the guard. They took me before the cadi, who sentenced me to receive a hundred blows with a cane on the soles of my feet, and then to be sent to the galleys. I was chained to the same galley and precisely the same bench as my lord the Baron. There were in this galley four young fellows from Marseilles, five Neapolitan priests, and two Corfu monks, who assured us that these things happen every day. My lord the Baron asserted that he had suffered a greater injustice than I; I, on the other hand, proposed that it was much more permissible to replace a bouquet in a bosom than to be found naked with an ichoglan. We were arguing the point continually, and getting twenty lashes a day with the bullwhip, when the chain of events within this universe brought you to our galley, and you ransomed us.

—Well, my dear Pangloss, Candide said to him, now that you have been hanged, dissected, beaten to a pulp, and sentenced to the galleys, do you still think everything is for the best in this world?

—I am still of my first opinion, replied Pangloss; for after all I am a philosopher, and it would not be right for me to recant since Leibniz could not possibly be wrong, and besides pre-established harmony is the finest notion in the world, like the plenum and subtle matter.[4]

---

3. The two callings of barber and surgeon, since they both involved sharp instruments, were interchangeable in the early days of medicine.
4. Rigorous determinism requires that there be no empty spaces in the universe, so wherever it seems empty, one posits the existence of the "plenum." "Subtle matter": describes the soul, the mind, and all spiritual agencies, which can, therefore, be supposed subject to the influence and control of the great world machine, which is, of course, visibly material. Both are concepts needed to round out the system of optimistic determinism.

CHAPTER 29

How Candide Found Cunégonde and the Old Woman Again

While Candide, the baron, Pangloss, Martin, and Cacambo were telling one another their stories, while they were disputing over the contingent or non-contingent events of this universe, while they were arguing over effects and causes, over moral evil and physical evil, over liberty and necessity, and over the consolations available to one in a Turkish galley, they arrived at the shores of Propontis and the house of the prince of Transylvania. The first sight to meet their eyes was Cunégonde and the old woman, who were hanging out towels on lines to dry.

The baron paled at what he saw. The tender lover Candide, seeing his lovely Cunégonde with her skin weathered, her eyes bloodshot, her breasts fallen, her cheeks seamed, her arms red and scaly, recoiled three steps in horror, and then advanced only out of politeness. She embraced Candide and her brother; everyone embraced the old woman; Candide ransomed them both.

There was a little farm in the neighborhood; the old woman suggested that Candide occupy it until some better fate should befall the group. Cunégonde did not know she was ugly, no one had told her; she reminded Candide of his promises in so firm a tone that the good Candide did not dare to refuse her. So he went to tell the baron that he was going to marry his sister.

—Never will I endure, said the baron, such baseness on her part, such insolence on yours; this shame at least I will not put up with; why, my sister's children would not be able to enter the Chapters[5] in Germany. No, my sister will never marry anyone but a baron of the empire.

Cunégonde threw herself at his feet, and bathed them with her tears; he was inflexible.

—You absolute idiot, Candide told him, I rescued you from the galleys, I paid your ransom, I paid your sister's; she was washing dishes, she is ugly, I am good enough to make her my wife, and you still presume to oppose it! If I followed my impulses, I would kill you all over again.

—You may kill me again, said the baron, but you will not marry my sister while I am alive.

5. Knightly assemblies.

CHAPTER 30

Conclusion

At heart, Candide had no real wish to marry Cunégonde; but the baron's extreme impertinence decided him in favor of the marriage, and Cunégonde was so eager for it that he could not back out. He consulted Pangloss, Martin, and the faithful Cacambo. Pangloss drew up a fine treatise, in which he proved that the baron had no right over his sister and that she could, according to all the laws of the empire, marry Candide morganatically.[6] Martin said they should throw the baron into the sea. Cacambo thought they should send him back to the Levantine captain to finish his time in the galleys, and then send him to the father general in Rome by the first vessel. This seemed the best idea; the old woman approved, and nothing was said to his sister; the plan was executed, at modest expense, and they had the double pleasure of snaring a Jesuit and punishing the pride of a German baron.

It is quite natural to suppose that after so many misfortunes, Candide, married to his mistress, and living with the philosopher Pangloss, the philosopher Martin, the prudent Cacambo, and the old woman—having, besides, brought back so many diamonds from the land of the ancient Incas—must have led the most agreeable life in the world. But he was so cheated by the jews[7] that nothing was left but his little farm; his wife, growing every day more ugly, became sour-tempered and insupportable; the old woman was ailing and even more ill-humored than Cunégonde. Cacambo, who worked in the garden and went into Constantinople to sell vegetables, was worn out with toil, and cursed his fate. Pangloss was in despair at being unable to shine in some German university. As for Martin, he was firmly persuaded that things are just as bad wherever you are; he endured in patience. Candide, Martin, and Pangloss sometimes argued over metaphysics and morals. Before the windows of the farmhouse they often watched the passage of boats bearing effendis, pashas, and cadis into exile on Lemnos, Mytilene, and Erzeroum; they saw other cadis, other pashas, other effendis coming, to take the place of the exiles and to be exiled in their turn. They saw various heads, neatly impaled, to be set up at the Sublime Porte.[8] These sights gave fresh impetus to their discussions; and when they

---

6. A morganatic marriage confers no rights on the partner of lower rank or on the offspring. Pangloss always uses more language than anyone else to achieve fewer results.
7. Voltaire's anti-Semitism, derived from various unhappy experiences with Jewish financiers, is not the most attractive aspect of his personality.
8. The gate of the sultan's palace is often used by extension to describe his government as a whole. But it was in fact a real gate where the heads of traitors, public enemies, and ex-officials were gruesomely exposed.

were not arguing, the boredom was so fierce that one day the old woman ventured to say: —I should like to know which is worse, being raped a hundred times by negro pirates, having a buttock cut off, running the gauntlet in the Bulgar army, being flogged and hanged in an auto-da-fé, being dissected and rowing in the galleys— experiencing, in a word, all the miseries through which we have passed—or else just sitting here and doing nothing?

—It's a hard question, said Candide.

These words gave rise to new reflections, and Martin in particular concluded that man was bound to live either in convulsions of misery or in the lethargy of boredom. Candide did not agree, but expressed no positive opinion. Pangloss asserted that he had always suffered horribly; but having once declared that everything was marvelously well, he continued to repeat the opinion and didn't believe a word of it.

One thing served to confirm Martin in his detestable opinions, to make Candide hesitate more than ever, and to embarrass Pangloss. It was the arrival one day at their farm of Paquette and Brother Giroflée, who were in the last stages of misery. They had quickly run through their three thousand piastres, had split up, made up, quarreled, been jailed, escaped, and finally Brother Giroflée had turned Turk. Paquette continued to ply her trade everywhere, and no longer made any money at it.

—I told you, said Martin to Candide, that your gifts would soon be squandered and would only render them more unhappy. You have spent millions of piastres, you and Cacambo, and you are no more happy than Brother Giroflée and Paquette.

—Ah ha, said Pangloss to Paquette, so destiny has brought you back in our midst, my poor girl! Do you realize you cost me the end of my nose, one eye, and an ear? And look at you now! eh! what a world it is, after all!

This new adventure caused them to philosophize more than ever.

There was in the neighborhood a very famous dervish, who was said to be the best philosopher in Turkey; they went to ask his advice. Pangloss was spokesman, and he said: —Master, we have come to ask you to tell us why such a strange animal as man was created.

—What are you getting into? answered the dervish. Is it any of your business?

—But, reverend father, said Candide, there's a horrible lot of evil on the face of the earth.

—What does it matter, said the dervish, whether there's good or evil? When his highness sends a ship to Egypt, does he worry whether the mice on board are comfortable or not?

—What shall we do then? asked Pangloss.

—Hold your tongue, said the dervish.

—I had hoped, said Pangloss, to reason a while with you concerning effects and causes, the best of possible worlds, the origin of evil, the nature of the soul, and pre-established harmony.

At these words, the dervish slammed the door in their faces.

During this interview, word was spreading that at Constantinople they had just strangled two viziers of the divan, as well as the mufti,[9] and impaled several of their friends. This catastrophe made a great and general sensation for several hours. Pangloss, Candide, and Martin, as they returned to their little farm, passed a good old man who was enjoying the cool of the day at his doorstep under a grove of orange trees. Pangloss, who was as inquisitive as he was explanatory, asked the name of the mufti who had been strangled.

—I know nothing of it, said the good man, and I have never cared to know the name of a single mufti or vizier. I am completely ignorant of the episode you are discussing. I presume that in general those who meddle in public business sometimes perish miserably, and that they deserve their fate; but I never listen to the news from Constantinople; I am satisfied with sending the fruits of my garden to be sold there.

Having spoken these words, he asked the strangers into his house; his two daughters and two sons offered them various sherbets which they had made themselves, Turkish cream flavored with candied citron, orange, lemon, lime, pineapple, pistachio, and mocha coffee uncontaminated by the inferior coffee of Batavia and the East Indies. After which the two daughters of this good Moslem perfumed the beards of Candide, Pangloss, and Martin.

—You must possess, Candide said to the Turk, an enormous and splendid property?

I have only twenty acres, replied the Turk; I cultivate them with my children, and the work keeps us from three great evils, boredom, vice, and poverty.

Candide, as he walked back to his farm, meditated deeply over the words of the Turk. He said to Pangloss and Martin: —This good old man seems to have found himself a fate preferable to that of the six kings with whom we had the honor of dining.

—Great place, said Pangloss, is very perilous in the judgment of all the philosophers; for, after all, Eglon, king of the Moabites, was murdered by Ehud; Absalom was hung up by the hair and pierced with three darts; King Nadab, son of Jeroboam, was killed by Baasha; King Elah by Zimri; Ahaziah by Jehu; Athaliah by Jehoiada; and Kings Jehoiakim, Jeconiah, and Zedekiah were enslaved. You know how death

---

9. An expounder of Muslim law. "Viziers": intimate advisers of the sultan. "Divan": a council of state. Everyone who takes part in affairs of state, whether civil or religious, dies, sooner or later, an atrocious death.

came to Croesus, Astyages, Darius, Dionysius of Syracuse, Pyrrhus, Perseus, Hannibal, Jugurtha, Ariovistus, Caesar, Pompey, Nero, Otho, Vitellius, Domitian, Richard II of England, Edward II, Henry VI, Richard III, Mary Stuart, Charles I, the three Henrys of France, and the Emperor Henry IV? You know . . .

—I know also, said Candide, that we must cultivate our garden.

—You are perfectly right, said Pangloss; for when man was put into the garden of Eden, he was put there *ut operaretur eum*, so that he should work it; this proves that man was not born to take his ease.

—Let's work without speculating, said Martin; it's the only way of rendering life bearable.

The whole little group entered into this laudable scheme; each one began to exercise his talents. The little plot yielded fine crops. Cunégonde was, to tell the truth, remarkably ugly; but she became an excellent pastry cook. Paquette took up embroidery; the old woman did the laundry. Everyone, down even to Brother Giroflée, did something useful; he became a very adequate carpenter, and even an honest man; and Pangloss sometimes used to say to Candide: —All events are linked together in the best of possible worlds; for, after all, if you had not been driven from a fine castle by being kicked in the backside for love of Miss Cunégonde, if you hadn't been sent before the Inquisition, if you hadn't traveled across America on foot, if you hadn't given a good sword thrust to the baron, if you hadn't lost all your sheep from the good land of Eldorado, you wouldn't be sitting here eating candied citron and pistachios.

—That is very well put, said Candide, but we must cultivate our garden.

Appendix

VOLTAIRE

Letter on the Subject of *Candide*

[When *Candide* was first published, in early 1759, Voltaire's name did not appear on the title page, which stated simply that the work was "translated from the German of Doctor Ralph." No one was intended to believe this, and the novel was widely attributed to Voltaire, though in private correspondence he continued to deny his authorship of the work. In March 1759, the *Journal encyclopédique*, a publication sympathetic to the cause of the *philosophes*, carried a review of *Candide* stating that "we do not believe at all in the existence of the German original of this novel, which is attributed to M. de V. . . ." The following letter is Voltaire's reply to this review. Its date, April 1, 1759, might be a hint to the reader to treat the letter as an April fool. Since the letter appeared in the *Journal encyclopédique* in July 1762, either the journal withheld it for three years (but why?) or, more likely, Voltaire sent the letter at the later date and predated it to add a further element of mystification. In any case, the reference to the power-hungry Jesuits was all the more relevant in 1762, when there was a series of crises that would lead to the final suppression of the Jesuit Order in France, in 1764.

The Socinians were originally a sixteenth-century sect that rejected the idea of the Holy Trinity and the doctrine of original sin. In the seventeenth century, the label *Socinian* came to be used loosely to describe skeptics and freethinkers. So Voltaire's suggestion here that the novel was designed to combat the beliefs of the Socinians is a further piece of mischief-making on his part, meant to confute critics who accused him of being irreligious. Voltaire constantly experiments with his authorial posture, and he especially relishes strategies that allow him to hint at his authorship of works that are ostensibly anonymous (see N. Cronk, "Voltaire and the Posture of Anonymity," *Modern Language Notes*, 126 [2011], pp. 768–84). This letter, inventing the character Demad, whose brother is alleged to be a friend of the invented Dr. Ralph, is a good example of the pleasure Voltaire takes in mystifying his authorial stance.—Nicholas Cronk]

Gentlemen,

You say, in the March issue of your journal,[1] that some sort of little novel called *Optimism* or *Candide* is attributed to a man known as Monsieur de V . . . I do not know what Monsieur V . . . you mean; but I can tell you that this book was written by my brother, Monsieur Demad, presently a Captain in the Brunswick regiment; and in the matter of the pretended kingdom of the Jesuits in Paraguay, which you call a wretched fable, I tell you in the face of all Europe that nothing is more certain. I served on one of the Spanish vessels sent to Buenos Aires in 1756 to restore reason to the nearby settlement of Saint Sacrament; I spent three months at Assumption; the Jesuits have to my knowledge twenty-nine provinces, which they call "Reductions," and they are absolute masters there, by virtue of eight crowns a head for each father of a family, which they pay to the Governor of Buenos Aires—and yet they only pay for a third of their districts. They will not allow any Spaniard to remain more than three days in their Reductions. They have never wanted their subjects to learn Spanish. They alone teach the Paraguayans the use of firearms; they alone lead them in the field. The Jesuit Thomas Verle, a native of Bavaria, was killed in the attack on the village of Saint Sacrament while mounting to the attack at the head of his Paraguayans in 1737—and not at all in 1735 as the Jesuit Charlevoix has reported; this author is as insipid as he is ignorant. Everyone knows how they waged war on Don Antequera, and defied the orders of the Council in Madrid.

They are so powerful that in 1743 they obtained from Philip the Fifth a confirmation of their authority which no one has been able to shake. I know very well, gentlemen, that they have no such title as King, and therefore you may say it is a wretched fable to talk of the Kingdom of Paraguay. But even though the Dey of Algiers is not a King, he is none the less master of that country. I should not advise my brother the Captain to travel to Paraguay without being sure that he is stronger than the local authorities.

For the rest, gentlemen, I have the honor to inform you that my brother the Captain, who is the best-loved man in his regiment, is an excellent Christian; he amused himself by composing the novel *Candide* in his winter quarters, having chiefly in mind to convert the Socinians. These heretics are not satisfied with openly denying the Trinity and the doctrine of eternal punishment; they say that God necessarily made our world the best of all possible ones, and that everything is well. This idea is manifestly contrary to the doctrine of

---

1. N.B. This letter was lost in the post for a long time; as soon as it reached us, we began trying—unsuccessfully—to discover the existence of Monsieur Demad, Captain of the Brunswick Regiment [Note by the *Journal*].

original sin. These innovators forget that the serpent, who was the subtlest beast of the field, tempted the woman created from Adam's rib; that Adam ate the forbidden fruit; that God cursed the land He had formerly blessed: *Cursed is the ground for thy sake: in the sweat of thy face shall thou eat bread*. Can they be ignorant that all the church fathers without a single exception found the Christian religion on this curse pronounced by God himself, the effects of which we feel every day? The Socinians pretend to exalt providence, and they do not see that we are guilty, tormented beings, who must confess our faults and accept our punishment. Let these heretics take care not to show themselves near my brother the Captain; he'll let them know if everything is well.

I am, gentlemen, your very humble, very obedient servant,

Demad
At Zastrou, April first, 1759

P.S. My brother the Captain is the intimate friend of Mr. Ralph, well-known Professor in the Academy of Frankfort-on-Oder, who was of great help to him in writing this profound work of philosophy, and my brother was so modest as actually to call it a mere translation from an original by Mr. Ralph. Such modesty is rare among authors.

BACKGROUNDS

RICHARD HOLMES

Voltaire's Grin[†]

His enemies said he had the 'most hideous' smile in Europe. It was a thin, skull-like smile that sneered at everything sacred: religion, love, patriotism, censorship and the harmony of the spheres. It was a smile of mockery, cynicism, and lechery. It was the sort of smile, said Coleridge, that you would find on the face of 'a French hairdresser.'

It was certainly the most famous smile in eighteenth-century Europe. But as reproduced in a thousand paintings, statues, busts, caricatures, miniatures and medallions, you can now see that it was more of a tight-lipped grin. Voltaire himself rather tenderly called it the grin of 'a maimed monkey' (*un singe estropié*). And he wrote to his fellow *philosophes*, 'let us always march forward along the highway of Truth, my brothers, grinning derisively.' To understand just something of that celebrated monkey grin—which symbolises both Voltaire's intelligence and his mischief—is to understand a great deal about the Europe he tried to change.

This last year, 1994, has been Voltaire's tricentenary. Learned foundations have been celebrating his birthday in Oxford, Geneva, Berlin, St Petersburg, and Paris. He has been, especially, the toast of the French intellectuals, publishers and media men. He has appeared (by proxy) on the influential Bernard Pivot television show, 'Bouillon de Culture' ('Culture Soup'). A great exhibition of his life and times, 'Voltaire et l'Europe,' has been running for two and a half months at the Hôtel de la Monnaie, Paris, organized by the Bibliothèque Nationale de France. The deputy editor of *Le Monde*, Edwy Plenel, has christened him 'the father of investigative journalism.'

The publishers did him proud. New critical studies (*Voltaire Le Conquérant*, by Pierre Lepape), new anthologies (*Le Rire de Voltaire* by Pascal Debailly), new paperbacks (*Voltaire Ecrivain de Toujours*, by René Pomeau). *Candide* appeared as a cartoon strip by Wolinski. The Pléiade library completed the publication of his correspondence in thirteen volumes. The Voltaire Foundation (by a quirk of fate, based at Oxford) continued its monumental edition of the *Complete Works* in 150 volumes, the *Life* in five volumes, and Voltaire for the desktop on CD-ROM. The magazine *Lire* sold terracotta busts of his monkey head by mail order, price 3,500 francs plus postage on the eight-kilo package.

† From Richard Holmes, *Sidetracks: Explorations of a Romantic Biographer* (London: HarperCollins, 2000), pp. 345–65. Reprinted by permission of HarperCollins Publishers Ltd. © 2000 Richard Holmes. Originally appeared in *The New York Review of Books*, Nov. 1995.

Although much of Voltaire's life was spent in exile (England, Holland, Switzerland, and Germany), he has become a palpable presence in Paris. A street, a lycée, a métro station, a café, a bank note, and even a style of armchair (upright, for hours of reading) have been named after him. His grinning statues can be found everywhere, in unexpected corners of the city, bringing the touch of irony to some grand historic purlieus: gingerly seated in the Comédie Française; niched like a Bacchus upstairs at his old Quartier Latin haunt in the Café Procope; hovering downstairs in the musty crypt of the Pantheon; genially hosting a reception room ('La Salle des Philosophes') in the Musée Carnavalet; or peering mockingly out of a little shrubbery outside the Institut de France at the bottom of the rue de Seine.

But there is a paradox in this stately, official spread of his works and influence. Voltaire was, par excellence, the free intellectual spirit. All his life he hated organizations, systems, canonizations, state authorities, and scholarly apparatus. He quarrelled continuously with the Church, the Government, the Law, and the intellectual Establishment of his time. He even quarrelled with his fellow authors of the great *Encyclopédie*, that monument to the French eighteenth-century Enlightenment, because he thought the edition was too big and too long for the ordinary reader, whom he championed.

Though Voltaire began his professional life as an author of epic poems (*La Henriade*, 1723), of vast histories (*Le Siècle de Louis XIV*, 1740–1751), and of mighty verse tragedies (*Œdipe*, 1718, *La Mort de César*, 1735), his true genius emerged as the master of brief forms. Speed and brevity are the hallmark of his gift and style. His great work is always scored allegro vivace. The short story, the pungent essay, the treatise, the 'portable' dictionary, the provoking letter, even the stinging single-sentence epigram: these now appear as the enduring and popular vehicles of his art.

Almost everything he has to say is somewhere touched on in the twenty-six *contes philosophiques* which he wrote between 1738 (*Micromégas*) and 1773 (*The White Bull*). All were the fiery distillations of age, observation, and bitter experience: an *eau de vie* of literature. They are set over the entire globe, and also out of it; and many of them take the form of fantastic travellers' tales. They were frequently published anonymously (like *Candide*), and while delighting in their success Voltaire often continued to deny authorship, and mocked the whole enterprise. His modesty was perverse. He once wrote: 'I try to be very brief and slightly spicy: or else the Ministers and Madame de Pompadour and the clerks and the maidservants will all make paper-curlers of my pages.'

His bon mots have travelled more widely than anything else, though their precision is often difficult to translate. They give some measure of the man. 'Use a pen, start a war.' (*'Qui plume a guerra a.'*) 'God is not on the side of the big battalions, but of the best shots.' 'In this country [England] it is thought a good idea to kill an admiral, from time to time, to encourage the others.' 'The superfluous, that most necessary commodity.' (*'Le superflu, chose très nécessaire.'*) 'If God did not exist, it would be necessary to invent him.' 'We owe respect to the living, but to the dead we owe nothing but the truth.' 'I disapprove of what you say, but I will defend to the death your right to say it.' This often-cited dictum of free-speech is actually an attribution, and has no precise French original. It is a paraphrase of Voltaire's letter to Helvétius (on the burning of Helvétius's *De L'esprit* in 1759), first made by S. G. Tallentyre (E. Beatrice Hall) in her book *The Friends of Voltaire* (1907).

Perhaps most famous of all is Candide's wry philosophic conclusion about the lesson of his terrible adventures: 'That is well said, replied Candide, but we must cultivate our garden.' These, and many like them, have remained part of that mysterious European currency of the ironic. They are the verbal equivalents, the linguistic icons, of Voltaire's mocking grin.

Brevity, irony, and a particular kind of fantastical logic were Voltaire's chosen weapons. They might appear curiously lightweight for his chosen targets: the great armies of the European night—fanaticism, intolerance, persecution, injustice, cruelty. But Voltaire was a natural-born fighter, an intellectual pugilist. He relished combat, and he committed himself absolutely to the battle of ideas. Like a later master of the ring, he 'floated' and danced like a butterfly but stung like a bee. For all his elegance, he could strike with stunning ferocity. A convinced anticleric, he could write of priests of every denomination who 'rise from an incestuous bed, manufacture a hundred versions of God, then eat and drink God, then piss and shit God.' He never pulled his punches, and he made enemies all his life, and he made them after it.

His commitment to the freedom of ideas is historically significant. The French rightly celebrate him as the first 'engaged' intellectual who attached himself to specific social and political causes. For them, Voltaire laid the foundations—in an almost architectural sense—of a unique European tradition. They see a line that runs straight as the 'Grand Axis' in Paris (that great vista from the seventeenth-century Louvre palace to the twentieth-century Arche de la Défense), from Voltaire via Hugo and Zola to Sartre and Camus. When General de Gaulle was urged to arrest Sartre for subversion during the 1960s, he replied 'one does not put Voltaire in the Bastille.'

For Voltaire, the essence of intellectual freedom was wit. Wit—which meant both intelligence and humour—was the primary birthright of man. The freeplay of wit brings enlightenment and also a certain kind of laughter: the laughter that distinguishes man from the beasts. But it is not a simple kind of laughter: it is also close to tears. Voltaire's symbolic grin (as we begin to examine it) contains both these elements when he surveys the human condition. Life amuses and delights him; but it also causes him pain and grief. In his *Questions sur L'Encyclopédie* (1772), he wrote this entry about 'Le Rire,' an epitome of both his thought and his style.

> Anyone who has ever laughed will hardly doubt that laughter is the sign of joy, as tears are the symptom of grief. But those who seek the metaphysical causes of laughter are not foolish. Anyone who knows precisely *why* the type of joy which excites laughter should pull the zygomatic muscle (one of the thirteen muscles in the mouth) upwards towards the ears, is clever. Animals have this muscle like us. But animals never laugh with joy, anymore than they weep tears of sadness. It is true that deer excrete fluid from their eyes when they are being hunted to death. So do dogs when they are undergoing vivisection. But they never weep for their mistresses or their friends, as we do. Nor do they burst into laughter at the sight of something comic. Man is the sole animal who cries and laughs.

The simple conclusion is profoundly deceptive. The sentences gather irony even as they shorten, and the blows strike home. What is this entry really about? Is it human laughter, or human stupidity, or human cruelty? Voltaire's wit is so often double-edged like this. His tales, his essays, his epigrams cut as we smile. And nothing is sacred. Consider what he wrote about human lovemaking, in one of his letters:

> Snails have the good fortune to be both male and female . . . They give pleasure and receive it at the same time. Their enjoyment is not just twice as much as ours, it also lasts considerably longer. They are in sexual rapture for three or four hours at a stretch. Admittedly, that is not long compared to Eternity. But it would be a long time for you and me.

This is the intellectual physiognomy, so to speak, of Voltaire's grin. But what gave it the particular historical twist that makes it seem like the insignia of the eighteenth-century Enlightenment? Voltaire's father, François Arouet (originally from Poitou), was a successful lawyer to the French aristocracy. His beautiful mother (Voltaire always travelled with her portrait) died when he was only six. The

youngest surviving child, he was born in November 1694 in the heart
of Paris, on the Ile de la Cité.

The comfortable house stood within sight of the Palais de Justice
(also the police headquarters) and the long rows of bookstalls already
established along the Seine. There is something symbolic in this
position. Voltaire's literary genius always contained both the lawyer's
delight in argument and the poet's sense of fantasy. His wit—from
childhood, swift, logical, and provocative—somehow combined
these two contradictory elements. (Flaubert said long afterward, in
Madame Bovary, that 'every lawyer carries inside him the wreckage
of a poet.')

Young François-Marie Arouet (*le jeune*) was hyperactive, almost
a child prodigy—clever, mischievous, and barely governable. He
started as he meant to go on. He flourished under his Jesuit teach-
ers at the Collège Louis-le-Grand, driving them to distraction with
his pranks. There is a famous story of how he got the school fires lit
earlier than usual one winter term. The rule was that no heating
was permitted until the water froze in the stone holy-water stoop in
the school chapel. Arouet accelerated this process by bringing in a
large sheet of ice from the schoolyard, and slipping it unnoticed into
the stoop. He was flogged when the trick was discovered, but in recompense the fires were also lit. It was a young poet-lawyer's solution: the letter of the law was observed, because the holy water did
indeed freeze; but the spirit of the law was made a mockery, because
Arouet had invented the ice. It was perhaps his first *conte philosophique* in action.

After graduation (rhetoric, classics, mathematics, and a first
brush with theology), a dangerously handsome young Arouet ran
riot as a junior diplomat in Holland. When he proposed to marry
his voluptuous Dutch mistress, Pimpette, he was brought home to
Paris in disgrace, and promptly moved into a libertine aristocratic
set and began publishing satires and political squibs. (He was supposed to be studying law.) He did his first stint in the Bastille
prison, having offended the Court, in 1717; and emerged with his
verse tragedy *Œdipe*, which made his name. Already it was allegro
vivace.

Having made his name, he promptly changed it. By a swift transposition of letters, 'Arouet Le J' became 'Voltaire.' (The sleight of
hand is rather puzzling here, but scholars explain that it was done
by assuming the 'u' to be a 'V,' and the 'J' to be an 'i,' which just about
works, though it would not appeal to Scrabble players.) But Arouet
had done something strikingly modern: he had repackaged himself
under a new brand name, carrying instant associations of speed
and daring: *voltige* (acrobatics on a trapeze or a horse), *volte-face*

(spinning about to face your enemies), *volatile* (originally, any winged creature). It meant he was a highflyer, and everyone would know it.

For the next decade, Voltaire soared to increasingly dizzy heights in France, writing plays, collecting gold medals and mistresses, moving in and out of royal favour with King Louis XV at Versailles. He was the supreme literary dandy about town, dining with the aristocrats as their *enfant terrible*, and 'passing his life from chateau to chateau.' His portrait was painted, his witticisms were admired, and his arrogance became insupportable. The portrait in the Musée Carnavalet from this period shows him rouged and powdered in an extravagant wig, a bottle-green coat over his pink silk waistcoat, lace frothing at his wrists, and an expression of delicate self-satisfaction on his impudent, unmarked face. Much of what he wrote at this time, except for a few erotic poems (*Épître à Uranie*), has since been forgotten. Then in January 1726 came nemesis.

Showing off in front of his mistress, Adrienne Lecouvreur, in her box at the Comédie-Française, Voltaire traded insults with a particularly brutish member of the French aristocracy, the Chevalier de Rohan-Chabot. The Chevalier queried the writer's name ('Arouet? Voltaire?') The writer queried the Chevalier's lineage. The mistress—having granted favours to both chevalier and writer—even-handedly and prudently fainted between them. Scandal.

Some nights later, Voltaire was wittily dining at the Duc de Sully's *hôtel particulier* on the rue Saint Antoine. (This superb baroque building, with decorated courtyard of naked nymphs and barrel-vaulted coach-entrance, is now visitable as the Caisse Nationale des Monuments Historiques.) Called down by an urgent messenger into the cobbled street outside, Voltaire was set upon by a posse of the Chevalier's hired thugs, and beaten with clubs until he collapsed. The Chevalier, meanwhile, looked on from a closed carriage, and shouted out to his men the one remark by which history remembers him. 'Don't hit his head: something valuable might still come from that!' The beating recalls the one delivered to the British poet John Dryden in Rose Alley, London, by henchmen of the Earl of Rochester. But the consequences were somewhat different.

Voltaire staggered back up to the Duc de Sully's dining room, but was mortified to discover that neither the Duc nor his delightful friends were prepared to take his part against a fellow nobleman. Bruised and bitterly humiliated, Voltaire attempted to challenge the Chevalier to a duel with swords, but was promptly put back into the Bastille. He had learned that the intellectual must defend himself with other weapons.

One might say that if the French Enlightenment began anywhere, it was on the cobblestones outside the hotel de Sully in 1726. A small plaque, beneath the nymphs, might not come amiss. Thenceforth Voltaire's career—he was thirty-two—followed a wholly different trajectory. He never forgot the beating, and years later Candide was to undergo a similar *bastonnade* in Lisbon, at the hands of the Inquisition. 'They walked in procession, and listened to a very moving sermon, followed by a beautiful recital of plainchant. Candide was flogged in time to the singing.'

Voltaire's travels now began. Despite brief returns to Court favour, he was not to feel really safe in Paris again until the last months of his life, fifty years later. First he fled to London, arriving 'without a penny, sick to death of a violent ague, a stranger, alone, helpless' (his own rather racy English). But being Voltaire, he was soon airborne again, and remained for two years, a decisive period of intellectual expansion. He met Pope, Congreve, and Swift, who became crucial influences on his writing. (His letter of introduction to Swift is delightfully dated from 'the Whiter Perruke, Maiden Lane, Covent Garden.') He read the works of Locke and Newton in detail, and judged them superior to Descartes (with his nonsense about 'innate ideas') and Pascal (with his gambler's view of heaven). He studied the liberal English civil code, which granted large freedoms of worship and citizenship. The British right of *habeas corpus* (as opposed to the arbitrary French *lettres de cachet*) deeply impressed him. He visited the Court, the Parliament, the lively and outspoken salons and coffeehouses, the bustling Stock Exchange. (Voltaire's brilliance as a private investor dates from this time, and he never again depended on book sales or aristocratic patrons.) He attended productions of Shakespeare's plays (then being revived), with their sublime ignorance of the three classical unities. He found 'a nation fond of liberty; learned, witty, despising life and death; a nation of philosophers.' It was an exile's idealization of course; but another *conte philosophique* as well.

Everything Voltaire saw went into his first distinctive prose work, a hymn to British liberty and eccentricity, *Les Lettres philosophiques* (1733), also known as his *Letters Concerning the English Nation*. An anthology of essays and travel sketches, it is a compendium of freethinking specifically designed to provoke established opinions and prejudices in France: the Quakers at worship, the Parliament in Debate, Newton doing experimental science, the stockbrokers trading, or Hamlet contemplating suicide. (Hamlet's 'to be or not to be' soliloquy is exquisitely rendered into classical French alexandrines, a perfect backhanded compliment to the Bard.) Each scene is given Voltaire's special spin of irony, as in his famous sketch of the British doing business, from the Sixth Letter.

> Go into the London Exchange, a place more dignified than many a royal court. There you will find representatives of every nation quietly assembled to promote human welfare. There the Jew, the Mahometan and the Christian deal with each other as though they were all of the same religion. They call no man Infidel unless he be bankrupt. There the Presbyterian trusts the Anabaptist, and the Anglican accepts the Quaker's bond . . . If there were only one religion in England, there would be a risk of despotism; if there were only two, they would cut each other's throats; as it is, there are at least thirty, and they live happily and at peace.

Voltaire's return to France was uneasy. He was no longer the darling of Paris, he was increasingly suspected of liberal and unpatriotic ideas, and his attempt at a sparkling satire of French cultural dullness, *Le Temple du Goût* (1733)—inspired by Alexander Pope's *Dunciad*—produced not dinner invitations but denunciations. He skulked in an aged comtesse's apartment in the Palais-Royal (no plaque), and indulged his lifelong love of amateur theatricals, while preparing for his next débâcle with the authorities. When the *Lettres philosophiques* was published, a warrant was immediately issued for his arrest.

But Voltaire was dancing again. He had met the remarkable woman who was to shape the whole middle period of his career. The Marquise du Châtelet was a handsome, headstrong eccentric of twenty-seven, with a passion for geometry and jewellery. A portrait shows her at her desk, in a tender flutter of blue silk ribbons, one milky elbow on a pile of books, an astrolabe at her shoulder, and a pair of gold dividers held thoughtfully, yet rather erotically, between her fingertips. She was married to a bluff and kindly career soldier, who was always away at some European front. Having born him two children, the Marquise was ready to take a lover of greater finesse, and she already had the mathematician Maupertuis in tow. She met Voltaire at a party in Saint-Germain, and they talked about Newton and fell in love. Voltaire said she had green eyes and could translate both Euclid and Virgil, and make him grin. It was an Enlightenment love match.

When the warrant for his arrest was issued, Voltaire decamped for Madame du Châtelet's charming château at Cirey, far away in the misty borderlands of Lorraine. Here they made a new life together over the next decade, redecorating the rambling apartments, establishing a garden, writing for ten or twelve hours a day, receiving inquisitive visitors, and occasionally playing host to the Marquis on his return from a dull military campaign. One of the first things they did together was to submit prize essays, without consulting each other's findings, on the subject of 'The Propagation of Fire,' for an award offered by the French Academy of Sciences. They were suitably outraged to find that both had lost.

There are many accounts of their stormy, and highly productive, ménage a trois. Nancy Mitford once wrote a diverting book about it, *Voltaire in Love* (1957), which she described as less of a biography and more 'a Kinsey report on his romps with Mme du Châtelet.' Both sexually and intellectually, it was a time of high stimulation. Encouraged by Madame du Châtelet, Voltaire turned away from pure literature, and began to publish a stream of histories and popular science, most notably his *Eléments de la philosophie de Newton* (1737). This contained the famous story of Newton and the falling apple, which 'demonstrated' the universal law of gravity. At their long suppers (the only meal their guests could rely on), they argued everything from physics to theology, and Voltaire did ludicrous imitations of their enemies. There were poetry readings, picnics, laboratory experiments, and financial investments. There were letters from all over Europe. And there was endless, enchanting talk, punctuated by the occasional amorous row. André Maurois once described Madame du Châtelet's main interests as 'books, diamonds, algebra, astronomy and underwear.' Voltaire shared them all.

Once, driving back to Cirey one freezing winter's night, their coach overturned and help had to be sent for. The servants were amazed to find them peacefully curled up together in a pile of rugs and cushions, deep in a snow drift, carefully identifying the outlines of the lesser constellations.

It was with Madame du Châtelet that Voltaire, complaining perpetually of ill-health and middle-age (he was now in his forties), began to concentrate on the problem of happiness. He viewed it not as a domestic matter, but as a profound philosophical conundrum in a world of ignorance, injustice, and fanaticism. His inquiries went into the short stories he began to write: the first of which was *Micromégas* ('Mini-Mighty'), begun at Cirey about 1738.

His initial target was the philosopher Leibniz, whose sturdy complacence had produced an immensely sophisticated argument to prove that, in accordance with the inevitability of Divine Providence, everyone lived 'in the best of all possible worlds.' All local suffering was part of a greater system of good. Curiously, this was a view highly fashionable among Enlightenment intellectuals, and had been popularized by Pope in his *Essay on Man*:

> All discord, harmony not understood;
> All partial evil, universal good;
> And, spite of pride, in erring reason's spite,
> One truth is clear: Whatever is, is right.

Voltaire attacked this absurdity with what was in effect 'An Essay on Space Monsters,' one of the earliest pieces of science fiction. Micromégas is approximately twenty miles high in his stockings, and comes from a deeply civilized planet near Sirius. He surfs through outer space on comets, making notes on everything he sees, because he, too, is a philosopher. Arriving on Earth (with a five-mile dwarf from Saturn as his companion), he believes it is uninhabited until he spots a whale in the Baltic, using his pocket microscope with a two-thousand-foot lens.

At last, Micromégas discovers a scientific expedition sailing back from the Arctic Circle, and questions the 'mite-sized philosophers' on the nature of human existence (he uses an improvised hearing trumpet made from a fingernail paring). They wisely quote Aristotle, Descartes, and Liebniz, which cuts no ice with Micromégas at all. Only a follower of Locke, who affirms that 'there are more things possible than people think,' makes any sense to the Space Giants.

Finally, a Thomist theologian, in full academic regalia, steps forward. He tells them that everything—the stars, the planets, the sun, and they themselves—is created by God uniquely for man's benefit. 'On hearing this, our two Travellers fell about, choking with that irrepressible laughter which, according to Homer, is the portion of the gods.' The philosophers' tiny ship is nearly engulfed, but the shaken survivors are sent home to report to the Paris Academy of Sciences.

Voltaire withheld the publication of *Micromégas* for several years. Meanwhile, on the strength of his growing reputation as an historian, he sought to place himself back at the centre of political power in Europe. It was the time of the 'Enlightened Despots,' and Voltaire flirted with them. He began a mutually flattering correspondence with Frederick the Great of Prussia, and much to Madame du Châtelet's consternation (she was not invited), Voltaire visited his court. He was then in turn invited back to Versailles, where he was appointed Royal Historiographer to Louis XV in 1745, and elected to the Académie Française in 1746. Again, Madame du Châtelet was largely excluded from this glory, and doubts and recriminations began on both sides.

Voltaire now wrote his second great *conte philosophique*, entitled *Zadig* (1748). This time he used the conventions of the Oriental tale, with its thousand and one twists, to show the absurdities of the sup-posedly benevolent workings of Providence. The young Zadig, 'an affectionate young man who did not always wish to be right,' pur-sues his fortune (he is briefly prime minister of Babylon) and the beautiful Astarte through a series of wildly improbable adventures, accompanied by talking parrots and other portents. The story is notable for its two, alternative endings. One is happy: 'Zadig glori-fied heaven.' The other is hopeless: 'But where shall I go? In Egypt they'll make me a slave. In Arabia they'll probably have me burned to death. In Babylon they'll strangle me. But somehow I must find out what has become of Astarte. Let us depart, and see what my sorry destiny still has in store for me.'

The second ending was nearer the truth, for Voltaire. In his absence from Cirey, Madame du Châtelet took a lover, became pregnant, and died in childbirth in September 1749. Voltaire was half-mad with grief and regret. At Cirey he fell down the stairs. In Paris he roamed through the streets at night, weeping, and believing his happiness was lost for-ever. He quarrelled with the French king, and unwisely accepted an official post at Frederick's court in Berlin. (The huge pink-and-blue marble working desk that Frederick gave him, presumably as a form of paperweight, has now somehow found its way to the Café Procope.) Voltaire remained for three unhappy years, finally fleeing in 1753, to be imprisoned briefly on Frederick's instructions at Frankfurt. The Enlightened Despots of Europe were finished with Voltaire.

But Voltaire, as it turned out, was also finished with them. With his amazing powers of resilience, he again chose independence. He moved to Geneva in 1754, rented an estate at Les Délices, and find-ing the intellectual air (and the banking) to his liking, finally set-tled just inside the French border (so he could slip easily into exile) at Ferney in 1758. This would be his home until the final months of his life. Immediately, he began to write his masterpiece, *Candide, or Optimism*, which became the epitome of all his adventures.

Voltaire was not alone at Ferney. He had taken a new lover: a fat, blond, domestically-minded young woman known to history as Madame Denis. It is said that she dressed like a Watteau but looked like a Rubens. Madame Denis also happened to be Voltaire's niece, his sister's daughter. This mildly incestuous arrangement seemed to work admirably. Voltaire's enemies said she was little more than a coarse housekeeper and crude bed-warmer. But she proved a skilled secretary and administrator, she obviously adored her capricious uncle, and Voltaire's erotic letters to her (he was now in his late fif-ties) are hymns of autumnal concupiscence.

He wrote from Germany, while they were still apart, in 1753: 'My heart is pierced by everything you do. None of my tragedies contains

a heroine like you. How can you say I don't love you! My child, I
shall love you until the grave. I get more jealous as I get older . . . I
want to be the only man who has the joy of fucking you . . . I have
an erection as I write this, and I kiss your beautiful nipples and
your lovely bottom a thousand times. Now then, tell me that I don't
love you!'

With Madame Denis at Ferney, Voltaire reconstructed the lost
happiness of Cirey on a grander basis. His investments had made
him rich, and he could create a little enlightened kingdom of his
own. He spread himself *en grand seigneur*, developing a model farm,
building a theatre and a chapel ('erected for God by Voltaire' over
the lintel), employing some sixty servants and even starting a silk
farm for the manufacture of fine stockings to the gentry. Not only
letters but visitors now came from all over Europe, including the
young James Boswell, who questioned him on the immortality of the
soul ('desirable, but not probable,' thought Voltaire) and excessively
admired his buxom Swiss serving girls. Voltaire's grin seemed genial
to Boswell. Voltaire told him: 'There is evidently a sun, and there is
evidently a God. So let us have a religion too. Then all men will be
brothers under the sun.' Voltaire, like Candide, had decided to cultivate his garden.

But *Candide* is not a treatise on gardening, or even on happiness. It is more like a treatise on misery. From his stronghold at
Ferney, Voltaire looked round the world and saw squalor, injustice,
disease, ignorance, cruelty, and fanaticism. The figure of Candide,
the young man from Westphalia 'whose soul was written upon his
countenance,' is a sort of brilliant animation or personification
of that all-seeing Voltairian gaze. Candide travels the Earth—
Germany, Portugal, England, Eldorado, Surinam, Constantinople,
Italy, France—and witnesses and suffers the absurdities and horrors of existence. It is a *catalogue raisonné* of historical disasters: the
Lisbon earthquake, the Spanish Inquisition, the German wars, the
South American Jesuits, even the English executing a heroic admiral
on his own quarterdeck.

The clear glassy fire of the narrative is unique. *Candide* has been
described as *The Thousand and One Nights,* condensed by Swift, and
translated by Montaigne. Yet its speed and wit and counterpoint are
wholly Voltairian. Journeying on with his faithful companions—
Pangloss the Optimist, Martin the Pessimist, Cunégonde the fat
Princess—Candide plays out a constant dialogue between hope and
despair, innocence and disenchantment.

> 'But for what purpose was this world created, then?' asked
> Candide.
> 'To drive us all mad,' replied Martin.

'But don't you find it absolutely amazing,' continued Candide, 'the way those two girls I told you about—the ones who lived in the land of Lobeiros—loved those two monkeys?'

The question is pure Candide; but it is Candide's reply that is pure Voltaire. Moreover Voltaire's world of rational absurdities is not safely fixed in the eighteenth century. Again and again, it flashes up toward our own. Fundamentalism, genocide, civil war, ideological persecution, environmental disaster: all are foreseen. Uneasy shadows stir at the edge of each bright page.

After the good Dr. Pangloss has been temporarily mislaid from the narrative in Germany (these sudden disappearances of the faithful companions are a favourite device), he turns up again in Bulgaria: gaunt, racked with coughs, and half his nose rotted away. The cause, he tells the appalled Candide, is love.

> You remember Paquette, that pretty lady's maid to our noble Baroness. Well, in her arms I tasted the delights of paradise, and in turn they have led me to these torments of hell. She had the Foul Disease, and may have died of it by now. Paquette was made a gift of it by a learned Franciscan, who had traced it back to its source. For he had got it from an old Countess, who had contracted it from a Captain in the Cavalry, who owed it to a Marchioness, who had it from a page-boy, who caught it from a Jesuit, who—during his novitiate—inherited it in a direct line from one of Christopher Columbus's shipmates. For my part, I shall bequeath it to nobody, because I'm dying of it.

Needless to say, Dr. Pangloss, being an optimist, survives. But he lives only to insist that his lethal infection was 'a necessary ingredient' in the best of all possible worlds. Without it, how could Columbus have discovered America, or the cafés of Europe have served delicious hot chocolate drinks?

Voltaire denied authorship of *Candide*, and called it 'une coïonnerie' (in effect, 'a load of old balls'). But it immediately bounced right across Europe, first published in Geneva, and then instantly pirated in Paris, Amsterdam, London, and Brussels. It was the greatest international best seller of its time. In its first year it ran over thirty thousand copies, an astonishing figure for a work of fiction in the mid-eighteenth century, over three times the sales of Swift's *Gulliver's Travels* (1726) in a similar period.

With *Candide*—'my diabolical little book'—Voltaire had broken through to a new international, middle-class readership, and created the voice that all Europe recognized. For the remaining nineteen years of his life at Ferney, stories, satires, squibs, and treatises poured from his pen. Largely ignoring the kings, the despots, the courts, and the academies, Voltaire wrote and published directly for a new liberal intelligentsia: a Fourth Estate who began to believe that the world could be changed through the battle of ideas. His first edition of *The Portable Philosophical Dictionary* was published in 1764, with 118 alphabetical entries, a true 'pocket' book. (Subsequent editions enlarged it to 600 entries.) Its compact declarations— some less than a page—on Love, Laughter, Fanaticism, Equality, Liberty, Torture, Tolerance, War, Dogma, Virtue, and Beauty, went round the world. Voltaire launched his fighting motto: '*Ecrasez l'infame*'—a vivid but almost untranslatable rallying cry to the liberal conscience everywhere. One version would be: 'Crush bigotry and superstition (the infamous thing).' Another, more spirited version, might run: 'Make war on the Fanatics.'

Voltaire now engaged with the authorities in a new and daring way. He began to take up specific causes, particularly cases of injustice or malpractice, and fight them through the press. The first and most famous was that of Jean Calas in 1762.

Monsieur Calas was an ordinary, middle-class citizen of Toulouse, in southwest France. He owned a successful cloth shop in the rue des Filatiers, and lived above the premises with his English wife, Rose, and their grown-up children. Monsieur Calas and his wife were Protestants, in a city that was overwhelmingly Catholic and had a long history of persecutions dating back to the Albigensian wars. Their eldest son, Marc-Antoine Calas, who was twenty-eight, had converted to Catholicism. One evening in October 1761, Marc-Antoine's body was found hanging from a rafter in the lower part of the shop. Jean Calas was arrested, tortured, tried for murder, broken on a wheel, and after a two-hour respite for 'confession' (which was not obtained), executed by strangulation. The Toulouse law court pronounced that Monsieur Calas's motive for murdering his son was Marc-Antoine's conversion to Catholicism.

When news of the case reached Ferney, Voltaire's lawyer's instinct was aroused. After extensive investigations and a long, searching interview with Calas's younger son, Voltaire took up the case in April 1762. He was convinced that there had been a grave miscarriage of justice, born out of fanatical religious prejudice in Toulouse.

His grounds for appeal rested on two salient points. First, Jean Calas was not in the least anti-Catholic. His family servant of many years was Catholic, and one of his other sons, after also converting to Catholicism, had continuing financial support from Calas. So there was no convincing motive for murder. Second, the twenty-eight-year-old Marc-Antoine had been the one misfit in the family. He had been an endless source of worry to his parents: moody, immature, theatrical. He had failed to marry, failed to become a lawyer, and failed to pay large gambling debts. He had dined with the Calas family on the very evening of his death, and left early, 'feeling unwell.' Almost certainly he had committed suicide in a fit of depression. So there had been no murder anyway.

Voltaire pursued justice on several fronts, with all his customary energy (he was now nearly seventy). He contacted government ministers in Paris, and drew Madame de Pompadour to his cause. He wrote letters to all the contributors to the *Encyclopédie*. He publicized the case in the English newspapers. Most important of all, he published his classic *Treatise on Toleration* (1762). It begins with a brilliant (and indeed thrilling) forensic analysis of the Calas case, and ends with a moving declaration of the principle of universal tolerance.

> Let all men remember that they are brothers! Let them hold in horror the tyranny that is exercised over men's souls . . . If the curse of war is still inevitable, let us not hasten to destroy each other where we have civil peace. From Siam to California, in a thousand different tongues, let us each use the brief moment of our existence, to bless God's goodness which has given us this precious gift.

In June 1764 the judgement against Jean Calas was annulled by the Supreme Paris court. Legal compensation for the family was never obtained, but the King was shamed into providing a large grant in aid. Voltaire had achieved a small legal victory, but a great moral one. He took up several similar cases over the next decade, and the authorities trembled whenever he moved. (The most terrible concerned a young man in Abbeville, twenty-year-old La Barre, who was convicted of singing blasphemous songs, urinating on a tomb, and possessing Voltaire's *Dictionary*. He had his tongue pulled out, his right arm was chopped off, and he was executed by burning. For years Voltaire supported his family and friends, seeking compensation. La Barre was a chevalier.)

Voltaire had established what were to become the crucial weapons of the 'engaged intellectual' over the next two hundred years: investigation, exposure, dispassionate argument, ridicule, and 'the oxygen of publicity.' Above all he had established the fighting power of plain truth, 'the facts of the case,' the small stubborn foot soldiers of veracity, which can rout the greatest armies of church or state by using 'the best shots.' He had become what Pierre Lepape calls 'Voltaire the Conqueror.'

Voltaire's *Treatise on Toleration* contains one vital exception to the universal principle. Philosophically this has profound implication for those who have inherited it, from the French Revolutionaries and the American Founding Fathers down to our present governors.

Chapter 18 is entitled 'The One Case in which Intolerance is a Human Right.' In it, Voltaire grasps the nettle that stings all liberals. How can we tolerate those groups in society who are themselves intolerant, and thereby threaten the principle itself?

Voltaire's answer is succinct: we cannot. For the individual, toleration is an absolute right and an absolute duty. But for society and its legislators, toleration has a limit. Where intolerance becomes criminal, the laws of the liberal state cannot tolerate it. And the fanatical intolerance of any social group, where it is sufficient to 'trouble society' at large, is always to be condemned as criminal. This is Voltaire's 'one case.'

Here is the vital passage. 'For any Government to abrogate its right to punish the misdeeds of citizens, it is necessary that these misdeeds should not class as crimes. They only class as crimes when they trouble society at large. And they trouble society at large, the moment that they inspire fanaticism. Consequently, if men are to deserve tolerance, they must begin by not being fanatics.'

The most problematic issue raised by Voltaire's 'one exception' to Tolerance is painfully illustrated by his own attitude to the Jews. How exactly do we measure the supposed 'fanaticism' of another social or religious group, who may merely hold strong beliefs and separate traditions, without falling into 'fanaticism' ourselves? Voltaire's weird, anti-Jewish prejudice runs like a barbed thread throughout his work; over thirty of the entries in the *Philosophical Dictionary* contain anti-Jewish statements; and the article on Toleration itself refers to the Jews as historically 'the most intolerant and cruel of all the peoples of Antiquity.'

It has been argued that Voltaire's position was essentially anti-Biblical and satirical—part of his general attack on the ludicrous extremes of Old Testament Christianity—rather than anti-Semitic in any modern sense. Certainly the persecution of the Jews by the Inquisition appalled him.

As Prince Hamlet says, 'Aye, there's the rub.' Voltaire had not shown how the battle could be won. But he had defined the field of combat. For him, 'fanaticism' is expressed essentially by religious or racial persecution, the two great curses of civilization. Two hundred years on, one might think he was still right. Wherever there are pogroms, lethal fatwas, book burnings, race riots, ethnic cleansing, apartheids, his spirit looks down grinning with pain. But out of that grin is born the notion of Human Rights, a term he specifically uses.

The British philosopher A. J. Ayer once observed that Voltaire's concept of toleration was based on one of the most noble dreams of the eighteenth-century Enlightenment. All religions and racial codes prepared us for the emergence of one universal, rational morality, which would gradually come to be accepted over the entire globe.

'Voltaire . . . wishes to maintain that there is a law of morality that holds universally, like Newton's law of gravitation.' The good action, the proper decision, the right thing to do, should be as obvious as the fall of an apple.

Voltaire lived on at his beloved Ferney until he was over eighty. There are many accounts of his kindly, eccentric household, and sheet after sheet of brilliant caricatures made by Jean Huber, a local Swiss artist, whom Voltaire allowed to make mocking sketches of his most intimate moments. (When Voltaire got irritated with his intrusions, Huber merely quoted from Voltaire on Toleration.) One of Huber's best paintings is of Voltaire in his bedroom, standing on one foot, pulling on his knickerbockers, and dictating a letter. Voltaire seems to have lived permanently in a series of brilliantly coloured dressing gowns, with silk slippers that were always falling off his feet.

He never stopped writing, and guests record that he was often at his desk for fifteen hours a day. In the 1770s he wrote or dictated over five hundred letters a year. In 1770 he began a series of philosophic essays, *Questions on the Encyclopaedia*, which eventually extended to nine volumes. He continued to add to his *contes philosophiques*, still usually published anonymously, slipped into newspapers or surreptitiously circulated in pamphlets purporting to be printed in Brussels or Amsterdam. Notable among these are *The Ingénue* (1767), a sly attack on Rousseau's theories of education; *The Princess of Babylon* (1768), an interesting excursion into sexual politics; and *The White Bull* (1773).

The White Bull was written when Voltaire was seventy-nine, and has the feeling of a will and testament. As in many of the later stories, it conjures a fantastic world where bigots rule, innocents travel, and animals speak the truth. In this case the beautiful Princess Amasida (who has read Locke's *On Understanding*) has fallen tenderly in love with a large white bull (who is really the young King Nebuchadnezzar). She is trying to save both him and herself from execution by the religious authorities, who fanatically disapprove. Amasida succeeds, and the last chapter is entitled, 'How the Princess Married her Ox.'

The story is unusual in that it contains a mocking self-portrait of Voltaire as the Princess's faithful companion, the philosopher Mambres, 'a former magus and eunuch to the Pharaohs,' who is 'about thirteen hundred years old.' Mambres gives exquisite dinners ('carp's tongue tart, liver of turbot and pike, chicken with pistachios') and dispenses wisdom. In his ironic, absent-minded fashion, Mambres succeeds in averting various catastrophes for the Princess and her Bull, and finally sees that the monstrous creature gets changed back into the handsome young king. 'This latest metamorphosis

astonished everybody, apart from the meditative Mambres . . .
who returned to his Palace to think things over.' To his great satisfaction he hears the people shouting, 'Long live our great King, who
is no longer dumb!'

It would be too much to expect Voltaire to die quietly and medita-
tively at Ferney. Instead, he decided on one last assault on Paris. He
succeeded in taking his native city by storm, not once, but twice.
Once, while he was dying; the second time when he was dead. In
1778, in the spring of his eighty-fourth year, he attended a performance of his last tragedy, *Irène*, at the Comédie Française, and sat
in on a session of the Académie. Both occasions were a personal
triumph. Over three hundred distinguished visitors called on him,
where he was staying at the Marquis de Villette's *hôtel*, now 27 quai
Voltaire (on the corner of the rue de Beaune, with the restaurant
Voltaire serving 'Candide cocktails' on the ground floor).

But amid this public glory, Voltaire was exhausted, and in the
privacy of his bedroom spitting blood. He died in much pain on
May 30, 1778. He had received a Jesuit priest in his dying hours,
whom he seems to have teased, as in the old days: on being urged to
renounce the devil, Voltaire gently replied, 'This is no time for making new enemies.' But to the relief of Enlightenment Europe, he
refused to renounce any of his works. His body was smuggled out to
a secret burying place in the Champagne region.

Thirteen years later, in July 1791, Voltaire came storming back
posthumously. He was reburied as a hero of the Revolution in the
crypt of the Paris Pantheon: and there (unlike many of his temporary cohabitants) his monument has always remained. The modern
inscription—probably written by André Malraux—describes him as
one of 'the spiritual fathers' of France, and as 'the immortal symbol
of the Age of Enlightenment.' His marble statue, with a quill in one
hand, and a sword beneath his foot, grins at that too.

Far above him, in the nave of the Pantheon, a curious law of physics is at work. The stonework of the great eighteenth-century vault
has become unstable, and chunks of masonry are imploding onto
the hallowed floors beneath. Safety nets have been set up, and the
public is warned to keep clear. The authorities announce that they
are making investigations. But they do not yet know the cause of
this disturbance in the great structure. Perhaps it is a *conte
philosophique*.

ADAM GOPNIK

Voltaire's Garden: The Philosopher as a Campaigner for Human Rights[†]

Voltaire, like God, whom he patronized, is always there. "No authors ever had so much fame in their own life-time as Pope and Voltaire," Dr. Johnson dogmatized in the late eighteenth century, and though Pope still sings for those with ears to hear him, Voltaire still squabbles, a more lifelike sound, and does it everywhere. On the Op-Ed page of the *Times,* he can ornament Paul Krugman or offend William Safire, and he is fun to read about, no matter what he is doing. In fact, he is most fun to read about when what he is doing is doing good, since he does good without being pious, an unusual mixture. For all that he was a mad egomaniac and an unabashed self-promoter, he remains matchlessly entertaining company, incapable of either shame or shoddy thinking.

There are at least three distinct Voltaires. First is the scandalous Voltaire, who by the seventeen-twenties had become the leading controversialist in France, with a series of topically loaded plays and poems, only to be thrown into the Bastille twice for being generally annoying, and in 1726 get exiled to England, where he absorbed and wrote about English learning and English parliamentary institutions. Next, there is the scientific Voltaire, who returned to France in 1728 and eventually became the lover and disciple of the brilliant Mme. Châtelet, and who, closeted with her at her Château de Cirey, wrote on math and science and did more than almost anyone else to bring the news of Newtonian physics to Europe. Then, from the seventeen-fifties until his death, in 1778, there is the socially conscious Voltaire, the Voltaire who became one of the first human-rights campaigners in Europe, and whose determination to remake the world one soul at a time W. H. Auden could still idealize in 1939, in his poem "Voltaire at Ferney." ("And still all over Europe stood the horrible nurses / Itching to boil their children. Only his verses / Perhaps could stop them: He must go on working.")

Although no single volume in English does justice to all the Voltaires, the second, scientific Voltaire, at least, inspired one of the most blissfully entertaining books in the language, Nancy Mitford's 1954 *Voltaire in Love,* an account of his great affair with Mme. Châtelet and of their joint introduction to the pleasures of sex and

† From *The New Yorker* (March 7, 2005): 74–81. © Condé Nast. Reprinted by permission.

calculus. It is de rigueur to dismiss Mitford as a reckless amateur who, as someone said, made the Enlightenment *philosophes* into members of her family. But they were members of her family—or more like them than they *were* like the kind of responsible, well-read, judicious dons, offering syntheses of current thought, beloved of academic historians. Voltaire spent his life with society people and show people, and lived in terror of boredom, not inconsistency. Mitford understands Voltaire's mixture of bad faith, irascible egotism, genuine altruism, and sporadic courage, all played out in an atmosphere of petty literary politicking—in part because the type remains intact in France to this day.

Ian Davidson, a longtime correspondent for the *Financial Times,* has, in his new book, "Voltaire in Exile" (Grove), taken on the story of the last Voltaire. This Voltaire evolves out of the two others; in fact, they are still right there. The old, good Voltaire was exactly the same man as the young rascal, and the rascality fuelled the goodness with energy and mischief. Yet the transformation is complete: in 1753, at the beginning of Davidson's story, Voltaire was, in contemporary terms, like Michael Moore and Susan Sontag all mixed up: a provocateur who was also a universal literary celebrity. By the end, he was more like a cross between Andrei Sakharov and Mr. Toad of Toad Hall—a conceited grand bourgeois with a big house who was also one of the first dissidents, embodying a whole alternative set of values, and who came to be treated even by the government almost as an independent state within a state. How this came about, and without any Tolstoyan repentance or self-remaking, is one of the great stories of literary evolution.

Davidson tells it well, too. In 1753, Voltaire was in flight from Frederick the Great, of Prussia, who had taken him in as a kind of house philosopher at Potsdam. Voltaire may have imagined that he would rule hand in hand, philosopher and king, but soon discovered that he was there merely as an exotic intellectual toy. ("We shall squeeze the orange," Frederick had said, secretly, "then, when we have swallowed the juice, we shall throw it away.") Even after the falling-out with Frederick, Voltaire knew that he had some big guns on his side. The foreign minister of France, the Duke de Choiseul, was a fan, as was Mme. Pompadour, the King's mistress, not to mention the Empress of Russia. He was also, luckily, very rich, in no small part because of his participation in a bizarre swindle devised by a mathematician friend, who, back in 1728, realized that the French government had authorized a lottery in which the prize was much greater than the collective cost of the tickets. He and Voltaire formed a syndicate, collected all the money, and became moneylenders to the great houses of Europe.

During his escape from Frederick, Voltaire first thought of going back to France, which he loved as only Frenchmen who have been away from it can. But a message from his old friend Mme. Pompadour confirmed the stunning news that the King had exiled him and forbidden him to return. (This turned out to be not quite true; the old man had probably said something merely pettish, like "Tell him to stay away!") The terms of his exile were unclear, but Voltaire decided to move someplace close enough to feel like France and far enough away to keep him out of the official grip. He chose Geneva, which was then a small, suspicious Calvinist Protestant city-state. Through the good offices of a prominent Geneva friend, he found, and managed to rent, a small estate. He moved in with his new love, Mme. Denis, and renamed the villa Les Délices, the Delights. Although it was his later, sister retreat at Ferney that became legendary (he moved there in 1765, after a series of feuds with the Calvinist authorities in Geneva), it was his escape to Les Délices that marked a new epoch in his life.

Voltaire's work, to this point, consisted essentially of a mass of journalism, essays, poems, potted, vivid histories, and historical plays all pulled together in the public imagination by a single strong personality. The "philosophy" that ran through it, though allergic to sectarian piety, was still officially Deist—partly because this was insurance against accusations of atheism, partly because, in a slightly condescending spirit, Voltaire was in favor of a benign, supervisory God in the way that British leftists used to be in favor of the Queen, or in the way that Yankee free agents are in favor of Joe Torre; it's nice to think that someone genial is overseeing things. But there doesn't seem to be any evidence that he actually believed, with any intensity or appetite, in "spiritual" experience, or found the sense of God's presence even momentarily engaging. But then Voltaire was never exactly a "philosopher" in the conventional sense; his philosophy is almost always a moral instinct rendered as a dramatic gesture, rather than consecutive thoughts turned into a logical argument. As with Victor Hugo and Zola, his moral instincts were so good that we still intellectualize the dramatic gestures they became.

He quickly turned his exile into a desirable condition—a version of the ancient Horatian ideal of escape from the corrupting city into a small enclosed country house. Pope had done the same thing when he built his grotto at his little house in Twickenham, and wrote about it as enthusiastically. Yet Pope's grotto is playful, an obvious mock hermitage. Voltaire's ideas were far more bourgeois; he wanted to play host to as many people as he could, and to build the sweetest garden he could, and, after renting the villa, he started shopping like Martha Stewart newly freed from prison.

There are few more premonitory or touching documents than
Voltaire's shopping lists. He demanded green olive oil, eight wing
armchairs, rosewood commodes, and furniture covers in red morocco.
He hired two master gardeners, twenty workmen, and twelve servants. He ordered the best coffee and crate after crate of wine
(though, odd reminder of another time, he drank his Burgundies and
laid down his Beaujolais). He decided to paint the trellises green, the
tiles red, and the doors either white or "a fine yellow." He wrote to
his agent asking for "artichoke bulbs and as much as possible of
lavender, thyme, rosemary, mint, basil, rue strawberry bushes, pinks,
thadicee, balm, tarragon, sariette, burnet, sage and hyssop to cleanse
our sins, etc." When he wrote that it was our duty to cultivate our
garden, he really knew what it meant to cultivate a garden.

It was a garden with a principle. It represented what he saw as a
new, French ideal of domestic happiness, windows wide and doors
open, "simplicity" itself. "We have finally come to enjoy luxury only
in taste and convenience," he wrote in those years, in his history
The Age of Louis XIV: "The crowd of pages and liveried servants has
disappeared." All that counted now was "affable manners, simple living and the culture of the mind." Of course, it was a very Petit Tri-
anon simplicity. As Davidson shows, though, it was deeply, emotionally
rich: "He was enjoying real happiness, for the first time in his life."

It was at this moment of delight and apparent retreat, of affable
manners and simple living, that he began the series of crusades that
eventually blossomed into the human-rights campaigns that came
to dominate the rest of his life. It would be nice to say that Voltaire was a courageous man whom no amount of comfort could
seduce. The truth is that, as his friend Condorcet wrote sadly, he
was easily terrified, and often a coward: "He was often seen to expose
himself to the storm, almost with temerity, but seldom to stand up
to it with firmness." And, of course, no man of fewer sublime feelings has ever lived; he was baffled by religion and spirituality, mate-
rialist and carnal to the core.

What motivated him, then, to start up? Partly it must have been
that he so much enjoyed vexing stupid powerful people that he kept
forgetting that stupid people who had gained power were never stupid about threats to their power. Each time he poked the silly tiger
and the tiger clawed back, he was genuinely shocked. And then there
is a kind of egotism so vast and so pleased with itself that it includes
other people as an extension of itself. Voltaire felt so much for other
people because he felt so much for himself; everything happened to
him because he was the only reasonable subject of everything that
happened. By inflating his ego to immense proportions, he made it
a shelter for the helpless.

But there was something else, too. His exile moved him away from court practices and court values, with their hypersensitivity toward status, toward family practices and family values, with their hypersensitivity toward security. (In these Délices years, he took in and later adopted a teen-age daughter, and began to sigh that he had never had children of his own.) As Tocqueville saw half a century later, home-making, which ought to make people more selfish, makes them less so; it gives them a stake in other people's houses. It is not so much the establishment of a garden but the ownership of a gate that moves people from liking a society based on favors to one based on rights. Enclosing his garden broadened Voltaire's circle of compassion. When people were dragged from *their* gardens to be tortured and killed in the name of faith, he began to take it, as they say, personally.

In those days, unspeakably cruel tortures were still routine in the French penal system. Condemned criminals were tortured by being broken on the wheel—that is, being bound on a scaffold to a wheel and then having their bones broken, one by one, with an iron bar. Davidson suggests (shrewdly and originally) that Voltaire's sense of outrage may have been galvanized by the hideous execution in Paris of the would-be assassin of Louis XV, the mad Damiens, in 1757. Damiens was pulled apart alive, his limbs attached to four horses and the horses driven in different directions, for public instruction in the center of Paris. Voltaire was no fan of regicide. It was because he was for the execution that the public torture frightened him: it was a sign of how quickly civilities could disintegrate under threat. ("Enlightened times will only enlighten a small number of honest men," he wrote. "The common people will always be fanatical.") He coined his most famous phrase, *écrasez l'infâme*—"Crush the horror"—and began to use it, in jauntily (and evasively) abbreviated form. Historians have fussed for centuries about exactly what Voltaire meant by it—the Catholic Church? the Court?—but it's clear. The horror was the alliance of religious fanaticism with the instruments of the state, and the two combined for torture and official murder.

It is against this background, of a garden built and the encroaching fanatics, that Voltaire wrote "Candide," in 1759. Two fine new translations of the book have just appeared, one by Burton Raffel (Yale) and one by Peter Constantine (Modern Library). The young Candide lives in the little German principality of Thunder-Ten-Tronckh, under the guidance of his tutor, Pangloss, a theorist of optimism. A liaison with his beloved Cunégonde causes him to be exiled, and soon afterward the principality is sacked by the Bulgars, who rape Cunégonde and leave Pangloss for dead. Candide then encounters every kind of eighteenth-century horror, from enslavement by the Turks to bondage on a French galley, and ends up on a little farm near Constantinople, wisely counselling Pangloss that the only worthwhile thing for people to do is to cultivate their gardens.

Candide is such a familiar book that it is easy to miss its real target. What marks it off from most other didactic literature, as Davidson says, is its gaiety; the disembowellings and rapes are drawn with breezily overdone matter-of-factness. The tone is like that of the Monty Python movies, which are genuinely appalled by violence but register their shock by making it absurd. Candide is said to have been occasioned by the 1755 Lisbon earthquake, a tsunami-like event, and is meant to satirize the optimism associated with Leibniz. It is also usually said to be unfair to Leibniz, a great philosopher, who was among the inventors of calculus. Leibniz's view, after all, was not that everything was good but that our world was the best possible. Given that God could have considered every world before he made it, he must have chosen the best one—so that if there is suffering and evil in it, these things must have a cause in the mind of God. Given that the deity is benevolent, small-scale pain must be part of some universal balance, or, as Pope puts it in his "Essay on Man," "All discord harmony not understood; / All partial evil, universal good." Leibniz and Pope after him are arguing not that life will always be happy but that the world is optimally designed. Suffering is explicable—not defensible but explicable.

But Voltaire was not unfair to Leibniz. He understood exactly what Leibniz was saying, and has Pangloss say it. On the tutor's first appearance, he gives the classic instance: pigs are made to be eaten and so we have pork. It seems hard only from the narrow point of view of the pig. "Those who have suggested that everything is good have spoken obtusely," Pangloss explains, in Raffel's rendering. "What they should have said is that everything is for the best." Voltaire's point was that the two ideas are, in concrete terms, the same idea. Insisting that everything is for the best means finding the best in everything. To subsume individual suffering or pain within a larger equilibrium is to accept the logic of the slaughterhouse. The pig has a right to his protest.

Voltaire's target throughout Candide is not optimism in the sense of fatuous cheerfulness but optimism in the sense of optimal thinking: the kind of bland reassurance that explains pain with reference to a larger plan or history. In this way, the Christmas tsunami cannot have for Voltaire's readers today anything approaching the force that a natural disaster like the Lisbon earthquake had for the eighteenth century. Few people any longer believe in a benevolent nature—much less a benevolent nature sitting in for a providential God. We can feel comfortably superior to Leibniz's particular brand of optimism, which is centered on natural law of this kind, since we no longer believe that nature is part of an inherently balanced or benevolent system.

But almost all of us still do believe, stubbornly, in some kind of optimal thinking. We believe, vaguely or explicitly, that liberal democracy, with all its faults, is the best of all possible political systems, that globalization, with all its injustices, is the best of all possible futures, and even that the American way is the best of all possible ways—with appropriate cautious Leibnizian emphasis on "possible." (One can track the path, and the travails, of modern popular optimism just by following Thomas Friedman's columns in the *Times*, agonized Tuesday to hopeful Sunday.) We are all optimalists of this kind, perhaps reinforced by the doctrines of evolutionary psychology (which say exactly that all discord is harmony misunderstood) or by faith in an inevitable evolving "future of freedom." Attacks on these beliefs—September 11th was the most acute—shake us up the way eighteenth-century people were shaken by the Lisbon earthquake. The realization that all may not be tending toward the best, that religious fanaticism and tribal intolerance could prevail over liberal meliorism, is the earthquake of our time.

Voltaire's radicalism, then and now, lies not in his refutation of optimism but in his refusal of belief. *Candide* is not really, or entirely, a satire on optimism. It is an attack on organized religion. The joke about optimism in *Candide* is always the same joke: something terrible happens, and Pangloss gallantly rationalizes it. The jokes about religious cruelty are mordant, varied, and encyclopedic: every kind of religious intolerance—Muslim, Jewish, and, particularly, Christian, dignified, crude, and greedy—is trotted out and exposed. The one thing that Voltaire is sure of in "Candide" is the idiocy of theodicy. What drives him crazy is the ability of religious fanatics to exploit the fatality of the world in order to enact their own cruelties.

In the famous early chapter, the Lisbon earthquake makes a brief Terry Gilliam–slapstick, scene-setting appearance. What happens immediately afterward is the point of the satire: "After the earthquake, which had destroyed three quarters of Lisbon, the country's wise men could find no better way of preventing total ruin than to give the people a beautiful auto-da-fé." Voltaire goes on to detail the hideous theatrics of the Inquisition: the yellow robes, the burnings and flogging set to Church music, the whole choreography of Christian cruelty. The point of *Candide* is that the rapes and disembowelments, the enslavement and the beatings are not part of some larger plan, not a fact of the fatality of life and the universe, but fiendish tortures thought up by fanatics. They may be omnipresent;

but they are not inevitable. Voltaire thinks optimism merely silly. It is the flight from failed optimism into faith that he fears.

Against the horrors of religious cruelty and the emptiness of religious apologia, Voltaire proposes—what, exactly? Burton Raffel, the more daring of the two new translators, takes that most familiar ending, *"Il faut cultiver notre jardin,"* and translates it not as "We must cultivate our garden" but, startlingly, as "We need to work our fields." (Raffel is a translator who doesn't mind shocking his readers—his version of "The Red and the Black" was one long provocation.) His change of the book's famous moral is obviously meant, in one way, to protect Voltaire from the charge of Petit Trianonism. After so much suffering, cultivating our garden seems too . . . *cultivated.* ("Crush the horror! Crush the horror!" Voltaire's friend D'Alembert wrote to him once. "That is easily said when one is a hundred leagues from the bastards and the fanatics, when one has an independent income of a hundred thousand livres!")

But Raffel is wrong, surely, in thinking that by cultivating one's garden Voltaire meant anything save cultivating one's garden. By "garden" Voltaire meant a garden, not a field—not the land and task to which we are chained by nature but the better place we build by love. The force of that last great injunction, "We must cultivate our garden," is that our responsibility is local, and concentrated on immediate action. In the aftermath of the tsunami, William Safire argued that this "surge of generosity" actually "refutes Voltaire's cynicism," as expressed in *Candide*. Yet American charity is not a refutation of Voltaire's cynicism; it *is* Voltaire's cynicism, an expression of the Enlightenment tradition of individual responsibility that he promoted. Voltaire was a gardener and believed in gardens, even if other people were gardening them. His residual optimism lies in that alone.

The horror that Voltaire wanted crushed, cruelty in the name of God and civilization, was a specific and contingent thing. His satire of optimism is in this sense an optimistic book—optimistic not only in its gaiety, which implies the possibility of seeing things as they are, but also in its argument. Voltaire did not believe that there was any justice or balance in the world, but he believed that bad ideas made people bad. The villains in the book are not, as in Samuel Johnson's exactly contemporary and parallel *Rasselas*, the fatality of the world and the mortality of man. The villains are the villains: Jesuits and Inquisitors and English judges and Muslim clerics and fanatics of all kinds. If they went away, life would be much better. He knew that the flood would get your garden no matter what you did; but you could at least try to keep the priests and the policemen off the grass. It wasn't enough, but it was something.

* * *

Though *Candide* seems to retreat from a confrontation with human cruelty to an enclosed garden, its publication marked Voltaire's, and his age's, moral development away from a passive Deism and toward a faith in liberal meliorism. Voltaire went on to a series of confrontations with the consequences of human cruelty that, two hundred-odd years later, remain stirring in their courage and perseverance. It is in the years *after* the publication of the supposedly cynical and even quietist *Candide* that he began the campaigns against persecution— and, more broadly, against torture and cruelty in punishment— from which, as Davidson says, most civilized societies can trace their liberation from organized cruelty and state killing.

Voltaire was no mere petition signer; he was intensely engaged with individual cases, and deserves credit for exposing at least two horrible judicial murders. He first took on the case of Jean Calas, a Protestant in Normandy who was wrongly accused of murdering his own son (it seems likely that the son committed suicide) to keep him from converting to Roman Catholicism. Calas was executed: publicly tortured by a judicial lynch mob of priests and local officials, and then broken on the wheel. Voltaire, after years of work, was able to show that Calas's execution had been a frame-up, and even managed to get official recompense for his family. He did the same thing, at greater personal risk, in the case of the teen-age Chevalier de La Barre, who had been accused by the Catholic authorities of desecrating a statue of the Crucifixion, under the influence of Voltaire's *Dictionnaire Philosophique*. Voltaire could not save his life—La Barre was tortured, and sentenced to have his tongue cut out, before he was killed and burned, along with Voltaire's book—but his writings helped make certain that La Barre was the last man to be murdered in France for blasphemy.

As though these crusades were not enough for an old man who was still busy writing plays and arguing with his neighbors about leases and noises, he also tried to demonstrate the possibilities of a garden-centered life by creating his own light industry at Ferney. He took several dozen Protestant watch-making refugees and supplied them with venture capital to start a watch factory in the village of Ferney. The thing should have gone the way of most virtuous communal schemes devised by well-meaning literary people—but it was a huge success, making as much as six hundred thousand pounds a year, and supplying watches to the Empress of Russia. (Voltaire turned out to be a brilliant salesman, using his high connections to force watches on people on consignment, and then blandly sending them bills.) It was a proof that one could do well by doing good. Ferney watches became the Ben & Jerry's ice cream of the later

Enlightenment, a luxury good that was also a sign of progressive values.

Of course, in the light of later horrors, the horror that Voltaire wanted to crush doesn't seem a horror at all. It was a half-aware, corrupt, guilty, placating horror, which watched nervously as he was fêted. His enemies were local lynch mobs, not centralized terror. A Nazi or Soviet regime would have crushed him, horribly, and everyone else with him. The argument has even been made that Voltaire's rejection of moral order and God helped lead to the later horrors. But unless one believes, against all the evidence, that faith in God keeps one from cruelty, this is a bum rap. There are absolutist and totalitarian elements in the Enlightenment, of the kind that Burke and Berlin alike opposed: the desire to rip up the calendar of the past and start over implies murdering whoever isn't with the program. This wasn't Voltaire's spirit by a mile. There couldn't be a better model of an improvisatory, anti-authoritarian intelligence, whose whole creed rests on individual acts and case-by-case considerations. He believed in the English model of trade and toleration, not the Jacobin model of ideology and intemperance. His intolerance of religion was nothing like religious intolerance; it was directed at institutions, not individuals. Even his notorious attacks on Judaism are largely of this kind. Like Gibbon, what he objects to in the Old Testament is the spirit of zealous intolerance it gave to the New; about the worst thing that he could say of the Jews is that they reminded him of Jesuits. Voltaire's spirit was one of tolerant cosmopolitanism, even though he didn't have the insight to see that one challenge for the cosmopolitan spirit would be how well it tolerated those who had no wish to be cosmopolitan.

It is still bracing, at a time when the extreme deference we pay to faith has made any attack on religious beliefs unacceptable, to hear Voltaire on Jesuits and Muslims alike—to hear him howl with indignation at the madness and malignance of religion—and to be reminded that that freethinking, which inspired Twain and Mencken, has almost vanished from our world. (There is, after all, as much of Voltaire in American life as in French life. Benjamin Franklin went to him for a blessing, and got it.)

Voltaire made a good end. No Frenchman can keep away from Paris forever. When he was eighty-four, he made the trip back at last; although there was no official "pardon" (there had never been an official condemnation), he thought it unlikely that the authorities would try to do anything to him. Seeing how old he was, the Church sent emissaries to try to get him to recant. Voltaire had the priests in, and perhaps even entertained the idea of confessing—partly because he always liked toying with priests, partly because he was genuinely afraid of being thrown into a common grave, as happened to the unshriven. But finally he sighed on his deathbed, told the priest who had arrived one last time to urge on him the virtues of Jesus, "Sir, do not speak to me any more about that man and let me die in peace," and turned away. The priests, furious, and knowing that it was against the law both to bury an unsacralized body and to move it, cruelly insisted that his body could be taken from Paris to a quiet burial only if the corpse was dressed up in clothes and the pretense made that Voltaire was still alive. The joke, on them, was that he was.

W. H. BARBER

[The Question of Optimism]†

Having proved itself still capable of attracting readers and giving them pleasure two hundred years after its first appearance, *Candide* may be felt to have achieved literary immortality. The appeal of such enduring works of art must obviously in a sense be timeless, but that does not mean that they are not better understood, and so more enjoyed, by those who are able to replace them in the historical context from which they sprang, to comprehend something of their meaning for the author and his contemporaries, to see how they are related to the preoccupations and the attitudes of their age. And this is especially true of a work of satire, intended by its author to be a weapon in a contemporary clash of ideas, ultimately to influence the course of events by its impact on men's minds. It remains for us, then, to look at *Candide* externally from this historical standpoint, and to say something, in particular, of the history of eighteenth-century 'optimism,' and of the development of Voltaire's own attitude on the subject.

The problem of divine justice or theodicy, of reconciling the existence of evil and suffering with the goodness and omnipotence of God, is one that clearly is of permanent concern not only to Christian theology but also to all believers in a creator rationally conceived as a Supreme Being. And it was a problem which became particularly acute in Western Europe about the beginning of the eighteenth century. The renewed confidence in the powers of human reason which characterizes so much of European thought in the seventeenth century, from Descartes onwards, contributed to this in two main ways. In the first place, as it led philosophers like Descartes

† From *Voltaire: Candide* (London: Edward Arnold, 1960), pp. 41–57. Reprinted by permission of the estate of W. H. Barber.

himself, Spinoza and Leibniz to conceive vast metaphysical systems in which every known feature of the universe was (ideally, at any rate) rationally accounted for and fitted into a comprehensive and coherent intellectual scheme, so also religious thinkers were impelled to emphasize the rationality of Christianity, to attempt to win or regain the allegiance of the now growing number of sceptics and freethinkers by demonstrating that Christian beliefs were entirely compatible with reason. In such an attempt, the problem of evil clearly constituted a major issue.

Secondly, the new rationalism was beginning to bear fruit where man's understanding of the world was concerned. New instruments like the telescope and the microscope, new mathematical techniques, a new awareness of the importance of experiment and observation, were making possible for the first time some scientific understanding of natural phenomena. Where formerly it had been assumed that, since the Fall, the world was predominantly given over to chaos and corruption, regularity and even purpose now began to be descried in the workings of nature. It seemed plausible to compare the universe to a watch, the most complex and delicately constructed machine of the age—a machine in which every part functioned regularly and purposefully, in accordance with the intentions of the watchmaker. If the arrangements of the Divine Watchmaker, however, proved accessible to human reason in such matters as the law of gravitation or the principles of optics (to quote the discoveries of Newton alone), the presumption seemed to follow that rational purpose pervaded every feature of the universe; and here too the problem arose as to how the existence of such manifest blemishes as evil and suffering could be reconciled with the necessary perfection of the divine scheme.

It is these two approaches to the problem, different in origin and emphasis but similar in their rationalism, which underlay respectively the two most influential and widely discussed formulations of the 'optimistic' solution, those of Leibniz and of Alexander Pope.

Leibniz's purpose in his *Essais de Théodicée* (1710: written in French) was essentially to defend the rationality of God and His creation against an attack which, in his eyes, was a potential danger to religion and to man's confidence in the divine purposes. The French Huguenot scholar and philosopher Pierre Bayle (1647–1706), a critical rather than a constructive thinker, had frequently emphasized the limitations of the human reason by drawing attention to philosophical paradoxes which appeared to admit of no rational solution; and one of these, in his view, was the problem of evil. In the articles 'Manichéens' and 'Pauliciens' of his *Dictionnaire historique et critique* (1697) he argued that the explanation propounded by the ancient Manichean heresy, namely that the world was the plaything of opposing gods, one good, one evil, was in fact the solution of the problem most in keeping with the facts, however illogical and incompatible with our notions of God it might be:

> Qui n'admirera et qui ne déplorera la destinée de notre raison: voilà les Manichéens qui avec une hypothèse tout-à-fait absurde et contradictoire expliquent les expériences cent fois mieux que ne font les orthodoxes, avec la supposition si juste, si nécessaire, si uniquement véritable d'un premier principe infiniment bon et tout-puissant ['Pauliciens,' note E].

Leibniz's book is a systematic discussion of Bayle's views, and in it he propounds an answer to the problem of evil which is in harmony with his own wider metaphysical thinking and also supports the claims of rational theology. He sees God as subject, like man, to the laws of reason: even God cannot make two and two add up to anything but four, nor create a spherical cube. Hence, when God is considered as deciding upon the creation of the world, Leibniz envisages him as having a choice only between *possible* worlds, that is, forms of creation which do not violate the laws of reason, which do not involve logical contradiction. And among such possible worlds God in His infinite goodness has inevitably chosen the best. This 'best of all possible worlds,' however, necessarily contains imperfections, and hence evil. While many evils are justifiable and even valuable as a means to good (e.g. the protective and warning function of much physical pain), other evils are merely the inevitable result of the imperfections inseparable from the status of created beings; man has limited power, limited knowledge: 'Il y a une imperfection originale dans la créature avant le péché, parce que la créature est limitée essentiellement: d'où vient qu'elle ne saurait tout savoir, et qu'elle se peut tromper et faire d'autres fautes' (*Théodicée*, I, §20). Evil of this sort is thus presented by Leibniz not as a positive force, but rather as something negative and privative; not anything willed by God, but an imperfection arising inevitably from the nature of things, and to which man must consequently reconcile himself. The fact of evil is not denied, but its presence in God's creation is morally justified and rationally accounted for.

The second version of the philosophy of optimism is linked with the name of Alexander Pope, not because he himself was an original thinker (he chiefly echoes the views of his contemporary, Bolingbroke, and the earlier English philosopher, Shaftesbury), but because he succeeded, in his *Essay on Man* (1733), in crystallizing and giving memorable expression to ideas on the subject which reflected the outlook of many contemporaries. It had become a common practice for Christian apologists to invoke the new scientific

discoveries as evidence: that the marvels of the universe bear witness to God's existence and His providence is the theme of such
works as the Rev. W. Derham's *Physico-Theology* (1713) and *Astro-
Theology* (1715), both of which were frequently reprinted and translated into French, and of the Abbé Pluche's equally successful
Spectacle de la nature (1732). The discovery of order and purpose in
the world of nature led less orthodox thinkers, however, to conclusions incompatible with the Christian doctrine of original sin. If scientific investigation revealed the working of universal laws, the
existence of rational purpose, in every phenomenon so far scrutinized, it seemed likely that greater knowledge would display the
ultimate regularity and purposiveness of *everything* in the universe:
that whatever now appeared as random, imperfect, evil, would be
revealed as playing its necessary part in the universal order. Man's
capacity for comprehending this order, it was argued, is inevitably
limited by his own quite restricted part in it, but the universe as a
whole is perfect, the unblemished product of the divine wisdom and
omnipotence, and it is merely human ignorance which makes us see
imperfection and evil in it. Such are the views Pope advances in the
First Epistle of his *Essay on Man*:

> Cease then, nor order imperfection name:
> Our proper bliss depends on what we blame.
> Know thy own point: this kind, this due degree
> Of blindness, weakness, Heav'n bestows on thee.
> Submit. —In this or any other sphere,
> Secure to be as blest as thou canst bear:
> Safe in the hand of one disposing power,
> Or in the natal, or the mortal hour.
> All nature is but art, unknown to thee;
> All chance, direction, which thou canst not see;
> All discord, harmony not understood;
> All partial evil, universal good;
> And, spite of pride, in erring reason's spite,
> One truth is clear, Whatever is, is right.

The distinction between this view and that of Leibniz is thus a
wide one. Leibniz, starting from a theological standpoint, admits the
reality of evil but sees it as an inevitable ingredient even in the best
of all possible worlds. Pope on the other hand, adopting an approach
which was of scientific inspiration, proclaims that evil is a mere illusion, a consequence of human ignorance. And the moral which the
two writers drew from their conclusions similarly differed, for while
Leibniz wished by his vindication of the ways of God to men to counteract the despair and helplessness which Manicheism might provoke, and to encourage men to collaborate actively with God in the

working out of His purposes, Pope seems to preach only passive submission to a Providence which, if universally rational and ultimately beneficent, is also beyond man's limited comprehension.

Such distinctions are important if we are to understand the history of optimism, but in practice they were seldom made by the eighteenth-century public. Pope's poem was enormously successful in France: no less than four different translations, two of which were frequently reprinted, appeared between 1736 and 1750; and it was very commonly, though erroneously, supposed that Pope had been influenced by Leibniz. Interest in Leibniz, indeed, which had somewhat languished in France since his death in 1716, was revived precisely by the controversy which sprang up over Pope's poem. It is significant that the fullest discussion ever accorded to Leibniz's *Théodicée* in a French periodical appeared, not in a review of the first edition of 1710, but in 1737, the year after the publication of the first French translation of the *Essay on Man*, when the Jesuit *Mémoires de Trévoux* devoted four articles to reviewing an edition of the *Théodicée* published in 1734.

The issue at stake in the controversy was a crucial one. The optimism expressed in Pope's poem, and which was commonly supposed to be that of Leibniz also, appeared in the 1730s as a characteristically deistic view. It presented God as a rational Supreme Being, the creator of a rational, ordered, perfect universe; it clearly left no room for such notions as the Fall, original sin, Christ's atonement, redemption by divine grace, or even, in the eyes of many, for freedom of the will. And at that date deism was the commonest form assumed by the growing European movement of free thought, the strongest enemy with which the Church had to contend. The forces of orthodoxy consequently reacted vigorously, condemning such doctrines as unchristian and above all fatalistic; but their attraction remained strong in an age which tended to complacency, was impressed by the achievements of the new science, and found the rationalistic notions of deism more congenial than the dogmas of revealed religion.

If Leibniz, who was little read, became better known, and by some better thought of, as a result of this renewed French interest in optimism, his reputation scarcely benefited in France from a further development, which served nevertheless to keep his name before the public in the following two decades. Owing chiefly to Leibniz's unwillingness to publish systematic expositions of his views, his philosophy, for all its originality and importance, exercised extremely little direct influence: but early in the eighteenth century there appeared in Germany an academic disciple of Leibniz whose impact was considerable. Christian Wolff (1679–1754), a professor in the universities of Halle and Marburg, was above all a systematizer and an expositor, developing some of Leibniz's principal conceptions into an all-embracing philosophical structure which covered every aspect of human thought, from logic to theology, from metaphysics to ethics. This he presented in lectures to students over a period of thirty years and published in some forty quarto volumes, in which his thought is set out in a rigidly organized pattern resembling that of a textbook of geometry. The apparently solid, 'mathematically' proven certainties of this arid and pedantic philosophical system had great appeal for his contemporaries, however, and before his death Wolff's philosophy had become the established orthodoxy in the universities of northern Germany.

It was in these Protestant areas of the country that many thousands of Huguenots had settled when in 1685 the revocation of the Edict of Nantes had forced them to leave France. These refugees, and especially the second generation, born in exile, while they preserved their religious traditions and their national language, also came inevitably under the influence of contemporary German movements. Some became enthusiastic Wolffians, and consequently tried to win further adherents by spreading knowledge of Wolff's system in the French-speaking world. French translations and expositions of Wolff were published in the late 1730s and the 1740s by Jean Deschamps, a little-known pastor in Berlin who later lived in London, and by the much more influential J. H. S. Formey, a Huguenot minister and professor who became the permanent Secretary of the Berlin Academy of Sciences in 1748, contributed articles to Diderot's *Encyclopédie*, and was extremely active throughout his career as a publicist and journalist. Formey's most ambitious attempt at presenting Wolff to French readers was *La Belle Wolfienne* (6 vols., 1741–53), a work which, in the early volumes at any rate, tried to emulate the conversational method of popular scientific exposition used so successfully by Fontenelle in his *Entretiens sur la pluralité des mondes habités* half a century before. But certainly more influential than this was his journalistic work. From 1734 until its disappearance in 1760 Formey was on the editorial staff of a periodical primarily concerned with presenting German literary and intellectual life to French readers, the *Bibliothèque germanique*, and in the 1740s and '50s he was able to use it as an organ of Wolffian propaganda, consistently publishing articles and reviews in which Wolff's philosophy was expounded and put forward in a favourable light.

The positive effect of this campaign in France itself was not very great. The only French convert to Wolffianism of any significance was Voltaire's mistress, Madame Du Châtelet. Won over, at least temporarily, by the enthusiasm of a disciple of Wolff whom she employed for a time as a mathematics tutor, Samuel König, she prefaced a popular introduction to physics which she published in 1741, the *Institutions de physique*, with an outline of the metaphysical conceptions of Leibniz (including the doctrines of the *Théodicée*), 'puisées dans les ouvrages du célèbre Wolff.' The general effect, however, of such pro-Wolffian activities was at least to keep the names of Leibniz and Wolff before the French public by provoking opposition. Apart from Madame Du Châtelet's book, during the twenty years preceding *Candide* virtually nothing was published on the subject in France itself which was not hostile to the Wolffian philosophy. It appeared to most French minds as an extreme example of a kind of dogmatic speculation which the new scientific progress, based upon observed fact only, had shown to be valueless. Condillac dealt this sort of philosophy a crushing blow with his devastatingly critical *Traité des systèmes* in 1749, and D'Alembert in 1751 recorded the decease of systematic metaphysics in his *Discours préliminaire de l'Encyclopédie*: 'Le goût des systèmes, plus propre à flatter l'imagination qu'à éclairer la raison, est aujourd'hui presqu'absolument banni des bons ouvrages.'

The interest in the doctrines of optimism which Pope's *Essay on Man* had stimulated in France was thus reinforced to some extent by the attempts of Madame Du Châtelet and the Huguenot enthusiasts in Germany to attract French support for the philosophy of Leibniz and Wolff. Pope and Leibniz were continually linked together by controversialists, 'le meilleur des mondes possibles' and Pope's 'tout est bien' ('Whatever is, is right') became the catchphrases of the discussion: but even those in France who sympathized with the optimistic solution of the problem of evil were rarely disposed to accept also the complete metaphysical system in which Wolff had embedded it. The outlines of that system became better known in France than Leibniz's own thought had ever been, thanks to the efforts of the Wolffian propagandists: but Frenchmen, it seems, if they were able now to recognize such technical phrases as 'l'harmonie préétablie,' 'la raison suffisante,' or 'les monades' as characteristically Leibnizian, saw no reason to take Leibnizian metaphysics seriously, and now also associated it with the pedantic aridity and prolixity of Wolff—who in these respects well exemplified the current French conception of German pedagogues and scholars.

Optimism itself, moreover, though defended by enthusiasts in Germany, continued to come under fire in France. As we have seen, the forces of religious orthodoxy condemned it, emphasizing especially the fatalistic implications which were inseparable from it; and to many men of sense it seemed less and less in accordance with the observable facts of existence—an impression which was of course enormously strengthened by the Lisbon earthquake of 1755.

We are now in a better position to understand the immediate success of *Candide*. In it Voltaire is making fun of a philosophy much discussed in France, but generally rejected there: one which aroused great interest, because it was concerned with a problem of acute importance for the age, but which had also acquired an aura of ridicule through becoming associated in the public mind with the academic jargon of German pedants and their infatuated disciples. In creating Pangloss, the German pedagogue, with his Leibnizian clichés, his irrepressible passion for metaphysical dogmatizing, and his blind devotion to optimism, Voltaire was setting up a butt for satire at which all France could laugh.

To describe the development of Voltaire's attitude to the question of optimism it is not necessary, or possible, to go back to the earliest years of his career: the successful young court poet and dramatist of the Regency had as yet no serious personal concern with such profound matters as the problem of evil. Yet, with his early interest in Bayle and impatience with religious orthodoxy, he can scarcely have failed, even as a very young man, to be aware of the importance of the question. He of course read his friend Pope's *Essay on Man* as soon as it appeared in 1733, and it is noteworthy that, although he qualified his first praise of it with the remark that 'Now and then there is some obscurity' (letter, in English, to Thieriot, 24 July 1733, Best. 614), his own earliest recorded opinions on the subject, which belong to this period, are on the whole in harmony with Pope's views. In his *Lettres philosophiques* (1734) he includes an attack on Pascal which opposes to Pascal's deep sense of original sin the assertion that all is well with creation, that man, even if he has his imperfections, is nevertheless in his rightful place in the divinely created order. Pope's optimism thus had its part to play as a weapon against Christian orthodoxy where doctrines of sin and redemption were concerned; but when, a year or two later, he attempts for the first time, in his *Traité de métaphysique*, to argue seriously the case for deism, he tries to exonerate God from responsibility for evil, from charges of cruelty and injustice towards man, by a new approach. He does not follow Pope to the optimistic extreme of maintaining that all evil is a means to good, but rather asserts that man is in no position to make judgments at all on the subject. To reproach God with injustice is to apply to Him a notion which is meaningful only with reference to one man's treatment of another; to condemn creation as imperfect is absurd unless we have some more perfect universe with which to compare it; God's ways, in short, are not our ways.

Such arguments give the impression of having been sought out as a way of answering the orthodox opponents of deism, rather than as springing from any very profound conviction. And Voltaire in the 1730s had little personal inclination to take the problem very seriously. As he makes clear in his epicurean poem of 1736, *Le Mondain*, he thought the world a pleasant place: 'le paradis terrestre est où je suis'; and, without denying the existence of evil in the world (he seems to have felt, indeed, that Pope tended too easily to gloss it over), he sees little point at this stage in his career in arguing over such problems, when life offers so much to enjoy:

> Sans rechercher en vain ce que peut notre maître,
> Ce que fut notre monde, et ce qu'il devrait être,
> Observons ce qu'il est, et recueillons le fruit
> Des trésors qu'il renferme et des biens qu'il produit.
>
> (*Sixième Discours sur l'homme*, 1738)

Voltaire's acquaintance with the philosophy of Leibniz began effectively only in 1736, when the future Frederick the Great, at that time a devotee, sent him some French translations of Wolff's works. Further contacts undoubtedly came through the Leibnizian enthusiasm of Madame Du Châtelet, which began in 1739: it seems to have been about this date that Voltaire first acquired some knowledge of the *Théodicée*. It is clear that Voltaire rapidly lost patience with the Wolffian enthusiasts, whose pedantic metaphysical dogmatism and supreme confidence in their own speculations he found exasperating—the complete antithesis of everything he admired in Locke and Newton, with their cautious scepticism and persistent refusal to go beyond the established facts. It is Leibnizian metaphysics, not the Leibnizian doctrine of optimism, that Voltaire makes fun of at this time, however; believing no doubt, with many of his contemporaries, that Leibniz and Pope were at one on the latter subject, he would have felt no desire to attack a view with which he was then largely in sympathy.

By 1744, however, the first signs of a different attitude begin to emerge. In that year, in a bitterly mocking reply to an attack which a Wolffian professor of philosophy, L. M. Kahle of Göttingen, had made on his *Métaphysique de Newton*, Voltaire includes Leibnizian optimism in his ridicule, closing his letter with the sarcastic gibe: 'Quand vous aurez aussi démontré en vers ou autrement pourquoi tant d'hommes s'égorgent dans le meilleur des mondes possibles, je vous serai très obligé' (Best. 2745). This sense that the realities of human suffering and evil are fundamentally irreconcilable with the doctrine of optimism, that, far from making them comprehensible and tolerable, optimism merely mocks at them, is one that comes more and more to dominate Voltaire's thinking on the subject in the ensuing years, and it is this which inspires *Candide*.

In the middle and late 1740s, too, Voltaire returned to the life of a courtier at Versailles. With its continual insecurity, its petty jealousies, its frivolous demands upon his time and literary energies, the flattery and insincerity which it necessitated, such an existence soon destroyed the sense of personal contentment which had underlain his earlier epicurean sympathy with Pope. At the same time, however, he had not altogether abandoned the intellectual conviction (implicit in his sincere deism) that, the universe being rational, a rational explanation of the fact of evil must exist. The conflict between the two attitudes, the one intellectual, the other at bottom emotional and personal, emerges clearly in the first of Voltaire's *contes* to be published, *Zadig*, the earliest version of which appeared in 1747.

In this tale the central theme is the problem of destiny: not whether it exists—Voltaire by this date was a convinced determinist, and his oriental hero has the traditional fatalism of his race—but why it treats men as capriciously and unjustly as it does.

Zadig is a young man of talent and virtue, yet his career is continually beset with undeserved misfortune: both men and events seem to conspire maliciously against him. Finally, after many adventures, he is on the point of winning the hand of his beloved, Queen Astarte, only to be cheated by the treachery of his last rival, a knight in green armour whom he had defeated in single combat. Zadig can endure no more: 'Il lui échappa enfin de murmurer contre la Providence, et il fut tenté de croire que tout était gouverné par une Destinée cruelle qui opprimait les bons, et qui faisait prospérer les chevaliers verts' (chap. 17). At this climax in the story, Zadig meets a mysterious hermit, who offers to enlighten and console him. On their way together, however, the hermit baffles and horrifies Zadig by his strange behaviour: he steals from one man who offers them generous hospitality, burns down the house of another, richly rewards those who treat them badly, and finally recompenses a hospitable and virtuous widow by deliberately drowning her nephew. The hermit, who has access to the book of destiny, is able to show Zadig how each of these actions was in fact beneficial, in spite of appearances: even the murder of the nephew was for the best, for if the boy had lived he would have killed his aunt, and Zadig too! The hermit now reveals himself to be the angel Jesrad, and the seal of supernatural authority seems to be set upon the interpretation of the workings of destiny which these episodes imply: whatever man, with his limited knowledge, may think, all is in fact for the best when it is seen from the transcendental viewpoint available to celestial beings.

Zadig, however, is not satisfied with these explanations. He continues to ask questions: would it not have been better to have changed the boy's destiny, and made him virtuous, rather than to have drowned him? Why should crime and unhappiness be necessary at all? What if there were only goodness, and no evil? These questions the angel tries to answer by again insisting upon the ultimate justice and beneficence of Providence: 'Les méchants, répondit Jesrad, sont toujours malheureux. Ils servent à éprouver un petit nombre de justes répandus sur la terre, et il n'y a point de mal dont il ne naisse un bien' (chap. 18). And to the question why evil exists at all, he answers merely that without evil this world would be a different world, nearer to the divine perfection, occupying a different place in the universal order from that to which God has in fact assigned it. Man must merely submit, and accept the purposes of Providence, which he cannot hope to understand. Zadig, inevitably, finds these answers unsatisfactory; but he is given no further opportunity for argument: '"Mais," dit Zadig . . . Comme il disait *Mais*, l'Ange prenait déjà son vol vers la dixième sphère.'

From a transcendental standpoint, Voltaire seems here to be implying, it may well be true that the universe is rationally and beneficently ordered, but for the individual this can never be more than a matter of faith. The sense of personal injustice and unmerited affliction remains and the reality of suffering is not mitigated by such remote and metaphysical considerations.

It is upon the inescapable fact of human suffering that Voltaire now begins to place the greatest emphasis in his treatment of the subject. In *Babouc* (1748), where he is concerned chiefly with satirizing French society and its institutions, he concludes, indeed, that 'si tout n'est pas bien, tout est passable'; but in the following year in another tale, *Memnon*, he returns to the dilemma of *Zadig*. Memnon too, after a horrifying series of undeserved misfortunes, including the loss of an eye, is confronted with an angelic mentor. He complains to him that this world must surely be the Bedlam of the universe—

> Pas tout-à-fait, dit l'esprit; mais il en approche: il faut que tout soit en sa place. Hé mais, dit Memnon, certains poètes, certains philosophes, ont donc grand tort de dire que *tout est bien*? —Ils ont grande raison, dit le philosophe de là-haut, en considérant l'arrangement de l'univers entier. —Ah! je ne croirai cela, répliqua le pauvre Memnon, que quand je ne serai plus borgne.

In this and the following years, moreover, Voltaire's own experiences led him to take an increasingly gloomy view of life, and strengthened his awareness of human suffering. The death of Madame Du Châtelet in 1749, the disappointment of his hopes for a congenial existence in an atmosphere of intellectual freedom at the Prussian court, the humiliations to which he was subjected when the inevitable break with Frederick came in 1753, his subsequent wanderings and ill-health: all this combined to create a pessimistic mood which is clearly reflected in Voltaire's correspondence, especially in the years 1752–5. All he seeks for himself is a refuge from the world's ills, a haven where he may enjoy in his now declining years some small measure of tranquillity. It is interesting to see Voltaire, in a poem written in March 1755, describing his hopes on taking possession of his new home at 'Les Délices,' near Geneva (the house which to-day is occupied by the 'Institut et Musée Voltaire'); the garden of *Candide* is already beginning to take shape:

> O maison d'Aristippe! O jardins d'Épicure!
> . . . .
> Empire de Pomone et de Flore sa sœur,
>   Recevez votre possesseur;
> Qu'il soit, ainsi que vous, solitaire et tranquille.
> Je ne me vante point d'avoir en cet asile
>   Rencontré le parfait bonheur;
> Il n'est point retiré dans le fond d'un bocage;
>   Il est encor moins chez les rois;
>   Il n'est pas même chez le sage:
> De cette courte vie il n'est point le partage;
> Il faut y renoncer; mais on peut quelquefois
>   Embrasser au moins son image.

In these circumstances, the Lisbon earthquake in November of that year seemed above all a confirmation of Voltaire's ideas, a further proof that 'la destinée se joue des hommes' and that the theories of the optimists were far too glib. His *Poème sur le désastre de Lisbonne* is not only a cry of horror at human suffering, but also a protest against those who, with their slogan 'Tout est bien,' would shrug off such suffering as a necessary ingredient in the divinely appointed order. Voltaire now insists that, in the face of a natural disaster of such magnitude, all the stock solutions of the problem of evil are unconvincing: the existence of such misery in a world created by a just and omnipotent God is simply incomprehensible. But the worst feature of optimism, Voltaire here maintains, is that by insisting on the rational perfection of the world as it is, by saying that 'tout est bien' here and now, it is in fact denying man any hope of improvement for the future, and thereby making life intolerable. The point is given an orthodox Christian emphasis, for publication, by being linked to the idea of hope for the life to come rather than for life on earth, but the force of Voltaire's criticism is not thereby weakened:

> Nos chagrins, nos regrets, nos pertes sont sans nombre.
> Le passé n'est pour nous qu'un triste souvenir;

Le présent est affreux s'il n'est point d'avenir,
Si la nuit du tombeau détruit l'être qui pense.
Un jour tout sera bien, voilà notre espérance,
Tout est bien aujourd'hui, voilà l'illusion.
Les sages me trompaient, et Dieu seul a raison.

Again, we are at the source of an idea central to *Candide*. It is hope, the hope of future happiness with Cunégonde, which supports Candide in his wanderings; and it is hope, of a less ambitious if more solid sort, which still inspires the labours of the little community at Constantinople.

The *Poème sur le désastre de Lisbonne*, however, as its preface makes clear, is primarily a critique of Pope's *Essay on Man*. The Leibnizianism which holds the centre of the stage in *Candide* plays no part here, and had, indeed, received very little emphasis in any of Voltaire's earlier discussions of the subject. Events in 1756, however, were to take Voltaire's thoughts again to Germany and to remind him of the German optimists and their theories.

The outbreak of the Seven Years' War in the summer of 1756 brought Germany into the forefront of events, and the long series of campaigns there during the ensuing years, with the devastation and poverty they brought in their train, gave that country the melancholy distinction of becoming the outstanding current example of extreme human misery. Voltaire himself was acutely conscious of this suffering, for he knew the country, had friends there who were involved, and of course had been on intimate terms with the German ruler chiefly concerned, Frederick the Great. Even more than those of the Lisbon earthquake, then, the horrors of the Seven Years' War had a personal immediacy for Voltaire which would by itself perhaps suffice to explain their appearance in *Candide*. But they are also relevant to the theme of the book in another, and uniquely direct, way: Voltaire was not insensitive to the irony of a situation in which the country which was *par excellence* the home of optimism had itself become that doctrine's most striking refutation. Rossbach and Leuthen and their aftermath formed a bitter contrast with the serene optimism of the Wolffians of Göttingen and Halle. Voltaire's correspondence at this period, and especially his letters to one of his German friends who had Wolffian sympathies, the Duchess of Saxe-Gotha, is sprinkled with sardonic allusions to Leibnizianism. In October 1756, after news of a Prussian victory, he writes: 'Voilà déjà environ vingt mille hommes morts pour cette querelle, dans laquelle aucun d'eux n'avait la moindre part. C'est encore un des agréments du meilleur des mondes possibles' (Best. 6333). And later, on 4 January 1758, at a time when he may well have been on the point of beginning *Candide*, he writes her a letter in the form of a comic proclamation to the mercenary troops occupying the Duchess's territories:

> A tous croates, pandours, housards . . . : il ne doit être rien de commun entre Mme la duchesse de Gotha et vous, vilains pandours . . . vous cherchez à rendre ce monde-ci le plus abominable des mondes possibles, et elle voudrait qu'il fût le meilleur. Il le serait sans doute, si elle en était la maîtresse. Il est vrai qu'elle est un peu embarrassée avec le système de Leibniz; elle ne sait comment faire, avec tant de mal physique et moral, pour vous prouver l'optimisme; mais c'est vous qui en êtes cause, maudits housards . . . [Best. 6855].

The setting and themes of *Candide* are thus of immediate personal relevance to Voltaire's own thought and experience. The intellectual problem which it discusses is one that had serious significance for him, for it was created by the conflict between the realities of life as he had himself experienced and observed them, and the implications of that belief in a rational God to which he was sincerely committed. His hostility to the optimist solution, though he found the optimists exasperating for other reasons too, springs also from the depths of his personality. He clearly sees that optimism is a doctrine of despair: by denying the possibility of improvement in a world in which, already, 'tout est bien,' it reduces man to passive acquiescence in his misfortunes; while Voltaire, even at his gloomiest, remains a man of energy, for whom life is meaningless and worthless if it is not a struggle—if it does not offer the individual some prospect of successful effort to escape from suffering and improve his condition. Finally, the historical events of the 1750s combined with his own misfortunes to give depth and immediacy to his compassion for suffering humanity, and at the same time provided him, in war-torn Germany, with a supremely ironic example of the follies of optimism.

DENNIS FLETCHER

Candide and the Philosophy of the Garden†

In his wide-ranging survey of the Enlightenment Peter Gay heads his stimulating discussion of *Candide* 'The Epicurean as Stoic.'[1] E. Rovillain, on the other hand, in the course of a detailed study of

† From *Trivium* 13 (May 1978): 18–30. Reprinted by permission of Trivium Publications, the University of Wales Trinity Saint David, Lampeter. Pages in brackets refer to this Norton Critical Edition.
1. *The Enlightenment: an interpretation* [1966], (London 1973), Vol. I, pp. 21, 197.

Stoic elements in *Zadig,* unequivocally classifies the eponymous hero of Voltaire's later *conte* as a representative of the philosophy of the Garden rather than an exponent of the philosophy of the Porch: "Il est amusant de constater que dans *Candide,* satire contre les systèmes, le héros finit en épicurien, vivant dans la solitude et la médiocrité, sans action, sans passions et sans amour, se contentant de cultiver son jardin."[2] René Pomeau refers to the "morale épicurienne de l'action qui est le dernier mot du conte,"[3] but is quoted disapprovingly by J. G. Weightman who detects "no trace of Epicurean serenity or moderation" in *Candide.*[4] These few examples of a more widespread divergence of opinion point to the need for an examination of the putative Epicureanism of Voltaire's tale and the extent to which it may be distinguished from any strain of Stoicism.

Assessing the total import and impact of *Candide* rather than the message offered in the final chapter, J. G. Weightman distinguished as one of the principal features of the *conte* "an instinctive zest for life."[5] The passionate attachment to this world, which takes the form of an apparent indestructibility in the case of the survivors who finally make up the little community, has often been remarked upon, though rarely, if ever, associated with Epicureanism. La Vieille, however, who illustrates *par excellence* the elemental urge to live, the ignoble aspect of bearing "the slings and arrows of outrageous fortune" ("Je voulus cent fois me tuer, mais j'aimais encore la vie . . ."),[6] may be fairly taken as exemplifying the New Hedonism of Epicurus, which posited that "life was the greatest good; it was a pleasure to be alive even if maimed or in pain."[7] Norman Wentworth De Witt's persuasive exposition of the ethical doctrine of Epicurus stresses how it gives precedence to the Feelings (or Nature) over reason. Epicurus, presented by De Witt[8] as a natural pragmatist intent upon stressing the inestimable boon of having survived calamity and impatient with Plato's tedious harping upon the meaning of 'good' recalls Candide's highly-developed instinct of self-preservation and his final irritation with the endless arguments of Pangloss.

2. 'Rapports probables entre le *Zadig* de Voltaire et la pensée stoïcienne,' *Publications of the Modern Language Association of America,* 52 (June 1937), p. 375, n. 10.
3. *Candide,* édition critique (Paris 1959), p. 71.
4. 'The Quality of *Candide,*' pp. 339–40 in *Essays presented to C. M. Girdlestone* (Newcastle upon-Tyne, King's College 1960), pp. 335–347. [See the Weightman article on p. 175 of this Norton Critical Edition.]
5. Op. cit., p. 338 [p. 178].
6. *Candide,* ed. J. H. Brumfill (Oxford 1968), p. 84 [pp. 26–27].
7. Norman Wentworth De Witt, *Epicurus and his Philosophy* [1954], (Cleveland and New York 1967), p. 246. Voltaire himself when we read of him at death's door, but despite having "lost the use of his eyes, his ears, his legs, his teeth, his tongue" [Theodore Besterman, *Voltaire* (London 1969), p. 522] still determined to make a visit to Paris, sounds like a real-life conflation of some of the characters from his *conte.*
8. Ibid., pp. 67.

In so far as it emphasises human resilience rather than super-human endurance, moral frailty rather than strength of character, *Candide* hardly deserves to be called Stoic. The unspectacular eking-out of a miserable existence has nothing in common with the Stoic aspiration after *la gloire*, to be realized by a Cornelian exercise of will and, if needs be, 'heroic' self-immolation. Among the Roman Stoics, suicide is condoned, advocated even, whenever a dispassionate consideration of the balance of advantage points to this course as the most sensible one to take. Seneca is frequently exhilarated by the prospect of painless, self-administered quietus. Epictetus and Marcus Aurelius both envisage the possibility of a voluntary exit at any time from an intolerable existence. Other Stoics stress considerations of personal advantage less but see suicide as a fitting end if committed for a noble ideal, such as the love of one's country.[9] The archetypal Stoic in this respect is the self-dramatising Cato of Utica, who, after a first attempt to evade capture by eviscerating himself had been foiled, manfully tore out his own entrails at the earliest convenient opportunity. A comparison with *Candide* is instructive here: Voltaire shows his hero (or anti-hero) as a deserter, shivering with fear and intent on picking his way through a mass of twitching limbs as he flees to save his own skin. The humble Epicurean ideal of safe obscurity is espoused by him and his fellow-refugees at the end of the tale. The rural retreat beside the Bosphorus illustrates Gilbert Murray's remark: "The best that Epicurus has really to say of the world is that if you are very wise and do not attract its notice, . . . it will not hurt you."[1]

It is, in our view, this shrinking back from the hurly-burly of life which constitutes the 'message' of Candide's "Il faut cultiver notre jardin" and gives it its pre-eminently Epicurean bias. The old Turk's choice of rural retirement and his distaste for political activity convinces Candide that peace of mind could be gained for himself and his own 'petite société' by imitating this model of disengagement. Both the ideal of inner tranquility and that of non-involvement in public affairs are essentially Epicurean. Epicurus's advice to his followers was: "We must release ourselves from the prison of affairs and politics"[2] and the condemnation of the envy, competition and factional spirit engendered by political activity is a dominant note in their writings. In this, Epicureanism is diametrically opposed to Stoicism which favours political commitment and stresses the citizen's civic obligations. In a more general perspective, the ideal of

9. For a discussion of suicide in the Stoic system of ethics, see F. H. Sandbach, *The Stoics* (London 1975), pp. 48–52.
1. *Five Stages of Greek Religion* (London 1946), Thinkers Library, No. 52, p. 110.
2. *Epicurus: the Extant Remains*, ed. Cyril Bailey (Oxford 1926), p. 115: Vatican Fragments, lvii.

withdrawal from the world which is presented in the concluding chapter of *Candide* is at variance with the expansive Stoic urge to extend to the full one's recognition of others. The doctrine of *oikeiô-sis*, one of the most important contributions of Stoicism to Western philosophy, was graphically presented by Hierocles in the second century A.D. as a number of concentric circles with man at the centre of the first circle, and in the others, his parents, wife, blood relations, more distant relatives, fellow-citizens, compatriots, and finally, in the outer circle, the human race.[3] This image is familiar to many from its use by Pope in his *Essay on Man;*[4] the convenient evaporation in a glow of cosmic optimism of the tensions between the relationships involved in this scheme is, of course, one of the targets for Voltaire's satire in *Candide*. Self-love does not automatically "serve the virtuous mind to wake" in Epicurean thought. The self-regarding impulses can be seen as still very near the basic animal instinct of self-preservation (Rousseau's *amour de soi*, characteristic of the state of nature). One can see much to be said in favour of the thesis, put forward in an invigorating article by Roy Wolper, that *Candide* finally shows he "has learned little about virtue." The expansive character of this key concept of Stoicism is succinctly underlined by Wolper: "Implicit in virtue is the consideration of the *other*, not self; the *world*, not the little group only."[5] The reverse of this medal is the scope which is offered in a small, tightly-knit community for close inter-personal relationships as opposed to a diffuse benevolence which aspires to the impossible aim of embracing all mankind. Epicureanism in its positive championship of the value of private moral obligations and of friendship lends an ethical content to the activities of *Candide* and his companions in their smallholding.

For the Epicureans, the way to happiness was through *philia*: friendship or affection; for the Stoics, such manifestations of human nature were considered as hindrances to the development of a sense of attachment to more important ideals. In its most extreme form this Stoic aversion to the Epicurean emphasis upon personal relations appeared as a distrust of all emotions. This opposition often appears in Voltaire's works as a tension between the rational and affective sides of his nature. It is associated specifically with the divergence between the Stoic and Epicurean attitudes in his play *La Mort de César*, which reflects preoccupations which were not confined to the period of its gestation in the early 1730's. Without analysing the tragedy in detail, one can say that the subordination of private emotions to patriotism is associated with Brutus, and his

3. Ct. Sandbach, op cit., pp. 32–35.
4. Ll. 363–368.
5. 'Candide, Gull in the Garden', *Eighteenth-Century Studies*, 3 (1969), pp. 265–277. See pp. 274, 276.

mentor, that supreme Stoic, Cato of Utica, whilst the values of friendship and love and the ideal of compromise as a means of achieving personal happiness are represented by the Epicurean Caesar, who reveals himself to be Brutus's father. Cassius appears as a complete fanatic who urges parricide upon Brutus as an inescapable duty. This connection between Stoicism and fanaticism was made elsewhere by Voltaire: the seventh of his *Discours en vers sur l'homme (Sur la vraie vertu)* includes both the Jansenist and the Stoic in a portrait-gallery of misguided zealots who have confused virtue with imperviousness to humane feelings. Brutus's disillusionment with the Stoic conception of virtue is referred to, and the *leitmotif* of *La Mort de César*—friendship, clemency, pity as opposed to a rigid and unfeeling conception of justice—are again vindicated. The Epicurean ideal of moderate hedonism is explicitly contrasted with the excessively lofty Stoic ambition of changing human nature in the fifth of these *discours (Sur la nature du plaisir)*; the values of industrious retirement from the world and of friendship which are approved reflect both Voltaire's own life-style at Cirey, Les Délices and Ferney and that of Candide and his companions in their *métairie*.

Voltaire's correspondence has been used with much penetration recently by such critics as Geoffrey Murray and Paul Ilie to show the persistence of certain preoccupations of Voltaire and their relation to the genesis of *Candide*.[6] In both cases attention has been concentrated upon the connection between the letters of the period 1755–1759 and the final chapter of the *conte*. Despite the undeniably valuable results of such restriction of the field of investigation, this approach has its drawbacks. The search for consistency and continuity in Voltaire's thought is a larger enterprise than that of exposing "the connective threads between Voltaire's letters and Chapter 30 of *Candide*"[7] and the evidence of all Voltaire's creative writings is relevant to it. The thread of continuity in Voltaire's life and works may be snipped up into sections for critical convenience, the letters of a given period may be put under the microscope, but this is obviously not the best way of seeing Voltaire steadily and seeing him whole. This is suggested by Ilie's handling of what he presents as the "core-problem" of his study: "the existence of a theme: Voltaire as an Epicurean."[8] The note which he appends to this statement of the problem points out that his interpretation "will stress contemplation and the senses, in contrast to

---

6. G. Murray, *Voltaire's Candide: the Protean Gardener, 1755–1762. Studies on Voltaire and the eighteenth century*, 59 (Geneva 1970); P. Ilie, 'The Voices in Candide's garden, 1755–1759: a methodology for Voltaire's correspondence,' *Studies on Voltaire . . . 148.* (Oxford 1976), pp. 37–113.
7. Ilie, op cit., pp. 44–5.
8. Ibid., p. 102.

Pomeau's idea that 'Il formulait la morale épicurienne de l'action qui est le dernier mot du conte.'" This interpretation clearly deserves close scrutiny in any discussion of the validity of attaching an 'Epicurean' label to *Candide*.

Of the 'Voices in Candide's garden,' that of egoistic hedonism tends to make itself heard, in Ilie's account, more insistently than the others. Epicureanism is associated predominantly with the creature comforts. The analogy which Voltaire offers between his position as owner of "the sumptuous Les Delices" (p. 107) and that of Aristippus, Cyrenaic exponent of extreme self-indulgence, is buttressed by Ilie with quotations from the correspondence to emphasise this love of luxury. The note of self-centred concern for personal survival is not absent from Chapter 30 of *Candide*. The "Epicurean aftermath of Libson,"[9] the "Epicurean garden" which "soothed both aching body and spiritual fatigue after years of Candide-like tribulation"[1] are certainly mirrored in the tale's final chapter. To distinguish in the *conte* so lush a "background orchestration" for the "thematic vocalisation" of Voltaire's letters,[2] however, is to misrepresent the true orchestral colour of the tale and to drown some of the familiar Voltairean voices in the correspondence. Ilie's deliberate contrasting of "contemplation and the senses" with Pomeau's emphasis upon the activist interpretation of Candide's message obscures the meaning of Voltaire's *conte*. Pomeau, as quoted, is referring to the dervish who originally put into Candide's mind, if not into his mouth, the famous final injunction with his "*Cultiver la terre*, boire, manger, dormir et te taire." The "morale de l'action" which is contained in the dervish's original pronouncement is underlined by the "bon Vieillard" whom Voltaire decided to use as the instrument of the final revelation to Candide and his companions of the gospel of work as an antidote for boredom. By shifting the emphasis from the old Turk's repeated stress upon what was to be echoed by Candide himself—the notion of useful industry—to that of the easeful leisure which was the reward of hard labour, Ilie misrepresents the authentic Epicurean colouring of Voltaire's work. The "bon Vieillard's" enjoyment of home-grown produce, and his admirable hospitality hardly make him a "Turkish epicure" any more than Voltaire's desire to send a friend some of his home-made jam make him a sybarite, in any except the most playful sense.[3] The Epicurean ideal, which is reflected both in Voltaire's way of life at Les Delices and in that of "la petite métairie" finally modelled on the old Turk's household, is closer to that of the moderation and sobriety of

9. Ibid., p. 89.
1. Ibid., p. 104.
2. Ibid., p. 113.
3. Ibid., pp. 53, 107 (n. 139).

Epicurus himself than to that of latter-day *bons vivants* who had given Epicureanism a bad name. When Voltaire greets his friend Formont as "un gros et gras épicurien de Paris" and depicts himself as "un maigre épicurien du lac de Genève" the contrast is more meaningful than the bantering tone might suggest.[4]

Ilie chooses to stress the quietist aspect of Epicureanism at the expense of its activist elements in his discussion of Chapter 30 of *Candide*. The "leisurely interval"[5] of the Les Délices period in Voltaire's life during which *Candide* was in gestation certainly exhibits certain features of Epicureanism. The sense of calm enjoyment of material ease which pervades Voltaire's letters at this time is reflected in the first phase of the grateful refugees' existence in their cherished retreat. At this point the "petite métairie" has affinities with the Epicurean *hortus deliciarum* of Renaissance poetry; one can detect affinities between the life of Candide's community and such Epicurean themes as *otium* and *voluptas* which represent one particular orientation of Epicurus's original doctrine, a refinement upon it later favoured notably by Saint-Evremond for whom the Epicurean sovereign good was (in 1647) "cette agréable indolence qui n'est pas un état sans douleur et sans plaisir; c'est le sentiment délicat d'une joie pure."[6] It is Voltaire's early association with pleasure-seekers of Saint-Evremond's persuasion who belonged to the *Société du Temple* which allows us to talk most positively of him as an Epicurean. This experience, related to the (somewhat over-played) *jouissance* of the proprietor of Les Délices, forms part of the "biographical matrix"[7] of *Candide* even if embedded deeper in Voltaire's psyche than that which is reflected in the letters of 1755–1759. A facet of Epicureanism, it is also a facet of Voltaire's life; but it should be distinguished from others. The "hedonistic glow"[8] with which Ilie surrounds Candide's "il faut cultiver notre jardin," for instance, seems unprofitable when this phrase is related to the quite different facet of Epicureanism which it clearly evokes.

This other facet is the activist strain which Professor Pomeau, rightly in our view, distinguishes as "le dernier mot du conte." In the history of ethical thought, Epicureanism reveals a polarity between the careless rapture of a *carpe diem*–type hedonism and that more circumspect eudemonism, ever-ready to rely on a felicific calculus, which produced the utilitarianism of Jeremy Bentham. The practical-minded Romans saw the dichotomy in terms of *voluptas*

4. Ibid., p. 107.
5. Ibid., p. 112.
6. Cited by René Ternois, 'Saint Evremond et Gassendi,' *Actes du VIIIe Congrès de l'Association Guillaume Budé*, 1969, p. 726.
7. Ilie, op cit., p. 112.
8. Ibid., p. 89.

and *utilitas*, and the more Romanized forms of Epicureanism veered far enough from the agreeable towards the useful, as to become almost indistinguishable from Stoicism. Horace's Epicureanism, faithfully reflected in his maxim: *utile dulci*,[9] is nearest to that suggested by Candide's final injunction, which presents purposeful and beneficial activity as a *sine qua non* of happiness. That this emphasis upon man's need for action is a restatement by Voltaire of one of the fundamental principles of his philosophy may be appreciated by extending the dimensions of the biographical matrix of *Candide* beyond the bounds set by the limited period immediately preceding its publication.

From this point of view, letter 25 ('Sur les Pensées de M. Pascal') of the *Lettres philosophiques* is certainly germane to a consideration of "la morale épicurienne de l'action" of *Candide*. The experience of Candide and his companions in the world at large before their retirement from it altogether offers as bleak a view of the human condition as that of the "sublime misanthrope" whose reflexions Voltaire had combatted so vigorously twenty-five years before. The Pascalian resonance of parts of Voltaire's *conte* is unmistakable; the responsive chord which had been struck but barely acknowledged so long ago vibrated more strongly as Voltaire's pessimism increased under the stress of private and public misfortunes. Inevitably, the optimism of the conclusion of the tale sounds lame after the intimations of existential absurdity which have gone before, but this should not obscure that fact that, however dour and dogged it appears, it is related to the buoyant confidence in humanity which characterises Voltaire's 'anti-Pascal.' This earlier *profession de foi* is a more explicit and spirited defence of the same values of moderate activist Epicureanism which are continually threatened by extremists. The latter include the Jansenists, whose estimate of human nature and potential is excessively low, and those who emulate the Stoics, who pitched their standards for mankind so high that "ils décourageaient le reste des hommes."[1]

In letter 25 Voltaire vindicated "le juste milieu" [the remark on *Pensée* 31]; he decries the contemplative life and is categorical in his championship of purposeful and useful activity: "L'homme est né pour l'action, comme le feu tend en haut et la pierre en bas. N'être point occupé et n'exister pas est le même chose pour l'homme. Toute la différence consiste dans les occupations douces ou tumultueuses, dangereuses ou utiles" [23]. Préfiguré here we find the superabundant tumult and danger which surround Candide and his companions, the initial attractions of the inactivity of their retreat from

---

9. *Ars poetica*, I. 343: "omne tulit punctum qui miscuit utile dulci."
1. *Le Philosophe ignorant*, xlv ('Des stoïciens').

all this sound and fury and, after such *douceur de vivre* has palled on them, the final satisfaction derived from the "occupations utiles" which they take up. Boredom, the specific cause of dissatisfaction amongst the members of "la petite société," is already being presented as a blessing in disguise: ". . . l'auteur de la nature . . . a attaché l'ennui à l'inaction, afin de nous forcer par là à être utile au prochain et à nous-mêmes." Idle hedonism is rejected in terms which will be echoed in the correspondence of the years 1755–59 ("Croire que le monde est un lieu de délices où l'on ne doit avoir que du plaisir, c'est la rêverie d'un sybarite" [4]). Gardening (a term which may be taken to embrace the upkeep of a *métairie* like Candide's and the estate-management of Voltaire himself) is opposed to the "fausse, jouissance" which lives only for the moment: the "semer, bâtir, planter" triptych serves as an image for that husbandry which looks hopefully to the future, as it will do later in Voltaire's letters.[2] "Si les hommes étaient assex malheureux pour ne s'occuper que du présent, on ne sèmerait point, on ne bâtirait point, on ne planterait point, on ne pourvoirait à rien: on manquerait de tout au milieu de cette fausse jouissance" [22]. This shift of emphasis from *voluptas* to *utilitas* will be characteristic of the predominance of *l'utile* over *l'agréable* in Voltaire's gardening activities at Ferney.[3] It would be unwise, however, to solicit Candide's "il faut cultiver notre jardin" too strenuously so as to make it symbolise the all-out effort towards "the reduction of social evil and the spread or social virtue"[4] which one associates with Voltaire's Ferney period. The restrictive utilitarian aspect of Epicureanism is more evident in Candide's garden than the expansive altruism of Stoic virtue. Unproductive inertia has been displaced by the ethic of work but personal welfare is still the paramount consideration. Fontelle's conception of happiness ("Celui qui veut être heureux, se réduit et se resserre autant qu'il est possible")[5] is mirrored there rather than that of Diderot ("Point de bonheur sans vertu").[6] "Epicure s'embourgeoise," Jean Ehrard comments à propos the moral climate of the first half of the eighteenth century in France.[7] The ending of *Candide* can be taken as an illustration of this development as far as such middle-class attributes as enterprise and industry are concerned. The diffuse "universal

2. Cf. *Complete Works of Voltaire, Correspondence*, definitive edition by Theodore Besterman: D8035 (Jan. 9, 1759); D6307 (June 13, 1755).
3. Cf. Christopher Thacker, 'Voltaire and Rousseau: eighteenth-century gardeners,' *Studies on Voltaire . . .* 90, p. 1597.
4. W. F. Bottiglia, *Voltaire's Candide, analysis of a classic, Studies on Voltaire . . .* 7, (Geneva 1959), p. 109.
5. *Pensée sur le bonheur* (1724). Cited by J. Ehrard, *L'Idée de Nature en France dans la première moitié du XVIIIe siècle* (Paris 1963), Vol 1, p. 564.
6. *Essai sur le mérite et la vertu* (1745); Dédicace 'A mon frère.' *Oeuvres complètes de Diderot*, ed. Assézat et Tourneux, Vol. 1, p. 10.
7. Op cit., Vol. 1, p. 544.

benevolence" which was to become a predominant feature of the *drame bourgeois*, however, is conspicuous by its absence from the *conte*.

"Epicure fut toute sa vie un philosophe, sage, tempérant et juste."[8] This image of the Philosopher of the Garden Voltaire could have derived from Gassendi, who had presented him in this way in his *De Vita et moribus Epicuri libri octo* (1647), or from one or other of his disciples. From Jean François Sarasin, for example, whose *Discours de Morale sur Epicure* (c. 1645) had appeared as part of the works of Saint-Evremond in 1683. Saint-Evremond rejected both the authorship of Sarasin's work and the view it propagated: in his *Sur la Morale d'Epicure* (1685) he is at pains to destroy the image of Epicurus as pre-eminently a paragon of self-denial.[9] However much respect the young Voltaire had for Saint-Evremond, it is clearly the essential temperance of the Epicurean life-style which found favour with him increasingly as he grew older. Bayle is a more obvious source for this attitude: ". . . il est certain qu'il [Epicure] vécut exemplairement, & conformément aux regles de la sagesse & de la frugalité Philosophique"; . . . "la sobriété, la tempérance, & le combat contre les passions tumultueuses & déréglées, qui ôtent à l'âme son état de béatitude, c'est-à-dire, l'acquiescement doux & tranquille à sa condition. C'étoient là les voluptez où Epicure faisoit consister le bonheur de l'homme."[1] Bearing in mind Saint-Evremond's suggestion that such a notion of *volupté* as this might be characteristic of the philosopher's old-age, but not of the vigour of his prime, it is possible to see Epicurus in the same light as "le bon vieillard" of Chapter 30 of *Candide*: an exemplary figure whose conception of happiness was reflected in the simplicity and sobriety of his life.

The old Turk who influences Candide's decision to imitate a life of useful labour and distinct moderation among the members of his little community bears some resemblance to another spry old man to whom Voltaire elsewhere directs the reader's attention: the Quaker whom the author describes in the first of his *Lettres philosophiques* as "un vieillard frais qui n'avait jamais connu les passions ni l'intempérance." This connection might well be taken further. 'The Society of Friends,' this title still borne by his sect today and amply

8. *Le Philosophe ignorant*, xliv ('D'Epicure').
9. *Oeuvres meslées*. (Londres 1705), 2 vols in 4. Vol. 1, p. 462: "Je ne croi pas qu'il [Epicure] ait voulu introduire une *Volupté* plus dure que la Vertu des *Stoïques*. Cette jalousie d'Austérité me paroît extravagante dans un Philosophe voluptueux, de quelque manière qu'on tourne sa Volupté.
1. *Dictionnaire historique et critique* (Amsterdam 1734), 5 vols. Vol. II: Art. 'Epicure,' p. 741, p. 740 (note H). Cf. La Rochefoucauld, *Lettre à la Duchesse de xxxx*, *Oeuvres* (Amsterdam 1692). Vol. II, p. 47: "Je crois que, dans la morale, . . . Epicure était un saint." Cited by J. S. Spink, *French Free-Thought from Gassendi to Voltaire*, p. 142, n. 2. The whole of Chapter VIII of this work ('The Rehabilitation of Epicurus') is invaluable for any consideration of Epicureanism during this period.

justified by the Quaker in his cordial reception of the narrator, could be aptly applied to "la petite société" of Candide, inspired by the friendly and hospitable atmosphere of the Turk's household. When Voltaire says of Epicurus: "Seul de tous les philosophes, il eut pour amis tous ses disciples, et sa secte fut la seule où l'on sût aimer . . ."[2] he clearly has in mind the gospel of love and brotherhood which provides a link between Epicureanism and the unadulterated doctrine of Christ which he never ceased to admire. The attraction of the erotic had as little place in their life as they have in Candide's *métairie* where the personal experience of almost all the inhabitants would prompt an endorsement of Epicurus's remark: "physical union of the sexes never did good: it is much if it does not do harm."[3] Though the radical Protestant sect of Quakers does not appear in *Candide* it is evident that another, the Anabaptists, through the saintly Jacques, with his combination of brotherly love and profitable industry, has left its mark on the mind of the *conte*'s hero. The philosophy of the Garden and the Protestant ethic of work may quite plausibly be regarded as having affinities with each other and with the philosophy of Candide's garden.

Although an abhorrence of war and an attachment to the ideal of useful labour provide links between the little community which is established at the end of *Candide* and certain Protestant sects, it might be said that the religious dimension is otherwise noticeably absent from Voltaire's tale. The author's expression of resignation to Divine Providence is more grudging than it had been in *Zadig*, where the hero's dogged attempts to articulate his doubts had been cut short by the angel Jesrad, who had only beat a retreat to the heavenly spheres after having been allowed to parade before Zadig (and the reader) all the arguments of Pope and Leibniz which buttress a position of respectful submission to the mysterious phenomenon of cosmic injustice. The earth-bound dervish in *Candide* is conspicuously unconcerned with justifying the ways of God to man, and shows none of Jesrad's angelic patience; indeed, revelling in his unsociability, he is first of all brusque in urging Candide to keep his mouth shut and then positively rude in slamming the door in the face of Pangloss's Jesrad-like philosophising. Jesrad's position, reduced to the level of parody for the expositions of Pangloss, is considerably closer to that of the Stoics than it is to the philosophy of the Garden. Stoic cosmology, based on Platonic ideas, presented the celestial bodies as a manifestation of a divine Reason which controlled all earthly happenings by inflexible law. The Stoic derived his inner tranquility from knowledge of the harmonious world-order

2. *Le Philosophe ignorant*, xliv.
3. Quoted by Gilbert Murray, op cit., p. 110.

and from his willing submission to it. The Epicurean universe, however, is devoid of a divine principle. The gods occupy a remote place in the world-picture of the Epicureans; they inhabit the interstices of outer space and are quite indifferent to human activity. Turning his eyes away from the comfortless heavens, man is driven back on to his own resources. This is much the same sort of universe as that of *Candide*, which is ruled by a *deus absconditus*. It is true that the vision of humanity presented by Lucretius will not be devoid of grandeur, but this grandeur is not of the Stoic kind which relates microcosm to macrocosm, and holds up man as an image of God.

The Stoic buoyancy of spirit, the outward-looking belief in man's ability to annex new areas of knowledge, to achieve mastery of his physical environment, contrasts with the very cautious Epicurean attitude to the concept of human progress, conceived basically, as *Candide* envisaged the future of his little community, in terms of limited and hard-won advance based upon constant effort.[4] The confident faith of the Stoics in the value of scientific enquiry blends with their sense of admiration before the wonders of the natural universe in the influential neo-Stoic strain of physicotheology in the intellectual history of the seventeenth and early eighteenth centuries. The Epicurean note is quite different: an intellectual humility which prompts a depreciation of the pursuit of knowledge when considered for its own sake and divorced from the goal of all human life: happiness. "To flee from science," Epicurus wrote to a disciple "hoist sail with all speed."[5] The 'science' he had in mind was the sort of airy Panglossian speculation surrounded by clouds of transcendental optimism which distinguished Stoicism from his own more lowly philosophy grounded on practical everyday reality and offering to all men a limited hope based on freedom from fear. The search for security and happiness leads Candide to his own 'philosophy of the garden.' The literal sense of his famous injunction to cultivate the soil has a great deal of relevance to a certain strain of anti-intellectualism which characterises Voltaire at certain phases of his life, when he compares the appeal of culture unfavourably with the attractions of agriculture. The Epicurean background of Voltaire's aspiration to be a happy husbandman and its reflection in *Candide* has been discussed elsewhere.[6] It may be noted, however, that the tendency to demote the cultivation of the arts and to glorify (in true Epicurean fashion) the more useful activity of cultivating the land becomes more marked as Voltaire grows older. In the *Dialogue de Pégase et du Vieillard* (1774), the artist dismisses

4. Cf. Ludwig Edelstein, *The Idea of Progress in Classical Antiquity* (Baltimore 1967), p. 165.
5. C. Bailey, op cit., p. 129: *Letter to Pythocles*.
6. Dennis Fletcher, '*Candide* and the theme of the happy husbandman,' *Studies on Voltaire* . . . 161 (1976), pp. 1–11.

his winged steed ("Va, vole au mont sacré; je reste en mon jardin."
[l. 80]) with the explanation (ll. 118–129):

> Dans ses champs cultivés, à l'abri des revers,
> Le sage vit tranquille, et ne fait point de vers.
> Monsieur l'abbé Terray, pour le bien du royaume,
> Préfère un laboureur, un prudent économe,
> A tous nos vains écrits, qu'il ne lira jamais.
> Triptolème est le dieu dont je veux les bienfaits.
> Un bon cultivateur est cent fois plus utile
> Que ne fut autrefois Hésiode ou Virgile.
> Le besoin, la raison, l'instinct doit nous porter
> A faire nos moissons plutôt qu'à les chanter;
> J'aime mieux t'atteler toi-même à ma charrue,
> Que d'aller sur ton dos voltiger dans la nue.

The old man's final words: "Je me tais. Je ne veux rien savoir, ni rien
dire" (1. 161),[7] besides reflecting the anti-intellectualist aspect of Epicureanism, inevitably recall, for the reader of *Candide*, the dervish's
curt advice to the hero of that tale.

Montesquieu in the *Esprit des Lois* had remarked upon the Stoic
'sect': "Elle seule savait faire les citoyens; elle seule faisait les grands
hommes; elle seule faisait les grands empereurs."[8] The disenchanted
author of *Candide* was not in the mood for admiration of such a
philosophy. The results of a policy of grandeur and an attachment
to 'heroism,' apparent in the suffering caused by the Seven Years
War, exercised a potent influence upon the tone and substance of
Candide. In Voltaire's correspondence with Frederick the Great the
concept of 'le grand homme' can be seen taking shape in his mind
as he reacts against his friend's ruthless imposition of his will in
the service of the State. Later he will sing the praises of enlightened Roman emperors like the Stoic Marcus Aurelius. In this tale
his horizons are narrower; he is concerned with the little man.
There is no sense of the desirability of man's reach exceeding his
grasp in *Candide*; moral improvement is not absent as an ideal but
it is not conceived of on the Stoic scale of self-mastery. "Si les Epi-
curiens rendirent la nature humaine aimable," observed Voltaire,
"les Stoïciens la rendirent presque divine."[9] If, in those words of
Pope admired and quoted by Voltaire,[1] "to err is human, to forgive

---

7. Cf. P. Toldo's interpretation of Candide's "il faut cultiver notre jardin": ". . . un pessi-
   misme qui, malgré tout, n'est qu'à la surface: une aspiration au silence et à l'oubli que
   tout homme éprouve à certaines heures," 'Voltaire conteur et romancier' in *Zeitschrift
   für französische Sprache und Literatur*, 40, (1913).
8. Livre 24, Ch. 10 ('De la secte stoïque').
9. *Le Philosophe ignorant*, xlv.
1. The epigraph to *Alzire* (1736) reads: "Errer est d'un mortel, pardonner est divin."

divine," then Candide, to judge by the way he consigns Cunégonde's brother to the galleys without compunction, has a long way to go before he becomes a god-like Stoic. If, as Voltaire said, the Stoics "décourageaient le reste des hommes," *Candide*'s creator, one feels, ranges himself with "le reste des hommes," most of whom are neither moral giants nor moral pygmies, and are capable of eventually becoming at least a little better. Having plumbed the depths of human fallibility and degradation in his account of Candide's adventures, Voltaire reaches the optimistic conclusion which, however muted, is virtually the same as that of his earlier more defiant 'anti-Pascal': "J'ose prendre le parti de l'humanité."

Gilbert Murray has written: "The glory of the Stoics is to have built up a religion of extraordinary nobleness; the glory of the Epicureans is to have upheld an ideal of sanity and humanity stark upright amid a reeling world."[2] Voltaire's particular glory in writing *Candide* is to have upheld the same ideal in the same spirit as the earlier Epicureans.

HAYDN MASON

[Gestation: *Candide* Assembling Itself][†]

[Gustave Lanson's enchanting picture of Voltaire's little "*metairie*" (farm) at Ferney—busy and prosperous, playful yet disciplined, cozy and intimate yet engaged in a vast semiclandestine conspiracy—had yet another aspect. In those hundreds of letters that Voltaire dispatched all across Europe, he accumulated (almost surely without realizing it) phrases and formulas and turns of thought that after lying dormant in his mind would emerge coated with crystals of Voltairean wit and anger to form part of *Candide*. Whether this material amounted in the end to a private language addressed to a special group of Voltairean *initiés* may be debated; the case is proposed by Geoffrey Murray in *Voltaire's Candide: The Protean Gardener*, published as volume 69 (1970) of *Studies on Voltaire*. Without getting into that argument, one can say that the materials assembled by Haydn Mason clearly demonstrate the inchoate preexistence of the book in Voltaire's mind and imply its assemblage, more abrupt than gradual, into the sparkling coherence we know. Where Mason does not do so, I have translated into English the French materials cited in the body of the text.—Robert M. Adams]

* * *

2. Op cit., p. 130.
† From *Voltaire* (London: Century Hutchison Publishing Ltd., 1975), pp. 79–92. Reprinted by permission of the author and The Random House Group Limited.

Let us return to an examination of Voltaire's own attitudes as they evolved in the period immediately preceding *Candide*. That *conte*, considered by general consent to be Voltaire's masterpiece, is a kind of summation of Voltaire's views in the late 1750s on the human condition, beset by suffering and wickedness yet not wholly without scope for initiative and improvement. This is not the place for an analysis of Voltaire's tale; but no biography of the *philosophe* can reasonably neglect a close look at the way his mind came to absorb and shape materials from the world around him and from his own reading. Such a consideration, involving as it does a careful review of detailed, even minute, matters, inevitably calls for a certain rigour of attention; yet without it we cannot hope to understand very much about the genesis of Voltaire's greatest work.

As we have seen, the news of the Lisbon earthquake in 1755 played an important rôle. Voltaire's immediate reaction is one of horror: 'One hundred thousand ants, our neighbours, crushed all of a sudden in our ant-heap, half of them perishing doubtless in inexpressible anguish.' The sole consolation is that the Jesuit Inquisitors of Lisbon will have disappeared with the rest. That, concludes Voltaire, should teach men not to persecute men, 'for while a few confounded rascals are burning a few fanatics the earth is swallowing up both' (D6597, 24 November [1755]).[1] Already the ironic perspective that informs Chapter VI of *Candide* on the Lisbon auto-da-fé has been glimpsed. Such expressions of horror resound through letters of succeeding days. The very size of the catastrophe is 'a terrible argument against Optimism' (D6605). Confronted by it, Voltaire feels his own problems shrink to such petty dimensions that he is ashamed of them (D6605, D6607). This attitude is somewhat reminiscent of the way his hero Zadig in an earlier *conte* had forgotten his own miseries in contemplation of the infinite heavens. But there is a sombre difference; Zadig's vision was sublimely consoling, whereas Voltaire's merely confirms the awful destructiveness latent in physical nature.

It is clear that the *Poème sur le désastre de Lisbonne* constituted an almost instinctive response. However, less attention has been paid to the fact that once the poem is completed Voltaire's attitudes are swiftly transmuted into a rather different stance. In a letter to the Protestant pastor Allamand on 16 December 1755 he writes: 'I pity the Portuguese, like you, *but men do still more harm to each other on their little molehill than nature does to them.* Our wars massacre more men than are swallowed up by earthquakes. If we had to fear only the Lisbon adventure in this world, we should still be

---

1. D preceding a number indicates the position of a letter in the immense Besterman edition of Voltaire's correspondence.

tolerably well off' (D6629: my italics). Two new notes are struck. Despondent alarm at the earthquake has given way to a more detached attitude; and the physical evils of the universe are set in a context in which man's wickedness to man, particularly in wars, looms far greater. Even in his very first letter after learning of the earthquake (D6597) he had, as we saw, found space to think also of the persecutions inflicted by the Inquisitors. It is this kind of consideration which, with more time for reflection, becomes paramount. Physical suffering, it is true, is a sufficient refutation of the belief that 'all is well'; but the true horror lies in the spectacle of what men do to one another. The same evolution of attitudes can also be glimpsed in the *Poème sur le désastre*, which begins with the actual catastrophe at Lisbon but then opens out onto a wider scene in which 'tout est en guerre.'[2]

Reasons to support this new-found awareness that war is the supreme evil were soon to be sadly abundant in the world around. On 29 August 1756 Frederick the Great invaded Saxony, thereby precipitating the Seven Years War. It accords well with Voltaire's darkening mood. In early 1756 he had passed from specific concern with the Lisbon earthquake to a more general brooding on the problem of evil. He tells Elie Bertrand (another of the Genevan clergy) in February that the myth of the Fall of Man, whether Christian or otherwise, is more reasonable in human terms than the Optimism of Leibniz and Pope, which beneath the disguise of a consoling name simply removes all hope: 'if *all is well*, how do the Leibnizians admit of a better?' (D6738: author's italics) It is the fatalistic quality of Optimism that is so cruel, for it invites man to acquiesce and therefore give up all striving for improvement. As we have seen, in the desolate picture Voltaire paints of the human condition, he allows man one single consolation: hope. Otherwise, the pessimism is general, and indeed increasing in the author's view of the world. He begins to become more interested in Manichean beliefs, according to which evil has a life of its own quite independent of the forces of good in the universe. A letter to Mme du Deffand in May 1756 talks of Jupiter's two casks, one for good and another, bigger, for evil. Not only does he pose the basic question—Why so? More daringly, he wonders whether the evil cask could have constructed itself. Here are the seeds of an outlook voiced in *Candide* by the self-styled Manichean Martin.

However, this increasingly sombre view of the world does not relate to a personal crisis as is sometimes claimed. Apart from worries over such matters as the widespread circulation, despite his

2. Everything is at war.

efforts to the contrary, of his notorious mock-epic *La Pucelle*, Voltaire is by and large happily established in Geneva. Les Délices has needed some improvements and from the early weeks he is busy planting, furnishing, building. Claude Patu, a visitor in autumn 1755, speaks wonderingly of Voltaire's vigour: 'Imagine, together with the air of a dying man, all the fire of first youth, and the brilliance of his attractive stories!' Never has one seen better fare or more engaging manners; the whole of Geneva is delighted to have him there and is doing all it can to keep him (D6562). The picture, in short, is not far short of idyllic. True, Voltaire looks like a corpse, as another visitor confirms (D6646). But the sense of returning vitality and purpose flows from the correspondence as it must have done at the dinner table. In 1758 Mme d'Epinay was also to find the *philosophe* full of gaiety and cheerfulness (D7704). Even the references to ill-health become less common. Voltaire has found 'a port after weathering so many storms' (D6842). To Thieriot he makes the touching confession that he is writing about the sufferings of his fellow-men out of pure altruism, for 'I am so happy that I am ashamed of it' (D6875, 27 May [1756]).

Yet this state of personal contentment in no way precludes a total divorce with the philosophy of Optimism, and from its outset the Seven Years War is invoked as a decisive refutation (e.g., D7001). To his friend the Duchess of Saxe-Gotha, who is to find herself in the thick of the battle, he never ceases to point up the absurd horror of it all, using the War polemically to express disagreement with her adherence to Optimism (e.g., D7023). To his more intimate acquaintance Thieriot, he voices an attitude of indifference: 'Happy is he who lives in tranquillity on the edge of his lake, far from the throne, and far from envy' (D7028). To the duc de Richelieu, also a friend but more distant as being of high rank and politically influential, another side appears. Richelieu being in charge of the larger of the two French armies, Voltaire turned to him to advocate his invention of an armed chariot which, he reckoned, would kill many Prussians, indeed would knock out everyone it met, so that two of the machines would be enough against a battalion and squadron combined (D7043, D7293). This particular notion (which the French Government did not take up) should of itself dispose of two long-standing myths about Voltaire: that he was a total pacifist, and lacked all sense of patriotism. Generally pacifist in outlook, he nevertheless was forced to accept the realities of preparing a military defence against the aggression of Prussia on land and the British at sea. Both countries fill him with consternation, though for rather different reasons.

He is appalled by the desolation wrought by Frederick's armies in central Europe, once they had won the decisive engagement at

Rossbach on 5 November 1757. But prior to that he had been moved by compassion for the Prussian King, who had intimated that he was contemplating suicide (D7373). Voltaire replied in urgent tones dissuading him from such a course, pointing out that it would dismay his supporters and give joy only to his enemies. Instead, Frederick should seek an honourable peace (D7400), show he is a *philosophe* and live for all the good things still remaining to him: possessions, dignities, friends (D7419). A further plea follows on 13 November (D7460). Ironically, it is written after Rossbach, which is Frederick's contemptuous reply to Voltaire's advice (the King had already expressed his scorn in a letter to his sister Wilhelmina, D7414, Commentary). The news of that Prussian victory reverses Voltaire's attitude. A despairing Frederick gains immediate access to his warm sympathy. Yet at the same time he is hoping for revenge over Frederick for the humiliating moment at Frankfurt when four bayonets had menaced Mme Denis, and he is disappointed when Frederick triumphs (D7471). His feelings towards the Prussian King are as strongly ambivalent as ever. Richard Phelps, a British visitor at this time, acutely observed: 'He was the most inconsistent, whenever he talked of the King of Prussia.'

By contrast, Voltaire's views on the British Navy are unequivocal. He fears their superior numbers (D7210) and wants to see their piratical ways punished (D7491). The British were exercising a direct influence upon Voltaire's life. Not only were they likely by their hostile actions and blockades to cause the price of sugar to rise (D7131, 7901). They were, more gravely, capturing French vessels in which the writer had considerable investments, especially the fleet sailing from Cadiz (D5719), and at times the Cadiz mercantile trade was to give him much cause for concern (e.g., D6811). Besides, the British Government had provided one of the more signal instances of horrible folly during the Seven Years War by the execution of Admiral Byng for failing to relieve Minorca against the duc de Richelieu's forces at Port-Mahon in May 1756. Voltaire and Richelieu had both intervened on Byng's behalf in the court-martial following the engagement, but to no avail; Byng was sentenced on 27 January 1757 to be shot, the sentence being carried out on 14 March. André-Michel Rousseau, providing a comprehensive account of the affair, sees it as Voltaire's baptism as champion of the oppressed. This time he was to gain nothing, save the achievement of making Byng, through his appearance in *Candide,* far more famous in death than he ever was in life and of turning the ironic remark that he had been executed 'pour encourager les autres'[3] into one of the very few

---

3. To encourage others.

phrases from French literature to have gained a proverbial currency in the English language.

After the outbreak of the Seven Years War, Voltaire's sense of the absurd aspect of warfare evolves considerably. Tales in that vein from the Duchess of Saxe-Gotha (D7040) might have heightened that impression, just as the Byng episode undoubtedly did. By February 1757 the acid tones of *Candide* are evident in a letter to the Englishman George Keate when Voltaire writes à propos of Byng: 'Your sailors are not polite,' going on: 'If you want to see some fine battles, Germans killed by Germans and a few towns pillaged, it is up to you to enjoy this little entertainment in the spring' (D7162). In June 1757 the same spirit of sarcasm appears in a letter to the Duchess of Saxe-Gotha. There would be much unhappiness, he tells her, if the warring armies did not destroy at least fifty towns, reduce some fifty thousand families to beggary, and kill four or five hundred thousand men. 'We cannot yet say "All is well" but it is not going badly, and with time Optimism will be conclusively proven' (D7297).

In early 1757, then, the essential tone of *Candide* is already present in Voltaire's mind. Other details too are beginning to appear in his letters. The final destination of Candide and his little band in the garden outside Constantinople is already foreshadowed in March 1757, when Voltaire cites a comparison between the view he has over the lake from Lausanne with a similar outlook in Constantinople (D7213). The writer who had drawn this parallel, so suggestive to Voltaire's imagination, was the seventeenth-century explorer Jean-Baptiste Tavernier, who had travelled widely in the East before retiring to Switzerland not far from Voltaire's house in Lausanne. Louis XIV had been offended that Tavernier had settled in Switzerland, to which he had replied that he wanted to own something that belonged entirely to him. Not surprisingly, Voltaire felt a kinship with this earlier Frenchman who had also shaken the dust of France from off his feet in order to find genuine independence; he adds that 'I am finishing up as he did' (D7215). One sees here a complex interweaving of elements. Lausanne view = Constantinople view, thanks to Tavernier. As Voltaire is retired and free outside France, so too Candide in his final retreat in Turkey. Whether yet consigned to paper, the lineaments of the *dénouement* to the *conte* are all mentally in place by March 1757.

On 26 October 1757 Voltaire laments the death of Patu, who had visited him two years before. His obituary notice is simple and touching: 'il aimait tous les arts, et son âme était candide' (D7434).[4] Thus

---

4. He loved the arts, and his soul was candid.

appears our hero's name. When Voltaire introduces it at the beginning of the *conte* the conjunction is much the same: 'Sa physionomie annonçait son âme . . . on le nommait Candide.'[5] A vital step in
the creation of the *conte* is prefigured here. Shortly afterwards on
9 November 1757 Thieriot is writing to Voltaire saying that they are
as ignorant as 'des souris dans un vaisseau de l'intention de ceux
qui le conduisent' (D7456).[6] This, as we have seen, is not the first
time the image has come to Voltaire's mind, as he had himself used
a similar expression to Frederick in 1736. But Thieriot probably
refreshed Voltaire's memory at a crucial moment, and his influence
is seen in one of the most trenchant observations in *Candide* about
divine Providence: 'Quand Sa Hautesse envoie un vaisseau en
Egypte, s'embarrasse-t-elle si les souris qui sont dans le vaisseau sont
à leur aise ou non?'[7]

Another important detail is added to the genesis of Voltaire's *conte*
at the end of November 1757 when he receives a letter from the Margravine of Bayreuth describing the battle of Rossbach. She wrote:

> Cette armée [i.e., prussienne] . . . fut rangée en ordre de
> bataille sur une ligne. Alors l'artillerie fit un feu si terrible que
> des Français . . . disent que chaque coup tuait ou blessait huit
> ou neuf personnes. La mousqueterie ne fit pas moins d'effet.
> Les Français avançaient toujours en colonne pour attaquer avec
> la baïonnette . . . L'infanterie . . . fut taillée en pièces et entière-
> ment dispersé.
>
> (This [Prussian] army was drawn up in battle order along a
> line. Then the artillery laid down such a terrible barrage that
> Frenchmen say . . . each shot killed or wounded eight or nine
> people. The musketry was no less efficacious. The French
> were still advancing in columns to attack with the bayonet . . .
> The infantry . . . were cut to pieces and totally scattered.)
>
> (D7477)

This must surely be at the origin of Voltaire's account in *Candide* of
the battle between the Bulgares and the Abares:

> Rien n'était si beau, si leste, si brillant, si bien ordonné que les
> deux armées. . . . Les canons renversèrent d'abord à peu près six
> mille hommes de chaque côté; ensuite la mousqueterie ôta du
> meilleur des mondes environ neuf à dix mille coquins qui en

---

5. His features admirably expressed his soul . . . they called him Candide.
6. As ignorant as mice in a ship of the intentions of those controlling her.
7. When His Highness sends a ship to Egypt, does he worry whether the mice on board
   are comfortable or not?

infectaient la surface. La baïonnette fut aussi la raison suffisante de la mort de quelques milliers d'hommes.

(Nothing was as beautiful, as sprightly, as well ordered as the
two armies. . . . The cannon first of all knocked over about six
thousand men on either side; next the musketry removed
from the best of worlds around nine to ten thousand rascals
who were infecting its surface. The bayonet was also the sufficient cause of the deaths of a few thousand men.)

The order of details is the same: the military line-up, the artillery,
musketry, bayonet. Voltaire simply transforms an honest and poi-
gnant account into a display of ironic brilliance. The rôles are similarly distributed in both passages, and the overall effect of utter
devastation is the same. But at Rossbach only the French were
routed. It is part of Voltaire's strategy to ensure that both sides in
his absurd and horrible battle are shot to pieces. The Margravine is
able to offer further help a week later when writing to Voltaire about
the starving soldiers who have fled after the defeat at Rossbach and
are now wandering about everywhere (D7483). This time the impact
upon *Candide* is less impressive, but it is true that Candide too flees
without direction and runs out of food.

   Such are the details that have begun to accumulate by the beginning of December 1757. At the turn of the year the number of parallels increases strikingly. Voltaire's bitter memory of the Frankfurt
incident where his niece had 'Four bayonets . . . in the stomach'
(D7521) is renewed, as we have noticed, after Frederick had tri-
umphed at Rossbach. This may be the starting point for the knife
wound which the heroine of the *conte* Cunégonde receives in the
side (Chapter 8) or the account of her disembowelling by Bulgarian
soldiers (Chapter 4). Voltaire advises the Genevan clergy not to
react to the *Encyclopédie* article 'Genève': 'Que faut-il donc faire?
Rien, se taire, vivre en paix . . .' (D7536, 27 December [1757]).[8] The
similarity is close with the dervish's brusque reply to Pangloss, who
wants to know the truths of metaphysics: 'Que faut-il donc faire? dit
Pangloss. —Te taire, dit le derviche.'[9] In January 1758 Voltaire is telling the Duchess of Saxe-Gotha that Prussians and the like are 'the
children of the evil principle' (D7554); we see here a further premo-
nition of the Manichean Martin in *Candide*, who believes that God
has abandoned this world to some evil being and cites war as one of
his strongest arguments for believing so. At the same time Voltaire
is working on his history the *Essai sur les moeurs*. The topics to which
he specifically refers include the English colonies in America and

8. What to do then? Nothing, keep quiet, live in peace . . .
9. 'What shall we do then? Asked Pangloss. —Hold your tongue, said the dervish.'

the Jesuits in Paraguay (D7559). Both enter into the make-up of *Candide*, Paraguay directly (Chapter 14) and the State of Pennsylvania in the disguise of Eldorado (Chapter 18), that Utopia where, as in Pennsylvania, there are no judges, doctors or priests. Just as, in Eldorado, the natives build a machine 'pour guinder [to hoist]' Candide and his companion Cacambo out of Eldorado, so too does Voltaire on 26 January 1758 use the same somewhat uncommon verb in writing that 'we would hoist' a visitor over the mont Cenis to Turin if he should wish to pass by Geneva (D7603).

On 8 January 1758 a reference to the efficient manoeuvres of Frederick's troops, including 'le pas redoublé [at the double]' (D7565), compares with the well-drilled Bulgar in *Candide* who also knew how to 'doubler le pas' (Chapter 2). Reference to the auto-da-fé recurs in a letter of 12 January (D7579). On the 15th mention is made of the mosques in Constantinople, as too of the Sultan's officers with the exotic title of 'azamoglans' (D7584); Cunégonde's brother is sent to the galleys for being found bathing with 'un jeune icoglan,' and Pangloss for making advances to a pretty girl in a Constantinople mosque (Chapter 28). On 29 January Voltaire sympathises with d'Alembert's problems over the *Encyclopédie*, adding that his colleague is a victim of the publishers: 'Vous avez travaillé pour des libraires' (D6708). So too in *Candide* has Martin suffered, and acquired his gloomy outlook on life, as the 'pauvre savant qui avait travaillé dix ans pour les libraires . . .'[1] Just as the 'Protestant ministers' of Surinam persecute Martin because they take him for a Socinian, so too d'Alembert suffers persecution because his article 'Genève' had suggested that the Genevan pastors were Socinian. On 12 February Voltaire writes that the War is a labyrinth from which one can hardly escape except over dead bodies, and he expresses regret that the nations must fight so ruinously for 'quelques arpents de glace en Acadie [a few acres of ice in Acadia],' a reference to the battles between the French and English in North America (D7630). Candide leaves his own battle by crossing over heaps of dead (Chapter 3), while Martin represents Voltaire's feeling of folly that England and France are at war for 'quelques arpents de neige vers le Canada.'[2] The next day Voltaire compares working on the *Encyclopédie* to rowing in the galleys (D7632); this latter occupation is what we find Pangloss and Cunégonde's brother doing near the end of the *conte*. Finally, Voltaire refers on 3 March to 'La canaille de vos convulsionnaires'[3] when writing of the odious Jansenist fanatics who went into convulsions (D7660); 'la canaille convulsionnaire' is known to Martin also.

1. Poor scholar who had worked ten years for the booksellers . . .
2. A few acres of snow near Canada.
3. The rabble of your convulsionaries.

These details, by their nature fragmentary, need to be assembled
if one is to obtain a comprehensive view of Voltaire's state of mind
during the period between late October 1757 and early March 1758.
His letters, we can see, are full of allusions that are taken up, often
without any virtual reworking, in *Candide*. The *conte* must have
been taking shape in his mind during those months. More specifically, the passages cluster around certain areas of the story: the
opening, and particularly the battle; the Eldorado episode; the
appearance of Martin soon afterwards; and the concluding sections
in and around Constantinople. Equally interesting, direct echoes of
Candide more or less vanish from Voltaire's correspondence after the
beginning of March 1758 and do not reappear until he pays a visit
to the Elector Palatine at Schwetzingen four months later.

This visit, which takes him away from Geneva in July 1758 for
about five weeks, appears to coincide with a change in Voltaire's
mood that has not been sufficiently noted by his biographers. Until
his departure he had led a relatively contented existence. A visitor
to Geneva just before he left remarks on how he seemed younger,
happier, healthier than before his stay in Prussia (D7784). But even
so, a period is coming to an end in Voltaire's life. The disappointments with the Genevan clergy have had their effect and he wishes
to leave the territory where they hold sway. The search is on once
more to find a property which combines the maximum of security
and independence. He thinks of Lorraine, which he had last seen
at the time of Mme du Châtelet's death; as he writes to Saint-
Lambert from Schwetzingen, he would like to place himself under
the protection of King Stanislas (D7795). But though the latter
appears to have been personally sympathetic to the proposal, he was
well aware that he could not afford to sanction it without first seeking the approval of his son-in-law Louis XV (cf. D7787). The latter
was to reply in August to Stanislas, clearly intimating his coolness
on the matter (D7787, Commentary); and Voltaire thereafter was to
look elsewhere for a home.

The visit to Schwetzingen, reluctantly undertaken, was made
apparently with business in mind in order to invest money for
optimum benefit. Perhaps Voltaire's maritime losses through the
activities of the British Navy had made the excursion indispensable. However, the journey permitted him also to sound out a number of influential people about returning to Lorraine or France, and
this in the end may have been the more important reason. Whatever the precise motives, it is clear that uncertainty about his future
has re-entered Voltaire's life. For a period he is transported back to
the climate of insecurity that prevailed during the years immediately preceding installation at Les Délices. Hopes of a return to
Paris flicker briefly, and for that he is willing to do obeisance to the

French King (e.g. D7762). But the nomadic life no longer brings him any pleasure at all. Although well fêted at Schwetzingen, he is also miserable and lonely. One of his letters to Mme Denis[4] is a *cri de coeur* such as has not been heard in his correspondence for some years: 'No letters from you, it is heart-breaking, it is abominable. I write to you daily, and you abandon me. I have never missed you so much and never been so angry with you' (D7803). It is the eloquent complaint of a man homesick for Les Délices and above all for the one person there whose company is essential to him.

Was *Candide* elaborated under such unhappy circumstances? Did Voltaire perhaps take with him a sketch, drafted out some months before, such as we now know preceded the composition of *L'Ingénu*? If so, he had probably written at least some sections in greater detail, as we have seen. But the composition of *Candide* may essentially date from the visit, when ample leisure time would have been available for it. It seems quite possible, as Voltaire's secretary appears to have made the first copy of the *conte* while at the château, the author then presenting it to his host. But the work was not necessarily finished even then, and one biography of Voltaire recounts an incident, which must remain unverifiable, to the effect that it was completed in three days' concentrated work back at Les Délices. However, Schwetzingen would seem to mark an important milestone in the genesis of the tale. When Voltaire wrote to Countess Bentinck in mid-August on his return journey that he had much to tell her when he saw her, adding that 'notre roman est singulier' (D7825)[5] he may well have been referring obliquely to *Candide* as much as to personal experiences. At any rate, the phrase he uses: 'nous reprendrons le fil de nos aventures [we shall pick up the thread of our adventures]' is echoed by Voltaire's observation in *Candide* about Cunégonde's narration of her own troubles: 'Elle reprit ainsi le fil de son histoire.'[6]

Unless *Candide* were virtually finished before Voltaire's visit to Schwetzingen, which appears unlikely, one must view it as written not simply in a state of ambivalent feelings about Paris and Geneva nor as a work of detached irony by a happy man but as the composition of someone who was once more plunged into despairing gloom. When he returned to Geneva he received definitive news from d'Argental that Mme de Pompadour had declared him *persona non grata* at Court. Besterman rightly notes: 'it is from this moment that can be dated his spiritual severance from his fatherland' (D7836, Commentary). A genuine sadness prevails in this letter,

---

4. His niece but also his mistress.
5. Our story is unusual.
6. So she took up the thread of her tale.

betokening the same kind of personal vulnerability as he had shown at Schwetzingen regarding Mme Denis. The buoyancy which had been uppermost even when he was deploring the horrors of the War has vanished. Comments are more direct, less ironic: 'tout le monde est ruiné. . . . Ah quel siècle!' (D7842, 2 September 1758). 'Quel triste siècle' (D7846, 3 September 1758); 'Le naufrage parait universel' (D7848, 5 September 1758). To the theme of shipwreck is added the despairing note: 'Une planche, vite . . . !'(D7839, 2 September 1758).[7] It is the dark mood of the Lisbon storm, when the one self-less man in *Candide*, Jacques, is drowned, while the sailor who murdered him swims to safety (Chapter 5).

One general factor must also not be overlooked in this pessimism. Voltaire is disheartened by the decline of French prestige and influence in the world. Concern is often expressed about cultural and military affairs together, as in a letter to d'Argental in March where he bewails the fact that since the battle of Rossbach 'everything has been in decline in our armies, as in the fine arts in Paris' (D7676). The *philosophe* had long been persuaded that *belles-lettres* in France were degenerating and that the French were living on past credit. This kind of comment proliferates in 1758. Voltaire notes that every French play now is hissed in Europe (D7836). The observation about living off the glory of the previous century returns in a letter where the author links together a series of charges against the French: a shortage of talent in every field; a profusion of writings on war, the navy and trade, yet French ruin and defeat on land and sea; a plethora of mediocre minds who possess a little wit, but not a genius anywhere; persecution and calumny as the lot of any man of merit who appears in France (D7846). Voltaire's professed response is to turn his back on all these lamentable happenings and enjoy the asylum he has discovered. But the very intensity of his reactions indicates a man who once again feels the need to be *engagé*, even if as yet he has no clear idea whether or how he will achieve it. When he eventually undertook negotiations to buy the Châteaux of Tournay and subsequently of Ferney, both just outside Geneva on the French-Swiss border, was his only idea, as he put it to the vendor of Tournay (President de Brosses), 'to die perfectly free' (D7871)? Or did he already have some inkling of what his new life would bring?

Be that as it may, the depressed tones of August and early September are closely related to the search for a new home. Voltaire approached de Brosses about Tournay on 9 September (D7853). A month later he has bought that château and, more important still for his future life, is about to buy the one at Ferney (D7896). He

---

7. The whole world is ruined. . . . Ah, what an age! —What a gloomy age. —The shipwreck seems universal. —A plank, quickly!

has taken a new decision, to renounce urban life (D7936). The tone of contentment begins to return to the correspondence. To his friend Formont he writes: 'I do not know of any situation preferable to mine' (D7888, [c. 3 October 1758]). True, he protests perhaps too much in his fulminations against a Paris that he can no longer hope to see; but elsewhere, too, the sense that the life of philosophers is much better than that of kings (D7936) and that he can now cultivate his garden in tranquillity (D7943) emerges clearly.

Thus far one might say that Voltaire is merely repeating in 1758 the search previously undertaken in 1755. But a remarkable letter of 18 November, the importance of which Besterman has rightly stressed, marks the beginning of a new and final period in Voltaire's life. He has been inspecting his new estate at Ferney and finding that there is more involved than the cultivation of plants. He has acquired peasants who depend on him. What is the state of the community? Half the land lies fallow, the *curé* has celebrated no marriages in seven years, the countryside is depopulated as people rush to nearby Geneva. Taxation (especially the salt-tax) destroys those who remain; either the peasants pay and are reduced to abject poverty, or they evade payment and are clapped in jail. 'It is heartbreaking to witness so many misfortunes. I am buying the Ferney property simply in order to do a little good there. . . . The prince who will be my liege lord should rather help me to drag his subjects out of the abyss of poverty, than profit from his ancient feudal rights ['du droit goth et visigoth des lods et ventes']⁸ (D7946, 18 November 1758).

This is a new voice in Voltaire's letters. We have seen how many times he had sought to intervene on the social or political scene and been frustrated. Here at last the right opportunity in time and place comes to hand. By acquiring seigneurial rights he is freer, he says, than when he possessed only his house in Lausanne and his 'country cottage [guinguette]' in Geneva, where the people were 'a little arrogant' and the priests 'a little dangerous'; Ferney and Tournay have added 'deux grands degrés'⁹ to his happiness (D7976). The rôles of 'maçon' and 'jardinier'¹ which he has long since arrogated to himself are now supplemented by a new one: 'seigneur' (D7985). Once again, as in 1755 (D6214), he claims that he is becoming a patriarch (D7970); this time the claim will have a firmer grounding. Already before he is even installed at Ferney he has taken up the cudgels against the *curé* of Moëns, who is the malefactor extorting moneys from Voltaire's peasants and forcing them to sell their own lands.

8. From the gothic and visigothic rights of dues and fines.
9. Two great rises.
1. Mason; gardener.

His appeal to the diocesan bishop at Annecy (D7981, 16 December 1758) marks the beginning of a long campaign against the priest.

This note of social concern enters into *Candide*, but only just. From late August 1758 another spate of parallels with the *conte* is to be found in the correspondence: Westphalia (D7838); shipwreck (D7839, 7848, 7862); the earth covered with corpses and beggars (D7852) reminding us of Chapters 3–4; the cultivation of pine-apples in India (D7875), as in Turkey in Chapter 30; *te deums* as thanksgiving after battle (D7890, 7908, 7928): these and other phrases reminiscent of the *conte* suggest that the latter was in the forefront of Voltaire's mind up to early November. But most of these are not new and indicate no more than elaboration of the finished product. However, one episode, that of the black slave in Chapter 19, is more important, because we now know that it did not figure in the earliest manuscript version of *Candide*. René Pomeau has shown that the source for this passage lies in Voltaire's reading of Helvétius's *De l'esprit*, which contains strikingly similar references to slavery, around 18 October 1758 (cf. D7912). Not that Voltaire was unaware of the horrors occurring to blacks in the colonies; he had already written about them in the *Essai sur les moeurs* the previous January. But Helvétius recalled the institution of slavery to mind as one of the horrors which no comprehensive account of the world's evils should ignore. It also linked up for Voltaire with his new experiences as *seigneur de Ferney*.

This passage in *Candide* is surely the one where the most direct assault is made on the reader's conscience: 'This is the price you pay for eating sugar in Europe.' It also leads to one of *Candide*'s few impassioned outbursts against Optimism. But it is poorly integrated into the plot, as was almost inevitable given the date of its interpolation, and has no direct impact upon anything subsequent to it. An element of hesitation can be discerned on the author's part. It relates to the ambiguity of Voltaire's views on social commitment in the *conte*. The Ferney epoch with all its glorious activities in social protest and reform is only just opening after virtually the whole of *Candide* has been completed. One of the reasons for the unique tragi-comic quality of the tale must surely be sought in its period of gestation: the relative contentment of the Geneva years is beginning to dissolve as Voltaire begins work on it, a sharp decline in morale accompanies the Schwetzingen phase when it is generally thought to have been for the most part composed, and the prospect of a new era opening out, as yet full of possibility but of uncertainty too, is descried as it is finished. No biography of a writer can, or should, attempt to explain his art through his life. Voltaire's *Candide*, infinitely complex, savagely lucid, is the author's most brilliant of his innumerable attacks on the strongholds and methods of obscurantism. Like all such creations, it will not yield its ultimate secrets. The biographer, confronted by such mysteries, has but one useful function. By delineating the area where echoes from the world of *Candide* overlap into the world of Voltaire's daily life, he may hope to catch an element that went into the amalgam of forces creating the *conte*.

At the end of 1758, Voltaire tells d'Argental with pride that he has created for himself 'a rather nice kingdom' (D7988). At last he has his own principality: he is now both *roi* and *philosophe*. His installation at Tournay on Christmas Eve 1758 was of fitting dignity and pomp, with sound of cannon, fife and drum, all the peasants bearing arms and girls presenting flowers to his two diamond-bedecked nieces. 'M. de Voltaire,' writes a spectator, 'was very pleased and full of joy . . . He was, believe me, very flattered' (D7998). Henceforth rank and authority will be used to advance social good. By the New Year Voltaire sees this as involving the overthrow of superstition (D8029); it is the tone of 'écrasez l'infâme,' and the famous phrase itself will make its appearance in 1760 (D9006).[2] As *Candide* begins to enjoy, a few weeks later, the success which has never since deserted it, so too does Voltaire enter at last into his kingdom. In his sixty-fifth year, François-Marie Arouet has finally realised himself as M. de Voltaire.[3]

NICHOLAS CRONK

The Voltairean Genre of the *Conte Philosophique:* Does It Exist?[†]

'The Voltaire *conte* does not work with established rules or procedures in the same way as, say, his tragedy. Part of its value is precisely its flexibility.'[1] So writes Richard Francis, in the Introduction to his authoritative critical edition of *L'Ingénu*. It is this important observation about generic flexibility that I would like to explore further in this essay. The widely-used term *conte philosophique* is a

---

2. "Ecrasez l'infâme" is a slogan many times repeated by Voltaire in the course of his crusades against bigotry, intolerance, and cruelty in the church of his day. "Wipe out the disgrace" is a literal translation, but the phrase implies much more.
3. François-Marie Arouet is the name of an insignificant Paris bourgeois; M. de Voltaire (wherever his name comes from) is a gentleman, a seigneur, a person of European repute.
† From *Enlightenment and Narrative: Essays in Honour of Richard A. Francis by Colleagues and Friends*, ed. Philip Robinson, *Nottingham French Studies* 48, no. 3 (Autumn 2009): 61–73. Reproduced by permission of *Nottingham French Studies* (www.nottinghamfrench studies.co.uk).
1. *L'Ingénu*, ed. Richard A. Francis, *Œuvres complètes de Voltaire* (Oxford: Voltaire Foundation, 1968–) [hereafter *OCV*], vol. 63c (2006), p. 104.

fixture of Voltairean criticism, though in the hands of some critics it has become anything but flexible. While Gustave Lanson regarded the *conte philosophique* as one of the 'formes fixes' of eighteenth-century French prose writing in general,[2] more recent critics have tended to reserve the term specifically for the short fiction of Voltaire. The venerable 'Lagarde et Michard' typically affirm that ideas are preeminent in Voltaire's *contes philosophiques*: 'Par une sorte de grâce, ces contes philosophiques où les idées sont souveraines nous paraissent de purs *divertissements*.'[3] Interestingly, they note the paradoxical tension between 'pure' pleasure and ideas, though they do not develop the point. More matter-of-fact is the presentation of this alleged 'sous-genre' in a modern volume aimed at French university students:

> Le conte philosophique: on peut fixer la naissance de ce sous-genre au XVIIIe siècle; il a pour ambition de mouler dans une fiction brève un contenu satirique et édifiant. Voltaire sera le meilleur illustrateur du genre (*Micromégas, Zadig, Candide*) et nous fournit implicitement un catalogue des règles du genre: l'utilisation de la fable (marquée par le surnaturel ou le merveilleux), la dimension parodique (on reprend, pour les transgresser ou les démystifier, les règles de l'écriture et de l'inspiration romanesques), la leçon philosophique (le conte philosophique vise à imposer un point de vue, à démontrer ou déconsidérer une thèse).[4]

Also writing in a book addressed to a student readership, Christiane Mervaud is exceptional in sounding a salutary note of warning about the use of this generic term: 'La définition du *conte philosophique* [. . .] privilégie souvent une démarche circulaire, prenant *Candide* comme point de départ pour le retrouver au point d'arrivée. Ou la question du genre ne paraît pas primordiale.'[5] We can understand why the category of *conte philosophique* was useful to Gustave Lanson, at a time in the Third Republic when *lycée* and university syllabuses were a matter of keen debate, and when it was felt important to bring Voltaire's 'message' to the fore. But we have continued to use the term ever since, perhaps because it seems a convenient pedagogic and critical tool, without always subjecting it to adequate scrutiny.

Literary critics working in the Anglo-American tradition have, ever since New Criticism, been wary of philosophical ideas inserted into literary structures. 'For some reason it has never been

2. Gustave Lanson, *L'Art de la prose* (Paris: Fayard, 1908), p. 182.
3. André Lagarde and Laurent Michard, *XVIIIe Siècle* (Paris: Bordas, 1970), p. 130.
4. Yves Stalloni, *Les Genres littéraires* (Paris: Nathan, 2000), p. 74.
5. Christiane Mervaud, *Voltaire en toutes lettres* (Paris: Bordas, 1991), p. 72.

consistently understood,' writes Northrop Frye, 'that the ideas of literature are not real propositions, but rather verbal formulas which imitate real propositions.'[6] Ronald Crane is emphatic that we cannot apply the same criteria of logic and coherence to ideas found in a literary work as we would to a work of philosophy.[7] The notion of a genre of 'philosophical fiction' can seem equally suspect to a philosopher too. Jonathan Rée has explored the literariness of philosophers such as Descartes or Hegel,[8] but is highly sceptical about the separate status of philosophical fictions: 'The difference between philosophy and non-philosophy is not a matter of literary genre. And philosophical non-fiction may contain as much fiction as philosophical fictions do; perhaps even more.'[9]

Turning to the Voltairean corpus, it is important to remember that the expression *conte philosophique*, though attested in the eighteenth century, is extremely rare, and certainly not a generic category. Angus Martin searched for instances of the adjective *philosophique* applied to eighteenth-century works of short fiction: 'In view of our familiarity with the term *conte philosophique*, it comes as something of a surprise to find this particular adjective occurring in *no* cases before 1750 and in only eleven cases thereafter [up to 1800]. On the other hand, while one would have expected the adjective *moral* to occur frequently, the overwhelming total of some 140 references (all but 4, it should be noted, after the mid-century) seems curiously disproportionate with the use of the term *philosophique*.'[1] In all, Martin can find only three works described by their authors as *contes philosophiques*—none of them of course by Voltaire.[2] The nearest Voltaire comes is when he adds the sub-title *histoire philosophique* to *Micromégas* (which he does for the first time in the Dresden Walther edition of 1754). It is certainly true that in the collective editions produced towards the end of his life, after 1770, the short prose fictions tend to be aggregated in one or more volumes, giving them for the first time a shared identity. This process begins with volume 13 of the Cramer quarto edition, published in 1771, which bears the title 'Romans, contes philosophiques, etc.' This is an important innovation, but several observations should be

6. Northrop Frye, *Anatomy of Criticism* (Princeton: Princeton University Press, 1957), pp. 85–86.
7. Ronald S. Crane, 'Literature, philosophy, and the history of ideas,' *Modern Philology*, 52 (1954), 73–83.
8. Jonathan Rée, *Philosophical Tales: an essay on philosophy and literature* (London: Methuen, 1987).
9. Jonathan Rée, 'Philosophical fictions,' *Notebooks* (Working Papers in Humanities, Middlesex University), 2 (1995), 39–43 (p. 42).
1. Angus Martin, 'Preliminary statistics on the practice and terminology of short fiction in eighteenth-century France,' *French Forum*, 3 (1978), 240–50 (p. 247).
2. Angus Martin (ed.), *Anthologie du conte en France 1750–1799: philosophes et cœurs sensibles* (Paris: Union générale d'éditions, 1981), p. 30.

made. Firstly, Frédéric Deloffre shows that it was clearly Cramer and not Voltaire who was responsible for the plan of the quarto edition, and that Voltaire was not consulted about the volume containing the fictions;[3] it would seem then that the title 'Romans, contes philosophiques, etc' was more likely the publisher's choice than Voltaire's.[4] Secondly, the corpus of *contes* is not entirely stable and several important tales, such as *Le Taureau blanc*, are omitted from volume 13 of the quarto edition. And thirdly, even if the corpus of short fictions is to some extent beginning to stabilise, the title given to it is not: volume 25 of the Lausanne Grasset edition has 'Mélanges, contenant des romans, ou contes philosophiques' (1772); the Paris Panckoucke editions have two volumes (24–25) of 'Romans, contes allégoriques, philosophiques et historiques' (1773); the 'encadrée' edition has two volumes (31–32) of 'Romans philosophiques' (1775), oddly placed together with the *Eléments de Newton*; while the Kehl edition presents us with two volumes (44–45) entitled simply 'Romans' (1784). While this clearly demonstrates that the corpus of prose *contes* was gradually acquiring a clearer identity, it also shows that the label *conte philosophique* was far from established as the usual description of that corpus. The term has come into its own in twentieth-century literary criticism, invariably in connection with Voltaire, and is not generally acknowledged as a generic category.[5]

It is notoriously difficult to pin down with precision the corpus of Voltaire's short fictions.[6] The term *conte philosophique* is problematic, for it is at one and the same time too inclusive and not inclusive enough. Too inclusive, because it lumps together works which are really rather different: *Micromégas*, with its roots in Lucianic satire, has little in common in terms of fictional techniques with *L'Ingénu*, clearly more indebted to contemporary fictional models. And too exclusive, because it fails to include many works which are evidently closely related to the canonical corpus of short prose fictions. Voltaire's narrative skills also manifest themselves in verse, and the *contes en vers*, restored to their rightful place thanks to the critical edition of Sylvain Menant,[7] resemble in style and

3. Voltaire, *Romans et contes*, ed. F. Deloffre and J. Van den Heuvel, Bibliothèque de la Pléiade (Paris: Gallimard, 1979), p. xv.
4. An earlier two-volume *Recueil des romans de M. de Voltaire* (1764) was clearly not authorised by Voltaire; nor was the three-volume collection *Romans et contes* (Bouillon, 1778). This last edition is however an interesting attempt to rethink the fictional corpus: it includes the *contes en vers*, and various prose fragments taken from the *Fragments sur l'Inde* and the *Questions sur l'Encyclopédie*.
5. There is no mention of the *conte philosophique* in, for example, the *Dictionnaire des genres et notions littéraires*, 2nd ed. (Paris: Encyclopaedia Universalis—Albin Michel, 2001).
6. F. Deloffre sets out clearly some of the difficulties of identifying the corpus, in Voltaire, *Romans et contes*, pp. xi–xix.
7. Voltaire, *Contes en vers et en prose*, ed. Sylvain Menant, 2 vol. (Paris: Garnier, 1992–1993).

manner some of the prose *contes*, even if they are not obviously *philosophiques*. There are also many short prose texts which contain fictional elements and are unquestionably *philosophiques* yet which are not conventionally classed as *contes philosophiques*. These are the works which Voltaire himself, with fake nonchalance, dismisses as his *rogatons*, his *fadaises*, his *petits pâtés*. Writing to his publisher Michel Lambert in 1751, Voltaire refers generally to these short prose fireworks (including the works we know as the *contes*) as 'ces petits morceaux d'une philosophie allégorique' (D4369)—as good a description as any. Gianni Iotti has edited an important anthology of these works, published in the Italian Biblioteca della Pléiade, under the title *Racconti, facezie, libelli*,[8] and he includes under this catch-all title the *Sermon des cinquante*, the *Sermon du rabbin Akib*, the *Relation du voyage de frère Garaisse*, and the *Relation de la maladie du jésuite Berthier*.

In the end, the category of the *conte philosophique* is a difficult critical concept to handle, because it begs too many questions, and leads too easily into circularity of argument. In one sense the term is too imprecise, since very nearly all the fiction produced in France in the eighteenth century has some content which might, in some sense, be described as *philosophique*. On the other hand, the term is too precise. In our search for the 'philosophical' 'content' of these fictions, we can all too easily forget to study their quintessentially self-reflexive novelistic qualities.[9] Thus once you have categorised *Candide* as a *conte philosophique*, you are immediately obliged to discuss its take on the problem of theodicy, and an alternative reading, for example that *Candide* is first and foremost an anti-novel, is almost excluded by the definition of its genre.

If we wish therefore to avoid the question-begging term *conte philosophique*, what other approach might the critic adopt towards Voltaire's short prose fictions? One possibility is to take a long historical perspective, and to examine Voltaire's *contes* as part of a tradition of menippean satire stretching back through Cyrano de Bergerac and Rabelais to Lucian.[1] The approach is certainly fruitful up to a point, as a certain number of the short fictions—*Le Monde comme il va, Zadig, Micromégas*—derive directly from Lucianic satire; in the case of other fictions, the link is looser or non-existent,

8. Turin: Einaudi, 2004.
9. See, for example, Richard A. Francis, 'Les critiques dans les Contes de Voltaire,' in M. Cook and M.-E. Plagnol-Diéval (eds.), *Critique, Critiques au 18ᵉ siècle* (Oxford: Peter Lang, 2006), pp. 137–49.
1. See Nicholas Cronk, 'Voltaire, Lucian, and the philosophical traveller,' in J. Renwick (ed.), *L'Invitation au voyage: studies in honour of Peter France* (Oxford: Voltaire Foundation, 2000), pp. 75–84. See also W. H. Barber, 'Voltaire's astronauts,' *French Studies*, 30 (1976), 28–42.

so again we have a label which is somewhat helpful but which is not sufficiently comprehensive to embrace all the short fictions.

Another starting-point is to look at the place of the short fictions in Voltaire's *œuvre* as a whole, and it is striking that he seems to have begun telling stories at an early age, long before he thought of publishing them. Voltaire began to publish *contes*, as we shall see, in the late 1740s, but before that there are two specific periods when he experimented with this form of composition. In the years 1714–1715 he composed *Le Crocheteur borgne* and *Cosi-Sancta*, which formed part of the entertainments staged by the duchesse du Maine at the court de Sceaux. These are works of considerable literary sophistication,[2] but Voltaire seems to have viewed them as ephemeral and he never sought to publish them. He embarked on a second phase of fictional creativity in the late 1730s when he worked on at least three tales. He almost certainly began *Le Songe de Platon* at this time, although it was not published until 1756.[3] In addition, in 1739 he sent Frederick what he called 'une fadaise philosophique'[4] about a certain baron de Gangan. He reshaped this piece subsequently and it was published in the early 1750s as *Micromégas*.[5] He also seems to have formed the idea for *Le Monde comme il va* during this period—in response to his visit to Paris in 1739; this tale was not published until 1748. The fictions of the Cirey period were created primarily as social entertainments, it would seem, rather than as pieces intended for publication, and Françoise de Graffigny, a guest at Cirey in 1738, offers a description of Voltaire in the mode of story-teller: 'Hier à souper, Voltaire était d'une gaieté charmante; il fit des contes qui ne sont bons que dans sa bouche.'[6] Thus Voltaire is a *conteur* before he is a publisher of *contes*. This quality of oral performance—which of course is etymologically part of the definition of the *conte*—is something which we more readily associate with Diderot (in *Jacques le fataliste*, for example) than with Voltaire, but it is a factor to be borne in mind in studying all his short fiction.[7] This means also that Voltaire is a *conteur* before he is a *conteur philosophique*, and he seems to have remained a storyteller to the end of his days. In one of Jean Huber's pictures forming

2. See Christiane Mervaud's edition of these tales, *OCV*, vol. 1B, pp. 47–129.
3. See Jacques Van den Heuvel's introduction to his edition of this work, *OCV*, vol. 17, pp. 539–42.
4. Voltaire, *Correspondence and related documents*, *OCV*, vols. 85–135 (1968–77), D2033. References to this edition will be included in the text hereafter.
5. For a summary of recent research on the dating of this work, see *Revue Voltaire*, 2 (2002), 264–65.
6. *Correspondance de Mme de Graffigny*, ed. J. A. Dainard and others (Oxford: Voltaire Foundation, 1985–), vol. 1, p. 211.
7. Yvon Belaval suggests that the *conte philosophique* has its roots, in part at least, in social spaces like the salon and the café, where the art of conversation was cultivated ('Le conte philosophique,' in W. H. Barber and others (eds.), *The Age of the Enlightenment: Studies presented to Theodore Besterman* (Edinburgh, Oliver and Boyd, 1967), pp. 308–17).

part of the series of images of the everyday life of the patriarch of Ferney, Voltaire is depicted seemingly telling stories to a group of peasants.[8]

This predilection for narrative performance makes all the more intriguing Voltaire's decision, finally, in the late 1740s, to begin publishing his tales. In the years 1745–1750, Voltaire composed *Zadig*, *Memnon* and the *Lettre d'un Turc*, and worked on two stories which have their origins in the Cirey period, the *Voyage du baron de Gangan* (which he recast as *Micromégas*) and *Le Monde comme il va*. Never before had he laboured on such a large body of fiction. Remarkably, all five works were published in the five-year period 1747–1752, marking a significant departure from his previous practice. Voltaire no longer told stories solely for the pleasure of his close friends; he now wrote fiction for his reading public.

How are we to account for this burst of fictional creativity in the form of short prose fiction? Clearly Voltaire's life underwent a great change when he left Cirey in August 1744 for Paris and Versailles. On the point of departure Voltaire wrote to Mme Denis: 'Je quitte la tranquillité de Cirey pour le chaos de Paris [. . .]. Je me sens un peu honteux à mon âge de quitter ma philosophie et ma solitude pour être baladin des rois' (D3015). After his long period of retreat, Voltaire's presence at court brought many new social contacts and demands. To Cideville in January 1745 he confided an impression of his new life: 'Je cours de Paris à Versailles, je fais des vers en chaise de poste. Il faut louer le roi hautement, madame la dauphine finement, la famille royale tout doucement, contenter la cour, ne pas déplaire à la ville' (D3073). It is possible, as Raymond Naves suggests, that Voltaire's encounter with court society encouraged him to explore new literary forms:

> C'est la vie de cour des années 1745–1748 qui semble avoir révélé à Voltaire tout le parti qu'il pouvait tirer de l'animation dramatique des idées. Après le long exil de Cirey, le contact intime et continu avec la société mondaine assouplit définitivement son génie et lui montre avec évidence ce qui peut le mieux conquérir ces esprits curieux et pressés: il leur faut des idées, mais il leur faut du plaisir piquant; aussi le conte, la facétie, le dialogue philosophique sont-ils les meilleurs véhicules de la pensée.[9]

8. 'Voltaire en conversation avec un groupe de paysans de Ferney,' Musée des Beaux-Arts, Nantes. Reproduced in Garry Apgar, *L'Art singulier de Jean Huber: voir Voltaire* (Paris: Adam Biro, 1995), pp. 139, 158. On Voltaire's skill as a story-teller, see also the testimony of the baron of Gleichen, quoted by William F. Bottiglia, *Voltaire's Candide: Analysis of a classic*, 2nd ed., *SVEC*, 7A (Geneva: Institut et Musée Voltaire, 1964), pp. 57–58.

9. Voltaire, *Dialogues et anecdotes philosophiques*, ed. Raymond Naves (Paris: Garnier, 1939), p. iii.

In addition to his experience of court life, Voltaire's visits to Sceaux in the late 1740s played an important role in the development of the tales. It was here, of course, more than thirty years previously, that Voltaire had composed *Le Crocheteur borgne* and *Cosi-Sancta* for the 'nuits de Sceaux,' and the place undoubtedly held a special significance for him. His hostess at Sceaux, the duchesse du Maine, leaves her mark on the genesis of *Zadig*, in the references Voltaire makes in that tale to yellow ribbons.[1] And it was at Sceaux that Voltaire found refuge in October 1747 after the 'jeu de la reine' incident—an episode to which he alludes in *Memnon*. There is also evidence that Voltaire may have worked on *Le Monde comme il va* while staying with the duchesse du Maine at Sceaux. If many of Voltaire's biographers emphasise his unhappy experiences of the late 1740s, an early chronicler, Duvernet, suggests that Voltaire took pleasure in the tranquillity and the civilised society he found at Sceaux:

> L'état de courtisan ne lui convenait pas: [Voltaire] rompit peu à peu les chaînes qui l'attachaient à Versailles, et donna la préférence à Sceaux. C'est là que Mme la duchesse du Maine, née Bourbon Condé, réunissait de jeunes seigneurs, et des savants très estimables. On ne voyait, dans la cour de cette princesse, ni intrigues, ni orages. Cette cour était composée de personnes aimables, spirituelles, s'amusant entre elles; et dans leurs amusements, n'ayant aucun des embarras de l'étiquette. On surnomma ceux qui y étaient admis, *les oiseaux de Sceaux*, comme autrefois on avait surnommé ceux de la société de Ninon, *les oiseaux des Tournelles*.[2]

The importance of Sceaux as a peaceful retreat where Voltaire composed, or at least revised, certain tales, is confirmed in the memoir of his secretary, Longchamp:

> M. de Voltaire ne descendait chez Mme la duchesse que lorsque tout le monde était retiré, mangeait un poulet dans sa ruelle, et était servi par un des valets de pieds de Mme la duchesse qui était dans la confidence. M. de Voltaire ne remontait à son appartement qu'un peu avant le jour. Lassé de cette vie oisive M. de Voltaire fit faire une provision de bougies et de lumières et se mit à travailler pendant le jour. Il fit plusieurs petits contes ou romans tels que *Zadig*, *Babouc* et autres; et il m'occupait à les mettre au net.[3]

1. See Jacqueline Hellegouarc'h, 'Encore la duchesse du Maine: notes sur les rubans jaunes de *Zadig*,' *SVEC*, 176 (1979), 37–40.
2. T. I. Duvernet, *La Vie de Voltaire* (n.p., 1787), pp. 106–07.
3. Sébastien Longchamp, *Anecdotes sur la vie privée de Monsieur de Voltaire*, ed. F. S. Eigeldinger and R. Trousson (Paris: Champion, 2009), p. 60. This passage was subsequently much rewritten by Decroix, cf. pp. 162–63.

The three tales, *Le Monde comme il va*, *Zadig* and *Memnon*, substantially the product of the same period, and partly, also, of place, share a good deal of common 'philosophical' ground. All three tackle the question of theodicy, along with other familiar topics such as tolerance. In all three Voltaire employs a fictional device in which an unconventional angel descends *ex machina* to expound the optimist cause to a bemused hero.[4] (It is only later, in *Candide*, that Voltaire will allow the optimist spokesman to assume human form.) In an attempt to identify 'Voltaire dans ses contes,' a number of critics examine the nuances of philosophical difference separating the angelic trio of Ituriel, Jesrad and Memnon's 'bon génie,' and many interpret Voltaire's sudden preoccupation with the problem of evil as evidence of a personal crisis, a crisis which, in this view, explains the emergence of the *conte philosophique* at this time. René Pomeau, for instance, asserts: 'Dans la crise de 1748, le mal n'est plus un sujet de controverse, il devient une pierre de scandale; et Voltaire l'aborde désormais par le conte. Car le conte voltairien naît définitivement de la crise de 1748.'[5] Laurence Bongie endorses this idea, suggesting that as Voltaire grappled with the problem of evil, it was only in the form of the *conte* that he found the means of freely expressing his complex, somewhat contradictory feelings about the question.[6]

Perhaps. But it is also possible that because we have decided in advance that these are *contes philosophiques*, we study first and foremost their philosophical content, even to the exclusion of other considerations. The philosophical arguments of *Zadig*, for example, are not particularly original, and Haydn Mason has shown that they are largely prefigured in the verse epistles of the *Discours en vers sur l'homme*, published a decade earlier, in 1738.[7] In purely formal terms, it can also be argued that these fictions display a certain continuity with those conceived a decade earlier. We need to be sensitive to the literary context of these tales, and in particular to the role played in these highly self-aware works by pastiche and parody. To take just one example: when modern readers encounter the angel Jesrad, they might well be tempted to focus on his 'message'; when Grimm encountered the same character, he immediately situated him in the realm of narrative fantasy, gleefully claiming that Voltaire

---

4. On this device, see Jean Sareil, 'Les anges de Voltaire,' *Kentucky Romance Quarterly*, 20 (1973), 99–112.
5. René Pomeau, *La Religion de Voltaire*, new ed. (Paris: Nizet, 1969), p. 248.
6. Laurence L. Bongie, 'Crisis and the birth of the Voltairean *conte*,' *Modern Language Quarterly*, 23 (1962), 53–64.
7. See Haydn Mason, '*Zadig* and the birth of the Voltaire conte,' *Rousseau and the Eighteenth Century: Essays in memory of R. A. Leigh*, ed. Marian Hobson, J. T. A. Leigh and Robert Wokler (Oxford: Voltaire Foundation, 1992), pp. 279–90.

had cribbed the entire chapter from a medieval tale.[8] If we believe that Voltaire was struggling in these fictions with a demon, or an angel, it was possibly with the demon of form rather than the demon of evil.

Another way of approaching and understanding this sudden flurry of fictional activity is to focus on the precise manner in which Voltaire chose to publish his short fictions. It was only in the late 1740s that he resolved to place his fictional works in the public realm for the first time. He began the venture in 1747 by publishing *Memnon, histoire orientale*. Of sufficient length to appear as a volume on its own, it was republished in a revised version the following year as *Zadig, ou la destinée, histoire orientale*. The appearance of this work paved the way for the publication of other shorter fictions. When *Zadig* was republished in the collected Dresden edition of 1748, it was accompanied in volume 8 by the first edition of *Le Monde comme il va*. In late 1749 there appeared the *Recueil de pièces en vers et en prose*,[9] which contained the first publication of *Memnon*, as well as *Le Monde comme il va* under the new title *Babouc, ou le monde comme il va*. In 1750 volume 9 of the collected Dresden edition appeared, containing the first publication of the *Lettre d'un Turc* and a reprinting of *Memnon*. In 1751 Voltaire prepared to bring out the first edition of *Micromégas*, but then withdrew it from the collective edition in which it had been placed; in 1752, the work was finally published separately, in a volume by itself.[1] That is to say, in the five years from 1747, Voltaire published five fictions, two of them long enough to appear as books in their own right. At no stage did Voltaire attempt to collect these fictions into a single volume, as he might easily have done. This is perhaps because he did not conceive of them as forming a coherent group (as we are inclined to do); or because he was aware of their similarities and wished his readers to come upon each tale serendipitously.

In any case, this series of publications marks a significant turning-point in Voltaire's carefully crafted public image as a writer, and with the appearance of these fictions, his position within the republic of letters undergoes a major change. After the *Discours en vers sur l'homme*, published a decade earlier, Voltaire wrote only two further philosophical poems, the *Poème sur la loi naturelle* and the *Poème sur le désastre de Lisbonne* (both published in 1756). To some extent, the *conte* of the late 1740s may be said to take over from

8. *Correspondance littéraire*, ed. M. Tourneux (Paris: Garnier, 1877–1882), vol. 12, pp. 381–82 (review of Le Grand, *Fabliaux ou contes*, April, 1780).
9. *Recueil de pièces en vers et en prose, par l'auteur de la tragédie de 'Sémiramis'* ([Paris: Lambert] 1750 [1749]). In this volume *Memnon* immediately follows the *Discours en vers sur l'homme*, to which it is closely related.
1. See D. W. Smith, 'The publication of *Micromégas*,' SVEC, 219 (1983), 63–91.

where the philosophical poem leaves off. If Voltaire often speaks dis-
missively of the novel as a genre, in particular the sentimental
novel,[2] he is always alert to changes in literary fashion. In this context *Zadig* may be read as a philosophical reply to the frivolous oriental fictions of recent years, notably Cazotte's *Les Mille et une
fadaises* (1742), Caylus's *Contes orientaux* (1743), and Voisenon's *Le
Sultan Misapouf* (1746). Voltaire's decision to have *Zadig* printed separately in two halves so as to avoid the risk of a pirated edition certainly gives the lie to the idea that he regarded the work with casual
indifference: nothing could have been more carefully stage-managed
than the publication of his first book-length fiction.

It has sometimes been suggested that the preoccupation with the
problem of evil in these works reflects Voltaire's personal lack of
'optimism' at this time (and of course there is a sleight of hand in
using 'optimism' in its colloquial, nonphilosophical sense). But the
(selective . . .) use of biographical information to explain the philosophical outlook of a literary work is a hazardous business. In
fact, the period of the second half of the 1740s was, notwithstanding
various personal setbacks, a time of remarkable professional success
for Voltaire. Enjoying unprecedented favour at court under the protection of Mme de Pompadour, Voltaire was elected to the Royal
Society in 1743, appointed *historiographe de France* in 1745, and in the
following year named to the lucrative position of *gentilhomme ordi-
naire de la chambre du Roi*.[3] In 1746, as well, Voltaire was finally
elected to the Académie française. In his fifties, and with his reputation in the canonical genres of tragedy, epic and history long-
established, Voltaire felt free to experiment with other genres,
publishing fiction for the first time from 1747, and also, from 1751,
philosophical dialogues. Publicly and deliberately, Voltaire was
embarking on a new direction as a prose writer.

But what can we say more precisely about his use of fictional
genre? A defamiliarising device straight from Lucian is used in *Zadig*
when the hero gazes down from above and sees men as 'des insectes
se dévorant les uns les autres sur un petit atome de boue.'[4] What
happens if we turn this device on the short fictions themselves, and
approach them from outside, like critics from Mars, with no pre-
conceptions? If we look at the *contes* simply in terms of their appearance in print, and for once leave on one side the issues surrounding
their ideological engagement, then the short prose fictions fall very

---

2. See David Williams, 'Voltaire on the sentimental novel,' *SVEC*, 135 (1975), 115–34.
3. Voltaire even boasted of the profitability of this latter position: see *Commentaire historique sur les œuvres de l'auteur de 'La Henriade,' Œuvres completes de Voltaire*, ed.
L. Moland (Paris: Garnier, 1877–85) [hereafter Moland], vol. 1, p. 88.
4. *OCV*, vol. 30B, p. 157.

clearly into two distinct categories. Firstly there is the category of
what I shall call 'stand-alone fictions,' that is to say, those works
which were long enough to constitute a book in their own right, a
separate publication: *Zadig*, and (though not initially so intended)
Micromégas. Secondly there are those works, *Memnon*, *Le Monde
comme il va*, and *Lettre d'un Turc*, which I shall call 'mosaic fictions,'
which were published as part of some larger structure. Modern critical editions of Voltaire's *Romans et contes* inevitably obscure these
distinctions of publishing history, but they would have been self-
evident to Voltaire's contemporary readership. As an example of a
'mosaic fiction,' we may take the example of *Memnon*, which is first
published in late 1749, in the *Recueil de pièces en vers et en prose*,
where it immediately follows the *Discours en vers sur l'homme*: 'Ce
petit ouvrage ayant quelque rapport aux Discours en vers ci-dessus,
on a cru devoir l'imprimer à leur suite.'[5] Subsequently the story is
included in various collective editions,[6] until finally, in 1771, over
twenty years after its first publication, *Memnon* resurfaces in the
fourth part of the *Questions sur l'Encyclopédie*, where, with an
added preliminary paragraph, it now appears as the article 'Confiance en soi-même';[7] and for once, Voltaire openly acknowledges
his manipulation of this mosaic fiction: 'Nous réimprimons ici ce
petit conte, qui est ailleurs: car il est bon qu'il soit partout.[8] Even
Voltaire himself seems sometimes to have lost track of these mobile
texts: whether by design or not, *Memnon* is printed twice in the
1775 *encadrée* edition, once as part of the *Questions* in volume 27,
where the dictates of the alphabet place 'Confiance en soi-même'
between the articles 'Confession' and 'Confiscation'; and again
among the 'Romans philosophiques' in volume 31, where it is sand-
wiched between *Le Monde comme il va* and *Les Deux consoles*. And
it is only a matter of time before some of these mosaic fictions break
away altogether from the Voltairean corpus, to lead a separate existence. Two of Voltaire's fictions, for example, appear anonymously
in a volume edited by Mlle Uncy, *Contes moraux dans le goût de
ceux de M. Marmontel, recueillis de divers auteurs* (4 vols, Amsterdam: Vincent, 1763). In this collection, *Ainsi va le monde* (vol. 3,
pp. 254–83) turns out to be *Le Monde comme il va*, while *Le sot
projet d'un homme sage* (vol. 4, pp. 359–69) is *Memnon* by another
name (the new title is taken from the opening sentence of the tale):
Voltaire's name is nowhere to be found, but in both cases, his text,
apart from the change of title, is reproduced faithfully.

5. *OCV*, vol. 30B, p. 249.
6. Voir *OCV*, vol. 30B, pp. 249–55.
7. *Questions sur l'Encyclopédie*, vol. 4 (1771), pp. 57–66.
8. Moland, vol. 21, p. 95.

In these multiple reincarnations, the text remains (more or less) stable, and yet our reading of the text is never settled. To the extent that we continue to read and reread the 'same' text, it may be said that Voltaire is successful in hammering home his ideas, multiplying variations on a theme. But it is also true that as the context of the text changes, so does the text itself, for meaning is generated by the larger structure into which the mosaic fiction is inserted. In these fictional kaleidoscopes, the individual pieces hold our attention by the shifting and dazzling patterns in which they appear, and Voltaire's ideas grip us in large part because we are unable to pin them down. The increasingly fragmentary nature of Voltaire's collections of prose works create an openness which implicates the reader.[9] This is Voltairean relativism in practice.

We may look more briefly at the short fictions written after 1750. Voltaire continues to write 'stand-alone fictions,' and following *Zadig* and *Micromégas* he writes many others, including *Candide* (1759) and *L'Ingénu* (1767). It continues to be the case that Voltaire's fictional writing seems to come in bursts: there are periods when he writes none, and periods when he writes several at once. Thus in March 1764, he informs Mme Du Deffand, 'Mon goût pour les contes est absolument tombé. C'était une fantaisie que les longues soirées d'hiver m'avaient inspirée. Je pense différemment à l'équinoxe' (D11791). But to Chabanon, in May 1772, he is in a teasing mood: 'Quand j'ai du chagrin je m'amuse à faire des contes. Mme d'Argental a une bégueule. Elle vous en fera part d'autant plus volontiers . . .' (D17736). After *L'Ingénu*, Voltaire composes three substantial stand-alone fictions in quick succession, *La Princesse de Babylone* (1768), *L'Homme aux quarante écus* (1768) and *Les Lettres d'Amabed* (1769); two more come in the mid-1770s, *Le Taureau blanc* (1774), and *Histoire de Jenni* (1775). As separate publications, these works could all be described in a very loose sense as 'romans'—or even as 'anti-romans,' given the significant presence of parody in these works. It is worth recalling that Grimm's immediate response to *Candide* had been to call it 'un petit roman.'[1]

But these stand-alone fictions (novels) are only a part of Voltaire's fictional output. Throughout the 1760s, he continues to produce 'tous ces petits morceaux d'une philosophie allégorique,' indeed they are a major tool in his campaign to 'écraser l'Infâme.' The one-volume *Contes de Guillaume Vadé* (1764) is an anthology including both prose and verse *contes*, as well as other works such as the *Discours aux Welches* and the *Lettre de M. Clocpitre à M. Eratou*; the

---

9. See Nicholas Cronk, 'Les dialogues de Voltaire: vers une poétique du fragmentaire,' *Revue Voltaire*, 5 (2005), pp. 71–82.
1. *Correspondance littéraire*, vol. 4, p. 85 (1 March 1759).

volume enjoyed great success and became Voltaire's best-selling work of fiction after *Candide*.[2] But this work aside, it is interesting that Voltaire never oversaw a collected volume of his short fictions. True, he seems to have proposed such a volume in 1751 to Michel Lambert (D4369); in 1764, Panckoucke wanted to publish a volume of *contes* (D11876, D11889); and in 1767, Voltaire speaks to Jacques Lacombe about a 'petit recueil de contes' (D14146, D14423): but not one of these projects was realised. Instead, Voltaire conceived miscellanies studded with mosaic fictions. The first edition of *Le Philosophe ignorant* (1766) contains two short fictions, *Petite digression* and *Aventure indienne*, which should of course be read as an integral part of the volume.[3] The first authorised edition of *Les Lois de Minos* appeared together with twenty-eight other short pieces, including *La Bégueule* and *Le Marseillais et le lion*.[4] And so the boundaries of the *conte* become increasingly blurred, as Voltaire incorporates mosaic fictions in a range of different works. The *Traité sur la tolérance* (1763) is made up of short chapters of contrasting genres, including one, a dialogue between a dying man and a priest, which is something of a fictional topos.[5] Both the *Dictionnaire philosophique* (1764) and the *Questions sur l'Encyclopédie* (1770–72) contain 'articles' which approximate to short fictions. Writing in 1765, in the wake of the Calas affair, an opponent of the *philosophes* attacked the deists for writing works which mixed genre and style, works he characterised as written 'à la mosaïque':[6] the subversive nature of mosaic fictions, a function of their form as much as of their content, was clearly felt.

Voltaire's essays in fiction are clearly not restricted to his *contes*. In the encounter between the French visitor and the Quaker at the start of the *Lettres philosophiques* or in the observations which open the *Traité de métaphysique*, Voltaire employs the devices of narrative fiction.[7] In this respect his technique echoes that of a prose writer he particularly admired: as Jacques Van den Heuvel observes,

2. See Edouard Guitton, 'Une singularité bibliographique et littéraire: les *Contes de Guillaume Vadé* (1764), ou Voltaire et l'impact vadéen,' in M. Delon et C. Seth (eds.), *Voltaire en Europe: Hommage à Christiane Mervaud* (Oxford: Voltaire Foundation, 2000), pp. 291–97.
3. See Nicholas Cronk, '*Le Philosophe ignorant*, volume de mélanges,' in N. Cronk (ed.), *Voltaire and the 1760s: essays for John Renwick* (Oxford: Voltaire Foundation), SVEC, 2008:10, pp. 195–205.
4. See Nicholas Cronk, 'Auteur et autorité dans les mélanges: l'exemple des *Lois de Minos, tragédie avec les notes de M. de Morza et plusieurs pièces détachées* (1773),' *Revue Voltaire*, 6 (2006), 53–68.
5. See Michel Delon, 'Le Mourant et le Barbare,' in N. Cronk (ed.), *Etudes sur le 'Traité sur la tolérance' de Voltaire* (Oxford: Voltaire Foundation, 2000), pp. 224–29.
6. *Le Philosophe dithyrambique* (Paris: de Lormel, 1765), p. xlvii.
7. Joseph Bianco, for example, points to narrative parallels between the *Lettres philosophiques* and *Zadig* in his article 'Zadig et l'origine du conte philosophique: aux antipodes de l'unité,' *Poétique*, 68 (1986), 443–61.

'la méthode de Locke était riche de certains prolongements dans le domaine de la fiction.'[8] In *Le Pyrrhonisme de l'histoire* (1769), as Voltaire recounts the litany of preposterous beliefs held in earlier ages, he ends up producing what Simon Davies has rightly called an 'anthology of *contes*.'[9] Roger Pearson puts this another way when, in a happy phrase, he writes that Voltaire 'thinks narratively.'[1] The term *conte philosophique* was an invention of Voltaire's publishers in the 1770s, and was given a further lease of life by critics after Lanson who found it a useful label. But to characterise a certain subset of Voltaire's short fictions as *contes philosophiques* is in the end to create an arbitrary category, and a misleading category moreover, in that it distracts us from the broader aesthetic questions which these short fictions pose. To understand how fiction forms part of Voltaire's polemical arsenal, it is necessary to appreciate his wholly original manipulation of the form of the *conte* as part of a broader strategy to create shifting miscellanies illuminated by fictional fireworks.

8. Jacques Van den Heuvel, *Voltaire dans ses contes* (Paris: Colin, 1967), p. 82.
9. See Simon Davies, '*Le Pyrrhonisme de l'histoire*, Voltaire's anthology of *contes*,' in N. Cronk (ed.), *Voltaire and the 1760s: essays for John Renwick* (Oxford: Voltaire Foundation), SVEC, 2008:10, pp. 207–15.
1. Roger Pearson, *The Fables of reason: a study of Voltaire's 'contes philosophiques'* (Oxford: Clarendon Press, 1993), p. 5.

CRITICISM

J. G. WEIGHTMAN

The Quality of *Candide*[†]

It may seem late in the day to ask how good a book *Candide* really
is. Has the world not been long agreed that it is a masterpiece? It
started triumphantly by being banned in Paris and Geneva, and has
gone on selling ever since. It has provided France and the world with
two or three proverbial expressions. Schopenhauer praised it in the
most emphatic terms;[1] Flaubert said that it contained the quintes-
sence of Voltaire's writings;[2] H. N. Brailsford declared that it "ranks
in its own way with *Don Quixote* and *Faust*."[3] So alive is it, indeed,
that it was recently turned into an American musical and has thus
shared with *Manon Lescaut* and *Les Liaisons dangereuses* the honour of being relaunched in the twentieth century as a work with a
universal appeal for mass audiences.

But, on second thoughts, this may appear a doubtful honour and
make us wonder on what level of success *Candide* has been operat-
ing. *Manon Lescaut* and *Les Liaisons dangereuses* are perhaps com-
promising connections, since their moral and aesthetic acceptability
has often been questioned by literary critics. And it is true that Voltaire himself is still often referred to as if he were, generally speaking, rather disreputable; irreverent, outmoded, a mere maker of
debating points. Faguet's 'un chaos d'idées claires' [a chaos of clear
ideas] is a Voltairean jibe that has been used, effectively, against Voltaire. Mr. Martin Turnell, a contemporary English critic with a
stern approach to French Literature, refers briefly to 'the flashy vul-
garity of *Candide*.'[4] Even those people who have a genuine interest
in Voltaire often imply that we should not look for depths or complexities in him. Carl Becker, after doubting whether Voltaire really
understood the brilliance of his own witticisms, suggests that his
scepticism did not amount to much, and that *Candide* is not a central text:

> The cynicism of Voltaire was not bred in the bone . . . It was all
> on the surface, signifying nothing but the play of a supple and
> irrepressible mind, or the sharp impatience of an exasperated

---

† From *Essays Presented to C. M. Girdlestone* (Durham, UK: University of Durham, 1960),
pp. 335–47. Reprinted by permission of the University of Durham. Quotations from the
French have been translated by Robert M. Adams.
1. "I can see no other merit in Leibniz's *Theodicy* except that of having furnished the great
Voltaire with the occasion of his immortal *Candide*." Quoted in *La Table Ronde*, Feb.,
1958, p. 111.
2. *Correspondance*, ed. Conard, 11, p. 348.
3. *Candide and Other Tales*, Everyman's Library, 1937, p. xxiv.
4. *The Novel in France*, Hamish Hamilton, 1950, p. 189.

idealist. In spite of *Candide* and all the rest of it, Voltaire was an optimist, though not a naïve one.[5]

The late Professor Saurat, introducing a selection of Voltaire's tales, differs from Becker in crediting Voltaire with deep feeling. However, he then goes on to deny him depth of intelligence:

> The jesting of *Candide* is the mournful levity of a belief expiring in the face of the facts, but which nonetheless persists. He would have preferred Leibniz to be right; but his intelligence, though so quick, was not deep enough to let him see that Leibniz was right.[6]

Professor Saurat does not explain in what way Leibniz is in the right.

Already in 1913, in his critical edition of *Candide*, André Morize had emphasized that Voltaire did not appear to have a detailed knowledge of Leibniz's arguments:

> *Candide* or *Optimism* is by no means the product of a metaphysician to whom Leibniz and the *Theodicy* were familiar.[7]

Richard Aldington, in his introduction to the Broadway Translation of 1927, gives a summary of the philosophical controversy from which *Candide* emerged, because—he says—the book 'is often represented as a merely amusing squib.' But his own conclusion seems strangely self-contradictory:

> Its popularity is due to its amusing adventures, its clear rapid style, its concentrated wit, its vitality and alertness, and *to its triumphant disposal of facile optimism. Whether it really proves anything may admit of doubt* . . .[8]

Dr. W. H. Barber, who gives a beautifully clear and meticulous account of the shifts in Voltaire's position with regard to optimism, makes a comment on *Candide* which might appear to reduce the book to personal satire on minor Neo-Leibnizians:

> Voltaire is not concerned to refute a doctrine by careful argument; his object is to ridicule a band of enthusiasts whose ideas he thinks absurd; and the immediate and lasting popularity of *Candide* is some measure of his success.[9]

A similar statement is made by Hugo Friedrich in a special number of *La Table Ronde* devoted to Voltaire:

5. *The Heavenly City of the Eighteenth Century Philosophers*, Yale University Press, 1957 edition, pp. 36, 37.
6. *Le Taureau blanc*, etc., The Hyperion Press, 1945, p. 5.
7. Librairie E. Droz, p. xiii.
8. Routledge, p. 16. My [Weightman's] italics.
9. *Leibniz in France*, O.U.P., 1955, p. 232.

At bottom it was not Leibniz whom Voltaire attacked, but the
cheap optimism fashionable in Paris salons, as seasoned with
obscure German lucubrations. We must not read *Candide* as a
novel with a thesis . . . we must let ourselves be amused by
watching a free spirit playing with very grave questions for lack
of power to resolve them.[1]

All these judgements must seem rather slighting to anyone who has
a high regard for *Candide*, because they suggest that the book is, in
fact, more of a squib than anything else. Consequently, there may
be a case for reopening the argument and trying to decide what
exactly *Candide* achieves.

The first thing to establish, if possible, is that *Candide* is basically
serious. Of course, Voltaire was never at any time fair-minded, and
there seems every reason to believe that he did not bother to reread,
or even read, Leibniz's *Théodicée* before writing his satire. As both
Morize and Barber point out, he mixes up the two main forms of
the theory of optimism: the belief that evil is an effect of the human
angle of vision, and the belief that evil is a necessary part of creation. He makes no attempt to distinguish between the different
degrees of sophistication represented by Leibniz, Pope and Wolff.
Leibniz neither denied the existence of evil nor held the simple final-
istic views which Voltaire attributes to Pangloss. Also, as Barber
shows, Leibniz was an activist whose purpose was to encourage men
to virtuous initiative within the all-embracing framework of God's
will, and as such he was, in a sense, on Voltaire's side. If one wished
to press the accusation of superficiality still further against Voltaire,
one could recall that he himself began by being an optimist who
declared in the *Traité de métaphysique* that moral evil was 'une
chimère' ["a dream"] and the notion of evil a relative one:

> To be quite sure that a thing is evil one must see at the same
> time that something better is possible.[2]

The Angel Jesrad in *Zadig*, which comes before *Candide*, is on the
whole Leibnizian in his statement that a world without evil would
be another kind of world. So is the Quaker, Freind, in the very
late conte, *L'Histoire de Jenni*. In other works of his later years—
the *Homélies prononcées à Londres en 1765*, *Questions sur
l'Encyclopédie*, *Il faut prendre un parti* and *Fragments historiques
sur l'Inde*—Voltaire contradicts himself, saying in one place that
God is obviously limited and repeating in another that evil exists

1. *La Table Ronde*, February 1958, pp. 111–115.
2. *Traité de métaphysique*, ed. H. T. Patterson, Manchester U.P., 1937, p. 16.

only from the human point of view and must be unknown to God in His perfection.

Have we to conclude, then, that Voltaire had a shallow mind which casually adopted different sets of ideas at different times? Is *Candide* an irresponsible attack on beliefs that he was capable of putting forward as his own, when they happened to serve his purpose? Is he simply a jester who does not understand what the philosophers are about? I do not think so. The extraordinary resonance of *Candide* and the strange frenzy in which Voltaire seems to have lived during most of his life, and particularly during the latter half, point to a very different conclusion. Here was a man who, through his personal experience, his reading of history and his observation of contemporary events, gradually came to be obsessed with the scandal of the presence of evil in the universe. At the same time, with his clear and vigorous brain he could only suppose that God was an immeasurably greater Voltaire who had organized the universe on rational lines and was not, ultimately, responsible for evil. How could God have willed evil since Voltaire, like any decent person, found it intolerable? Yet evil existed, and God must be good. But how could a good God . . . etc. He never escaped from the dilemma, but tried out different verbal solutions at different stages and was presumably never convinced by any of them. Through some psychological accident of which we shall no doubt always remain ignorant (perhaps he went through a phase like Shakespeare's tragic period), he produced *Candide* at a time when his awareness of evil was at its most violent and his vitality at its strongest. In this one book, the horror of evil and an instinctive zest for life are almost equally matched and it is the contrast between them, inside the paragraph and even inside the sentence, which produces the unique tragicomic vibration. The lesson of *Candide* is the permanent one that there is no verbal, that is intellectual, solution to the problem of evil, but that we go on living even so, and even when we think we have no faith.

If this interpretation is correct, two consequences follow. In the first place, Voltaire is not simply attacking Pope or Leibniz or the Neo-Leibnizians or J.-J. Rousseau; he is also attacking himself, because when he trusted to the philosophical use of language, he found himself arguing like them. He himself is Pangloss, just as he is Candide, Martin and Pococurante. The book is a transposition of his inner debate. And it is surely an underestimation of his wit to imply that his rapid jokes are not valid against the more elaborate explanations of evil. They are genuine caricatures. To the question: 'Why, if God is good (and we must suppose that He is), does evil exist?' there is no articulate answer which is not a juggling with words. Book VII of St. Augustine's *Confessions* is quite elaborate, but are its logical fallacies not obvious? Chapter VII of Book III of St. Thomas's *Summa Contra Gentiles* seems no less purely verbal. And when we open Leibniz to see how Voltaire misunderstood him, we find this sort of argument:

> For God sees from the beginning of time that there will be a certain Judas; and the notion or idea that God has of him contains this future free action. Only this question now remains, why this Judas, the traitor, who is only a possibility in the idea of God, exists in actuality. But to this question there can be no answer here below, except that in general one can say that since God found it proper that he should exist in spite of the sin He foresaw, it must be that this evil will be repaid with interest somewhere else in the universe, that God will derive a greater good from it, and in short it will be found that the sequence of events which includes the existence of this sinner is the most perfect of all those which were possible. But to explain in every instance the admirable economy of a particular choice, that cannot be done while we inhabit this transitory sphere; it suffices to know it without understanding it.[3]

The 'admirable economy' of a choice we know nothing about and only suppose to have existed is an excellent example of Panglossian applauding of the cosmos. Before Leibniz wrote the *Théodicée*, Bayle had said all there was to be said about this kind of circular argument in dealing with Lactantius, St. Basil and Maximus of Tyre,[4] and he was not adequately refuted by Leibniz. In particular intellectual gifts, Bayle and Voltaire may have been much inferior to Leibniz, but on this precise issue they saw more clearly the futility of verbalizations. As Barber says:

> Leibniz . . . never really abandons *a priori* argument. He bases his knowledge of God's nature on *a priori* rational considerations . . . and once God's infinite goodness and wisdom have thus been established, all else also follows deductively. Thus he never really meets Bayle on his own ground. To all Bayle's paradoxes he has at bottom only one reply, though his subtlety of argument sometimes conceals the fact; the world as it is is God's creation, therefore no better world is possible.[5]

In the second place, *Candide* is not in the last resort a message of hope, or at least not exactly in the way suggested by some critics who

---

3. *Discours de Métaphysique*, 30, in *Leibnizens Gesammelte Werke*, Hannover 1846.
4. Voltaire's incisive analysis of verbal circularity in Lactantius (above, pp. 85–86) illustrates sufficiently the character of Bayle's more wide-ranging exposés [Adams].
5. *Leibniz in France*, p. 88.

take a favourable view of it. Morize, Barber and René Pomeau, the author of *La Religion de Voltaire*, all seem to me to underestimate the virulence of the work. Morize writes:

> The world is in shambles, blood flows, Jesuits and Molinists rage, innocents are slaughtered and dupes exploited; but there are in the world delicious asylums, where life remains possible, joyous, and sweet: let us cultivate our garden.[6]

This suggests an ability to shut out the spectacle of the world which Voltaire never possessed, and does not correspond to the tone of dogged persistence in the final chapters of *Candide*. According to Barber:

> The practical philosophy to which Candide finally attains is the application to the limited field of personal activity of that *espérance* [hope] which Voltaire had offered to humanity on a transcendental level in the conclusion of the *Poème sur le désastre de Lisbonne*.
>
> In rejecting the doctrines of Pangloss and his like . . . he is seeking . . . a safe foundation in an insecure world for that profound belief in the value of activity which is characteristic of European man and was particularly strong in him.[7]

But does he find any such foundation? There is no evidence in *Candide*, and very little in his biography, that he had a profound belief in the value of activity. He believed in man's need for activity and he himself had a tremendous urge to be active, but these can be independent of any conviction of value. Would it not be more plausible to suppose that his feverish busyness was the only relief he could find for his acute awareness of evil? Pomeau speaks of the "epicurean motive for action which is the last word of the tale" and says that Voltaire "will make a philosophy of activity . . . A lesson revolutionary in its banality." No doubt, Voltaire borrowed the image of the garden from Epicurus,[8] but he has no trace of Epicurean serenity or moderation. Actually, Pomeau is uncertain about the ultimate significance of the work. In *La Religion de Voltaire* (1956), he declares roundly:

> Is the philosophy of *Candide* a philosophy of the "absurd"? Certainly not. Candide is not, any more than Jacques or Figaro, a hero tragically abandoned in a wrong world. Whatever surprises existence may hold for them, these wanderers are not

---

6. Librairie E. Droz, p. xlvii.
7. *Leibniz in France*, p. 233.
8. Epicurus, the classical philosopher who made pleasure the supreme goal of life, had a famous garden, where he lived an impressively moderate and contemplative existence [Adams]. See the article by Dennis Fletcher on p. 130 of this Norton Critical Edition [Cronk].

"outsiders" . . . Amid the worst disasters, Candide's universe always furnishes a lifesaving plank.[9]

However, in his critical edition of 1959, after making some excellent remarks about the poetic quality of *Candide*, he contradicts his earlier statement:

Spontaneously, from the poetry of the unforeseen, there arises a philosophy of the absurd.[1]

Only one critic appears to have stressed unequivocally the strength of the dark side of Voltaire's temperament, which is so obvious in *Candide* and in the correspondence. This is André Delattre, in his stimulating little book, *Voltaire l'impétueux*, where we read:

It is only when, in *Candide*, he accepts certain perspectives of Pascal's, it is only when he ceases to strain against a dark and healthy pessimism, and ceases to hold open the empty sack of his optimism, that he finally creates, after his sixtieth year, his real masterpiece.[2]

This is a good pointer to the quality of the work. *Candide* is not just a clever, unfair satire on optimism which concludes with the bracing recommendation that we should do what we can to improve matters in our immediate vicinity. It is a work in which an unappeasable sense of the mystery and horror of life is accompanied, at every step, by an instinctive animal resilience. Negative and positive are juxtaposed (as they are, indeed, in some religious temperaments) with no unsatisfactory ratiocinative bridge between them. Voltaire has a faith, but it is not a political faith nor an easily defined religious one. It is the sort of faith that keeps the severed fractions of a worm still wriggling, or produces laughter at a funeral. In this sense, Voltaire's humanism is a very basic and simple characteristic, exceptional only in that it has at its service extraordinary intelligence and wit.

I say 'at its service' advisedly, because *Candide* is not, in the first place, an intellectual work. Its driving force is an intellectual bewilderment, which is felt as a strong emotion. Pomeau makes the interesting suggestion that the chronological irregularity in the composition of the *contes* is proof of their springing from a level well below Voltaire's everactive, normal consciousness:

The intermittent quality of the invention in the tales makes clear that here a deeper self is finding outlet, which does not get expressed every day.[3]

9. Librairie Nizet, 1956, p. 305.
1. Librairie Nizet, 1959, p. 70.
2. Mercure de France, 1947, p. 69.
3. Edition critique, p. 7.

He also adduces evidence to show that *Candide*, instead of being a rapid improvisation as has often been thought, was probably written at intervals over a period of a year. He concludes that it shows signs of deliberate artistry:

> A work of spontaneous fantasy, no doubt, but in the course of working on it, retouchings and additions appear, which make plain a very conscious impulse toward artistic form.[4]

I think it is possible to accept the first suggestion, while remaining unconvinced by the second. The alterations and additions Pomeau mentions are comparatively slight, and although *Candide* may have been in the making for a year, it could still be a happy fluke in which the artistry is largely unconscious. Voltaire himself seems never to have realized that it was his masterpiece, and he probably devoted more deliberate attention to denying its authorship than he had to its composition. His still-born tragedies he composed with great care, passing them round amongst his friends for comment and improvement. His tales were rattled off much more spontaneously, and he does not appear to have understood how original and gifted he was in this *genre*. If he had, he would presumably have taken more pains with some of the others, which are all either imperfect or slight. It is impossible not to agree with Delattre on this score:

> As for the tales, apart from *Candide* which is in a class by itself, they are really thin, quite slender.[5]

There is no progression up to *Candide*, nor any sign of further development afterwards. Good *contes* and less good were written higgledy-piggledy. *Zadig*, which came twelve years before *Candide*, and *L'Ingénu*, written eight years after, are probably the next best, but the first is uncertain in design and ends feebly, while the second begins in one tone and finishes rather abruptly in another, without the transition having been properly justified. Neither is firmly centered on a major theme. Other *contes*, such as *Le Monde comme il va* and *Micromégas*, which keep to one theme, repeat the same effect rather monotonously. It is very curious that, in *Zadig, Le Monde comme il va, Memnon* and *Scarmentado*, Voltaire should appear to be fumbling towards *Candide* and then, having produced his masterpiece, that he should go on to imperfect works such as *L'homme aux quarante écus* and *L'Histoire de Jenni*, which we would be tempted, on artistic grounds, to place before *Candide*, if we did not know their date of composition. *Candide* is the only *conte* which has an overall pattern, a major theme worked out with a variety of

4. Edition critique, p. 46.
5. Op. cit., p. 96.

incidental effects, a full complement of significant characters and an almost constant felicity of style.

Some slight discrepancies show that Voltaire did not finish the work with absolute care. Pomeau mentions the abrupt change, between Chapters I and II, from a springlike atmosphere to a shower of snow. Voltaire could, no doubt, have replied that fine spring days are quite often followed by snowstorms. More definite slips are the attribution of young wives to old men in Chapter III, the use by the inhabitants of El Dorado of gold and precious stones for the adornment of their houses, while referring to these commodities as '*boue*' [mud] and '*cailloux*' [pebbles] and the implication in Chapter 20 that Manicheism is a belief in the all-powerfulness of evil. But these flaws pass unnoticed in the general effectiveness of the work.

I think H. N. Brailsford is right in saying that *Candide* "ranks in its own way with *Don Quixote* and *Faust*," and the reason is that, like them, it is a parable of an aspect of the human plight. It is a pilgrim's progress, only this pilgrim can find no meaning in life nor establish any relationship with the transcendent. Candide has, of course, a clear literary ancestry; he is adapted from the hero of the picaresque novel of adventure, who could so easily represent the post-Renaissance displaced individual engaged on some more or less significant journey. More immediately, he is Voltaire himself, who was *déclassé* [a social outcast] like the picaresque hero, had been beaten and snubbed, 'tremblait comme un philosophe' ["trembled like a philosopher"] and had been frequently on the move. But he is also a symbol of the central part of the human soul which never loses its original innocence and, as Simone Weil says, always goes on expecting that good will be done to it rather than evil. And again, in spite of Pomeau's denial, he is *l'étranger* [the outsider], a fatherless bastard whose cosy sense of belonging to a coherent society and a comprehensible universe is a childhood illusion, soon to be shattered at the onset of puberty. Cunégonde is at first Eve who tempts him, with the result that he is driven out of the early paradise by the irate master of his little world. Then Cunégonde becomes the symbol of a lost happiness which will be recovered in the future, when the world falls again into some pattern reminiscent of the patriarchal social cell which preceded adulthood. But gradually it becomes clear that the world has no pattern, all human communities are in a state of perpetual flux and strife, and the best Candide can do is to reconstitute the battered Westphalian society of his childhood as a refugee colony on the borders of barbarism, with himself as its disillusioned head, in place of the self-confident Baron Thunder-Ten-Tronckh. Pangloss, the linguistic part of the brain, is still looking irrepressibly for explanations, but the numbed soul now knows that the quest is futile.

Just as the Candide/Cunégonde conjunction is far more significant than the parallel couples, Zadig/Astarte and Ingénu/St. Yves,
so the structure of *Candide* is more complex and much better
balanced than that of the other *contes*. It is not just one story, like
the adventures of Zadig or the Ingénu; it is an interweaving of several different stories, which are linked and knotted and contrasted
in an almost musical way. Dorothy M. McGhee, in her study, *Voltairian Narrative Devices*,[6] gives an interesting diagram showing
that one method of analyzing *Candide* is to see it as a series of oscil-
lations between Candide's "mental path of optimism" and the "level
of reality" to which he is always being brought back by disaster. But
there is much more to it than this. In addition to the up-and-down
movement, there are complexities in the linear development. The
stories of Candide, Cunégonde and La Vieille [the Old Woman] follow each other like three variations on the same theme, each slightly
more preposterous than the previous one and with an increasing
urbanity of tone as the events become more shocking. The pope's
daughter, whose exquisite breeding has remained unaffected by
the excision of a buttock, gives her account while the scene of action
is shifting from Europe to America. In the New World, the same
figure is repeated once more with a final flourish in the Jesuit's
story, which leads into the El Dorado episode. This is an interlude of
calm, coming in Chapter 17, almost exactly in the middle of the
book. Candide is now as far away as he ever will be from Europe
and from the realities of ordinary life. Then, since the beatific vision
can never be more than a fleeting experience, he begins on his long
return journey, picking up the threads in the reverse order. The second half is, however, different from the first in two important
respects. Candide is no longer an underdog; he has acquired money
and he sees the world from a new angle. At the same time, he has
lost his initial freshness; Martin has replaced the absent Pangloss
and the accumulated experience of horror has added a permanent
sob to the gaiety of the music. The hero has mastered life to some
small extent, in that the terrible accidents no longer happen so
often to him, but this is a hollow achievement since it leaves him
freer to contemplate the sufferings of others. The second half of
the book may seem weaker, artistically, precisely because Candide
has become a spectator, but it is psychologically true in the sense
that adulthood involves awareness of general evil.

Other aspects of the musical dance of the characters provide further refinements in the pattern. Each is killed once or more and bobs
up again with heartening inconsequentiality. Voltaire expresses the

6. Menasha, Wisconsin, George Banta Publishing Co., 1933, p. 55.

strength of man's unconquerable soul by making Pangloss and the Baron, for instance, step out of the galley and begin at once behaving with characteristic foolishness, as if they had never been hanged, stabbed or beaten. He also balances the horror of evil by never leaving the hero in solitude for very long. Candide is always part of a group of two or more, and he is always assuming solidarity until it is proved illusory. A minority of human beings are, like himself, decent and well-meaning; the majority are selfish and stupid, but the implication is that all are involved in evil in more or less the same way. In this respect, Candide is both fiercely critical of human nature and curiously tolerant. The Grand Inquisitor, the brutal sailor and the *levanti patron* are carried along on the same inevitable melody as Maître Jacques or Martin. In this one work, especially, Voltaire strikes a note which is very much deeper than propaganda and which is perhaps in the last analysis, not very far removed from inarticulate religious faith.

The parallel with music can be carried further. *Candide*, more clearly than the other *contes*, is written in such a way that the reader has to perform it mentally at a certain speed. As Pomeau says:

> That this style is not everyday prose, the loose style of the marketplace, is apparent in the first lines of the text.[7]

Voltaire is by no means the only eighteenth century author who can write *allegro vivace* [quick and lively]. Lesage, in parts of *Gil Blas*, is almost his equal.[8] Voltaire has Lesage's main qualities: an overall rhythm, a euphemistically noble vocabulary and an ability always to imply more than is actually said. But he also has features not to be found in Lesage or the other gay stylists of the century. He uses repetition and recapitulation very effectively in *Candide* to produce a constant impression (which at first sight would seem difficult to achieve in a typically eighteenth century style) of the welter of chance events. It is astonishing that so short a book should create such a vision of the teeming multifariousness of incomprehensible Necessity. His elliptical expressions are more frequent and more startling than those to be found in the prose of his contemporaries, and so he jerks the reader again and again into awareness of a metaphysical perspective behind his apparently innocent recital of events. Each important character has his or her *motif* which sounds at appropriate intervals; less obvious, but no less telling, than Candide's simplicity or Pangloss's silliness are Cunégonde's accommodating sensuality and Cacambo's practical good sense. And the

---

7. Edition critique, p. 55.
8. See the excellent '*récit de Lucinde*' (Book 5, Ch. 1), which may have helped to suggest the stories of Cunégonde and La Vieille.

mixture of rapidity, irony, allusion, ellipsis, merciless satire of human nature and affectionate understanding of the human plight produces an unmistakable, singing, heartrending lilt, of which only Voltaire is capable in prose and that only Mozart, perhaps, could have transferred to the stage. Admittedly, there are passages in *Candide* that might have been written by Lesage, for instance, parts of the Old Woman's account, in Chapter 11, of her sufferings at the hands of the pirates:

> It's a very remarkable thing, the energy these gentlemen put into stripping people. But what surprised me even more was that they stuck their fingers in a place where we women usually admit only a syringe. This ceremony seemed a bit odd to me, as foreign usages always do when one hasn't traveled.

But in the more characteristic passages, Voltaire infuses feeling into this bright, eighteenth century melody, without falling into the sogginess of *sensibilité*, the usual weakness of eighteenth century writers when they try to be serious. Chapter I, in its deceptive simplicity, is no doubt the most perfect example of his style and one of the highest achievements in all French writing. However, practically every chapter contains what can only be described as unique, ironical prose poetry.[9] I quote, at random, the description of the auto-da-fe in Chapter 6:

> . . . Candide's mitre and *san-benito* were decorated with inverted flames and with devils who had neither tails nor claws; but Pangloss's devils had both tails and claws, and his flames stood upright. Wearing these costumes, they marched in a procession, and listened to a very touching sermon, followed by a beautiful concert of plainsong. Candide was flogged in cadence to the music; the Biscayan and the two men who had avoided bacon were burned, and Pangloss was hanged, though hanging is not customary. On the same day there was another earthquake, causing frightful damage
> Candide, stunned, stupefied, despairing, bleeding, trembling, said to himself: —If this is the best of all possible worlds, what are the others like? The flogging is not so bad, I was flogged by

---

9. An exhaustive and useful analysis of Voltaire's irony has been made by Ruth C. Flowers in *Voltaire's Stylistic Transformation of Rabelaisian Satirical Devices*, The Catholic University of America Press, Washington, D.C., 1951. Dr. Flowers distinguishes (pp. 63 et seq.) eight varieties of 'Satirical Detail Elements' and nine varieties of 'Compound Satirical Devices' and concludes: 'Unquestionably, Voltaire is the greatest master of satire by "small art," a witty almost epigrammatic satire, a satire whose ironical impact depends entirely and exclusively on little things, strategically placed."

It is ironical, however, that Dr. Flowers should not notice the emotion which governs the strategic placing of these little things. She says (p. 90) that Voltaire's heart is 'coolly detached, superficially moved.'

the Bulgars. But oh my dear Pangloss, greatest of philosophers, was it necessary for me to watch you being hanged, for no reason that I can see? Oh my dear Anabaptist, best of men, was it necessary that you should be drowned in the port? Oh Miss Cunégonde, pearl of young ladies, was it necessary that you should have your belly slit open?

He was being led away, barely able to stand, lectured, lashed, absolved, and blessed, when an old woman approached and said. —My son, be of good cheer and follow me.

Candide was of very bad cheer, but he followed the old woman. . . .

It is one of the mysteries of literary composition that the *Poème sur le Désastre de Lisbonne* should be so flat and unpoetical, whereas Voltaire's treatment of the same theme in prose is at once rich, funny and deeply moving. Perhaps the explanation is to be sought in the fact that there is a philosophical ambiguity running through Candide, in addition to the contrast between vitality and awareness of evil. The *Poème* is a direct, but feeble, reproach to God, which ends with a still feebler hope that life will be better in the world to come than it is here. Voltaire was not, temperamentally, a God-defier. He invokes God convincingly only when it is a question of enlisting Him on the side of virtue, as in the *Traité sur la tolérance*. He was incapable of saying outright, with Baudelaire:

> For truly, Lord, this is the highest gage
> That we can offer of our dignity,
> This ardent sigh, which rolls from age to age,
> Dying on the shore of your eternity.

He can only criticize God freely when he does so, by implication, through human nature. It may be that the almost pathological violence of his onslaughts on the Church is to be accounted for, to some extent, by the transference of an unexpressed exasperation with the unknowable Creator onto a part of creation which is particularly irritating precisely through its claim to understand something about the Creator. At any rate, it is remarkable that, in *Candide*, the distinction between evil which is an act of God (and therefore from the human point of view gratuitous) and evil which is an effect of human wickedness or stupidity, is not clearly maintained. It is made, in Chapter 20, when Candide and Martin are watching the shipwreck, but in the form of a joke against Candide. God's indifference to humanity is again stressed in Chapter 30 when the dervish slams his door in Pangloss's face, and this time the joke— admittedly a rather sour one—is on Pangloss. It seems almost as if Voltaire were unwilling to come out into the open and accuse God, so much so that, from one point of view, the El Dorado episode can be seen as a logical flaw. That happy country, where the inhabitants never quarrel and worship God without a church, does not provide a fair contrast with the ordinary world; how would the people of El Dorado retain their serenity if their capital were shattered by an earthquake? The only way to justify the El Dorado chapters is to suppose that they are really a conscious or unconscious criticism of God. They occur as a sunny interlude between two series of disasters to show how happy and pious we might have been, had God not given us our ungovernable natures and put us into a world containing inexplicable evil. And the book as a whole, although so critical of mankind, tends to show human nature as a blind and passionate force driving helplessly on against a background of mystery. In other words, Voltaire, like Diderot, had not made up his mind about free-will, because the determinism/free-will dilemma is just another formulation of the God/no-God issue. The question is left open in Chapter 21:

> —Do you believe, said Martin, that hawks have always eaten pigeons when they could get them?
> —Of course, said Candide.
> —Well, said Martin, if hawks have always had the same character, why do you suppose that men have changed?
> —Oh, said Candide, there's a great deal of difference, because freedom of the will . . .
> As they were disputing in this manner, they reached Bordeaux.

Yet the whole weight of Voltaire's emotion is obviously against accepting the parallel between men and animals. *Candide* throbs from end to end with a paradoxical quality which might be described as a despairing hope or a relentless charity, and which comes from seeing the worst steadily, without either capitulating to it or sentimentalizing its impact. Although, as Delattre says, no great writer wrote more often below his best than Voltaire did, in this short tale he managed to hold fundamental opposites in suspense and so produced, from the heart of a century that wished to deny evil, an allegorical prose poem about evil which is still perfectly apt, exactly two hundred years later.

ROBIN HOWELLS

Does Candide Learn? Genre, Discourse, and Satire in *Candide*†

According to some critics, the protagonist of *Candide* develops. He progressively learns, finally attaining a form of wisdom. This view is argued at some length by Jacques Van den Heuvel in the 'Notice' to *Candide* in the authoritative Pléiade edition of the *Romans et contes*. Van den Heuvel calls *Candide* a 'roman d'apprentissage': 'L'aventure de Candide, en effet, est essentiellement une prise de conscience.' Moreover, 'les étapes de son cheminement intérieur ont été soigneusement marquées par Voltaire, bien que sans insistance de sa part.' The most important are the episodes of Eldorado (chs 17–18), the 'nègre de Surinam' (19) and his discovery that Cunégonde has become ugly (29).[1] Roger Pearson, in his recent book treating all the *Contes*, agrees in the main. He too identifies the first two of these episodes as key moments for Candide, though adding the final chapter (30) as the completion of the third: 'All the time he is turning [his] experiences to account so that his final comment that "il faut cultiver notre jardin" grows necessarily out of his past experience.' *Candide* exhibits 'the characteristics of what would come to be known as the "roman de formation," or *Bildungsroman*. . . . Each narrative incident fits in to a carefully ordered "argument" running through the *conte*.' In retrospect we observe 'the Lockean "steps by which the mind attains several truths." Movement through time means movement towards increased knowledge and wisdom.'[2]

I want to consider first how far the notion of Candide's development is supported by the text. I shall then look at the wider question to which it is significantly linked by these critics—that of genre.

---

† From *Journal of the Institute of Romance Studies* 4 (1996): 145–54. © Institute of Romance Studies, 1996. Reprinted by permission of Berghahn Books Inc. This article is based on a lecture given at the Institute of Romance Studies on 24 November 1994.
1. 'Enfin, c'est la réapparition de Cunégonde vieillie et enlaidie qui achève de le former': *Voltaire, Romans et contes*, ed. Frédéric Deloffre and Jacques van den Heuvel (Paris; Gallimard, 1979), 834–35. We may note that Van den Heuvel repeats here—often word for word—what he said in *Voltaire dans ses contes* (Paris: Armand Colin, 1967), 289–91.
2. Roger Pearson, *The Fables of Reason. A Study of Voltaire's 'Contes philosophiques'* (Oxford: Voltaire Foundation, 1993), 116, 119. Nevertheless for Pearson 'the final, famous aphorism fails to hide much uncertainty and gives on to as much of a white page as *Micromégas*' (123). Among other recent commentators, David L. Langdon seems to incline to development and final wisdom ('On the meanings of the conclusion of *Candide.' Studies on Voltaire and the Eighteenth Century*, 238 (1985), 397–432). Haydn Mason regards the conclusion as ambiguous, and is cautious about development (see below, note 5). On the other side, André Magnan argues for a non-realist, self-ironic reading (*Voltaire: 'Candide ou l'optimisme'* [Paris: Presses universitaires de France, 1987]); so do I (*Disabled Powers: A Reading of Voltaire's 'Contes'* [Amsterdam: Rodopi. 1993]).

How we read is affected by generic expectations and assumptions. My argument will be not only that the case for Candide's development is rather weak, but that the evidence requires a different account. To understand what kind of text this is, and to make more satisfactory sense of it, we must read the 'characters' as well as their utterances within wider discursive systems.

Candide gives some appearance of development in that he becomes in the course of the narrative a stronger presence. In the story he becomes more self-assertive, and in the narration too—for a time at least—he acquires greater consciousness. In chapter 1 he is totally passive or reactive. He is assigned neither independent will nor an interior life at all. Both first appear when he deserts the Bulgar army in chapter 2: the account of his first positive act is preceded by the notations 'il s'avisa,' 'il se détermina.' His first verbal assertion of his own needs appears in chapter 3: '. . . mais je manque de pain.' His first protest against Pangloss's doctrine appears in chapter 4, when he is told of Cunégonde's death: 'Ah! meilleur des mondes, où êtes-vous?' In chapter 9 he not only kills the Jew. He (rapidly) deliberates and resolves before killing the Inquisitor. And he briefly reflects upon these acts as an index of change in his own personality. 'Quand on est amoureux, jaloux et fouetté par l'Inquisition, on ne se connaît plus.'

In chapter 10 he is assigned the capacity to identify the transition between stages in his own story, and to assess their significance. '"Nous allons dans un autre univers," disait Candide; ". . . on peut gémir un peu de ce qui se passe dans le nôtre en physique et en morale."' Similarly he identifies and evaluates the episodes in chapter 16 (the Oreillons: 'la pure nature') and chapter 17 (Eldorado: 'le pays où tout va bien'). In chapter 19, confronted with the negro slave, he voices the famous and apparently decisive judgement: 'O Pangloss! . . . c'en est fait, il faudra qu'à la fin je renonce à ton optimisme.' He is now rich. This enables him to live, and especially to travel, as he chooses. He pensions Martin; he aids Paquette and Giroflée (24), and the ex-King of Corsica (27); he ransoms Pangloss and the Baron (28), Cunégonde and La Vieille (29). He acquires the 'métairie' (29). In the last chapter we are told 'Candide . . . fit de profondes réflexions.' It is then he who articulates twice, in contradistinction to the utterances of Pangloss, the famous closing formula on the necessity of cultivating the garden. Taken in the literal sense, his injunction seems to be being followed, to the collective benefit. Through experience and then through wealth, Candide goes progressively from passivity to self-assertion, while acquiring a modicum of mental life.

Even on this level however there are difficulties for the developmental account. The fundamental one, which we shall return to later, is that the utterances assigned to Candide resist a reading in terms of character. As in the examples above, they are too foolish or too wise, functioning to thematise and satirise beyond his competence. Then the supposedly key points in his development pose problems. Awkwardly, we happen to know that the 'decisive' episode of the negro slave in chapter 19 was a late insertion in the text—though that does not make it necessarily less intrinsic to the internal logic. More notable is the fact that just before the conclusion Candide appears thoroughly feeble. The idea of acquiring the 'métairie' (the future 'garden') is not his—it is proposed by La Vieille (29). How to get rid of the Baron is solved not by him but by Cacambo (30). On the matter of the marriage with Cunégonde, his good will seems to be accompanied by weakness and even spite. Faced with Cunégonde's insistence, 'le bon Candide n'osa pas la refuser.' Then we are told 'Candide dans le fond de son cœur n'avait aucune envie d'épouser Cunégonde. Mais l'impertinence extrême du baron le détermina à conclure le mariage' (29–30). The imminent end of the narrative is not signalled by any sense that Candide is now ripe for wisdom. It is signalled by these arbitrary events—the gathering of the group, the marriage and the halt—along with the narrator's announcement at the head of chapter 30.

At the start of the final chapter all on the farm are discontented, and Candide has no more idea than anyone else what to do about it. It is the old Turk who furnishes him with the solution. And what of the famous last line itself? '"Cela est bien dit," répondit Candide, "mais il faut cultiver notre jardin"' is often hailed as the demonstration that Candide has finally learned to abandon Pangloss's abstract words in favour of practical deeds. But, firstly, that is not what he says. The latter clause qualifies rather than negates the former. Secondly, the last line is very similar to his responses to Pangloss's harangues in early chapters. '"Voilà qui est admirable," dit Candide, "mais il faut vous faire guérir"' (4). '"Rien n'est plus probable," dit Candide; "mais, pour Dieu, un peu d'huile et de vin"'[3] (5). Practical concern, rendered rhetorically as the deprecation of abstract reasoning, is assigned to him from almost the beginning. Certainly there are differences. At the end we have a collective reference (not 'me' or 'you' but 'us'). The formulation possesses epigrammatic and figurative force. 'Cultivating the garden' has considerable resonance within the text, and a vast resonance beyond it. Pangloss by his reference to Eden in the penultimate paragraph helpfully reminds us of this. But Candide seems not to have taken it in. There is no

---

3. On the importance of 'l'adversative *mais*' in the binary discourse of the *Contes*, see Jean Starobinski, 'Le fusil à deux coups de Voltaire' (1966), reprinted (as the latter half of a longer piece under this collective title) in *Le Remède dans le mal* (Paris: Gallimard, 1989), 144–63.

evidence that Candide himself understands the wider implications of what he says.[4]

It is doubtful, then, whether Candide becomes progressively wiser in philosophical understanding. Nor is it clear that he becomes morer sophisticated in his dealings with the world.[5] Experience seems to make little difference. In chapter 22 we still read of 'l'innocence de Candide.' In chapter 23 he is still 'si étourdi et si choqué de ce qu'il voyait' (Byng); and in chapter 25 he is 'fort étonné de ce qu'il entendait' (Pococurante). His responses, that is, remain primary. If he is Lockean man, this cannot be in the sense of a progression of the mind (from simple impressions to complex ideas, to 'attain several truths'). But it might still be in the sense that he continues to react to experience on a primary level.[6] In relation to the doctrine of philosophical Optimism, he exhibits a certain development. We find a more or less consistently growing resistance up to the crisis of the encounter with the slave. A period of depression— 'une noire mélancholie' (19)—follows, and a denunciation of mankind throughout history is posited in the most extreme terms. '"Croyez-vous," dit Candide, "que les hommes . . . aient toujours été menteurs, fourbes, perfides, ingrats, brigands, . . . ?"' (21). Yet two chapters later he exclaims 'Tout est bien, tout va bien, tout va le mieux qu'il soit possible' (23)! And later still, 'Mon cher Martin,

4. As the message of *Candide*—not of Candide—I think that one could call the final formula rueful but positive (a reduction of ambitions). To find here a call to action in the world though seems rather against the textual evidence of the preceding paragraphs. However it has also been shown that there is a message here to the *initiés*, from Voltaire-at-Ferney. In his voluminous correspondence Voltaire uses the language he will assign to the Old Turk and Candide ('je ne m'en mêle pas,' 'cultiver,' '[devenir] jardinier') before the publication of *Candide* and after it (where he may actually attribute it to *Candide*—which also, remember, has nothing to do with him), especially in connection with the follies of the Seven Years War. An ironic sense is implied by his overemphasis and by the contexts. Thus too 'Constantinople' becomes Geneva or Paris (with whose affairs Voltaire was very much involved—compare 'j'y envoie les fruits du jardin que je cultive'). At this third level, we are invited to read the final message of *Candide* as playful, evasive and antiphrastic, suggesting a secret activism. *Candide* and its epistolary intertexts are studied together in: Geoffrey Murray, 'Voltaire's *Candide*: the Protean gardener 1755–1762,' *Studies on Voltaire and the Eighteenth Century*, 69 (1970); Paul Ilie, 'The voices in Candide's garden 1755–59: a methodology for Voltaire's correspondence,' *SVEC* 148 (1976), 47–113 (read as retreat); and more recently by David Langdon (n. 2 above) (read as moderate engagement). Thus the text, and intertexts both public (The Bible) and semi-private (Voltaire's *Correspondance*), offer us meanings beyond Candide's understanding.
5. The distinction between growing personal assertion and lack of cultural sophistication is adumbrated by Haydn Mason. 'Candide achieves personal autonomy,' 'he is his own master at last' (53, 92); but he exhibits 'a continuing naïveté on the level of abstract reflection,' 'he continues [to be cheated] as naïvely as ever' (84, 90): '*Candide': Optimism Demolished* (New York: Twayne, 1992).
6. Both senses appear in Pierre Cambou, 'Le héros du conte voltairien: sa genèse dans les Œuvres historiques,' *Littératures* 23 (1990), 89–101. Of the 'héros . . . de conception lockienne' in the tales he says 'il bâtit une science nouvelle' (98), yet refers in his conclusion to 'le point de vue réducteur du héros' (101).

encore une fois Pangloss avait raison: tout est bien' (27). The propo-
nents of development pass off these unconditional affirmations of
Optimism as best they can.[7] The contradiction can be 'naturalised' by
the explanation that Candide is now entirely identifying the philosophical issue with the amorous pursuit.[8] However, that account not
only supports the view that his reactions remain primary and affective. It means that he becomes more self-centred rather than more
generous in his concerns as the narrative progresses.[9] Another and
broader defence is to claim that it is such inconsistencies which make
Candide and others not puppets but 'real characters.'[1] For the kind of
inconsistencies (and the kind of writing) that we are talking about, I
think this is a false argument, though it also raises fascinating and
fundamental questions about the relations between art and reality.

In fact in this last third of the narrative Candide contradicts himself more directly, and repeatedly. In the same chapter 23 as he
says 'Tout est bien' he rhetorically proposes the opposite extreme:
'Quel *démon* exerce *partout* son empire?' (23, my emphasis). In successive chapters he seems to affirm 'le libre arbitre' (21) and then
say that men are determined to evil, 'ils ne peuvent pas s'en dis-
penser' (22). Later in successive chapters he says 'Pangloss avait
raison, tout est bien' (27), then challenges him to maintain this
doctrine after all that he has suffered (28). Even at this stage he
poses the silliest questions. '"Qui pensez-vous," dit-il, "qui soit le plus à
plaindre, de l'empereur Achmet, de l'empereur Ivan, du roi Charles-
Edouard, ou de moi?"' Even at this stage he affirms that Pangloss has
the answers. '"Ah!" dit Candide, "si Pangloss était ici, il le saurait et
nous l'apprendrait"' (27).

The explanation of course is that Candide scarcely develops, is not
self-consistent, and is arguably not a 'character' at all in the modern

---

7. 'Il lui arrive encore d'osciller entre l'espérance et la noire mélancholie, . . . mais on le
   sent dans la bonne voie,' says Van den Heuvel (n. 1 above, 835). Pearson (n. 2 above)
   makes no specific reference to them, but in effect transcribes the problem by saying
   both that 'Candide seeks to think more independently' (117) and that 'Candide is unable
   to judge safely for himself' (118).
8. William F. Bottiglia, despite his general resistance to psychologising, offers this explanation: *'Candide': Analysis of a Classic*, Studies on Voltaire and the Eighteenth Century,
   7A (1964), 170ff.
9. That Candide actually becomes more selfish is part of the revisionist reading of *Candide* by Roy S. Wolper, who sees the protagonist of this and other tales as targets for
   Voltaire's satire rather than his messengers. See 'Candide: gull in the garden,' *Eighteenth
   Century Studies* 3 (1969), 265–77. Wolper's salutary but overly sweeping approach is
   discussed in commentaries by Vivienne Mylne and Theodore E. D. Braun in *SVEC* 212
   (1982), 312–30.
1. 'Numerous inconsistencies [. . .] make him less of a type': Douglas A. Bonneville. *Voltaire and the Form of the Novel*, Studies on Voltaire and the Eighteenth Century, 158
   (1974), 54. 'Continually the characters in *Candide* do or say surprising things which run
   counter to the expectations which their name, class, nationality or literary ancestor may
   lead us to entertain, thus forcing us to recognise them as real people who are not easily
   categorized, as human beings not ciphers': Pearson (n. 2 above), 130. The latter is really a
   very strange statement.

(individual, psychological, realist) sense. Any element of personhood is subordinated to wider purposes within the narrative discourse. Candide continues to evoke Pangloss because it is his function to juxtapose the doctrine of Optimism and reality.[2] The narrator tells us that 'Candide . . . avait été élevé à ne jamais juger de rien par lui-même' (25). This statement appears not near the beginning but near the end of the narrative—surely another embarrassment for those who maintain that Candide develops. But even if we do not, it seems to contradict a fundamental quality in Candide announced by the narrator at the start: 'il avait le jugement assez droit.' The explanation must be that his primary judgement—essentially affective and moral, in a word *natural*—is right, but he is also the vehicle for every kind of received idea of order, centrally that of Panglossian Optimism. His other fundamental quality of mind, 'l'esprit le plus simple,' ensures that he will continue to do his job of failing to understand either Optimism or the world. More exactly, he will only partially understand. The Fool utters the truth beyond his own awareness. Candide's dislocated utterances function comically and satirically. They mime the incoherence of the doctrine and of the world.

But we must go back further. Candide is the innocent sent into the world. 'L'innocence de Candide' functions, prior to any thematisation, to show forth the world by contrast, and to keep him perpetually open to it. For satire, for comedy and for our sympathy he must continue to bear the world's assaults. At this most basic level too he must fail to learn. His stupidity functions to invite or force the world to reveal its hand clearly. It is precisely because he fails to understand that he serves to unmask—for our benefit—Bulgar punishment, Dutch charity, ecclesiastical theft, female lust or primitive cannibalism.[3] Even when protected by his new wealth—itself the result of a satirical Chance, not of his own abilities—he continues to function affectively in this way. (His name is, after all, a programme.) He remains open to what one might call moral and cultural assault. His stupid amazement endures—'fort étonné,' 'si choqué'—to expose the inadmissibility of what we have learned to accept. These simple responses mark the second level of his inability to

---

2. It is notable that, although Pangloss is present in the story in only eight chapters out of the thirty of *Candide* (1, 4–6 and 27–30), his name appears in twenty-six of the thirty. See Pierre R. and Marie-Paule Ducretet, *Voltaire: 'Candide'—étude quantitative. Dictionnaire de fréquence, index verborum et concordance* (Toronto, 1974).

3. Because he fails to understand that one may not simply walk out of the army ('il s'avisa' is not of course an index of Candide's inner life, but an ironic signal to us), he exposes—metaphorically, and literally on his body—its underlying violence. Because he fails to understand that sectarianism is more important than another simple human expectation ('Je manque de pain'), he brings out the limits of Christian charity. And so forth.

learn. Violence done to his moral and cultural sensibility belongs somewhere between violence done to his body (the rudimentary level) and violence done to the doctrine (the third level).

His openness or stupidity also makes him repeatedly the recipient of the experiential stories of others. He hears—on our behalf—the 'histoires' of La Vieille, Pangloss, Martin (more abstractly), Cunégonde, Paquette, Giroflée and the young Baron. Each is an *abyme* or double of his own. It is mainly a sequence, rapid yet random, of calamities. Its meaning—overwhelmingly the negation of Optimism—is more or less explicitly thematised. Like Candide, the subject of each story has been repeatedly assaulted by the world. Like him, each has stupidly persevered, to show forth more of it. Because they narrate, the discourse of these speakers is more extended than Candide's. It exhibits greater understanding. But no more than his own discourse can it be read as the expression of character. It delivers too little or (more often) too much, foregrounding trivia or offering epigram. It distances us from events and individual responses, figuring or thematising dislocation.[4] These speakers, unlike Candide, are clear about the meaning of their experiences—which makes them more wise but more limited than he. He debates their understanding with them. This allows us to see his interlocutors also allegorically, as aspects of himself or different views of the world. Optimism and 'Manichean' pessimism, perhaps also sexual desire, prudence and practicality, engage discursively. After much argument the speakers are, as the narrator confirms, none the wiser. It is of course the discourse of that narrator which runs through the whole. It is both epigrammatic and polemically incomprehending, continually drawing attention to itself and to meaning.[5] That voice, which we cannot call Voltaire but might call Voltaire-in-this-genre, is heard through the voices of all the characters. As André Magnan excellently summarises it, 'les personnages sont traversés par le discours' (1st n. 2 above, p. 80).

We must nevertheless continue to differentiate between Candide and the other characters. He provides the title of the work, his adventures the narrative thread, his experiences and those told to him by others the object of interpretation, his voice the last word. He and the other main characters alike are comic, but he more richly

4. An extract from Paquette's account of her present life provides a nice example. 'Etre souvent réduite à emprunter une jupe pour aller se la faire lever par un homme dégoûtant' (24) comically foregrounds the particular yet aphoristically summarises the whole. The satiric wit and the global judgement alike are manifestly beyond the competence of the fictional 'character,' and they take us beyond her fictional situation.

5. The famous description of a battle as 'cette boucherie héroïque' (3) offers an example. The narrator pretends not to understand that 'boucherie' and 'héroïque' belong to incompatible—low and high—registers. By yoking them together he speaks the truth about the battle, with witty and epigrammatic force.

and for more reasons. In common, he and they are caricatural 'types'; all are launched on accidental trajectories through the world; all are repeatedly assaulted; all tenaciously persevere. All are thus the object of satire, but also of our sympathy and affection. (The only 'bad' character, the Baron, is expelled from the group.) Candide however differs from them in a number of ways: his naivety (both innocence and cultural deference); his vulnerability as innocent, youth and social outcast; his looks and the affection he prompts in others; his own sensibility, companionability and active goodness; his pursuit of an ideal love as well as philosophical understanding; his world-pilgrimage; and the instability of his judgement. In all these respects he is especially the object of satire and of sympathy. He above all will not learn. His indomitable folly is central to his appeal. It is no less central to his function—to go on questioning, suffering, prompting our amusement and anger.

Candide is at the centre of a narrative whose signification goes beyond him. He is the protagonist in not one but two quests: the quest for Cunégonde as well as the quest for philosophical understanding. The narrative is a satire on epic romance as well as on philosophy. But they are the same, because epic romance affirms Providential order, and Providential order is an epic romance. The dislocated plot, the series of disasters, the internal narratives and reviews, Candide's eventual loss of belief in the ideal, are a satire on both. (At this level it is the *writer* who fails to understand how epic romance and philosophy should be written.)[6] The status of philosophy and of literature as truth are collapsed through parody. *Candide* functions to 'défabuler la fable' (Magnan). All wisdom is ironised—mocked or maimed. The *Contes* are themselves 'fallen fables' (Pearson), 'disabled powers.' They mime 'ce monde qui cloche' (Starobinski). But *Candide* is unique in its breadth, force and focus. It shows forth the grotesque body of narrative and of philosophy, representing that of the world. Its microcosm is dislocation of the body of discourse, and its burlesque literalisation is the battered body social and human.

The competence to grasp the full meaning is not given to Candide. Nor does the narrative discourse (which deals *wittingly* in polemical stupidity, whereas Candide deals in it unwittingly) give

---

6. The writer also fails to understand, it appears, how narrative of any kind should be written. Minor inconsistencies include the climatic change from outdoor weather in chapter 1 to snow in chapter 2, and the irreconciliability of Cunégonde's chronology in chapter 8 with Candide's (see Magnan [1st n. 2 above], 81–2). Absurdities include Candide's familiarity with the *Journal de Trévoux* (16) and with Milton (25). Need we mention such broader infractions of the rules as the telescoping of contemporary historical events, or the survival of protagonists who are repeatedly killed? We should however recall the narrator's joky 'je crois' (chapter 1)—foregrounding and ironising at the start the convention of narratorial omniscience.

it directly to us. But that discourse constantly—mockingly and flatteringly—prompts us towards it. The meaning is reserved for the reader. Can we say then that although Candide does not learn, the reader does? Is it the reader who is led progressively towards the truth? This seems to me highly questionable. As Carol Sherman thoroughly demonstrates, the *Contes* deal in massive redundancy.[7] One might add that the 'message' which critics are wont to find is usually pretty trite. If the message of *Candide* is the contrast between ideal philosophy and a disorderly world, it is more than evident to us within half-a-dozen chapters. It certainly does not need thirty chapters. If the message is the necessity of practical action, it seems to have been forgotten—after Jacques and Lisbon—for the next two dozen. The shape of *Candide*, surely, is not the shape of a learning curve. It is the shape of a myth. Indeed it could hardly be otherwise, for the parody of all of our myths must be a parodic myth.

Any attempt to define the genre of *Candide* must begin with the fact that it is a narrative. Having related it to 'epic romance,' we might opt for one of these two categories. Arguably (by breadth of narrative reference and fixity of heroic purpose) it is closer to *epic*. We have the eponymous protagonist (albeit young and handsome and pure as in romance), the faithful band, the world-journey and ideal quest, the reiterated terrible trials and the final attainment of the goal. But these are fools, precipitated through calamities at high speed, in very short chapters with mock-medieval titles, who eventually reach disillusion. Heroes, narrative scale, and achievement, that is, are all radically reduced. It is a *comic* (satiric, parodic) epic. The subtitle, the quest for understanding, the order of the story (its logic of theme not plot), and the discourse require us to add a third term: a *philosophical* comic epic. Setting it within contemporary history perhaps requires a further qualification; but one might subsume that, as an ironic modern transposition of epic, under the comic. The power of *Candide* does not lie in some worthy meliorism; still less in the message that we must replace words by deeds (for *Candide* itself is words, and a considerable deed). It lies in the rewriting of pagan epic, romance (including utopia), fable (exemplarity and moral), and of the Judeo-Christian epic (from 'le paradis terrestre' and expulsion to very modest secular hopes).[8] They are rewritten—with amusement, derision and ferocity—against

---

7. In particular, 'rendundancy abound[s] in *Candide*': Carol Sherman, *Reading Voltaire's 'Contes': A Semiotics of Philosophical Narration* (Chapel Hill: University of North Carolina Department of Romance Languages, 1985), 272.

8. Probably the best accounts of *Candide* as the mock-epic of mankind are: Patrick Henry, 'Sacred and profane gardens in *Candide*,' SVEC 176 (1979), 133–53; and Jean-Marie Apostolidès, 'Le système des échanges dans *Candide*,' *Poétique* 48 (1981), 449–59.

the hold that they still have on us and against the world which is so grotesquely inadequate to them. But Voltaire knew that he too would not learn.[9] Neither will we.

Finally we might look at the *Bildungsroman* reading in historical terms. Its two main elements—that Candide progressively learns, and that his final formula about the garden is a wise and positive message—have not always been associated.[1] To look for character and its development is perhaps a particularly British tendency, influenced by our tradition of realist narrative. (The lack of an English critical term equivalent to 'Bildungsroman' or 'roman d'apprentissage' implies that we see this category as natural rather than generic.) I think however that as a reading of *Candide* it belongs to the present century. The affirmation that the conclusion constitutes a call to practical action is certainly modern. I suspect that both, and the *Bildungsroman* reading itself, arose in reaction to the negative view of Voltaire and especially of *Candide* in the previous century. The Romantics and much of the nineteenth century—from de Stael to Flaubert and beyond, in differing registers—saw Voltaire's tale as heartless and cynical.[2] For much of our own century it was regarded as immoral and indecent.[3] The humanist account (characters and positive message) has been a kind of corrective. It has served as a liberal and progressivist defence of Voltaire and of the Enlightenment in general. My own reading reflects the structuralist approaches, focussing on genre and discourse within a reflexive literary system, fashionable in the later twentieth century. It is unlikely in turn that this has finally established the right way to read *Candide*. But we go on trying. We will not learn.

9. Having affirmed that the satiric voice of 'Voltaire' pervades the voices of all the main characters, we may go on to propose the obverse. Their quest for meaning, and the differing holistic accounts of the world that are assigned them (to Martin and Pangloss too, to La Vieille and Pococurante, and—radically unstable—to Candide) are exercises in self-irony by Voltaire.
1. Gustave Lanson in his excellent brief account of the *Contes* sees the characters in *Candide* as 'fantoches,' but finds in the conclusion a call to practical action: *Voltaire* (Paris, 1906), 152–53. Nearly a century later, Roger Pearson as we have noted takes the opposed positions: Candide learns, but the conclusion is open and ambiguous.
2. See the Introduction to René Pomeau's edition of *Candide* (Oxford: Voltaire Foundation, 1980), 76–78.
3. Not until the late 1960s did *Candide* appear in an edition for schools, in France or in England: Pomeau, *ed. cit.*, 79. Jean Sareil, 'Le massacre de Voltaire dans les manuels scolaires,' *SVEC* 212 (1982), 83–161, claims that the *Contes* were widely deprecated until 1945 if not 1965 (125–30). André Magnan (who writes from the opposite position from Sareil, not to approve but to attack the increasing integration of *Candide* into the literary institution) dates the 'promotion' of the *Contes* back to the nineteenth century, but agrees that it was accompanied by moral disapproval until the 1960s. Indeed, he points out that two extracts from *Candide* in the classic student manual by Lagarde et Michard (*XVIIIe Siècle*) appeared in bowdlerised form until as recently as 1985: *Voltaire: 'Candide' ou l'optimisme* (1st n. 2 above), 110–15.

JAMES J. LYNCH

Romance Conventions in Voltaire's *Candide*†

Source studies of Voltaire's *Candide* are in such general agreement about the romanesque background of the *conte* that the very idea of a fresh view seems impertinent.[1] Most critics are content to say that Voltaire either compresses or parodies conventions common to the general romance tradition: separations of lovers, surprising and improbable accidents while one lover pursues the other, and a wish-fulfilling reunion at the end of the novel. While it is easy enough to recognize the general romanesque parody in the story, unless one has a more specific knowledge of how romance conventions function in a serious context, it is difficult to see the comic use Voltaire makes of those conventions. I propose to define Voltaire's burlesque of the romance tradition by comparing *Candide* to one tradition of seventeenth-century romance, the Heliodoran novel. By no means is this tradition the only one Voltaire may have known and by no means does it embrace all of the romance elements in *Candide*. Nevertheless, it is useful for comparison because the Heliodoran tradition results from a desire to refine and make regular earlier traditions of romance. By comparing *Candide* to the Heliodoran novel, we will be able to identify the unifying romance structure of the novel and parodic romance elements in the characters of Candide and Cunégonde.

I call this tradition the Heliodoran novel because its principal influence is Heliodorus's post-classical Greek novel, the *Aethiopica*—a work rediscovered in 1526 and first translated into the vernacular by Jacques Amyot in 1547.[2] By the end of the sixteenth century,

---

† From *South Atlantic Review* 50 (1985): 35–46. Reprinted by permission of the publisher. Page numbers in brackets refer to this Norton Critical Edition.
1. Jacques Van den Heuvel sees *Candide* as parodying romanesque forms and using the realistic elements of the picaresque. He argues that Voltaire parodies the surprising accidents of the adventure novel but also derides the dreams on which such a romance view is founded. Pierre de Saint Victor notes that, unlike Voltaire's other *contes*, *Candide* relies on the formal literary artifices of romance narratives to establish aesthetic distance. For other discussions of *Candide* and the adventure novel genre see: Barber (13–14), Bonneville (282–87), Bottiglia (134–35; 201–02), Mc Ghee (13–14), Morize (L), Sareil (77–88).
2. Works I call the Heliodoran novel, such as Cervantes's *Persiles*, are often given the confusing label *novela bizantina* in Spanish literary historiography. Yet post-classical Greek works such as the *Aethiopica* antedated Byzantine civilization, and the very label "Byzantine" connotes an intricacy of structure and an ornateness of style that is not present in the sixteenth-century and seventeenth-century works influenced by Heliodorus.

I use "Heliodoran novel" as a neutral label, suggesting rather that the works in this subcategory of romance display many of the formal principles that Renaissance theorists admired in Heliodorus's novel. Similarly, I use the term "novel" simply to refer to works of long prose fiction. I use the term "romance" to describe the forms and rhetorical conventions of works such as the Heliodoran novel that present a wish-fulfillment world in which literary providence prevails. For a general theoretical discussion of romance as I use the concept, see Frye.

the *Aethiopica* had won critical praises from such theorists as Tasso, Scaliger, and El Pinciano (Forcione 49–87). To them, Heliodorus's novel was the prototype of the epic in prose because it possessed the unity and verisimilitude which chivalric novels lacked. During the sixteenth century, it influenced a variety of novels, including Alonso Nuñez's *Clareo y Florisea* (1552) and Montemayor's *Diana* (1559) in Spain, Sidney's *Arcadia* (1590) in England, and Chappuys's translation of the *Amadis* (1581) and Ollenix du Mont Sacré's *Oeuvre de la Chastété* (1595–99) in France (Sandy 102–20).

In the first half of the seventeenth century, the *Aethiopica* became even more widely associated with literary theories about the prose epic. Cervantes's Canon of Toledo, although he does not actually cite Heliodorus in his discourse on romances, recapitulates the arguments of Tasso, Scaliger, and El Pinciano (Forcione 91). Indeed, Cervantes's final novel, *Persiles y Sigismunda* (1617) in many ways attempts to create the kind of ideal romance that the Canon envisioned; it is a work that the author himself claimed "dares to compete with Heliodorus" (*Novelas* 100). In seventeenth-century France, the *Aethiopica* influenced the heroic novels of Gomberville, La Calprenède, and particularly de Scudéry, who cites the *Aethiopica* as a source in the prefaces to both the *Ibrahim* and the *Grand Cyrus*. By the time Pierre-Daniel Huet wrote his treatise on the origin of the novel in 1670, the association of the *Aethiopica* with the prose epic had become so much a part of literary theory that he calls Heliodorus "the Homer of the novel" (78).

Although individual works in the Heliodoran tradition (such as the *Persiles*, the *Ibrahim*, and the *Grand Cyrus*) differ dramatically among themselves, they share a common aesthetic theory and a common narrative structure. Because the Heliodoran novel is a synthesis of romance and epic, it strives for a balance between unity and diversity, verisimilitude and the marvelous, instruction and delight. After the fashion of verse epics, these novels typically begin *in medias res*—a narrative decision that produces suspense and provides a unified framework within which the authors can introduce diverse and marvelous accidents conventional to romance in general. The plot typically consists of a journey of two lovers who are betrothed, but whose marriage is prevented by some problem of identity. They travel to a specific destination, usually the center of their civilization; there the impediments to their marriage are removed, and they wed. In the *Aethiopica* and the *Persiles*, the lovers disguise themselves as brother and sister, but in all of the Heliodoran novels, either the hero or the heroine assumes a different identity. In the *Ibrahim*, for instance, Justinian is forced to assume the name Ibrahim at the court of Soliman; in the *Grand Cyrus*, Cyrus assumes the name Artamène in order to mask his real identity in the court of Cyaxare.

The journey itself, which typically comprises the bulk of the novel, consists of the kind of adventures we think of as romanesque: separations, shipwrecks, enslavements, abductions, apparent deaths, miraculous resurrections, apparent infidelities, and tender reconciliations. These accidents are unified because they are connected to the principal event of the novel—the marriage of the lovers—but they also provide the expansiveness characteristic of both romance and epic. Moreover, the loosely unified format of the novels allows room for stylistic embellishment. Separations often prompt lengthy rhetorical complaints and stylized descriptions of absent lovers. Reunions prompt recitals of offstage action that recreate in miniature the suspense of the larger plot line. The various companions met on the journey give way to interlaced histories which often mirror the providential schema on which the novel as a whole is based.

In the last half of the seventeenth century, when prose fiction turns away from the stylized conventions of the heroic novels, the Heliodoran tradition as a distinctive literary influence ceases. Indeed, it becomes part of the generally indiscriminate romance background of the novel. Nevertheless, its distinctive features emerge in *Candide*, almost as a unified romance thread that generates expectations which are comically thwarted by the end of the novel.

There is no evidence that Voltaire had the *Aethiopica* especially in mind while writing *Candide*. He did own a French translation of it, however, and according to his correspondence he was at least familiar with the *Grand Cyrus*.[3] In addition, there were at least six French editions of the *Persiles* before 1759 (Stegmann 229). I suggest the Heliodoran novel tradition not as a source, but as a paradigm of literary romance. I will use it as an analytical model by which we can identify particular romance conventions in the *conte* and see how Voltaire shatters both *Candide*'s and our expectations for a best of all possible endings.

Parallels with the Heliodoran form can be found both in the larger structure of *Candide* and in several minor episodes. One of these minor episodes—Candide's meeting with Don Ferdinando d'Ibaraa in chapter 13—provides a useful starting point, for here the hero is placed in a romance role he is incapable of playing.

---

3. *Bibliothèque de Voltaire* (440). Voltaire makes reference to the *Grand Cyrus* in a letter to Charlotte Sophia (*Correspondence* 103: 121). His correspondence also suggests at least a passing knowledge of the *Aethiopica*. In a letter to the count and countess Argental, he is familiar with the legend that Racine had memorized the *Aethiopica* when his tutor threatened to take away his copy (*Correspondence* 110: 118).

After Candide's and Cunégonde's arrival in Buenos Aires, Don Ferdinando lustfully inquires about the hero's relationship with the heroine. Having a spirit that was "trop pure pour trahir la vérité," Candide is flustered but unable to tell the polite lie that Cunégonde is his wife or his sister (165–66) [28].[4] His inability to lie reminds us of his persistent naivete, but the narrator's parenthetical observation suggests a displacement of romance convention. He observes that the kind of lie Candide avoids was "très à la mode chez les anciens et . . . pût être utile aux modernes" (165). Morize (74–75) and Pomeau (165) explain this comment as an allusion to Abraham's disguise as Sarah's brother. Yet the juxtaposition of "ancient" and "modern" suggests a literary context as well as a biblical one; it points toward the expedient lies told by romance heroes and heroines in order to protect their identities and to deceive their assailants. Indeed, disguise and the accompanying lies are central to the Heliodoran novel, for its unity and suspense depend upon our recognizing that the lovers' real identities will eventually be unmasked.[5] By indicating that such lies were "très à la mode chez les anciens," Voltaire gently criticizes romance conventionality. But by adding that such a lie might also be "utile aux modernes," he suggests that such lies—even if conventional—are more practical than Candide's naive allegiance to truth. The parenthesis, in short, signals the intersection of romance and realism that can be found throughout the novel.

When we look at the larger elements of form, we can draw even more ironic parallels between *Candide* and the Heliodoran novel. As in the Heliodoran tradition, Candide and Cunégonde fall in love despite her father's and, later, her brother's objections; they are both separated, reunited, and they begin a journey during which they are once again separated. At the end, they are finally reunited and married. But while the separations in the Heliodoran novel are designed to create suspense, the two separations in *Candide* seem real. We have no reason to doubt that Cunégonde has been killed by the Bulgars and no reason to expect the hero and heroine to be reunited after their separation in Buenos Aires—that

4. All references to *Candide* are to Pomeau.
5. In the *Aethiopica* Theagenes and Chariclea pretend to be brother and sister to deceive Thyamis, a suitor of the heroine. Cervantes exploits the convention more fully in the *Persiles*; not only do Persiles and Sigismunda pretend to be brother and sister, but they assume different names (Periandro and Auristela). Much of the narrative tension of the novel, in fact, depends on this disguise: we recognize that they are actually lovers not siblings, even though many of the other characters they meet do not, and even though we are not aware of their real identities until the very end of the novel. In the *Roman comique* Scarron also plays with the conventionality of this device; Destin and Etoile (pseudonyms which curiously echo Periandro and Auristela) pretend to be brother and sister, much to the disbelief of the realist, Rancune.

is, of course, until Candide sets off on his quest for the heroine after the Eldorado episode.

In the Heliodoran novel the journey of lovers usually has thematic as well as narrative significance, which is one reason that it became the model for the epic in prose. For example, in the *Aethiopica* Theagenes and Chariclea journey from the barbarous lands of the Nile delta southward to Meroë, the capital of Ethiopia, where the heroine is revealed to be the daughter of the king and queen. There, too, the hero and heroine are finally able to marry. Similarly, in the *Persiles* Periandro and Auristela journey from the barbarous North (where Christianity had strayed from the true faith) to Rome, the seat of Roman Catholic civilization. This geographical movement enacts a Counter-Reformation journey of man; Auristela, having been instructed in the true faith at Rome, recovers her religious birthright, in effect, and is thus able to marry Periandro. The journey in *Candide* is similar, although it is geographically and thematically different. Starting off in Germany—a Germany barbarously overrun with Bulgars, in fact—the lovers journey to the New World, back to Europe and finally to Constantinople. It is an epic that almost traces the progress of western civilization in reverse and brings the hero and heroine to a qualified, if not disputable, happiness. A disillusioned Candide and a prematurely aged Cunégonde end up on a small, impoverished farm near the seat of a faded empire.

Although the journey in *Candide* generally resembles that of the Heliodoran tradition, the narrative is significantly different from works such as the *Aethiopica* and the *Persiles* that begin *in medias res*. Voltaire's arrangement is chronological from the start and thus follows the realistic pattern of such quasi-picaresque novels as Fielding's *Tom Jones*. In the Heliodoran tradition, the *in medias res* opener signals a connection with the epic tradition (and thereby legitimizes its claim to be art), but, more importantly, it provides a unified framework thought to be absent in earlier romances. Jacques Amyot, one of the first Renaissance commentators on Heliodorus, noted that the epic style opener links the chronological start of Theagenes's and Chariclea's history with the beginning of the *Aethiopica* and then establishes "an ingenious liaison" between that beginning and the "long-awaited joy" one experiences at the end. The followers of Heliodorus in the seventeenth century used the *in medias res* opener with such regularity that it no doubt appeared to eighteenth-century writers such as Voltaire merely another romance improbability. By choosing a chronological ordering, Voltaire thus follows a typical eighteenth-century pattern of subordinating romance elements to a realistic structure. In *Candide* as well as in such chronologically structured novels as *Tom Jones*, the journey itself takes on romance characteristics once the historical setting is established.[6]

There is, however, an even more important reason for Voltaire's choice of a chronological ordering—one that implicitly criticizes the wish-fulfillment dream of romance. In the Heliodoran tradition, the *in medias res* beginning makes the hero and heroine question their faith in divine providence; when we reach the "long-awaited joy" that Amyot finds in the ending, that faith is restored. In *Candide*, the hero's hopes for a happy ending are tied up with the causal logic of Pangloss's optimism. Thus a chronological narrative, with all of the improbability of romance, makes even more absurd the Panglossian notion that seemingly adventitious events will result in the best of all possible worlds.

Voltaire uses romance conventions to lead the reader through a process of disillusionment with romance just as Candide is to be disillusioned with Pangloss's philosophy. An understanding of the Heliodoran novel conventions thus sharpens our awareness of modes of irony in Voltaire's characterization.

Candide is cast in a romance role, even though his character suggests conventions of the picaresque. Like Tom Jones after his dismissal from Paradise Hall, when Candide is booted from the Baron's "paradis terrestre," he seems destined to wander "sans savoir où" (122) [5]; his destiny, like Jones's, seems to be that of the *picaro*. Yet, like Tom Jones, Candide nevertheless dwells on the heroine, and he soon finds himself praising her in a company of soldiers. He thus follows the pattern of the heroes in the *Aethiopica*, the *Persiles*, the *Grand Cyrus*, and the *Ibrahim*, who all go to war after their initial separation from their mistresses. Although in the Heliodoran novel this convention lends heroism to their roles as lovers, in Voltaire's novel Candide's romance heroism is undercut by realistic struggles. Not only does he encounter the savagery of war, but Voltaire ironically qualifies his heroic stature. He is predicted to be "le soutien, le défenseur, le héros des Bulgares" (123) [6], yet he fails to understand either his heroic potential or the realistic motives of the Bulgar recruiter. By undercutting Candide's heroic potential, Voltaire places Candide in a wasteland between romance and realism: he can neither be a romance hero nor, because of his Panglossian optimism, can he understand the realities of war.

6. In *Tom Jones*, for example, the hero's quasi-picaresque journey after leaving Somerset becomes the mutual journey of separated lovers about midway through the novel. Sophia pursues Jones to Upton, where they nearly meet. He then pursues her to London. There—after many complications that oppose our expectations for a happy ending against our knowledge of Tom's unheroic behavior—the two are reunited and finally married.

Other conventions of the romance hero are negated and inverted in Candide's character as well. Theagenes, Periandro, Ibrahim, and others are depicted as noble lovers; their physical appearance mirrors both their heroic nature and their noble love. Periandro, for example, is described as "more beautifull than could be well expressed" (*Persiles* 2). Similarly, Ibrahim is described, with elaborate rhetorical embellishment, as noble and heroic:

> His Physiognomy was promising and sprightful; his soul was seen in his eyes, his courage and affability appeared equally in them; and without having ought of the beauty of a woman, he was goodliest man that ever was beheld. In fine there was seen in his whole person, a lofty ayr without pride, a gallanterie without affectation, a neglectful handsomeness, a freeness without artifice, a civility without restraint, and something so great and so high therein, as one could not behold him without judging him to be worthy to bear a crown. (Scudéry 373)

It is not difficult to see from this passage the degree to which Voltaire ironically compresses romance embellishment in chapter 1: "Sa physionomie annonçait son âme" (118) [3]. Innocent in appearance, Candide is innocent in spirit and name—a trait that replaces the conventional romance hero's courage.

Even though Candide lacks the conventional prowess of the hero in Heliodoran novel, he possesses that hero's conventional idealism about love. After his first reunion with the heroine (ch. 6), he is conventionally jealous (a device used for narrative complication in the Heliodoran novel); but unlike Theagenes, Periandro, or even Cyrus, Candide's jealousy quickly forsakes romance idealism and stretches toward deterministic realism: "Ma belle demoiselle, répondit Candide, quand on est amoureux, jaloux, et fouetté par l'Inquisition, on ne se connaît plus" (149) [20]. It would not be surprising to find Cyrus or Ibrahim so casual about the enemies he had vanquished, but Candide's reaction seems naiveté, rather than heroic pride.

During his second separation from Cunégonde, comprising the second half of the novel, Candide is again cast in a romance role. Like Periandro, Cyrus, and Ibrahim, he is filled with romance aspirations: "il espérait toujours revoir mademoiselle Cunégonde" (201) [47]. His hopes are sustained despite Martin's pessimism and despite his own mounting frustration. Even after being deceived in Paris by a false Cunégonde (an episode recalling a variety of romance episodes), Candide remains naively optimistic. When he expects to find his mistress in Venice, he is overcome with Panglossian hope and believes: "Tout est bien, tout va bien, tout va le mieux qu'il soit possible" (224) [61]. This romance hopefulness reaches its height in chapter 27, on the journey to Constantinople, during which

Candide discovers that Cunégonde has become quite ugly. He remarks in the manner of a gentleman and a romance hero: "Ah! belle ou laide . . . je suis honnête homme, et mon devoir est de l'aimer toujours" (244) [72]. *Devoir*, of course, suggests distinctively romance motivations, but in light of her change in appearance, these motivations suggest a resignation to an unhappy fate.

Cunégonde's character, like the hero's, parallels the basic pattern of the heroine in the Heliodoran novel, but unlike Candide's, her very role inverts romance behavior. In the Heliodoran novel the heroine is distinguished by her nobility, beauty, and intelligence. Chariclea's and Auristela's beauty make them forever the object of desire by virtually every male they encounter. Yet because of the conventional powers associated with their chastity, their virtue survives whatever attacks are made on it. Similarly, their nobility, even though concealed, manages to survive all attempts to taint it: captured by pirates, sold as slaves, the heroines are always treated royally. Even their jewels, the concealed evidence of their noble births, always remain in their possession. In addition, each possesses the wit to deceive assailants—a quality that enhances a romance belief in wish-fulfillment.

Cunégonde directly parodies this pattern. Chastity, we learn at the outset, is not one of her strong points. Unlike Chariclea and Auristela, who withstand every attack, Cunégonde's virginity is quickly dispatched by the Bulgar soldiers. Although Heliodoran novel heroines typically pit one rival against another, preserving their own chastity by a combination of duplicity and delay, Cunégonde treats her lovers with duplicity but not delay. She plays the Jew off against the Inquisitor for material gain. Indeed, instead of inflexible fidelity to the hero, she seems quite willing to abandon Candide in Buenos Aires.

Like the conventional romance heroine, Cunégonde is of noble birth, although only the daughter of a minor Westphalian baron. Yet, even this small degree of nobility is made ignoble. Taken captive after her rape in Germany, she is forced to become cook, laundress, dishwasher, and pastry cook—menial tasks that a romance heroine would never undertake. In spite of all these vicissitudes, her brother still insists that she cannot marry Candide because he is not her equal. Like Chariclea and Auristela, Cunégonde possesses some jewels that should function as marks of her nobility, yet these are the results of her affairs with the Jew and the Inquisitor. Furthermore, the jewels are stolen, in direct violation of their function in the Heliodoran novel. Whereas the beauty of Chariclea and Auristela is pure and heavenly—a parallel to their virtue—Cunégonde's is less rarefied. Hers is an earthly, even earthy beauty, she is "haute en couleur, fraîche, grasse, appétissante" (119) [3]. Her plump beauty comically inverts the conventional flower and jewel clichés found in the embellished descriptions of romance heroines; indeed she sounds more like a pastry than a rarefied flower or gem.

Although the realistic way in which Voltaire depicts Cunégonde seems to negate her romance role, there are nevertheless a variety of incidents that parallel romance conventions of the Heliodoran novel. In works like the *Aethiopica* and the *Persiles*, the initial separation of the lovers seems permanent—often because either the hero or the heroine is assumed to be dead. When the lover is "resurrected," their adventures appear once again to be guided by providence. Cunégonde's resurrection and her recital of events after her initial separation from Candide invert the pattern of the Heliodoran novel. Instead of convincing the hero and the reader of her constancy, Cunégonde's recital convinces the reader, if not Candide, of her promiscuity. The mere suggestion of a romance convention underscores the irony of her ignoble actions. Indeed, Cunégonde's rape and reported disembowelment recalls Leucippe's reported disembowelment in book 3 of Achilles Tatius's *Clitophon and Leucippe* (165–73), another post-classical Greek novel associated with the *Aethiopica* and the Heliodoran novel vogue. Notably, Voltaire owned a French translation of Achilles Tatius's novel as well (*Bibliotheque* 10).

In novelistic terms Cunégonde's resurrection is contrived and improbable, but it is a contrivance and an improbability that Voltaire tacitly invites the reader to accept. Instead of reassuring us of the designs of providence, her resurrection convinces us of the caprices of fate. Although it momentarily restores Candide's faith in the best of all possible worlds, her resurrection makes us laugh at its unreality rather than hope, along with Candide, for the couple's eventual happiness. Apparent deaths and miraculous resurrections occur thrice more: two times with the younger Baron and once with Pangloss. It is as if Voltaire is stretching the convention to its breaking point.

After the second reunion of the hero and the heroine in the penultimate chapter, even Candide's romance hopes are negated. In the Heliodoran novel the heroines survive the ravages of time and travel; in fact, at the end they are frequently more beautiful than when they set out. Much the reverse, Cunégonde's beauty disappears entirely. After Candide's long quest, he finds the heroine dishearteningly ugly: "rembrunie, les yeux éraillés, la gorge sèche, le joues ridées, les bras rouges et écaillés" (252) [77]. Her physical appearance is purposefully the reverse of the rosy cheeks, coral lips, and marble skin of the romance heroine. And just as the beauty of the romance heroine mirrors her virtue, Cunégonde's ugliness suggests her lack of it. Whereas the constant beauty of the romance heroine kindles the hero's hopes, the change in Cunégonde's appearance sparks Candide's final demystification.

That Cunégonde should turn out to be ugly at the end of the journey suggests a further parallel with the *Persiles*. In the last book of Cervantes's novel, after Auristela and Periandro arrive in Rome, the hero is besieged by a worldly-wise courtesan, Hipólita who, when she fails to win him by seduction, attempts to destroy what she believes is causing his fidelity to the heroine: Auristela's beauty. Hipólita thus arranges with a witch to afflict Auristela with an infirmity that will make her ugly. Almost immediately, the heroine's poetic beauty disappears: "It was not above two houres after shee fell sicke, but the naturall roses of her cheeks were of a leaden colour; the carnation of her lippes wanne; and the pearles of her teeth, black" (*Persiles* 377). The traditional features that define Auristela's beauty are momentarily destroyed, but they are restored when she recovers. Periandro, all the while, is perfectly constant in his affections. In Cervantes's novel, the ugliness afflicting Auristela is temporary: it is the revenge of an evil spirit, and it ultimately serves as a final test for the hero. In Voltaire's novel, Cunégonde's ugliness is permanent, unpoetic, real: the revenge of time and work. It eradicates any hope for a conventional romance ending.

Like Periandro, Candide is initially constant in his affections. When he learns of Cunégonde's ugliness, he promises to love her forever. Yet when he meets her face to face, her appearance causes him to react with a horror born of disillusionment and to recoil "trois pas saisi d'horreur" (252) [77]. This negation of romance convention is evident also in the cause-effect relationship surrounding the change in the heroine's beauty. Hipólita's design was to remove, by sorcery, the cause of Periandro's love. Although there is no sorcery in Voltaire's novel, Cunégonde's ugliness certainly removes the last possible source of Candide's optimism—his hope that, when he reunites with Cunégonde, all will be for the best.

Voltaire's use of romance conventions is not merely parodic, although parodic elements are present. His compression of narrative recitals, for instance, clearly parodies the use of those devices in the heroic novel. As Pierre de Saint Victor notes (383–84), the compression not only parodies the convention but also makes the reader aware of the aesthetic distance separating the reader and the author. *La vieille* remarks that she would not have told her story if it were not conventional to recite personal histories on board ships. Chapter titles also are more direct signals to the reader that the author is telescoping romance conventions. The title of chapter 5, for example, jumbles a series of romance devices: "Tempête, naufrage, tremblement de terre, et ce qui advint du docteur Pangloss, de Candide, et de l'anabaptiste Jacques" (134) [12].

For the most part, however, Voltaire is less concerned with making light of the literary excesses of romance than with using the romance conventions to shock the reader, as he has shocked Candide, into reality. Indeed, at the end of the novel he pokes fun at the expectations of a romance ending: "Il était tout naturel d'imaginer qu'après tant de désastres, Candide marié avec sa maîtresse, et vivant avec le philosophe Pangloss, le philosophe Martin, le prudent Cacambo et la vieille, ayant d'ailleurs rapporté tant de diamans de la patrie des anciens Incas, mènerait la vie du monde la plus agréable" (254) [78]. This is a penultimate smile before the final twist. The possibilities of a romance ending grow more and more remote as Cunégonde becomes uglier every day and as Martin and Pangloss become more contentious.

The ending of the novel thus presents us with a deliberate negation of romance conventions. In the Heliodoran novel, the marriage of the hero and heroine almost always occurs near the last page. Little remains to be said, for a romance world view implies a prosperous life. Voltaire, however, leaves us with a realist's analysis of such a view. He extends the characters' lives a page or two beyond the conventional finale. Martin and Pangloss argue; Cunégonde cooks; Paquette embroiders; and Candide, at last, resigns himself to the necessity of work.

Works Cited

Achilles Tatius. Ed. S. Gaselee. London: Heineman, 1947.

Amyot, Jacques. "Le Proesme du Translateur." In *L'Histoire éthiopique de Héliodore.* Paris: 1547.

Barber, W. H. *Voltaire: Candide.* New York: Barron's Educational Series, 1960.

Bibliothèque de Voltaire. Moscow: L'Académie de Science de l'URSS, 1961.

Bonneville, Douglas. *Voltaire and the Form of the Novel.* Vol. 158 of *Studies on Voltaire and the Eighteenth Century.* Oxford: Voltaire Foundation, 1976.

Bottiglia, William F. *Voltaire's Candide: Analysis of a Classic.* Vol. 7 of *Studies on Voltaire and the Eighteenth Century.* Oxford: Voltaire Foundation, 1959.

Cervantes Saavedra, Miguel de. *Novelas ejemplares.* Vol. 1 of *Biblioteca de autores españoles.* Madrid: 1944.

Cervantes Saavedra, Miguel de. *The Travels of Persiles and Sigismunda.* Trans. M. L. London: 1619.

Forcione, Alban K. *Cervantes, Aristotle, and the Persiles*. Princeton: Princeton UP, 1970.

Frye, Northrop. *The Secular Scripture: A Study of the Structure of Romance*. Cambridge: Harvard UP, 1976.

Heuvel, Jacques Van den. *Voltaire dans ses contes*. Paris: Armand Colin, 1967.

Huet, Pierre-Daniel. *Lettre-traité sur l'origine des romans*. Paris: Nizet, 1971.

McGhee, Dorothy M. *Voltairian Narrative Devices as Considered in the Author's Contes Philosophiques*. 1933; rpt. New York: Russell, 1973.

Saint Victor, Pierre de. "Candide: de la parodie du roman au conte philosophique." *Kentucky Romance Quarterly* 15 (1968): 377–85.

Sandy, Gerald N. *Heliodorus*. Boston: Twayne, 1982.

Sareil, Jean. *Essai sur Candide*. Genève: Droz, 1967.

Scudéry, Madeleine de. *Ibrahim, or the Illustrious Bassa*. Trans. Henry Cogan. London: 1674.

Stegmann, Tilbert Diego. *Cervantes' Musterroman Persiles*. Hamburg: Lüdke, 1971.

Voltaire. *Candide, ou l'optimisme*. Ed. André Morize. Paris: Didier, 1957.

Voltaire. *Candide, ou l'optimisme*. Ed. René Pomeau. Vol. 48 of *The Complete Works of Voltaire*. Oxford: The Voltaire Foundation, 1980.

Voltaire. *Correspondence*. Ed. Theodore Besterman. Vol. 103 of *The Complete Works of Voltaire*. Oxford: The Voltaire Foundation, 1973.

Voltaire. *Correspondence*. Ed. Theodore Besterman. Vol. 110 of *The Complete Works of Voltaire*. Oxford: The Voltaire Foundation, 1973.

PHILIP STEWART

Holding the Mirror up to Fiction: Generic Parody in *Candide*†

For many of Voltaire's stories there are rather evident models with regard to subject-matter, narrative form, or both. *Micromégas* owes of course much to Swift, *Zadig* to the *Arabian Nights*; *Le Monde comme il va*, *La Princesse de Babylone*, and even more *Le Taureau blanc* are parodies of the Old Testament. The model in each instance is copied only up to a point, as must be the case if the many ironies of Voltaire are to be immediately perceptible. But by the same token, parody is appreciable only when the identity of what is parodied is

† From *French Studies* 33 (1979): 411–19. Reprinted by permission of Oxford University Press.

obvious to the reader. Gulliver, Scheherazade, and the Bible have remained rather more current in readers' minds of all ages than has a kind of antecedent which seems to me relevant for a reading of the best-known of all the tales, *Candide*. I am referring to the long, heroic novel (or romance), which, although it had had its heyday in the seventeenth century, had not altogether died and was certainly not altogether unread well into the eighteenth.

I will centre this discussion on Prévost's *Cleveland* (1731–1739),[1] both because it typifies many of the commonplaces of such fictions, and because Voltaire certainly was familiar with it and arguably—though not demonstrably—had it in mind at some points in composing *Candide*. (The work's true title was *Le Philosophe anglais*, but it was more frequently designated by Voltaire and his contemporaries by the name of its hero, a bastard son of Cromwell.) To a lesser extent, other novels of Prévost might also be invoked, particularly *Manon Lescaut*. Happily, it is possible to read *Candide* profitably without first having assimilated all the novels of *Cleveland*'s type; but the literary public of 1759 was familiar with them, and likely to be familiar as well with the derisive opinion in which Voltaire, resolutely classical in most areas of literary taste, held such manner of fictions. In any event, the narrative style of *Candide* would have sufficed, for them, to make this attitude clear. To pursue some of the informing parallels between *Cleveland* and *Candide*, therefore, may well add in some measure to an understanding of the latter's processes of signification.

There are first the commonplace situations and events, the repetitive repertory of picaresque peripetaia, of adventure fiction in general. The most obvious of these are shipwreck, capture, and ensuing slavery. Cleveland, Fanny, and their party are capsized by a storm in the Channel, and later they are sold to traders by the Rouinton Indians who have taken them captive. Similarly, Candide and Pangloss are barely saved off the coast of Lisbon, and several characters in Candide are sold at one time or another into slavery. En route for the New World, Cleveland bares his soul to Captain Will, explaining, 'les premiers jours qu'on passe dans un vaisseau s'emploient à lier des connaissances' (p. 90); the setting for the old woman's story in *Candide* is an ironic allusion to just such narrative devices (frequently a strategy for intercalations), as she too, with Candide and Cunégonde, is crossing the Atlantic: 'Je ne vous aurais même jamais parlé de mes malheurs,' she explains, 's'il n'était d'usage, dans un

---

1. References in the text are to my edition of *Cleveland* (in *Œuvres de Prévost*, vol. II, Presses Universitaires de Grenoble, 1977); to chapters in *Candide* following the Bénac edition of *Romans et contes* of Voltaire (Garnier, 1960); to the Deloffre/Picard edition of *Manon Lescaut* (Garnier, 1965). Some of the parallels which this article will note have of course been observed earlier; see especially Jean Sgard, 'Prévost et Voltaire,' in *Revue d'Histoire Littéraire de la France*, 64 (1964), 545–64.

vaisseau, de conter des histoires pour se désennuyer' (Chapter 12). Poison, the symbol of intrigue and passion, appears in both stories, killing the old woman's fiancé as it would have killed Cleveland had he actually consumed it.[2] Another such element might even be the downstream movement whereby the hero is swept from danger or captivity into a region of release and renewed adventure. Cleveland and Fanny are transported down the Alabama River to be sold, but then are liberated by the Europeans of Pensacola; Candide and Cacambo escape both Oreillons and Jesuits likewise: 'jetons-nous dans cette petite barque, laissons-nous aller au courant; une rivière mène toujours à quelque endroit habité' (Chapter 17). The *toujours* here can refer only to a context of novels, the pattern of which is thus characterized by their mechanical predictability within certain situations; Voltaire's irony mocks such reflexes of narrative banality, much as do Diderot's asides in *Jacques le fataliste*.[3]

The cataclysmic reversals of fortune which are equally basic to the themes of both *Cleveland* and *Candide* are not of course peculiar to either, although Voltaire, like Diderot, doubtless considered Prévost a prime abuser of systematic plot alternation. Perhaps the fear of Candide and Cacambo that they will be roasted on a spit by the savage Oreillons (Chapter 16) is a reminiscence of the frightful manner in which Mme Riding and Cécile, in *Cleveland*, were presumed to have perished; however that may be, the fact that the assassinated and re-assassinated characters of *Candide* spring irrepressibly back to life—Cunégonde after being gutted by soldiers, her brother who is first slaughtered and later run through by Candide himself, Pangloss who was 'mal pendu'—is surely a satire on the kind of fictional recall through which Mme Axminster, thought like Cunégonde to have expired, recovers her breath, and Mme Riding and Cécile turn up years after their supposed death, in a village through which Fanny chances to be passing. Such rebounding and fortuitous encounters are a constant of paper characters from *Le Roman de Renart* to the comic books, and their concentrated over-use in *Candide* implicitly links melodramatic novels like *Cleveland* to that tradition. Even the naïve 'optimism' of *Candide*'s sub-title is an ingredient of novels as well as a philosophy, and contributes to the romantic theme.

All these are reinforced too by use of the fixed formulas of narrative staging. For instance, as Mme Riding's story is introduced with the words: 'Elle nous satisfit en ces termes' (p. 536), that of her analogue in *Candide*, the old woman, is preceded by: 'La vieille leur

2. *Candide*, xi; *Cleveland*, p. 597. Cleveland is spared thanks to an experiment with it carried out first on his dog.
3. That Diderot is thinking of *Cleveland* is explicit: 'J'aurais bien su appeler quelqu'un [au secours de Jacques]: mais cela aurait pué le *Cléveland* à infecter' (in *Œuvres romanesques*, Garnier, 1962, p. 526).

parla en ces termes' (x). Similarly, there is the fictional licence which rationalizes the listener's impeccable memory:

> [Fanny] entreprit aussitôt cette intéressante narration, dont on ne sera pas surpris dans la suite que j'aie pu répéter ici jusqu'au moindre mot. [p. 380]

> [Cunégonde] parla en ces termes à Candide, qui ne perdait pas une parole . . . (Chapter 7)

The way a story is told thus becomes as much the object of satire, or nearly so, as the elements of the plot.

Staples like these are referred to in *Candide* precisely as 'ces situations qu'on trouve dans tous les romans' (Chapter 22). But there may also be more specific relations between the two works, beginning with the philosophical association of the themes of each announced in their titles. Cleveland starts out as a 'philosophe' of much the same sort as Candide, that is to say, '[un] jeune métaphysicien fort ignorant des choses de ce monde' (ii). As the earlier work is 'traduit de l'anglais,' so is the latter 'traduit de l'allemand'; and the old yarn about a manuscript finally falling into the editor's hands, used in the preface of *Cleveland* as in other Prévost novels, finds its ironic parallel in the sub-title Voltaire appended to *Candide*: 'avec les additions qu'on a trouvées dans la poche du docteur [Ralph], lorsqu'il mourut à Minden, l'an de grâce 1759.' Even the names of the heroes sound somewhat alike.

From the outset, each is stigmatized and rendered vulnerable by his illegitimate birth. There is first, however, a period of security—Cleveland in Rumney-Hole and Candide in the château—coupled with an idyllic juvenile passion, Cleveland's for Fanny and Candide's for Cunégonde (who, like Fanny, is the legitimate daughter of the hero's noble protector). Then the orphan is expelled from the adoptive maternal/paternal haven, and separated from the love without which he cannot henceforth conceive happiness. At this point both stories take on some of the traits of picaresque narrative, Candide's career being more bouncily episodic, as the oft-lonely hero pursues a sinuous journey which is also a quest for a happiness embodied in the object of his first simple attachment. He roams self-obsessed through the mine-field of history, taking some note, but not much, of the major events which explode about him as he goes.

In each case too the vulnerability is compounded by that other fundamental trait already alluded to, naïveté. The green and credulous provincial had been common in picaresque fiction, and there are, for example, episodes in the early chapters of *Gil Blas* which parallel Cleveland's being duped in Rouen by an ostensibly generous merchant. But Cleveland's faith in the certifiable sincerity of others is persistent, and he never comes to doubt it more than slightly. In this Candide resembles him—'l'esprit le plus simple,' repeatedly deceived because of his almost incorrigible good faith. By having the recalcitrant Indian Moou executed in the name of public order (book iv), Cleveland becomes a murderer, albeit without losing his essential goodness and innocence; the same is true of Des Grieux (who slays a jail-house servant in *Manon Lescaut*)—and of Candide, a double and even triple assassin despite himself.

The crossing of the Appalachians by Cleveland, Axminster, and Fanny being pursued by Captain Will is comparable in function to Candide's flight with Cunégonde and the old woman towards Cadiz (ix–x). The motivation for undertaking the voyage to America is similar too in the two stories, as are the circumstances surrounding it. Cleveland is enrolled in the service of Charles II against Cromwell, specifically to assure the submission of the American colonies; Candide is signed on to help to quell a revolt against the Portuguese king among his American subjects. If Cleveland for his part tries to make Mme Lallin pass as his aunt, Candide for his almost calls Cunégonde his sister: Voltaire mocks this commonplace whether it is found in the Bible ('ce mensonge [. . .] autrefois très à la mode chez les anciens' [Chapter 13]) or in modern romance, which are thereby reduced to the same level. A spirit of optimism accompanies the liberation from European constraints. Candide's confidence resembles that of Bridge, Cleveland, and Des Grieux at comparable moments:

[. . .] je me crus transporté dans un nouveau monde. (p. 103)

C'est au Nouvel Orléans qu'il faut venir, disais-je souvent à Manon, quand on veut goûter les vraies douceurs de l'amour.
(*Manon Lescaut*, p. 188)

Nous allons dans un autre univers, disait Candide; c'est dans celui-là, sans doute, que tout est bien [. . .]. C'est certainement le nouveau monde qui est le meilleur des univers possibles. (Chapter 10)

Moreover, in each of the instances just cited there arises a serious complication owing to an obstructed or contested marriage. Bridge's unofficial betrothal, though consummated, is not recognized by the authorities. Cleveland's is performed in the wilds of America, also without the church's benediction, so its status can later be disputed. The resemblance is even closer between *Manon Lescaut* and *Candide*, where the couple want to marry after disembarking, but see their plans frustrated by the colonial governor's imposition of his own authority to marry the heroine to someone else. The old woman moreover advises Cunégonde to take advantage of this to 'faire la fortune de monsieur le capitaine Candide' (xiii), which recalls to mind the indelicate means Manon had been known to propose for assuring her own and Des Grieux's financial security. Finally, Candide's hiring of a valet upon arrival in Buenos Aires presents resemblances with both these Prévost novels. Cacambo is reminiscent of Iglou, an Indian servant; and this step by Candide suggests that he, like Des Grieux, who engages a valet and chambermaid in New Orleans, similarly pretends to live in the New World as a gentleman.

And then there is El Dorado, very much like the Nopande kingdom where Mme Riding and Cécile arrive after a year of peregrinations in the vague interior topography of Prévost's North America. Voltaire's pair of travellers survey 'un horizon immense, bordé de montagnes inaccessibles,' mountains 'droites comme des murailles' (Chapters 17–18): such terrain might have been suggested by descriptions of the Andes like those cited by André Morize,[4] but equally well by any number of utopian fictions, among them *Cleveland*. The island colony in Bridge's story is itself surrounded by cliffs 'd'une hauteur qu'il ne me semblait pas possible de surmonter' (p. 103), and Mme Riding finds herself before 'un mur fort élevé [. . .] qui s'étendait d'une montagne à l'autre' (p. 543). The Nopande kingdom lying behind it has none of the surface glitter of El Dorado, which plausibly might derive from the fame of Incan wealth, but on the other hand could just as well have been inspired by an obvious literary model which no editor seems to have cited as a source: the new Jerusalem of the Apocalypse, all encrusted with jewels, paved with gold, and spectacular in its dimensions. And Voltaire's harnessing of the famous 'gros moutons rouges' parallels the entrance of Mme Riding: 'On attelait à une petite voiture deux animaux dont l'espèce m'était inconnue' (p. 544); in both cases it takes a ride of just four hours to reach the palace.

Each of the authors makes of the mysterious mountain refuge the sole society encountered by any of their characters where people are authentically happy:

> [. . .] cette nation la plus douce peut-être et la plus polie qui existe dans l'univers [. . .] (p. 543)

> C'est probablement le pays où tout va bien [. . .] (Chapter 17)

Yet ultimately in both instances they insist on leaving over the objections of the ruler, because happiness is perceived as reunion with persons who are elsewhere:

---

4. Critical edition of *Candide* (Paris: Hachette, 1913), chs. 17–18 and notes. Christopher Thacker, in a more recent critical edition (Geneva: Droz, 1968), does list *Cleveland* among the sources, but without giving specific references.

> Je n'ai point d'autre vue que de chercher des personnes dont je
> ne puis supporter l'absence [. . .] (p. 553)

> [. . .] mais enfin mademoiselle Cunégonde n'y est pas [. . .]
> (Chapter 18)

The departure of Candide and Cacambo by virtue of 'une machine
pour guinder ces deux hommes extraordinaires hors du royaume'
(Chapter 18) has been compared to a similar machine in *Histoire des
Sévarambes*,[5] but an equally plausible source is the moment where
Mme Riding first sees the Nopandes atop their mountain wall: 'Sur le
champ je leur vis préparer une machine qu'ils laissèrent couler
jusqu'à moi, et de laquelle sortirent deux hommes' (p. 543). El Dorado
and the Nopande land are both left behind forever, a memory of happiness which, once renounced, can never be recovered.

Cleveland, being English, is subject to that famous ailment, mel-
ancholia (Martin says the English are atrabilious [Chapter 23]); but
so is Candide: the theft of his sheep 'le plongea dans une noire
mélancolie' (Chapter 19), and the same happens later in Venice
(Chapter 24). Experience of course contributes to their gloom, especially since each of the heroes returns to Europe without the heroine
of his quest, whom a traitor has stolen away. His philosophical and
emotional depression leads Cleveland to imagine that suicide would
be sanctioned by his Author:

> En permettant que je sois tombé dans l'extrémité de l'infortune
> et de la douleur, il m'a excepté du nombre de ceux qu'il con-
> damne à vivre longtemps. (p. 290)

Candide comes close to succumbing to the same desperate
temptation:

> A quoi me servira de prolonger mes misérables jours, puisque
> je dois les traîner loin d'elle dans les remords et dans le déses-
> poir? (Chapter 16)

The evidential value of this comparison, in terms of possible allusion specifically to *Cleveland* on the part of Voltaire, is the stronger
if one bears in mind that at this time suicide was hardly a common
theme in novels: *Candide* appears before the long letters on suicide
in *La Nouvelle Héloïse*; the first literary suicide I know of is in the
Histoire du marquis de Cressy of Mme Riccoboni (1758).[6]

5. Ibid., p. 124, n. I.
6. If it is specifically *Cleveland* which Voltaire does have in mind in this passage, then the
   aside which follows the above quotation—'Et que dira le Journal de Trévoux?'—would
   have an additional piquancy, since Prévost was much upbraided about the rationaliza-
   tions of Cleveland before and after his suicide attempt, and the *Journal de Trévoux* in
   addition accused him of 'declaring war' on it and slandering the Jesuits. See *Le Pour
   et Contre*, VII, 5–9; *Mémoires de Trévoux*, Nov. 1735, 2386–88; and the response of

There is obviously a clear philosophico-religious theme in both stories. The minister's insistence in *Cleveland* (book 3) that the fall of the dice—that consummate symbol of chance—in fact betokens the divine will has perhaps its analogue in Pangloss's dictum that all is arranged for the best. Cleveland's vague discussion of deism (book 4), and especially the arguments involving protestants, Jesuits, and Jansenists (books vi–vii), could be likened to the religious debates running through *Candide*. Bridge's persuasion that he is plagued by 'quelque puissance maligne' (p. 147) is even worthy of comparison to Martin's Manicheanism: God has abandoned the world, in the latter's opinion, to 'quelque être malfaisant' (Chapter 20).

Each of these odysseys finally leads to a Parisian episode which is essential to its resolution, clearly because, thematically speaking, France and its culture must be reckoned with before the philosophical voyage can be entire. Significantly also, although each hero returns without his idol, he possesses on the other hand a fortune which secures him definitively from want: as Cleveland has inherited the riches of Fanny's Spanish grandfather, so Candide has the limited yet considerable remnant of his El Dorado treasure, and like the former he enters Paris in the opulent style of 'quelque milord anglais' (Chapter 22). Cleveland's systematic exposure to all the pleasures of the capital (books 12–14) is a precedent both for Candide's less ordered initiation and, because of its ultimate disappointment, that of the rich but profoundly disabused Pococurante. In Paris, Cleveland barely overcomes the seductions of La Cortona—the only episode of his life which causes him genuine remorse. There too, Candide succumbs to his first real temptation since Cunégonde, and feels 'quelques remords d'avoir fait une infidélité' (Chapter 22).[7]

Candide's eventual recovery of Cunégonde does not belie Cleveland's eventual reunion with Fanny, but it recalls even more specifically, as André Morize has noted, another novel by Prévost, his *Mémoires pour servir à l'histoire de Malte*: 'le héros retrouve enfin sa maîtresse Hélène enlaidie et défigurée comme Candide revoit Cunégonde, et comme elle impérieuse.'[8] And despite obvious differences, there are philosophical discussions at the very end of both *Cleveland* and *Candide* which determine, or at least precipitate, the conclusion. The Lord Clarendon of *Cleveland* is hardly a 'derviche,' but he serves an analogous function as the voice of wisdom which is at once serene and free from fanatical certitudes.

Prévost in Henri Harrisse, *L'Abbé Prévost* (Paris, 1896), 239–44. As a matter of fact, the suicide section of book vi was suppressed, for reasons that cannot be precisely determined, in the first Paris edition of the novel.

7. From France, each will also set out for England. Candide never actually goes ashore, however, and sets sail instead for Venice.

8. Ed. cit., p. liv.

Nevertheless, despite these numerous comparisons, it cannot be said that any passage in *Candide* is an undeniably specific reference to *Cleveland*. The point indeed is not so much that it is meant to be the topical parody of *Cleveland* alone, as that it is the parody of a certain variety of novel which *Cleveland* can be held to represent. *Candide*, to be sure, satirizes much more than one particular genre; but it is also true that Voltaire generically situated his own tales in part by the ways in which they differed from *romans*, a name he was reluctant to see applied to them.[9] In 1733 (just when *Cleveland* was half completed) he wrote: 'Si quelques nouveaux romans paraissent encore, et s'ils font l'amusement de la jeunesse frivole, les vrais gens de lettres les méprisent.'[1] Such a judgment is not aesthetic alone: the novel addresses a *public* which Voltaire, although a vulgarizer in his own way, did not wish to claim. Twenty years later that view had scarcely changed, even if by then Voltaire was himself penning *contes*:

> On est bien éloigné de vouloir donner ici quelque prix à tous ces romans dont la France a été et est encore inondée; ils ont presque tous été, excepté *Zaïde*, des productions d'esprits faibles, qui écrivent avec facilité des choses indignes d'être lues par les esprits solides.[2]

Thus, although the novel was not necessarily in his eyes an intrinsically inferior genre, it usually was so in practice, and was unworthy company for an author concerned for the seriousness of his work and for his intellectual reputation.

We are accustomed to thinking of *Tristram Shandy* and *Jacques le fataliste* as anti-novels; less so of *Candide*, since it is not itself similar in form to a novel, and yet in significant measure it is a comparable sort of generic parody. But it reflects in addition Voltaire's personal refusal to participate in a genre which he was not alone in associating both with base popularizing and with extravagance; doubtless too he was motivated by the fact that the novel was frequently the vehicle for a kind of sentimental righteousness which he mistrusted—and Prévost represented. Certainly this connexion is suggested by his sarcasms concerning *La Nouvelle Héloïse*.[3] Such emotive fulsomeness is not identical with the 'optimism' which *Candide* in particular derides, but it contains at least the seeds of a

---

9. Although *Romans et contes* is now a standard title for his collected tales, the word *roman* never appeared on any edition before 1764.
1. *Essai sur la poésie épique* (in *Œuvres complètes*, Paris: Garnier, 1877–1885, vol. 8), p. 362.
2. Article 'Villedieu' in the 'Catalogue des écrivains français' appended to *Le Siècle de Louis XIV* (*Œuvres complètes*,14).
3. See the mordant *Lettres à M. de Voltaire sur la Nouvelle Héloïse*, in *Mélanges* (Paris: Gallimard, 1961), pp. 395–409.

self-contained assurance and self-satisfaction which to Voltaire was equally indefensible. Neither it nor the commonplaces of novelistic plots, both exemplified in *Cleveland*, are given any quarter in *Candide*, since they are part and parcel of a literary practice that, through parody, he condemns.

ERICH AUERBACH

[Voltaire's Style: Tone, Pace, Insinuation][†]

[Voltaire's prose, which at first glance looks like a simple taut string on which to hang a set of one-liners, is a great deal more complex and interesting than that. Nobody has been more deft and patient at unraveling the way a piece of writing actually works than Erich Auerbach, the much-admired German humanist, whose classic *Mimesis* traces through European literature the way in which a thread of social realism intertwines with other themes and literary modes, bending syntax subtly to its purposes.

The chapter dealing with Voltaire begins by discussing a passage from the Abbé Prévost's novel *Manon Lescaut* (1731). Here the surface of things is colorful, varied, lively, and graphic; the feelings depicted, on the other hand, are serious, almost tragic. Yet the language is almost invariably charming and elegant. Very different is the manner cultivated by Voltaire in one of his *Lettres Philosophiques*, then in a late verse narrative, and finally in *Candide*.—Robert M. Adams]

* * *

Quite different is the stylistic level of the realistic texts which serve the propaganda purposes of the Enlightenment. Examples are to be found from the Regency on, and in the course of the century they become more frequent and increasingly aggressive polemically. The master of the game is Voltaire. As a first example we choose a fairly early piece, from the sixth of the *Philosophical Letters*, which deal with his impressions of England.[1]

> Entrez dans la bourse de Londres, cette place plus respectable que bien des cours; vous y voyez rassemblés les députés de toutes les nations pour l'utilité des hommes. Là, le juif, le mahométan et le chrétien traitent l'un avec l'autre comme s'ils

---

[†] From *Mimesis: The Representation of Reality in Western Literature*, trans. Willard Trask (Princeton, NJ: Princeton University Press, 1953), pp. 401–13. Reprinted by permission of Princeton University Press.

1. Voltaire's involuntary visit to England lasted three years (1726–29) and put the finishing touches on his literary and political education. The *Letters concerning the English Nation*, which appeared in 1733, were powerful and important in themselves and laid the foundations of many of Voltaire's future attitudes. The work appeared in French as *Lettres philosophiques* (1734) [Adams].

étaient de la même religion, et ne donnent le nom d'infidèles qu'à ceux qui font banqueroute; là, le presbytérien se fie à l'anabaptiste, et l'anglican reçoit la promesse du quaker. Au sortir de ces pacifiques et libres assemblées, les uns vont à la synagogue, les autres vont boire; celui-ci va se faire baptiser dans une grande cuve au nom du Père, par le Fils, au Saint-Esprit; celui-là fait couper le prépuce de son fils et fait mar-motter sur l'enfant des paroles hébraïques qu'il n'entend point; ces autres vont dans leurs églises attendre l'inspiration de Dieu leur chapeau sur la tête, et tous sont contents.

(Enter the London stock exchange, that more respectable place than many a court; you will see the deputies of all nations gathered there for the service of mankind. There the Jew, the Mohammedan, and the Christian deal together as if they were of the same religion, and apply the name of infidel only to those who go bankrupt; there the Presbyterian trusts the Ana-baptist, and the Anglican accepts the Quaker's promise. On leaving these peaceful and free assemblies, some go to the synagogue, others go to drink; one goes to have himself bap-tized in the name of the Father, through the Son, to the Holy Ghost; another has his son's foreskin cut off and Hebrew words mumbled over him which he does not understand; others go to their church to await the inspiration of God with their hats on their heads; and all are content.)

This description of the London exchange was not really written for a realistic purpose. What goes on there, we are told only in a gen-eral way. The purpose is much rather to insinuate certain ideas, which in their crudest and driest form would run as follows: "Free international business as dictated by the egotism of individuals is beneficial to human society; it unites men in common pacific activ-ities. Religions, on the other hand, are absurd. Their absurdity needs no proof beyond the observation that they are very numerous while each claims to be the only true one, and that their dogmas and cer-emonies are nonsensical. However, in a country where they are very many and very different, so that they are forced to put up with one another, they do not do much harm and can be regarded as an innoc-uous form of madness. It is only when they fight and persecute one another that things get really bad." But even in this dry formulation of the idea there is a rhetorical trick which, however, I find it impos-sible to eliminate because it is contained in Voltaire's conception itself. It is the unexpected contrast of religion and business, in which business is placed higher, practically and morally, than religion. The very device of coupling the two, as though they were forms of human endeavor on the same plane and to be judged from the same viewpoint, is not only an impertinence; it is a specific approach or, if one prefers, an experimental set-up, in which religion is ipso facto deprived of what constitutes its essence and its value. It is presented in a position in which it appears ridiculous from the start. This is a technique which sophists and propagandists of all times have employed with success, and Voltaire is a master of it. It is for precisely this reason that here, where he wants to demonstrate the blessings of productive work, he chooses neither a farm nor a business office nor a factory but the stock exchange, where people of all faiths and backgrounds congregate.

The way he invites us to enter the stock exchange is almost solemn. He calls it a place deserving of greater respect than many a court, and its frequenters deputies of all nations foregathered in the interests of humanity. Then he turns to a more detailed description of its frequenters and observes them first in their activity at the exchange, then in their private life; in both cases he emphasizes their differing in religion. As long as they are at the exchange, the difference has no importance. It does not interfere with business. This gives him the opportunity to introduce his play on the word *infidèle*. But as soon as they leave the exchange—that peaceful and free assembly, in contrast to the assemblies of battling clerics—the disparateness of their religious views comes to the fore. What was just now a harmonious whole—a symbol as it were of the ideal cooperation of all human society—now falls asunder into numerous unrelated and indeed incompatible parts. The remainder of the passage is given over to a lively description of a number of these. Leaving the exchange, the merchants disperse. Some go to a synagogue, others go to have a drink. The syntactic parallel presents the two as equally worthy ways of passing the time. Then we get a characterization of three groups of pious frequenters of the exchange: Anabaptists, Jews, and Quakers. In each case Voltaire emphasizes a purely external detail which differs from and is in no way related to the next but which in every instance is intrinsically absurd and comic. What comes out is not really the true nature of Jews or Quakers, not the grounds and the specific form of their convictions, but the external aspect of their religious ceremonial, which, especially to the uninitiated, looks strangely comic. This again is an example of a favorite propaganda device which is often used far more crudely and maliciously than in this case. It might be called the searchlight device. It consists in overilluminating one small part of an extensive complex, while everything else which might explain, derive, and possibly counterbalance the thing emphasized is left in the dark; so that apparently the truth is stated, for what is said cannot be denied; and yet everything is falsified, for truth requires the whole truth and the proper interrelation of its elements. Especially in times of excited passions, the public is again and again taken in by such tricks, and everybody knows more than enough examples from the very recent past. And yet in most cases the trick is not at all hard to see through; in tense periods, however, the people or the public lack the serious desire to do so. Whenever a specific form of life or a social group has run its course, or has only lost favor and support, every injustice which the propagandists perpetrate against it is half consciously felt to be what it actually is, yet people welcome it with sadistic delight. Gottfried Keller[2] describes this psychological situation very finely in one of the novellas in his Seldwyla cycle, the story of lost laughter, in which a campaign of defamation in Switzerland is discussed. It is true, the things he describes compare with what we have seen in our time as a slight turbidity in the clear water of a brook would compare with an ocean of filth and blood. Gottfried Keller discusses the matter with his calm clarity and lack of prejudice, without softening the least detail, without the slightest attempt to whitewash the injustice or to speak of it as a "higher" form of justice; and yet he seems to sense in such things an element that is natural and at times beneficial, because after all "more than once a change of government and the expansion of freedom have resulted from an unjust cause or untrue pretense." Keller was fortunate in that he could not imagine an important change of government which would not entail an expansion of freedom. We have been shown otherwise.

Voltaire concludes with an unexpected turn: *et tous sont contents*. With the swiftness of a prestidigitator he has, in three sharp phrases, parodied three creeds or sects, and the four concluding words are sprung at us just as swiftly, surprisingly, and merrily. They are extremely rich in content. Why is everybody satisfied? Because everybody is allowed to do business and grow wealthy in peace; and because everybody is no less peacefully allowed to cling to his religious madness, with the result that no one persecutes or is persecuted. Long live tolerance! It lets everybody have his business and his fun, whether the latter is taking a drink or persisting in some absurd form of worship.

The method of posing the problem so that the desired solution is contained in the very way in which the problem is posed, and the searchlight technique, which overilluminates the ridiculous, the absurd, or the repulsive in one's opponent, were both in use long before Voltaire. But he has a particular way of handling them which is all his own. Especially his own is his tempo. His rapid,

2. Keller, a Swiss-German novelist of the late nineteenth century, serves Auerbach as a contrast-comparison with Voltaire's focusing devices in the *Lettres philosophiques*. The examples from the very recent past, to which Auerbach quietly alludes, were provided by the anti-Semitism of Hitler's Third Reich, which drove Auerbach himself into exile [Adams].

keen summary of the development, his quick shifting of scenes, his surprisingly sudden confronting of things which are not usually seen together—in all this he comes close to being unique and incomparable; and it is in this tempo that a good part of his wit lies. As one reads his marvelous rococo sketches, the point becomes strikingly clear. For example:

> Comme il était assez près de Lutèce,
> Au coin d'un bois qui borde Charenton,
> Il aperçut la fringante Marton
> Dont un ruban nouait la blonde tresse;
> Sa taille est leste, et son petit jupon
> Laisse entrevoir sa jambe blanche et fine.
> Robert avance; il lui trouve une mine
> Qui tenterait les saints du paradis;
> Un beau bouquet de roses et de lis
> Est au milieu de deux pommes d'albâtre
> Qu'on ne voit point sans en être idolâtre;
> Et de son teint la fleur et l'incarnat
> De son bouquet auraient terni l'éclat.
> Pour dire tout, cette jeune merveille
> A son giron portait une corbeille,
> Et s'en allait avec tous ses altraits
> Vendre au marché du beurre et des œufs frais.
> Sire Robert, ému de convoitise,
> Descend d'un saut, l'accole avec franchise:
> "J'ai vingt écus, dit-il, dans ma valise;
> C'est tout mon bien; prenez encor mon cœur:
> Tout est à vous. —C'est pour moi trop d'honneur,"
> Lui dit Marton. . . .

(Not far from Paris, at the corner of a wood which borders Charenton, he saw the dashing Marton, with her blond hair bound by a ribbon. Her waist is trim and her little skirt permits a glimpse of her slim white leg. Robert approaches: he finds a face which would tempt the saints in Paradise; a beautiful bouquet of roses and lilies lies between two alabaster apples which none can see without adoring; and the freshness and bloom of her complexion would have dulled the brightness of her bouquet. To speak plainly, the young miracle of beauty was carrying a basket in her arms and, with all her attractions, was on her way to market to sell butter and fresh eggs. Sir Robert, shaken with unholy desire, dismounted at one jump and frankly embraced her. Said he: "I have twenty crowns in my valise; it is my entire fortune; take my heart to boot: the whole is yours." "The honor is too great," Marton replied. . . .)

This passage is from a fairly late narrative in verse: *Ce qui plaît aux dames*. It is composed with great care, as may be inferred from the successive impressions the knight receives of Marton's beauty as he admires it first from afar and then from nearer and nearer. A great part of its charm lies in its tempo. If it were drawn out longer, it would lose its freshness and become trite. And the tempo determines the wit of the piece too. The declaration of love is so comical only because it states the essential data with such astounding brevity. Here as everywhere else, Voltaire's tempo is part of his philosophy. In this instance he uses it to set in sharp relief the essential motives of human actions as he sees them, to unmask them as it were and show their extreme materialism, without ever permitting himself anything crude. This little love scene contains nothing sublime or spiritual, all that comes out in it is physical lust and the profit motive. The declaration of love begins with an unrhetorical statement of the business side of the transaction, and yet it is charming, elegant, and far from pedestrian. Everybody knows—and Robert and Marton are no exception—that the words, *prenez encor mon cœur, tout est à vous*, are nothing but a flourish to express the desire for instantaneous sexual gratification. And yet they have all the charm and bloom which Voltaire and his time inherited from classicism (in this case specifically from La Fontaine)[3] and which he presses into the service of the materialistic Enlightenment. The content has changed completely, but the pleasing clarity, *l'agréable et le fin*, of the classics has remained. It is present in every word, in every phrase, in every rhythmic movement. A specifically Voltairian feature is the swift tempo, which never becomes unaesthetic despite the author's boldness, not to say unscrupulousness, in moral matters and his technique of sophistic surprise attacks. He is completely free from the half-erotic and hence somewhat hazy sentimentality which we have tried to demonstrate in our analysis of the text from *Manon Lescaut*. His unmaskings in the spirit of the Enlightenment are never crude and clumsy; on the contrary they are light, agile, and as it were appetizing. And above all, he is free from the cloudy, contour-blurring, overemotional rhetoric, equally destructive of clear thinking and pure feeling, which came to the fore in the authors of the Enlightenment during the second half of the century and in the literature of the Revolution, which had a still more luxuriant growth in the nineteenth century through the influence of romanticism, and which has continued to produce its loathsome flowers down to our day.

Closely related to rapidity of tempo, but more generally in use as a propaganda device, is the extreme simplification of all problems.

---

3. La Fontaine, who lived in the seventeenth century, is best known for his *Fables*, light, quick, charming poems that seemingly don't take their moralities too seriously [Adams].

In Voltaire's case the rapidity, one feels almost tempted to say the alertness, of the tempo is made to serve the purpose of simplification. This simplification is almost always achieved by reducing the problem to an antithesis which is then exhibited in a giddy, swift, high-spirited narrative in which black and white, theory and practice, etc., are set in clear and simple opposition. We can observe this point in our passage on the London stock exchange, where the contrast business versus religion (the one useful and advancing human cooperation, the other senseless and raising barriers between men) is displayed in a vivid sketch which vigorously simplifies the problem in terms of a partisan approach; with this, and no less simplified, the contrast tolerance versus intolerance appears. Even in the little love story, if not a problem, at least the subject of the occurrence is reduced to a simplified antithetical formula (pleasure versus business). Let us consider yet another example. The novel *Candide* contains a polemic attack upon the metaphysical optimism of Leibnitz's idea of the best of all possible worlds. In chapter 8 of *Candide*, Cunégonde—who was lost and has been found again—begins her relation of the adventures she has undergone since Candide's expulsion from her father's castle:

> J'étais dans mon lit et je dormais profondément, quand il plut au ciel d'envoyer les Bulgares dans notre beau château de Thunder-ten-tronckh; ils égorgèrent mon père et mon frère, et coupèrent ma mère par morceaux. Un grand Bulgare, haut de six pieds, voyant qu'à ce spectacle j'avais perdu connaissance, se mit à me violer; cela me fit revenir, je repris mes sens, je criai, je me débattis, je mordis, j'égratignai, je voulais arracher les yeux à ce grand Bulgare, ne sachant pas que tout ce qui arrivait dans le château de mon père était une chose d'usage: le brutal me donna un coup de couteau dans le flanc gauche dont je porte encore la marque. —Hélas, j'espère bien la voir, dit le naïf Candide. —Vous la verrez, dit Cunégonde; mais continuons. —Continuez, dit Candide.

> (I was in my bed, in a deep sleep, when it pleased Heaven to send the Bulgarians into our fair castle of Thunder-ten-tronckh; they cut my father's throat and my brother's, and chopped my mother to pieces. A huge Bulgarian, six feet tall, observing that I had fainted at the sight, began to rape me; that brought me to, I recovered consciousness, I screamed, I struggled, I bit, I scratched, I tried to tear out the big Bulgarian's eyes, not knowing that everything that was happening in my father's castle was perfectly customary: the brute gave me a knife-thrust in my left side, of which I still bear the scar. "Alas! I hope that I shall see it," said the simple Candide. "You shall

see it," said Cunégonde; "but let us go on." "Go on," said
Candide.)

These dreadful incidents appear comic because they come hammering down with almost slapstick speed and because they are represented as willed by God and everywhere prevalent—which is in
comic contrast to their dreadfulness and to the aims of their victims. On top of all this comes the erotic quip at the end. Antithetical simplification of the problem and its reduction to anecdotal
dimensions, together with dizzying speed of tempo, prevail throughout the novel. Misfortune follows upon misfortune, and again and
again they are interpreted as necessary, proceeding from sound
causes, reasonable, and worthy of the best of all possible worlds—
which is obviously absurd. In this way calm reflection is drowned in
laughter, and the amused reader either never observes, or observes
only with difficulty, that Voltaire in no way does justice to Leibnitz's
argument and in general to the idea of a metaphysical harmony of
the universe, especially since so entertaining a piece as Voltaire's
novel finds many more readers than the difficult essays of his philosophical opponents, which cannot be understood without serious
study. Indeed, even the observation that the supposed reality of experience which Voltaire builds up does not correspond to experience
at all, that it has been artfully adjusted to his polemic purpose, must
have escaped most contemporary readers, or if not, they would
hardly have made much of it. The rhythm of the adventures which
befall Candide and his companions is to be nowhere observed in the
reality of experience. Such a relentless, unrelated torrent of mishaps
pouring down from a clear sky on the heads of perfectly innocent
and unprepared people whom it involves by mere chance, simply
does not exist. It is much more like the mishaps of a comic figure in
a farce or a clown in a circus. Even apart from this excessive con-
centration of mishaps and the fact that in all too many cases they
bear no inner relation whatever to their victims, Voltaire falsifies
reality by an extreme simplification of the causes of events. The
causes of human destinies which appear in his realistic propaganda
pieces for the Enlightenment are either natural phenomena or accidents or—insofar as human behavior is admitted as a cause—the
promptings of instinct, maliciousness, and especially stupidity. He
never pursues historical conditions as determinants of human destinies, convictions, and institutions. This applies both to the history
of individuals and to that of states, religions, and human society in
general. Just as in our first example (the London exchange) Anabap-
tism, Judaism, and Quakerism are made to appear meaningless,
stupid, and accidental, so in *Candide* the wars, troop-levies, religious
persecutions, and the views of the nobility or the clergy are made to

appear equally meaningless, stupid, and accidental. For Voltaire, it is a perfectly self-evident premise that no one in his senses can believe in an inner order of things or an inner justification for views. With equal assurance he assumes as a demonstrated premise that any individual in his personal history may encounter any destiny which is in accordance with the laws of nature, regardless of the possibility of a connection between destiny and character; and he sometimes amuses himself by putting together causal chains in which he explains only the factors which are phenomena of nature and purposely omits anything to do with morals or the history of the individuals concerned. By way of example we may turn to the fourth chapter of *Candide*, where Pangloss discusses the origin of his syphilis:

> . . . vous avez connu Paquette, cette jolie suivante de notre auguste baronne; j'ai goûté dans ses bras les délices du paradis, qui ont produit ces tourmens d'enfer dont vous me voyez dévoré; elle en était infectée, elle en est peut-être morte. Paquette tenait ce présent d'un cordelier très savant, qui avait remonté à la source; car il l'avait eue d'une vieille comtesse, qui l'avait reçue d'un capitaine de cavalerie, qui la devait à une marquise, qui la tenait d'un page, qui l'avait reçue d'un jésuite qui, étant novice, l'avait eue en droite ligne d'un des compagnons de Christophe Colomb. . . .

> (. . . you knew Paquette, our august Baroness's pretty attendant; in her arms I tasted the joys of Paradise which produced the infernal tortures which you see devouring me; she was infected with them; perhaps she has died of them. Paquette had received the gift from a most learned Franciscan, who himself had gone back to the source; for he had got it from an old countess, who had received it from a cavalry captain, who owed it to a marquise, who had it from a page, who had received it from a Jesuit, who, as a novice, had received it in the direct line from one of the companions of Christopher Columbus. . . .)

Such an account, which regards only natural causes, and on the moral plane merely lays a satirical emphasis on the mores of the clergy (including their homosexuality), at the same time merrily whisking out of sight and suppressing all details of the personal history of the individuals concerned, although it is these details which brought about the various love affairs—such an account insinuates a very specific conception of the concatenation of events, in which there is room neither for the individual's responsibility for acts he commits in obedience to his natural instincts nor for anything else in his particular nature or his particular inner and outer development which leads to particular acts. It is not often that Voltaire goes as far as he does in this instance and in *Candide* in general. Basically he is a moralist; and, especially in his historical writings, there are human portraits in which the individuality comes out clearly. But he is always inclined to simplify, and his simplification is always handled in such a way that the role of sole standard of judgment is assigned to sound, practical common sense (the type of enlightened reason which began to come to the fore during his time and under his influence) and that from among the conditions which determine the course of human lives none but the material and natural are given serious consideration. Everything historical and spiritual he despises and neglects. This has to do with the active and courageous spirit with which the protagonists of Enlightenment were filled. They set out to rid human society of everything that impeded the progress of reason. Such impediments were obviously to be seen in the religious, political, and economic actualities which had grown up historically, irrationally, in contradiction to common sense, and had finally become an inextricable maze. What seemed required was not to understand and justify them but to discredit them.

Voltaire arranges reality so that he can use it for his purposes. There is no denying the presence, in many of his works, of colorful, vivid, everyday reality. But it is incomplete, consciously simplified, and hence—despite the serious didactic purpose—nonchalant and superficial. As for the stylistic level, a lowering of man's position is implied in the attitude prevailing in the writings of the Enlightenment, even when they are not as impertinently witty as Voltaire's. The tragic exaltation of the classical hero loses ground from the beginning of the eighteenth century. Tragedy itself becomes more colorful and clever with Voltaire, but it loses weight. But in its stead the intermediate genres, such as the novel and the narrative in verse, begin to flourish, and between tragedy and comedy we now have the intermediate *comédie larmoyante* [sentimental comedy]. The taste of the age does not favor the sublime; it seeks out the graceful, elegant, clever, sentimental, rational, and useful, all of which is more properly intermediate. In its intermediate level the erotic and sentimental style of *Manon Lescaut* coincides with Voltaire's style in propaganda. In both instances the people introduced are no sublime heroes detached from the context of everyday life but individuals embedded in circumstances which are usually intermediate, on which they are dependent, and in which they are enmeshed materially and even spiritually. A certain seriousness in all this cannot be overlooked, not even in Voltaire, who after all takes his ideas perfectly seriously. And so we must conclude that, in contrast to classicism, a mixing of styles now occurs once again. But it does not go far or very deep either in its everyday realism or its seriousness. It continues the aesthetic tradition of classicism inasmuch as its realism remains always pleasant. Tragic and creatural penetration and historical involvement are avoided. The realistic elements, however colorful and amusing they may be, remain mere froth. With Voltaire the pleasantness and frothiness of the realism, which is present only to serve the ends of Enlightenment ideology, have developed into such an art that he is able to use even the "creatural" premonitions of his own decrepitude and death, which come to him during his last years, as material for an amiably jocular introduction to a popular philosophical disquisition. In this connection I will cite an example which has already been analyzed by L. Spitzer (*Romanische Stil- und Literaturstudien*, Marburg, 1931, 2, 238ff.). It is a letter which the gaunt seventy-six-year old patriarch with the fleshless mask, whom everybody remembers, wrote to Mme Necker[4] when the sculptor Pigalle had come to Ferney to do a bust of him. It reads:

A Madame Necker.
Ferney, 19 juin 1770
Quand les gens de mon village ont vu Pigalle déployer quelques instruments de son art: Tiens, tiens, disaient-ils, on va le disséquer; cela sera drôle. C'est ainsi, madame, vous le savez, que tout spectacle amuse les hommes; on va également aux marionnettes, au feu de la Saint-Jean, à l'Opéra-Comique, à la grand'messe, à un enterrement. Ma statue fera sourire quelques philosophes, et renfrognera les sourcils éprouvés de quelque coquin d'hypocrite ou de quelque polisson de folliculaire: vanité des vanités!

Mais tout n'est pas vanité; ma tendre reconnaissance pour mes amis et surtout pour vous, madame, n'est pas vanité.

Mille tendres obéissances à M. Necker.

(When the people of my village saw Pigalle lay out some of the instruments of his art: "Why, look," said they, "he's going to be dissected; that will be curious." So it is, Madame, as you well know, that any spectacle amuses mankind; people go indifferently to a marionette-show, to a Midsummer Eve bonfire, to high mass, to a funeral. My statue will make a few philosophers smile, and knit the practiced brows of some villainous hypocrite or some depraved hack: vanity of vanities! But all is not vanity; my fond gratitude for my friends and above all for you, Madame, is not vanity. A thousand fond homages to Monsieur Necker.)

4. This is the married name of Suzanne Curchod, wife of the financier Jacques Necker and mother of the woman of letters Mme de Staël [Cronk].

I refer the reader to Spitzer's excellent analysis, which pursues and interprets every shade of expression throughout the text, and shall limit myself to adding or summarizing what is essential for the problem of style here under discussion. The realistic anecdote which serves as point of departure is either invented or at least rearranged for the purpose. It is not at all likely that peasants about the year 1770 should have been more familiar with anatomical dissection than with the sculptor's craft. Who Pigalle was must have been widely discussed; and that portraits should be made of the famous châtelain who had lived among them for a decade must have seemed more natural to them than the idea of dissecting a person who had quite recently still been seen alive. That some half-educated wit among them could have made a remark of this sort is of course not entirely impossible, but I imagine most readers confronted with this question will find it much more probable that Voltaire himself was the wit. However that may be, whether he arranged the setting himself (as I suppose he did) or whether chance supplied him with it exactly as he describes it, in either case, it is an extraordinary, much too pat, theatrical piece of reality, admirably and exclusively suited to what he appends to it: the trite bit of worldly wisdom, charmingly and amiably presented, the fireworks display of examples in which the sacred and profane are mixed together with the characteristic impertinence of the Enlightenment, the irony in regard to his own fame, the polemic allusions to his enemies, the summing up of the whole in the basic theme from Solomon,[5] and finally the recourse to the word *vanité* to find the turn of expression which concludes the letter and which radiates all the charm of the still amiable and still lively old man, all the charm of the entire century in the formation of which he played so prominent a part. The whole thing is, as Spitzer puts it, a unique phenomenon, the *billet* of the Rococo Enlightenment. It is so much the more unique in that the texture of worldly wisdom and amiable wit is here linked to an anecdote which conjures up the creaturality of the old man's decrepit body, but a step from the grave. Yet even with such a subject Voltaire remains witty and pleasing. How many different elements this text contains: there is the artfully arranged realism; there is the perfection of charm in social relations, which combine great warmth of expression with a high degree of reserve; there is the superficiality of a creatural self-confrontation which is at the same time the exalted amiability which refuses to let one's own somber emotions become a burden to anyone else; there is the didactic ethos which characterized the great men of the Enlightenment and which made them able to use their last breath to formulate some new idea wittily and pleasingly.

---

5. The basic theme of the book of Ecclesiastes, supposed to be written by King Solomon, is "Vanity of vanities! All is vanity!" [Adams].

JEAN STAROBINSKI

On *Candide*'s Philosophical Style[†]

A narrative? Most certainly. But more than that, it is the simulation—a parody, a pale reflection—of a narrative. In *Candide*, the fictional is a caricature of the fictional, an exaggerated version that mixes up generic conventions, be they of the adventure story (of Hellenistic origin), the picaresque novel, or—most susceptible of all to the implausible—the fairy tale. If asked to pin down *Candide*'s literary genealogy, we would identify the tradition originating with Lucian and Petronius, and continuing with Rabelais and Cyrano de Bergerac. Events in *Candide*, especially in the way one follows on from another, fly in the face of probability; their random nature makes it clear that they are not trying to persuade readers, they are leaving them free. Announced deaths, unexpected meetings, accelerated turns of plot, fabulous lands, undreamed-of riches— everything indicates that we should not pay serious heed to the story itself; everything refers to literary commonplaces that one by one are deformed through mockery into a parable whose moral is that we should mistrust all morals.

So is this just a game? For sure. But a game of parody in which all the situations described reflect present reality: war, massacre, rape are taking place in Germany; heretics are being burned in Portugal; American savages eat their captives; and in Paris gamblers cheat and prostitutes rob unwary travelers. Candide is, in many respects, no more than a cover name, the minimal identity necessary for a person whose essential function is to encounter, and so reveal, the world as it is.

The hallmark of *Candide* is the multifaceted, the potpourri: this applies not just to the kaleidoscopic succession of episodes, but also to the mix of self-reflective fiction and unavoidable truth, to the unstable combination of the arbitrariness of the narrative and the intrusion into it of a climate of violence. The freedom of the story line goes hand in hand with obsessive, omnipresent evil. Wherever the individual turns, all freedom is crushed by ludicrous violence. *Candide*'s journey, by virtue of its implausible speed, reviews all the countries of the globe; this economy of narrative time ensures movement from one place to another, and makes possible multiple

† Originally published in French, "Sur le style philosophique de *Candide*," in *Comparative Literature* 28 (1976), pp. 193–200. This translation, by Nicholas Cronk, is based on the slightly revised version that appeared in *Le Remède dans le mal* (Paris: Gallimard, 1989), pp. 123–44. © Editions Gallimard, Paris, 1983, 1989. Reprinted by permission of Georges Borchardt, Inc., for Editions Gallimard.

experiences of foolishness, intolerance, and the abuse of power.
The narrative's lack of realism permits journeys of every kind and
allows horrifying realities to be described without their ever seeming
doubtful or merely the result of authorial fantasy.

Through the systematic use of mockery, and thanks to the
invulnerability of a hero who narrowly escapes all dangers, Voltaire is able to multiply evocations of the most appalling abuses,
all in the service of a strategy of repeated denunciation. Voltaire's
writing progresses by means of cuts, ellipses, litotes—all forms of
subtraction—whereas the expression of indignant emotion would
have inflated the sentences, drawn out the complaints, taken up time
for the "truth" of feeling to express itself. The time for feeling is thus
cut short, and emotional impact is intensified. By playing deliberately off-key, Voltaire avoids the perils of overdone sentiment and
failed eloquence. The evil of the world stands out all the more clearly
and tenaciously in a dessicated atmosphere that leaves no room for
feeling or consolation. Nothing atrocious is made up in *Candide*;
Voltaire gives us a documentary account, admittedly somewhat simplified and stylized, but an anthology of atrocities that any educated
European could have found in the newspapers. In *Candide*, we
experience, perhaps for the first time in fictional form, that attitude
which improved means of communication have today made common in the West: the sense that a nervous system extending across
the face of the Earth allows us to suffer all the woes of humanity.
Voltaire shivers at the world's suffering; he knows, or thinks he
knows, all the authors of injustice, all the parties making unjust
demands: he details them, confronts them, and opposes them. He
is too intelligent to denounce only the wrongs on one side; he sees
the same crimes being committed by rival princes, by opposed
churches, by "civilized" and "savage" peoples.

The sinuous line, with its suggestion of surprise and caprice, is one
of the hallmarks of rococo taste, and the journeys of Candide, of
the old woman, and of Cunégonde clearly trace such a line on the
map of the world: chance, desire, persecution all provoke endless
detours, to the point where nothing seems like a detour and no particular direction seems privileged. Fully present here too—another
aspect of the rococo—is an appetite for the new and the piquant.

Play, parody, satire, the denunciation of violence in the modern
world, philosophical enquiry: together these form not just a compos-
ite work, but a text *without precedent*, a text seeking a purely
polemical relationship with its predecessors. Through its diversity, through the unexpected and scabrous nature of the adventures, through the unforeseen itinerary, through the succession of
surprises, through the efficient brevity of each episode, *Candide*

brings together all the causes of the piquant, to produce the supreme stimulus of novelty. The visit to Pococurante's library (chapter 25) reviews the models of the past, encompassing the literary world in its entirety: the disabused amateur speaks of all this with disdain. Literature seems to have come to an end, and *Candide* is the supplementary volume that catalogues the past and follows on from the catalogue. This is a book beyond literature, beyond philosophy, that mocks literature and philosophy, and that in its turn can of course do nothing but propose a different literature, a different philosophy. "It's a great pleasure," says Cacambo, "to see and do new things" (chapter 14).

Yet it is not difficult to assimilate *Candide* to an age-old type: that of clownish narration or pantomime deploying enormous virtuosity to conjure up its very opposite, misfortune and clumsiness.

There is no need to insist here, in the wake of so many other critics, on the gaiety of this light and weightless writing, nor on the stylistic agility—with its supreme command of repetition, contrast, and ellipsis—that can manipulate at will the beat of the sentence to create or disrupt effects of balance. This mastery, which does so little to hide itself and which shows its own mechanism so openly, does not of itself generate comic effect; it becomes comic, in taking nonmastery as its subject—that is to say, the story of a boy without malice who is unable to control what happens to him and who runs from one misfortune to another. His adventures, like those of so many clowns, begin with kicks in the backside: we laugh, while he weeps, sighs, and despairs.

The writing of the narration is supremely active; it calculates and governs all its effects; and one of its principal effects is to represent its contrary, in dedicating Candide, almost until the very end of his adventures, to passivity[1] and astonishment. Candide—who, at the start, is dependent on others to speak and act—sees his words and deeds have disproportionate consequences: he is constantly transported further than he could have hoped or expected. With sly malice, the narrator allows us to witness the misadventures of a character easily duped who has no control over his own destiny—except in the final moment, which seems to inaugurate a period of stable activity. It's the same, on stage or at the circus, with the character who suffers an avalanche of failures, regulated like ballet steps, always concluding with a spectacular reversal. The spectator feels delightful dizziness in observing such technical wizardry used to mimic a victim's fate.[2]

---

1. On the theme of passivity, see the pertinent remarks of Christopher Thacker in the introduction to his critical edition of *Candide* (Geneva, 1968), p.10ff.
2. Literary and pictoral aspects of this theme are explored in J. Starobinski, *Portrait de l'artiste en saltimbanque* (Geneva, Skira, 1970; Paris, Gallimard, 2004).

To be precise, this is a destiny where desire misses and loses its object only to recover it degraded, forever different from the image that had been kept alive. For if, after the visit to Eldorado, Candide avoids vexation, he remains fundamentally frustrated; he misses Cunégonde and dreams only of finding her again. And when he does finally find her, it is to discover that she is so ugly that he reels back "three steps in horror." A Gilles or a Pierrot is frustrated in the same way: everything conspires to deprive them of what they think they are on the point of possessing: they remain empty-handed, their hearts heavy. Candide's only memory of the first paradise in Westphalia is of a furtive caress behind a screen (a caress, it should be remembered, initiated by Cunégonde). This "appetizing" fruit, offered without resistance, will be defended as it passes through the most brutal hands: violated, stabbed, sold, pimped, humiliated, profaned in every way possible, Cunégonde, before being bought back by Candide, will find her flesh marked by all the stigmata of "physical" and "moral" evil, the sign of an evil world and the mark of the destructive passage of time. The feminine being whom Voltaire makes the cause of all Candide's peregrinations—expulsion, wandering, quest—is no more than the lure of freshness and youth, qualities liable to deteriorate: desirable only as long as she is missed and because she is missed, once she is found again, Cunégonde is no more than an ugly shrew with whom life would be intolerable were it not for the garden to be cultivated, the productive refuge of hard work. Candide is tricked by love: foremost among the ideals that the narrative is determined to destroy is the myth of passion. Candide is the object of an experiment: he is motivated by an illusion that vanishes at precisely the moment that the loved one ceases to be an image and a name and appears as a "real" person. The comedy derives from the fact that this final possession, so long deferred, is doubly disappointing.

An author who is clairvoyant, omniscient, and free; a hero who is naïve, clumsy, deluded, and under the sway of violent men: this relationship between author and hero is grounded on irony. It is marked from the start by frequent recourse to what classical rhetoric narrowly defines as *irony*—that is, destructive antiphrasis, the use of words to say the opposite of what they mean: "a *beautiful* auto-da-fé."

What is the function of irony here? Its purpose is not to give the author (and the reader) an easy victory over an ignorant, narrow-minded hero. Nor is it to exalt, from the author's perspective, a sense of freedom rising above finite reality—Voltaire does not aspire to that disengaged liberty with which, in Romantic irony, the spirit defines its separate realm. Irony in *Candide* works like an offensive weapon: it faces outward and spearheads the fight of reason against everything that usurps the authority that should properly belong to rational thought alone.

Usurped authority: this is how theological discourse, and its successor, metaphysical discourse, are made to appear, once the gap between the world as it is and the world of Optimistic theodicy has become clear. A critique of the contemporary world, *Candide* is also just as much a critique of the abstract assertions that smug theorists make about the world. In their singularity and relentlessness, the events of the journey inflict one defeat after another on Pangloss's teaching. It's hardly necessary to give voice to the opposing philosophies, those of the Anabaptist Jacques and of Martin the Manichean. Facts are responsible for Candide's education, and the result is seen in the contrast between the first chapter, in which Candide gives his master a respectful hearing, and the last, in which he cuts him off. The irony of Voltaire's narrative endorses the way the facts of the world give the lie to the euphoria of systems. The "point" and "shaft" of ironic diction joyously give succour to the cruelty of the real and confer on it a hyperbolic ferocity: refutations are conducted with the selfsame energy as the evil violence that Voltaire simultaneously condemns. All the affirmations of ultimate perfection are undercut, literally in human flesh, with mutilations, castrations, and amputations. Pangloss loses an eye and an ear, the old woman a buttock, and so forth. The devastation caused by illness, war, and inquisition is told with a narrative verve expressing delight in the destruction of the Optimist illusion: the characters' bodies are subject to savage wounds, defects, and unreasoning brutality, and in its very style (what we have called a style of subtraction), *Candide* mimics the physical diminution that evil inflicts on whole human beings, and thus it mimics the world's response to Optimism's proposed solution. Against a metaphysical view postulating the eternal presence of an all-embracing view of the universe (poorly grasped by us), Voltaire imagines a reason that discerns inadequacy everywhere, and that, by this very fault, by this scandalous absence of sense, finds the spur for militancy.

But after identifying with the ferocity of the world to refute preconceived systems, irony then turns against violence and injustice. Despite the dizzying speed with which he demonstrates the victory of smallpox, tempests, Bulgarian heroes, black pirates, and inquisitors over the articles of faith of Leibnizianism, Voltaire is scandalized by the suffering inflicted. Despite the hint of Sadism detectable in the way he trumpets the victory of cruelty and intolerance, he does not share Sade's belief that evil in all its forms is the expression of the natural order—put simply, he does not believe that natural law should be hailed as benevolent. The determinism that produces gallstones, smallpox, and earthquakes shows that Nature has no care for humanity. In addition to the unavoidable evils that must be painfully endured, there are the superfluous evils that people inflict on one another: how can these be described without revulsion? Voltaire cannot accept the miseries that he so joyously allows to rain down on his characters' heads.

The irony is redoubled, the sharpness of the response reinforced. Having given free rein to the images of evil to counter Optimist dogma, Voltaire opposes evil because he hates injustice and fanaticism. Voltaire's style—generally described as "witty," "incisive," "sarcastic"—owes its specific character to this double aggressive charge. Most of the events narrated in *Candide* are *bivalent*: they joyously demonstrate the inanity of Pangloss's system; but once they have fulfilled their polemical purpose, they instantly become unbearable. These events that decry the Optimist illusion are in their turn decried on account of their violence. They belong to that category of events that invariably make Voltaire "shiver with horror" (the expression is frequent in his correspondence and his historical writings). The "grinding" that Flaubert rightly discerns in Voltaire is precisely the effect caused by the coincidence of this polemical verve with a shiver of horror; it is due to the fact that each of the "realities" that intrude to destroy Pangloss's pronouncements is made in turn the object of a pitiless critique. The atrocious event designed to deny the preceding dogma becomes in its turn the object of moral, aesthetic, and emotional repudiation.

To deploy effects such as these, the act of writing must have been granted the privilege of *last resort*. Voltairean mockery presupposes hindsight: experience has run its course, and we know the final outcome. The game is played out, and irony reflects retrospectively on the world. Looked back on, Pangloss's first speech is already absurd; as it is told to us, it is already marked by the superior mockery and wisdom resulting from the damage inflicted by reality on metaphysics and then on reality by the demands of practical reason. Think of the role played in *Candide*, after so many ups and downs, by the reflective responses of the hero and his comrades. Such commentaries, taken separately from the narrative, are described in rhetoric as *epiphenomena*. Their function is to express a maxim of general import, suggesting self-assured knowledge, as the culmination of a sequence of *individual* events or feelings. We should not hesitate to use this apparently erudite term: the epiphenomenon is a final declaration that distils a lesson and condenses it into a maxim or "moral." Whenever this figure of style occurs, we know there is at work a faculty of judgment and a power of reason that can keep distant and operate on a general level. Candide's final exclamation—"but we must cultivate our garden"—despite its connection to the particular situation (the farm on the Bosphorus) confers on the entire narrative an epiphenomenal conclusion—a "wise" conclusion, of universal bearing, confirming what was said to the hero in the very first lines ("he had fairly clear judgement . . ."), after his trials and tribulations had equally confirmed the subsequent phrase (". . . with the most simple mind"). Irony then works retrospectively, according to the process of learning we have undergone by the end: the wanderings and illusions of the naïve adventurer are narrated from the stand-point of stability and security guaranteed by the final conversion to gainful employment. We know with hindsight (but Voltaire knows *already* when he takes up his pen) that, despite all the losses, disappointments, mutilations, and so forth, work remains always as a safe resource. Moreover, the assessment of the epiphenomenon and of retrospective irony in the text of *Candide* can be fully reapplied to characterize the function of *Candide* in Voltaire's existence. After the death of Mme Du Châtelet (whose philosophical doctrine inclined towards Wolffian or Panglossian Optimism), after the Prussian episode and the arrest in Frankfurt, after the search for a place of exile and the purchase of properties in Geneva and Lausanne, *Candide* has the status of a summary entertainment. In a single breath, an idea is narrated, travestied, caricatured, and expressed; Voltaire thus delivers himself of the past by means of a comic performance that transforms it into fiction.[3] But the duties and satisfactions of the landowner on the shores of Lake Geneva, i.e. the Bosphorus, are anything but fiction. These represent belatedly won wisdom, a guide to conduct that reliably distinguishes between truth and falsehood, the illusory and the solid. *Candide* is the epilogue, the sententious lesson, the stylized profession of faith of practical wisdom belatedly discovered. The transposition of personal disasters into tragicomic fiction is part of true wisdom and leaves the way clear for productive activity.

In all that happens to Candide, we see at work a displacement of authority that from one episode to another carries the whole movement of the narrative. Authority is affirmed, then questioned, then reaffirmed in a different way, then questioned again, and so on. This is the overarching dynamic of the tale in its most abstract formulation. Any interpretation must necessarily refer to the concept of authority if it is to capture not just the style of *Candide* but what is at stake in the work.

3. On the movement of the narration, see Geoffrey Murray, *Voltaire's Candide: The Protean Gardener, 1755–1762.*

In the beginning, in the closed universe of the tiny Westphalian province, the hero is clear about authority: it resides in the head of the household, in the aristocratic hierarchy, in Pangloss's philosophical system, which affirms that the world has a sense and that humanity is the beneficiary. To start with, Panglossian metaphysics is all of a piece with the status quo, in that it justifies and reinforces the master's authority. But immediately the malice of the narrator, who has a broader view, undermines this ostensible authority. Candide, as a bastard, is living proof of the challenges that love poses to aristocratic requirements. By the fact of his birth, Candide embodies the fragility of the established order: the quarter of nobility that he lacks is a lacuna from birth, a gap at the heart of the system. The narrator thereby denounces the verbal artifice by which the baron's rural household pretends to the status of a real court: a shift of substantives turns "barnyard mutts" into a "pack of hunters," "stable-boys" into "huntsmen," and a "country vicar" into a "chaplain." Similarly, by crediting Panglossian learning with the suffix *nigologie*,[4] Voltaire instantly devalues it with the ringing endorsement of his scorn. The tutor's lecture, supposedly celebrating the transparent order of the world, is pronounced with chronic lack of logic; in the very moment that it is given, its intellectual authority is undermined (for anyone who knows how to read). But as for Candide, he is full of admiration.

The kiss behind the screen is an allegory of the sly intrusion of what is traditional authority's stubborn rival: feeling, desire. Cunégonde is prepared to repeat with her cousin the transgression to which he owes his birth. After a momentary eclipse of authority, a few kicks and slaps quickly restore order—in what is also the first manifestation of violence. But at this level, minor potentates and minuscule states are not guaranteed to keep the upper hand. Noble titles and the vestiges of the old military order cannot hold out against the princes with larger numbers of crack troops. At the heart of a world governed by a single principle of political authority, princely sovereignty and military might play a decisive role: and so the province, the castle, the baron, whom in his naïvety and gullibility Candide took to be absolutes, are all quickly relativized. The facts—ruins and massacres—stand as sufficient proof. If nothing in existence lacks *sufficient reason*, whosoever controls the biggest army has sufficient reason on his side. Power can quickly change hands. The resort to force triggers a "chain of events" whose end is uncertain. Voltaire enjoys delivering up the violent to violence, letting tyrants perish at

---

4. *Nigaud* is French for "fool," hence the undermining comic effect [Cronk].

the hands of rival tyrants or in a victorious rebellion. The baron who chases out Candide vanishes in the disasters of war, the Bulgarian who rapes Cunégonde is instantly killed by his captain, the kidnappers of Urban X's daughter are slaughtered by a rival faction, the Grand Inquisitor who holds Cunégonde and who has had Pangloss hanged is killed by Candide, the Dutchman who stole from Candide is sent to the bottom of the sea, and so on. These are so many twists of fate that are too sporadic, too unexpected to suggest a sense of immanent justice: violence is not confined to the violent, and innocents perish while thugs go unpunished. Worse still, those characters who are sincere and good, such as Candide, find themselves helplessly sucked into the whirlpool of violence. It's not easy to find one's bearings, and in this game of slaughter, effective power is never held for long; as we watch the demise of the baron, the Grand Inquisitor, the Reverend Father Commandant, the English admiral, one after another, the narrative acquires a sense of generalized destitution, affecting not only those holding civil and religious authority, but authority itself, the very principle that gives legitimacy to the exercise of power. Neither the Church nor even the monarchy emerges unscathed; when Candide is passing through Paris, there has just been an attempt on the life of the king, and all foreigners are arrested. Except in Eldorado, no representative of supreme power is exempt from danger: in Venice, the dinner of the dethroned kings, with its remarkable comic repetition, epitomizes this frenzy of lèse-majesté. It is clear that the target here is not just the vanities of greatness and the caprices of fate, but rather the ultimate impotence reserved for those who have held, or have hoped to hold, sovereign authority. One does not have to be an authority in psychoanalysis to notice that throughout *Candide*, Voltaire is determined to inflict subtly calculated humiliation on the image of the father, multiplied indefinitely: what satisfaction, what revenge, when one can poke fun at "his miserable Highness"! It wouldn't be difficult to discern a similar attack, but this time on literary authority, in Pococurante's assessments of the great writers: no matter that this profanation comes from a tired dilettante, it has the effect of depreciation, of denying traditional approbation, of amputating—more mutilation!—celebrated works by criticizing their weak parts.

When the young baron, the last representative of restrictive authority, is finally sent back to the galleys, the position is clear. No haughty inquisitors or reverend fathers are left in the Propontis. The survivors are foreigners who possess a "small farm": political power, far distant, seemingly respects ownership of property and is disinclined to intervene officiously. Where is authority now? Is it reduced to this nonintervention, to this spirit of laissez-faire that benefits all those who don't come too close to the Court? After their trials, have

Candide and his friends simply found the place where they are beyond the reach of authority? Or will they themselves instigate a new authority, different from the one that had oppressed them, that they had tested, and that they found sometimes laughable, sometimes tyrannical, and sometimes laughable and tyrannical both at the same time?

Let's reconsider the problem from a philosophical angle. The question we began with concerned the harmony of the universe, the finality discernable in all things. Optimism consists not just in affirming that we must discern that finality, but that discerning it is our first duty. The debate about theodicy assumes that humanity gives priority to the search for contemplative knowledge, to the effort of capturing meaning: it is necessary to understand the world and to recognize its order. The Optimist response believes it has attained this goal. There is no more to be *done*. The question of theodicy is interesting only if, as an ancient injunction has it, humanity finds happiness in *theoria*, in the contemplative apprehension of meaning. According to the Panglossian principle, authority then resides in the reason inherent in the world itself, and in its unfolding of the whole sequence of events. Absolute will, intelligence, power (those of God, of whom Pangloss hardly speaks, but who is always implied in his arguments) have chosen for the universe ultimate perfection; humanity's task is not to intervene in the course of events (Pangloss only interprets them), but to decipher the course of meaning as it emerges, includng its accompanying evils. Before it can be resisted, evil has to be understood as one of the transitory means that a just Creator requires to achieve his ends: the general good, and, looking forward, universal happiness. Panglossian Optimism is inclined to overlook Leibniz's argument against "idle sophistry."

The method of Voltairean critique consists in cutting out of the chain of putative causes everything that is not accessible to the *candid* eye: divine origins and harmonious finality. Voltaire's polemical technique denounces as fanciful every wish to return to a first cause, and every presumption to pontificate on final causes. To pretend that one can assign a place to every event in some divine plan is idle banter, and the perfection of the universe is no more than a consoling deception, deaf to contrary arguments, at odds with the "fact of reality."

The story of Candide unfolds in brief episodes based on immediate cause and effect, the exact opposite of the interminable causal chains invoked by Pangloss. Following an assumption of radical empiricism that refuses to make conjectures about what cannot be observed, only the immediate cause and its subsequent effect are considered here. Sufficient reason is in this way reduced to mere efficient causality. Voltaire deliberately exaggerates this restriction on causality: his strategy is to isolate the event, detaching it from the context that would have given it meaning, to make it exist for itself alone. The absurdity leaps out at us. An example would be the chapter of the battle. What are the political aims of the Abar and Bulgarian kings? Voltaire intentionally says nothing about them: the omission of distant causes and of the aims of the war leaves only the *fact* of the war: the murderous acts, the weapons, the corpses. The war seems all the more appalling because it is conducted literally for no reason. Only the mechanisms and the arithmetic of combat survive: "The cannons first killed about six thousand men on each side. . . .' We certainly have cause and effect here: the instrumental cause and the murderous effect; but we remain spectators of "quivering limbs," and all "profound reason" is lacking. We have observed only a single day of battle. (It was not like this in the *Poème de Fontenoy*, when Voltaire spoke as the official eulogist of the king and his victory; that battle was justified by high political purpose: the victorious king "will pacify Europe, will bring calm to the Empire.") What revolts Voltaire most is the way in which people excuse the illogicality and brutality of their actions by attributing them to a Providence overseeing the destiny of humankind: the battle (the effect of short-term causality) is an absurdity, but the two kings have the *Te Deum* sung, as if the event formed part of the long-term causality of some divine plan. When religion sanctions absurdity, Voltaire's fury knows no bounds.

Voltaire has sporadic recourse to the terminology of systematic philosophy in order to underline the critical impact of fragmented causal links. He introduces these terms into the narrative to test them against specific reality. Concepts such as "physical experiment," "effects and causes," "sufficient reason," "best of worlds," taken out of context, detached from their system and trivialized, can only shrivel: their incongruity in this new context disqualifies them entirely. They are henceforth fundamentally inadequate, void of authority. The infinite chain of being, the "great chain of beings and events," simply does not exist. To put it more precisely: this hierarchy expands by sprouting new branches, and these curtailed branches and sterile boughs are numerous and unpredictable. Everything is not therefore the cause of everything else. It suffices to look at the entry "Chain of Events" in the *Philosophical Dictionary*, where Voltaire sets out his arguments very clearly:

> Let's get this straight: every effect obviously has its cause, going back from cause to cause in the abyss of eternity, but not every cause has its effect, down to the very end of time. I freely admit

that each event is produced by the next, and that if the present is born of the past, the present in turn gives birth to the future; all things have progenitors, but all things do not necessarily have progeny. Here it's just the same as in genealogy: every family tree goes back to Adam, as we know, but in every family there are always people who die without issue.[5]

The causal cul-de-sac, whereby many events remain without consequences, deprives them of all real function and prevents us from invoking them as necessary links to a "future good."

In the end what dominates in *Candide* is not the chain, but the procession of events, in which miseries and absurdities occur totally at random: the genealogy of smallpox or the list of assassinated kings are jumbled sequences, in which moral and physical evil goes on repeating itself in a never-ending sterile cycle. Pangloss, who would like to justify providence, just maunders on. One of the last images of a procession occurs in the final chapter, when ships sail constantly back and forth before Candide's eyes, bringing the disgraced Effendis, Bachas, Cadis, severed heads, and so on. In a ludicrous chain and a nonsensical rhythm, tyrannical arbitrariness is repeated indefinitely. Faced by this spectacle ("there is a dreadful lot of evil on earth"), the last representative of religious authority, the Dervish, falls silent; he enjoins the manifestation of the System, in the person of Pangloss, to hold his tongue. The last external authority abdicates, or at least renounces the attempt to interpret God's will. From that moment, God retreats into an unfathomable distance, and humanity is left to itself, alone, without the comfort of universal order, exposed to "convulsions of anxiety" or the "lethargy of boredom." The world is no longer governed by Reason: we see at work an unbenevolent law that determines the regularity of natural effects. What remains? It remains to *know* this merciless law, not so as to celebrate it meekly, but to take control, as Bacon advises, by obeying it. Individuals, restricted to their space and confined to their garden, discover in themselves and by the quantifiable results of their productive efforts, the new authority that will take the place left vacant by the old authority. "The small farm yielded a great deal." When Martin exclaims, "Let's work without reasoning," he is formulating the cry of the new human order, which is closely linked to the (unreasonable) refusal of reason that had previously sought to construct an acceptable image of the universe. Authority, henceforth, is not to be found outside of humanity; it is reduced to this "Let's work without reasoning," which gives absolute primacy to the

5. Voltaire, *A Pocket Philosophical Dictionary*, trans. John Fletcher, Oxford World's Classics (Oxford University Press, 2011), p.56 [Cronk].

activity of labor. There is no longer an order to contemplate, only land to work.

Is this simply about the symbolic advent of the bourgeois ethic of work and productivity? Things are less simple than contemporary literary sociology would have us believe. In Candide's formulation of the imperative to work, we can still recognize one of the great precepts of Christian moralists preaching to cure the boredom of cloistered monks: manual activity is essential to those who experience *acedia*, the *taedium vitae*; and this is precisely the psychological state of the survivors on Turkish soil: "When we were not arguing, the boredom was unbearable. . . ." Work, at the end of *Candide*, is a psychological remedy.

It is also at the same time a response to an economic necessity. Voltaire has fun, by first making Candide extremely poor (when he leaves his first "paradise"), then extremely rich (when he leaves Eldorado). Candide has lost all his treasure, partly through people's dishonesty and partly through his own generosity, when he buys nearly all his companions out of slavery. There comes a moment when the reserves of "yellow mud" and of the pebbles gathered so easily are exhausted. Life must go on.

In extreme poverty, Candide had observed that all was not for the best on Earth; when he has become excessively rich, he begins to ask a different question: Who is happy? How can we be happy? For money, without Cunégonde, brings no happiness. And Cunégonde, belatedly recovered, does not bring happiness either. Work, in the final resort, masks the absence of happiness, and brings in its place other benefits—less precious, no doubt, but preserving us from a void: "Cunégone was in truth very ugly; but she became an excellent *pâtissière*."

A more exact way of describing this *transfer of authority* would be to note how, in *Candide*, the emphasis first placed on the question of the world's *order* is displaced finally to the question of humanity's happiness. Through the link that Voltaire establishes between happiness and work, he is already sketching in outline the lesson that Goethe will propose in *Faust*, Part Two. The new age that is dawning is not properly characterized by the currently fashionable term *bourgeoisie*: we are in fact witnessing the emergence and triumph of the moment when humanity, no longer the admiring spectator of an all-encompassing universe, makes itself the creator of its own world, a world that is partial, specific, and provisional.

But there is nothing yet to anticipate the Industrial Revolution and the technological domination of nature. What Voltaire draws in miniature is an agrarian society deriving the essential part of its income from the land, supplemented by the modest luxury of embroidery. But is it in fact a *society* at all? Have we not here rather an example

of withdrawal into private life? The group around Candide form neither a state nor even a family. They are at most a tiny enclave in a
world given over to evil; a refuge, a place of asylum (as they said at
the time) for a group of cripples whom chance and misfortune have
brought together. None of the farm's residents is a native of the place;
they reconstitute a miniature homeland in a place where they can
lead a better life—and they can lead a better life when they are not
dependent on either religious or political power. It's important to
note that the group of exiles is cosmopolitan: in addition to the West-
phalians (Candide, Cunégonde, Pangloss, Paquette), there are the
Italians (the old woman, brother Giroflée), a Dutchman, more or less
(Martin), and the Metis Cacambo. This group would come close to
being a symbol of all humanity, were it not for the individual nuances
of skin color and opinion that Voltaire holds precious and that he
will always want to preserve in all his calls for toleration. The group
is marginal, so small that it can dispense with the problem of political organisation. Voltaire's evocation of productive labor checks any
thoughts of utopia. This small society is in no way a model. "The
small farm yielded a great deal." That is all. It's very little, some will
say. Voltaire does not need more. (As for Rousseau, he offers far
greater emotional and social riches with the image of Clarens in *La
Nouvelle Héloïse*.) Voltaire has kept his variations on the theme of
utopia for the kingdom of Eldorado, suggesting perhaps that the best
of political organizations is conceivable only as the attribute of a
nonexistent place. In the Propontis, at the end of this unsatisfying
odyssey, we are far from absolute perfection. We have a bastard, surrounded by a prostitute, a renegade priest, a pox-ridden pedant, an
ugly and abused young baroness, and a half-breed valet—impure
guilty beings, in short, seemingly scarred by moral conventions—
who take charge of their destiny and who, by what they undertake,
by what they make with their hands, seek in the final resort to
become less unhappy. They manage an accommodation that can
never quite compensate for life's wear and tear. A political reading
of *Candide* should ask if the small territory of the farm is more likely
to endure than the tiny barony—the pocket-sized Eden swept away
by violence at the beginning of the narrative. At a time when small
feudal lands have been swallowed up in the conflicts of the nation-
states, what do we make of the fate of a private domain in a despotic
state? Does even this compromise have a future? Voltaire perhaps
wants to make us feel the fragility and *eccentricity* inherent in any
semblance of regained stability.

We should not reason excessively about a text that warns us precisely against excessive reasoning. We can think about *Candide* as
a parable. But this book is only a parable in its general outline and
in some of the questions and maxims that punctuate it. The caprice

and even *folly* that flourish all around are not without a hidden link to the central message. How, for example, are we to interpret the paired figures, the ballet of minor characters who enter and exit *in twos*? This game of pairs is repeated indefinitely: two recruiting officers, two rival kings (the Abar and the Bulgarian), the servant of the Inquisition and his attendant, the Grand Inquisitor and Don Issachar, Cunégonde and the old woman, the two girls pursued by two monkeys, Giroflée and Paquette, the two girls in the service of Pococurante, the young baron chained next to Pangloss, the two sons and the two daughters of the good old man, and so on. This is only a summary list of these *simultaneous* dualities. We can identify other dualities that occur in rapid succession: the Protestant preacher followed by good Jacques; the Spanish kingdom, then the Jesuit kingdom; the Parisian experience, then the English experience; the dervish, then the good old man. . . . These games of pairs allow Voltaire to fall back sometimes on the comic effects of *symmetry* (when dealing with the companions), sometimes on the troubling effects of *disparity* (when dealing with more important characters and when there is a succession of episodes). Disparity, contrast, difference, all arranged as paired figures, bring to the fore the image of a world irregular in its regularity (we think of Pangloss's one eye, the old woman's single buttock), dedicated to the law of geometry while also denying it. Nothing is organized; nothing matches the harmonious *pattern* spoken of by the metaphysicians and theologians. To make the point, Voltaire must resort to excess, even frenzy: the Grand Inquisitor, who consigns Jewish converts to the flames, shares his mistress with a Jew; the priests, meting out sentences including hanging and burning, debauch young girls and boys; and not one woman who is not, willingly or otherwise, prostituted. No, *Candide* is not even remotely a *representation* of the world. The elements of reality it contains are caricatured beyond measure. But here the *principle of disparity* intervenes once more: *Candide* produces meaning by virtue of being paired with the world—a pair that is willfully asymmetric, in which the fictive image, reduced and preposterous, forces us to see better the perverse seriousness, the rigidity, the evil weightiness, the dogmatic intolerance that humans accept as the necessary order of their existence.

246

JACK UNDANK

The Status of Fiction in Voltaire's *Contes*†

[*Candide* has been routinely described as a "philosophical fiction": Voltaire is a philosopher, so the argument runs, and he uses fiction to "sugar the pill," to wrap up his philosophical truths in an attractive fictional cloak. But what if the fictions themselves are the "message"? Or to put it another way, what if Voltaire is using the complexities of fiction to say something that simply cannot be said in any other way? Examining *Candide* alongside Voltaire's other tales, Jack Undank shows here that Voltaire's fictions are highly self-conscious constructs. These works call attention to their status as fictions, foreground the processes of narration, and perhaps even critique the idea that a fiction can encapsulate a straightforward truth. Undank calls these tales "visionary structures," which seem to offer a solution to problems by means of an escape into fantasy—*Candide* on two occasions declares that his life is a dream; but the fantasy is typically brought to an abrupt end that leaves readers wondering how to make sense of what has happened, as with the concluding chapter of *Candide*, which, Undank claims, is "violently yoked to the bruised body of the rest." Employing what are called here "ironies of disjunction." Voltaire in telling his tales challenges us to stand back from the narrative to think about the processes of tale-telling. In so doing, he finds a language and a structure that can communicate the intricacies and ambiguities of his thinking.—Nicholas Cronk]

What kind of dreaming is it that Plato managed to produce in visions like those of *The Republic* or *Timaeus*? His work is not all "rubbish" ("galimatias"), Voltaire reassures us; it contains "de très belles idées."[1] And one knows that Plato's "dream" in Voltaire's *Songe de Platon* is something of both: beautiful rubbish. A faintly Leibnizian and Popean explanation of the imperfect Creation, this dream was once, for Voltaire, beautiful; by 1756 it has become a damaged thing. Why is it worth repeating? Above and beyond its value to Voltaire as a structure for equivocation (justifying God and subverting this justification), it seems to suggest that a Platonic dream is not far different from a Voltairian one, that the equivocation to be found in the message is also present in the question Voltaire very guardedly raises about the efficacy and purpose of certain kinds of fiction—or "dreams"—not merely Plato's beautiful rubbish but his own. The fact that Plato uses an apologue, a cosmological fable, a deliberately archaic genre, ought not (though Voltaire encourages it) draw

† From *Degré second: Studies in French Literature* [Blacksburg, VA], vol. 6 (July 1982), pp. 65–88. Reprinted by permission of the author and the publisher.
1. *Essai sur les moeurs*, ed. R. Pomeau (Paris: Garnier, 1963), vol. 1, 94.

attention away from the way fiction here, as elsewhere in Voltaire's works, speaks of its own processes with mixed comfort and contempt.

Already as the *Songe* opens the narrator hedges every bet, and form begins to predict and imitate the uneasy condition of what will be the substance of Plato's "dream." Plato, he warns us, dreamed a lot, "et on n'a pas moins rêvé depuis."[2] Like Mambrès in *Le Taureau blanc*, he claims that dreams used to confer great reputations; in these enlightened days they no longer do. We're prepared not to believe a word of what Plato says. But all the same: "Voici un de ses songes qui n'est pas un des moins intéressants" (p. 473). The frame advises distance and discrimination; it also simultaneously produces an illusion of historicity or authenticity and so invites us to become absorbed. Irony suddenly flags, Voltaire disappears behind Plato's voice, and the dream begins. We have moved from the narrator to Plato to a dreamwork, which takes us, in turn, from the words and deeds of Démiourgos, the eternal Geometrician, to Démogorgon, who is directly responsible for the Creation. We slip not only from reflections on mind to the inner matter of those reflections; we seem to be advancing through a series of Chinese boxes or frames toward an inner sanctum in which truth is held and displayed. What in fact we pass through is a series of voices, each with its own authority—making it seem as if the "dreaming" mind were searching within its own substance, its dream (or fiction), for the simulacrum of truth and explanation. The recessive progression of the structure suggests a metaphor (would in fact be a metaphor, if we allowed that the plasticities of whole works could constitute one) that houses and also replicates several other metaphors: for thought turned probingly back upon itself; for a movement back in time; for a pursuit not merely of what is but of all causality and origins. Yet to any retrospection and "dreaming" there must be a stop. The path leading in and back also leads out, and as we leave Démogorgon, we again hear, in sequence, the voices of Démiourgos, Plato, and the narrator. The concluding sentence, however, is a nasty jibe by one of Plato's disciples, and it is also Voltaire's final comment, a kind of *coup de grâce* performed, as I've suggested, with a double-edged sword: "*Et puis vous vous réveillâtes*" (p. 475). The metaphor of a dream with which the narrator began is used to crush Plato's message but this time from within, issuing from a voice that finds its place in the narration itself. The disciple's words break the scheme of the narrative progression as I've traced it. The entire tale, which toys with formal symmetries—rhetorical, semantic, structural—abruptly collapses into a swift, unbalanced, unframed,

2. *Romans et contes*, ed. H. Bénac (Paris: Garnier, 1960), p. 473. Henceforth, references to the stories, all drawn from this edition, will appear parenthetically in the text.

italicized line. The narrator appears briefly before it to say, "Voilà ce que Platon enseignait à ses disciples" (p. 475). But his words cannot serve as a counterweight to his introductory remarks; and the story now protrudes briefly beyond what we had taken to be its frame. It is as if the disciple's lethally silencing "pointe" had to disrupt the carefully laid strata through which it surfaces, just as Plato's "awakening," or any intrusion upon an effort so strenuous, is necessarily rude and seems to violate what precedes it. It is the awesome contradictions of different fields of consciousness that Plato (and Voltaire and we) must now face—outside the story. The dream, having ventured several improbable solutions, subsides into its originative perplexity.

But this is to simplify the *Songe*. The fact is that remnants of the wakeful mind are already operative in Plato's dream. Even before the smart aleck student calls a spade a spade, a dream a dream, we get some sense of the critical threat that inheres in the troubled conscience of the dreamer dreaming, that is, telling his tale. As soon as Démogorgon reveals his world, a group of querulous genii question the form and purpose of the Creation that this dreamwork has constructed. Their protests in fact take up the largest portion of the text. Démigorgon betrays his own misgivings; and all these celestial beings are brought to heel only by the return of the Démiourgos himself and by his (as it turns out) not fully adequate explanation. If this is a dream, it is one that reaches vainly for its own subliminal, dialectical exegesis—and fails. As an imaginative fiction, it ends up describing the law of limits, limits not only of knowledge—one of the themes of the work—but of poetic and metaphorical supposition. As long as the restless dream lasts, it generates, in spite of its internal problems, at least the compelling satisfactions of invention and absorption. But the final pinprick, *Et puis vous vous réveillâtes*, rouses the dreamer and the reader to see in this art of storytelling a process of gestation comparable to the production of imperfect but self-sustaining worlds, or dreams, that partially subvert their own figurative supports and aims.

There would appear to be no need in the *Songe* or elsewhere in Voltaire's stories for the usual kind of narrative frame to score the ironic point, since negativity saturates the narration itself, most obviously through parody but also through many other casually embedded ironies of disjunction. These opening and closing frames, wherever they occur, speak eloquently and, at first glance, rather repetitiously, of what the stories make abundantly clear: that right reason and metaphysical understanding are incompatible with life as it is perceived or lived. But they also allow Voltaire to represent more overtly than elsewhere the complex and ambiguous moods he must have experienced while thinking—thinking while writing. The two are emphatically connected in more than the ordinary sense: like so much of the literature for and about salons and social life in the early century, Voltaire's stories promote the illusion of an oral, impromptu performance.[3] They digress, forget their direction or earlier intention, and end either abruptly or with the promise of a sequel; they exist, in short, as much if not more for the momentary pleasure of the segment than for the concerted harmony of the whole. Like all performances of this kind, they are spiritedly self-conscious, and, however modified, the sense of an audience and of a special milieu persists, affecting and often confounding sense and meaning.

A story like *Le Crocheteur borgne*, one of the earliest, which undisguisedly betrays its wayward impulses, gives us some notion of how Voltaire's mind dances with its thoughts and some idea of its characteristic rhythms. As it happens, something altogether typical occurs in the very first sentence: "Nos deux yeux ne rendent pas notre condition meilleure; l'un nous sert à voir les biens, et l'autre les maux de la vie" (p. 602). Two statements apparently joined in a symmetry of apposition turn out, on closer inspection, to have been forced together for the sake of rhetorical balance. The first clause invites the conclusion we find elsewhere in Voltaire that one had best not look at things around us, or at ourselves; the second takes flight on the notion of *two* eyes and, while pretending syntactically to modify the first, actually sets up a vague contradiction and produces still another binary structure. Once this self-impelling, self-adjusting two-step has begun, Voltaire succumbs as much to its playful beat as Mesrour, his protagonist, to alcohol. The opening paragraphs virtually sway with contrasting pairs of clauses, eyes, people, human conditions, etc.; and at the end of the first, the narrator exclaims that those people are fortunate who see only with the eye that perceives the good. Mesrour, he tells us, is an example. We expect to discover a character morally and psychologically blind to evil; but in fact the metaphor is used, quite literally, to put out an eye! And none of us, says the narrator, still playing with his polarities, is so blind that he will not see that Mesrour is one-eyed. Mesrour is so happy that, to express exactly how, Voltaire sets him up as a conventionally primitive "philosopher," an impoverished porter who lives not, as we would say, from hand to mouth, but from moment to moment, in a "jouissance du présent," untroubled, like the wealthy Epicurean

---

3. See Jacqueline Hellegouarc'h, "Genèse d'un conte de Voltaire," *SVEC*, 176 (1979), 7–36. I read this article after I had completed my own and was delighted to discover that she refers to "le halo onirique" of an impromptu composition. Mme Hellegouarc'h's "conte" is *Le crocheteur borgne*, and her analysis is superb; I do not however agree that "le *Crocheteur* est différent de tout ce qu'a écrit Voltaire" (p. 36), and it does not seem to me, as it does to her, that "la morale annoncée se trouve illustrée" (p. 31).

who serves as his real model, by thoughts of the future. Yet all of this, as Voltaire takes his next spin, is totally irrelevant. The story turns out to be not at all about a one-eyed man who can see no evil, and even less about the pleasures of living with bare but satisfied necessities. Poor Mesrour, we find, was maimed for no purpose at all—except the whimsical, antithetical, momentary *jouissance* of the writer. What really inspires Mesrour's bliss and saves him from evil is liquor, not philosophy, not a missing eye—even though, in an attempt to bring his performance to a matching, unifying close, Voltaire reminds us, pointlessly now, that Mesrour had no eye for evil.

Like Plato, Mesrour dreams; both are victims of their own and of Voltaire's imagination; and all three of them clarify or intensify desire in the process. The "present" of the dream, which complements the Epicurean, *occasional* present of Mesrour's happy life outside the dream, is also the intoxicating, occasional present of the narrator's dance—even as it leads Voltaire and the reader away from the ordinary logic of fiction. It is fiction, the making of it, that matters; and our narrator is willing, with typical *sprezzatura*, to acknowledge or to insist on his artlessness: "Mélinade (c'est le nom de la dame, que j'ai mes raisons pour ne pas dire jusqu'ici, parce qu'il n'était pas encore fait) avançait . . ." (p. 604). This is what we're asked to appreciate—less a coordinated, relentless philosophical argument disguised as fiction than a story celebrating its own quick inventiveness (while speaking, thematically, of the inventions of the imagination). What is "philosophical" in *Le Crocheteur* is banal and confused. The narrator's freedom momentarily to release his protagonist, the world—and himself—from disorder, and from thoughts of ugliness, poverty, and filth, is not. The frame returns at the end as Mesrour awakens and as the narrator faces his audience with a firmer (changed) grasp of the realities of Mesrour's wretched life—that is, with the need for closure and a final "pointe." The dream, the drunkenness of writing (or speaking) is over; there is no *sagesse* achieved, no connecting of the processes of mind with the ways of the world, only the miming of the two and of their disjunction.

Not all dreams are good ones, and, as I've suggested, consciousness and negativity usually engulf them. Even in the case of *Le Crocheteur*, the oriental narration sneers at itself. And, of course, not all of Voltaire's fictions are concerned with actual dreams. But where they are not, most of them evoke in one way or another the elements of the configuration I've been dealing with: an intransigent problem or situation that inspires a search; an illustrative fantasy (its form borrowed from a familiar genre or source—which serves both to isolate its discourse and to heighten its symbolic content); and a rude awakening. In this particular sequence—and not accidentally—one can find a grotesque version of Kenneth Burke's Purpose, Passion, and Perception, the X-rayed soul of Aristotelian "action." But this is not really as shocking as it appears. The reverse of tragedy is not comedy but burlesque or parody;[4] and it would not be wrong to find in Voltaire's stories the precise, dialectical extension of his theatre. In the stories, however, one has to contend with a shifting center of gravity, an identifiable murmur of consciousness that floats freely between narrators and protagonists, so that when the awakening or enlightening Perception occurs there is often a blurring of the distinction. Someone opens his eyes—literally or figuratively—and the fantasy together with its problems are abruptly erased in a formal closure that cannot pretend to resolve the issues raised. The closure itself often acknowledges this, thematizes its own impotence or misgivings, and frequently insists instead on the satisfactions of a debriefing—the movement not simply out of the dream or fantasy but away from thought itself and into the compensatory pleasures and urgencies of the *reader*'s world, which is precisely, when all is said and done, Voltaire's world as well. Human presence returns, and with it the realities, the lingering present of the salon, the site and inspiration of the dream performance and of Mesrour's "jouissance."

In *Le monde comme il va*, written at approximately the same time as *Le Crocheteur*, the confluence of narrator and protagonist is complete. Though it is subtitled "vision de Babouc, écrite par lui-même," its narrator, oddly enough, does not speak for himself but is spoken about. This is because he deliberately walks between first and third personhood, conveying the perfect emblem of a vision (or dream) now over but lingering as an object of thought. At the close of the tale, when the audience giggles to learn that the "lui-même" of the subtitle is Voltaire, it is overjoyed to discard what it now takes to be a mask and to hear itself praised. Babouc, commissioned by the celestial Ituriel to decide whether to exterminate Persépolis (Paris), eventually offers what is a not unusual conclusion to Voltaire's fantasies: a recapitulation, in conglomerated form, of the already evident— here, a symbolic statue composed of "tous les métaux, des terres et des pierres les plus précieuses et les plus viles" (p. 80). This is as much as "visions" can produce: a suspensive testimony, an eloquent but inert lump of pros and cons, the very same that provoked the vision to begin with. But Babouc does decide to let Persépolis stand. Why? Generations of readers have given what is actually Ituriel's interpretation of the statue: "si tout n'est pas bien, tout est passable" (p. 80). Babouc, his story-vision told, has other reasons,

---

4. See A. Kibédi Varga, "Le burlesque: le monde renversé selon la poétique classique," in *Image du monde renversé et ses représentations littéraires*, eds. J. Lafond and Al Redondo (Paris: J. Vrin, 1979), pp. 153–160.

only obliquely congruent with his dialectical narrative and its artistically frozen complement, the statue: he is happy ("de si bonne humeur"), physically, morally, not simply with opera, theatre, and delicious food, but—we have to suppose—with having to think no more. Unlike Jonah (the narrator's example), trapped in the dark intestine of his mind, Babouc-Voltaire opens his eyes to crystal and candlelight, a bright island of civilized, untroubled, and no doubt adoring company. Thought is a cloud passing over "la jouissance du présent"; it ends up celebrating not a solution, but its own artfulness and, ultimately, a *place*, which happens to be a place of origin as well as repose. Babouc-Voltaire, facing his audience, exorcized and smiling, manages to include that posture, as flattering as it is witty, in the message of his story.

We can recognize in these visionary structures a prefiguration of Voltaire's general manner, his style of argument and disengagement. Thought or imagination continually goes down, self-consciously and publicly, to defeat. What we are left with at the end of *Micromégas*, for example, is a book opening onto another book, the first, an imaginary voyage, the second, a book of whys and wherefores which is supposed to resolve the issues raised in the first. If only the Sirian who wrote the second and disappeared (as dreams disappear), leaving it as a legacy to the Académie des sciences, had been able to write something in it, we might be convinced that this "philosophical" fantasy could engender irrevocable and stable truths from within itself. But it can't. After the usual sparring of opposites, the familiar dance, all riddles and visions blank out; worse, they confirm their chronic anxiety and so encourage repetition, another search, another fantasy. Instead of a narrator explaining his book, we have one who cannot read it; and this incapacity is not weakness but truth. In *Zadig*, Jesrad is there, like Babouc's statue, symbolically to encapsulate the episodic action of the whole—and to provide his inadequate explanation. Immediately after Zadig's "Mais" and his submission, as it were, to fantasy, the rude awakening is not the protagonist's but the narrator's, at the protagonist's expense. The happy ending, like *Candide*'s, is violently yoked to the bruised body of the rest. So violently in fact that it cannot adhere and is not meant to. Both Zadig and Candide, after surviving the fantasticated, parodic yarns of their lives—Candide actually says, twice, that his life is a dream—the heaving to-and-fro of good and evil, are packed off to live in other moral climes. Neither Zadig nor Candide have any longer to be involved with the *Lebenswelt* of the initial fantasy. Life for both of them, as if its fever had subsided, is a matter of rational control, something firmly within their grasp and unlike what it had been heretofore: a thing assaulted from

within and without. It is hard to imagine Candide, in the heat of
sexual and occasionally metaphysical pursuit, wondering, as he
does in the end, what to do about boredom or vice; and harder still
to imagine that his garden, had it come into existence a few chapters sooner, would not have been trampled or seismically convulsed.[5]
The wakeful, disenchanted garden of *Candide* and Zadig's enchanted
Babylonian court are emphatically not solutions to the swirl of shifting problems that generate now one narrative move, now another.
Both tales come to rest in a domesticated and domesticable space.
Zadig's doesn't escape Voltaire's ironic sense of the inadequacy of
his ending; Candide's, which more closely approximates the sense
of the social space of the earliest tales, offers itself not as a solution
to the worst of all possible worlds but, once again, to the mind that
cannot read its own book—as an end to the search for answers. But
this end, as we know, is perpetually a beginning, just as surely as
nagging questions follow us into the most fertile or blissful of
gardens. The instabilities of these conclusions are not unlike the
instabilities of the swerving, evasive explorations within the stories.

If Voltaire's most remarkable accomplishment is the parodic harnessing of unseemly forms of fiction to provide an exact but hyperbolic metaphor for the forms of life; and if mimesis thereby becomes
an *impersonation* of an imitation, the projection of Voltaire's voice
through exotic figures and structures, then no rhetorical gesture
used to indicate a separation from his model can save him from
being partially or wholly caught within its premise. Having erected
the Byzantine world of *Candide* or the "Oriental" one of *Zadig*, how
can he resolve it "philosophically"? Can non-sense be recuperated
by sense? Every conclusion must come as a separation, a radical
escape from or denial of the vision (fiction) itself—at least in those
stories where resolutions exist. And there are further complications
having to do with where Voltaire locates truth or thinking—never
in the world but apart from it, in spite of it, an interruption in time
and a consequent benumbing, blinding expansion in space.[6] Lost
in the stars or in the abstractions of resolutely remote Reason, solutions, resolutions, and critical thought itself turn away from the
particularities and variousness of existence toward what is obvious chiefly to celestial travelers and "philosophers" alike: eternal,

---

5. This is to concur wholeheartedly with the work of Roy S. Wolper, especially with the
analysis of *Candide* in "Candide, Gull in the Garden?," *ECS*, 3 (Winter 1969), 265–277.
6. We have all been struck by two passages, one in *Zadig*, the other in *L'Ingénu*, both commonplaces of baroque contemplative literature, in which men, thinking *in extremis*,
experience a beatific exhilaration. Zadig gazes at the vast expanse of the heavens and
his misery disappears; his soul "s'élançait jusque dans l'infini, et contemplait, détachée
de ses sens, l'ordre immuable de l'univers" (p. 23). And Gordon and l'Ingénu, "par un
charme étrange," diminish their pain and the *noche oscura* of their ignorance by contemplating the great network of calamities spread throughout the universe (p. 251).

universal verities. Sub specie rationis, the world and its ways are—it
is a spatial, temporal, psychological, and moral corollary—repetitious.
And just as Voltaire's impersonations are predominantly episodic,
repetitions with variations, as one moves from story to story one
becomes aware of a hectic reprise of theme and motif. When boredom arrives suddenly on the scene, at the end or even at the dinners
of the wealthy, it sums up a condition not only of life but of a special
kind of fixed, rational attention to life. Thought, impotent because it
cannot stoop to conquer, anxious to create a distinction between
itself and the world—both characters and narrators repeatedly
insist on this disjunction—loses what Adorno refers to as its "field of
tension" and maintains instead a "safety zone" from which it can
ultimately only issue proclamations "relaxing the claim of ideas to
truth."[7] The result is that the stories project a final, master symmetry within which disconnection from life, from what is below the
mind, finds its mirror image in disconnection from what is above—
the answer to what is below. A fullness of reason, the scaffolding of
Voltaire's "mediate"[8] or satiric ironies, collapses into this avowal of
weakness and emptiness, contained but partially obscured within
his texts, in voices like Candide's, Plato's, Babouc's, or Zadig's or situated between the layers of story and irony or in the final, unexpected
warp of plot or frame. In the contest (rather than interaction) between
reason and the world, the world, paradoxically, proves "unreal," a
dream-fiction, an extravagant, violently attractive, often exotic
fantasy, and thought takes cognizance of its limits. It returns home,
to its *place*, its "Pénates"—or hidden, centering gods—as does Scarmentado, who invokes them when he too, obeying the dying, erratic
swerve of his author's will—a buried figure of the author's mind—
decides never to travel or search again.

With *Le blanc et le noir* and *Le taureau blanc*, life is once more,
respectively, a dream and an enchantment vainly striving to understand itself. Rustan's dream lives up to what has always been
expected of dreams: taken as a whole, it has a message that must be
deciphered. But inside the dream, the dreamer struggles, as he
moves from sequence to sequence, to interpret oneiric omens and
oracular pronouncements that intimate, as they structure themselves repetitiously into the familiar binary oppositions, that all
would be well if he could understand. The questions we're left with
after dreams end are here, as in Plato's fable, injected into the dream
itself—a kind of second degree of interrogation that makes the very
procedure of questioning a central theme. Only when he is dying

---

7. *Minima Moralia*, trans. E. F. N. Jephcott (London: NLB, 1978), p. 127.
8. See n. 1 on p. 258.

does Rustan have the paltry satisfaction of hearing, still within his
dream, and more clearly now, what he (and we) had already guessed:
that destiny is good and bad, white and black, and that God's ways
are mysterious. Though this message is hardly worth dying for, it
allows Rustan to wake up, abruptly and in a sweat, to the "real" world
around him and, more importantly perhaps, to the wonder of what
he—or rather Voltaire—has done. Wisely, Rustan-Voltaire chooses
less to think of the content of the dream than to be amazed that so
much has been compacted into the single hour of its duration. What
in fact Rustan discovers is what Babouc had already found in his
statue and what Amazan (of *La Princesse de Babylone*) will find
reason to admire in an English map containing "l'univers en rac-
courci" (p. 386)—the miraculous astringencies of symbolic form,
their capacity, as Rustan experiences them, to abbreviate an entire
life of desire even to the moment of death. But just as Babouc's
statue sums up his mission and neither answers nor explains the
gods, providing only a denser semiosis of his "vision," so Rustan's
restless dream, for all his delight at its remarkable brevity, is oddly
cyclical and redundant, issuing finally not in a responsive wakeful-
ness but in this fascination with the act of telling. And as if further
to contract what has already been suggested about the contractive
power of discourse, a parrot, planted in the very last line of the tale,
parts its beak, ready to divulge the entire secret of Time and—since
it was born before the Flood—History. Again the whiteness of the
page, which neither Rustan, Voltaire, the Academy of Sciences, nor
celestial travelers can read. The final reduction or message would
have been, we're told, simple, unrhetorical, and unself-conscious
(p. 128), that is, unlike Rustan's dream or Voltaire's stories, neo-
classical in spirit—if that were possible (which it is not) *within*
those stories or the texts they imitate. (The parrot sounds suspi-
ciously like Gresset's Ver-Vert.) Voltaire's impersonations of the ways
of the world long to shed their stylized language, to dissolve
beneath a bright gleam of truth, making expendable the kinds of
signs and portents that control Rustan. Instead that radiance turns
out to be an unutterable blankness, an open beak. It is not that the
truth does not exist; it neglects to come.

If we could disenchant the world, that is to say, our thoughts, our
language, there might be an end to "dreaming." Every voice would
speak like the parrot, without wit and no doubt without metaphor;
and there would be no such thing as the unverisimilar or the inde-
corous, no kingdom, in short, like the one described in *Le Taureau
blanc*. Making their way through the messiness, the sheer density
of this setting, the lists of creatures, smells, sounds, foods, most of it
deliberately cacophonous, the characters suffer from the confusions
and frustrations of the world. At the center of this enchantment,

overwhelmed by it but also, paradoxically, responsible for it, are the linked energies of desire and curiosity (Amaside), reason (Mambrès), and narration itself (the serpent). The story, which probably began with the intention of constructing itself into a Biblical satire, ends up by appropriating fairy tales and Greek romances and by continually drawing its author's consciousness into its web. It is not only, as critics have said, that the images of Mambrès and the serpent are, in part, self-portraits of Voltaire, but that Voltaire devises a way of speaking about himself and his reader in the specular scene of the serpent telling his tales to the Princess Amaside. Her response has become famous: she's bored and yearns for a story "fondé sur la vraisemblance" (p. 594): "Je veux . . . qu'il ne ressemble pas toujours à un rêve" (p. 594). She is of course entangled in a "dream" as unbelievable as the stories she's heard; and when the serpent aims for something more seemly or rational, a parable of jaded prophets, she misses the point and couldn't be less interested. What is a serpent to do? Amaside's (the reader's) needs, her unflagging attention to the bull, eroticize Voltaire's (the serpent's) fictions; her need for consolation in view of the interminable postponement of love provokes the kind of imitation, fantastic and digressive, that corresponds to her predicament. She is no happier with the serpent than she is with the life Voltaire has meted out to her. What she actually longs for are lies—the magical clarification and dematerialization of world and body so that when Mambrès asks the serpent to tell her tales, he adds, knowingly, that "ce n'est que par des contes qu'on réussit dans le monde" (p. 592)—"contes," stories; "contes," lies.

The verisimilar story exists, like the parrot's explanation, as an hypothesis, wrapped in abstraction, that fails to find real or verbal substance. Where could it find these things—given the contravening vision that ties Amaside and the others into an inescapable, intertextual knot? The hope for verisimilitude, which Mambrès also shares—seeing, as he puts it, "une foule d'incompatibilités que je ne puis concilier," and unable to find reasonable explanation for what has happened to him and for history in general—is ultimately, at its furthest reaches, a hope for a vast negation of the very conditions of existence, not simply of the metaphors that describe them but of the laws and procedures of nature itself: the foul proliferation of a flawed creation and of the violent predators that inhabit it. The wheels within wheels of time, as they are described in *Le blanc et le noir*, are drawn here into Voltaire's vision along with the syncretisms of the *Notebooks* and the histories: all the serpents and white bulls of myth and fable, characters from different books, times, and places. They converge to provide some sense of the mind's perennially irrational and reiterative response to the nature of things. This static flow, these recurring symbols also speak of the consoling and reductive power of abstraction, language, fiction, and "dreams," their capacity to arrest proliferation and to draw time, event, and human presence or belief into the harness of symmetrized values: white, black, or any of the other terms of Voltaire's favorite dualities. But in the last analysis, the exercise is useless. Mambrès-Voltaire wanders about like Quijote in the Cave of Montesinos, a magician sunk in a conflated, magical world he himself sustains, waiting for the final disenchantment. Yes, the white bull becomes a king, but his very metamorphosis and the entire ending—the feast, the abrupt and ironic enumeration of what happens to each of the characters—cannot and is not meant to dispel, any more than the voice of Démiourgos, the problems raised earlier.

Are there fictions of another kind, wakeful, rational, verisimilar, that might please the Princess—and Voltaire? She tries contemporary novels and stories, including some by Crébillon fils, Hamilton, and the Chevalier de Mouhy; like Formosante, that other Princess, she finds them inadequate and irrelevant. If life is, upon reflection, like a driving, preposterous fiction, authors and characters alike will have to tread their crooked way through plots that seem to pile up whimsically but insist, as if by reaction, on concatenations, flash-backs, and previews of things to come. The purpose of shunting between past and future is not, as in Heliodorus or Gomberville, to create suspense or to settle matters into a reassuring order; it is to call attention both to the blight of most temporal progressions, whether forward or back, and to underscore what other, so-called verisimilar fictions deliberately omit. In order, for example, to rouse the one-eyed porter from his sleep, Voltaire invents a typically elaborate arabesque of causes: an irreligious servant woman, whose master, too lazy to make the trip, has holy water delivered from the mosque, dumps the used water unknowingly on the porter's head. Explanations like these, even as far back as *Le Crocheteur*, offer virtuoso occasions for satire, but what they have more profoundly in common is their insistence on the base, physical events that force life forward, events that histories, tragedies, and ordinary novels tastefully pare away. And if I choose this one incident from among hundreds, it is in order to suggest as well that all origins for Voltaire are vile, including those two paradigms of origin, the Creation and human birth. In the accidental, watery drama of the porter, in the notion of being flushed into awareness or life with tainted water, even, I think, in the witless female intercession that brings it about, there is already, at this early stage, a striking emblem of Voltaire's permanent and ever more aggravated and metaphysical disgust with all bodily functions but especially procreation—or with what amounts to the same: things slipping into or surfacing in the hidden crevasses of the body, life, or art. What Wolfgang Iser refers to as "blanks" or "places of indeterminacy" and Seymour Chatman nicely calls the *unbestimmt*, necessary "gaps common to all narrative"[9]—among which one must include secondary or unutterably offensive moments in the verisimilar, "historic," or classical novel as it moves from one "significant" event or passion to another—become *primary* sources of interest, awe, and significance in Voltaire's stories. A provocative mass of *intermediate* detail spreads into what were heretofore silent intervals, as "uselessly hidden" as that "stinking membrane" in which we all lay at the moment of birth, "entre de l'urine et des excréments"—according to Sidrac in *Les Oreilles du comte de Chesterfield* (p. 556). It is in these glamorless "gaps" that most of Voltaire's narratives vengefully and self-consciously expand, so much so that all the rest is made to seem both a cause and an effect, a series of hinges connected not to larger, solid planks but to one another. And, as if to make amends for this loose suspension of material, Voltaire most frequently provides a firm armature of simple but overarching necessities, legacies of the past and inescapable commands from the future. Rustan, Cosi-Sancta, and Formosante obey oracles; others, like Adate, witness omens or, like Shastasid and Memnon, have presentiments or providential visions. These unverisimilar underpinnings, together with the episodes that prove their strength, are as fanciful as Plato's "dream" explanation of the Creation—and as lawlessly lawful as all creations metaphorically constituted to resemble it. Voltaire discovers in this simulacrum of writing represented by the urgencies of impromptu composition and in the voices and genres that display them best a proximity to the divine "dream" and a distance from it that is an endless source of pleasure and revulsion.

Oddly enough, the true antidote for unverisimilar fantasies and abstractions based on negation is not the "real" world or verisimilar truths, from which they violently extract their symbols, but utopia. This helps explain why Voltaire has such difficulty articulating an anironic[1] ideal *within* the action or flow of the story, why he has to force the ironic eruption of utopian islands: theatre and dinner parties that keep life at bay, Eldorados, prisons (*L'Ingénu*), private

---

9. *The Act of Reading* (Baltimore: Johns Hopkins University Press, 1978), ch. 8; *Story and Discourse* (Ithaca: Cornell University Press, 1978), p. 30.

1. Distinctions between different forms of irony are brilliantly elucidated by Alan Wilde (*Horizons of Assent* [Baltimore: Johns Hopkins University Press, 1981]), dealing principally with fiction of this century. The terms "mediate" and "anironic" are his. For Wilde, irony is not merely rhetorical form but a vision of things, and dwelling within this vision there is a pulsing desire or countervision: the anironic—which shapes the ironic and is shaped by it. Voltaire's utopian hopes become, in this good light, the product of a universe marred by ironic disjunctions and by his narrators' separation (another disjunction) from it.

chambers (*Les Oreilles*), and even the precincts of the contemplative mind (*Zadig, L'Ingénu*). In a sense, as we know, these are all moments of thought essaying or celebrating its detached powers, powers often evident in the narrator's voice from the start, but pausing at these times to take stock of themselves. They are ultimately dedicated to discovering their utopian separation from the real, so that as the mind contemplates itself or its relationship to the world it senses its impotence and sequestration. *Et puis vous vous réveillâtes.*

But chronology does matter in Voltaire's fiction after all, and if we watch the progress of these privileged moments, we may be able to detect something else: a compensatory, growing desire for connection and communication. The suggestion is again and again that though the "dream" of explanation or resolution may be defeated and though the world may remain as fantastic as fiction, speech softens the blow and establishes a ground for civility and constancy. More than this, language defines our intellectual grasp and locates or even produces a community of intelligence. Like many of his contemporaries, Voltaire is awed by the very fact of discourse, its origins and abuse, and he too is involved in the ongoing Cartesian search for a stable, diaphanous language.[2] But there is more at stake in the fictions of the sixties and seventies—and here again Voltaire's case is only the most spectacular, largely because he lived long enough to have been able to allow submerged impulses to play themselves out in times that legitimated them. In fact what Voltaire's work helps make plain are the desperate reasons for a vast cultural shift of sensibility. Once concerned with frustrations of connection and understanding, the stories begin to highlight successful acts of persuasion and even, in the case of *Histoire de Jenni*, display them theatrically, boxing them off like showcase abditories, exemplary specimens within the fiction. Yet nobody now is convinced by argument alone. Ordinary discourse and positive knowledge, always shaky at best, surrender in the end to a semiotics of "charm" and authoritative presence.

Amid the narrative and epistemological uncertainties of *Micromégas*, three beings—the Sirian, the Saturnian, and the narrator—manage to converse, using the same linguistic categories, in spite of enormous facultative differences. Just as the narrator's voice remains strangely unanchored, of this world but somehow outside of it, neither puzzled nor vexed by its situation, so the celestial creatures are content only when conversing, outside their planetary sphere, away from slander and the treacheries of women, voices merely affixed to or rather limited by bodies, shadows of beings,

2. See Maureen O'Harra, "*Le Taureau blanc* and the activity of language," *SVEC*, 148 (1976), 117–118.

neither living nor touching down. This projection of a commanding voice flows naturally from Voltaire's search for a "disinterested" one many years earlier, in the *Traité de métaphysique*, a voice "hors de [la] sphère [de l'homme]" and sounding from a body "n'ayant point la forme humaine."[3] But it is only in the stories that the full implications of this willing sacrifice—if it is that—can be drawn. Memnon had already been visited by a "bon génie" whose happiness depended on the fact that he had no body like ours, required no sex, money, or food; and the angel Jesrad, who drew people to him "par un charme invincible" and "une éloquence si vive et si touchante," was, of course, a hermit. Holy or angelic, supernal blessings grant a release from the confining attachments and identities of the flesh and, correlatively, an overpowering eloquence. As with Reason in the *Eloge de la raison*, incarnation can be achieved only with great difficulty and never permanently. In fact the mind appears to drain and absorb the body's potency and to replicate the body's separation from itself in its separation from the world. At the furthest end—or at the source?—of what might be called celestial envy is the desire to dematerialize, to take positions behind a mask, speaking by way of ventriloquism[4] or impersonation, writing within a thicket of given tones and turns.

This is, more than a matter of camouflage, a quest for voice as powerful and efficacious as the jaws that in the stories increasingly and emblematically tear at animal flesh—flesh of tender birds particularly, flesh of women. The strength of this voice is assured, paradoxically, by its compensatory displacement of sexual teeth, or it is inspired by the felt absence of those teeth. Mambrès, who is literally castrated, bears the thematized burden of an accumulated fear of the slicings and maimings perpetrated or threatened throughout the stories. He is, as Voltaire notably said of himself, "une ombre," longing for the lost, restorative power of language. Chesterfield, whose ears are drying up and so precipitate the communicative failure that causes Goudman's misfortune, presides over a story haunted by death and blockage (kidney stones and constipation) and celebrating the untrammeled, asexual exchange between men. Communication (or the lack of it) had always been a rather hidden theme in the stories, but in the sixties and seventies it swells into a major preoccupation among primary figures. Martin talks with Candide; there's no agreement, "Mais enfin ils parlaient, ils se communiquaient des

---

3. Ed. H. Temple Patterson (Manchester: University of Manchester Press, 2nd ed., 1957), p. 2; see also p. 31.
4. See Julia L. Epstein, "Voltaire's ventriloquism: voices in the first *Lettre philosophique*," *SVEC*, 182 (1979), 219–235. I prefer the notion of impersonation only because it implies the *assumption* of a voice, a partial merger with the object imitated, a reciprocity of influence.

idées, ils se consolaient" (p. 188). Gordon and the Huron not only console, they "convert" each other: it is the central scene and turning point of *L'Ingénu*. After this it hardly matters that Mlle de St. Yves dies. Exchanges and conversions ricochet to the end in ways that grow less convincing, like the exhausted outer circles of a splash fully willed and believed in. Voltaire still pushes against resistant grain. The two rival princesses, Formosante and Aldée, unexpectedly thrown together in a distant land, "mirent dans leur entrevue un charme qui leur fit oublier qu'elles ne s'étaient jamais aimées" (p. 375). Sidrac invites Goudman to a dinner where, as he puts it, two "thinking faculties" will have the pleasure of signifying by means of language—"ce qui est une chose merveilleuse que les hommes n'admirent pas assez" (p. 554). And when they agree on an epistemological and linguistic matter that men have argued about for centuries, Goudman exclaims: "Et j'admire que nous soyons d'accord" (p. 555). In spite of the rather flimsy reason for this instantaneous agreement—the fact that both are "de bonne foi"—nothing can detract from the characters' and Voltaire's joy.

What has to be attended to in all these works is the way difficult problems and differences of many kinds are overcome in a gesture that turns away from earlier impasses. Thought, which once dwelt on irreconcilables, faced the enemy, attacked, and darted away, now, though still locked within small areas and moments of exchange, concentrates as much if not more on its mediative role—its function in the strictly human and interpersonal equation, its process of dissemination—than on content and truth. The purposes of union and consolation now win over the disjunctions of falsehood or vanity and the misapprehensions and misconceptions of language. Voltaire had prepared us for this triumph of an inescapable and conciliatory presence with characters from the "marchand de magnificences inutiles" and "l'homme judicieux" of *Le monde comme il va* to "le bon et respectable sage" in *Candide* and Pythagore in *Aventure indienne*, all of whom bring down to earth, in virile, lapidary speech, a wisdom as irresistible as the Word. But in the last decade of his fictions, these characters are lovingly and ever more amply tended. M. André, "l'homme aux quarante écus," like Sidrac, uses supper as his bait, but he hardly needs Sidrac's special learning or his powers of argument: "l'autorité qu'il se concilie n'est due qu'à ses grâces, à sa modération, et à une physionomie ronde qui est tout à fait persuasive" (p. 334). And finally, in what is fittingly one of the last of the stories, Freind, whose very name tells us what means even more than knowledge, is repeatedly described as "respectable," "vénérable," "grave," "calme comme l'air d'un beau jour," "sage et charitable," "tolérant." When he speaks, he's heard in silence; nobody dares interrupt: "Hear him, hear him," they cry (p. 509). The natives of the Blue Mountains learn that Penn was his ancestor, and they feel immediate respect. In a single conversation, he wins them over: "c'était Orphée qui apprivoisait les tigres" (p. 520). Orpheus serves as a perfect metaphor: there is little need for language at all—and, incidentally, women whose names suggest nothing more than gashes and mounds, Boca Vermeja and Las Nalgas, are squarely routed to make way for the less exigent Miss Primrose. Freind refuses to lecture his son ("les exemples corrigent" [p. 571]) and, at times, to answer Birton head on. No matter. His long discussion with the atheist is surrounded by the breathless approbation of the Parouba family, Jenni, and the narrator himself, all exemplary readers in the text, inciting us to agree. The civilized and the uncivilized capitulate; narrative time hangs suspended as it had for Gordon and the Huron. The model is ecstatic, and in this prescriptive, self-congratulatory, and sentimental mood, truth comes as a quasi-divine, patriarchal revelation. It so saturates will and flesh (whatever remains of it) that, in the manner of Karl Jaspers' "paradigmatic philosophers," philosophy becomes a state of being, seizing its witnesses, forcing them sweetly and willingly to bend. Birton falls to his knees; he no longer thinks, he believes: "Oui . . . je crois en Dieu et en vous" (p. 548), he calls out to Freind. Nothing need rouse Freind from *his* "dream." He is the dream, the magical solution to whatever resists explanation—or quite simply to whoever resists.

Toward the end of his career, utopian moments—gaps within the gaps I mentioned earlier—overwhelm Voltaire's landscape. Slowly, not fictional models but outrageously fantastic forms of fiction disappear and with them, ostensibly,[5] Voltaire's habitually subversive and perplexed accompaniment. His final stories spell out the victory of will and desire over the unverisimilar world. These shroud themselves in a "discours ferme et serré" (p. 508), the language and sign of stoic authority, marmoreal but tender, no longer persuading in the old way (perhaps weary of it) or "invoking" laws and testimonies, but providing them, insisting on them: "il les attestait, il les citait, il les réclamait" (p. 508). Truth descends through charmed and perfected vessels, and oracles—or Démiourgos' final words—are no longer quite so ridiculous as once they seemed. In the end, speaking or writing in order to think, "dream," exorcize, and survive matters less than the power, evident, like so much else, in even the earliest stories, to create a spiritual home for the speaker, a theatrical climate of worship and accord within which his voice can at last gain the strength to govern.

---

5. Actually, it could be argued, he continues to cast doubt on the efficacy of thought and language even as he appears to be disenchanting the world. Is the world disenchanted or merely transformed into an endearing theatrical fiction?

Bibliography

The best modern biography of Voltaire is Roger Pearson's *Voltaire Almighty: A Life in the Pursuit of Freedom* (London, Bloomsbury, 2005). On Voltaire more generally, *The Cambridge Companion to Voltaire*, ed. Nicholas Cronk (Cambridge University Press, 2009), provides an overview of modern readings of his works. On the historical, philosophical and cultural background, see W. H. Barber, *Leibniz in France from Arnauld to Voltaire: A Study in the French Reactions to Leibnizianism, 1670–1770* (Oxford, Clarendon Press, 1955); Daniel Roche, *France in the Enlightenment*, trans. Arthur Goldhammer (Harvard University Press, 1998); Steven Nadler, *The Best of All Possible Worlds: A Story of Philosophers, God, and Evil in the Age of Reason* (Farrar, Straus & Giroux, 2008); and Anthony Pagden, *The Enlightenment and Why It Still Matters* (Oxford University Press, 2013); and John Robertson, *The Enlightenment: A Very Short Introduction* (Oxford University Press, 2015).

Readers may also like to sample one of the early English translations: Eric Palmer's edition of *Candide* (Broadview, Peterborough, ON, 2009) uses the translation published by John Nourse in London in 1759, *Candide, or All for the Best*. Readers who would like to read other tales by Voltaire should look at *Candide and Other Stories*, translated by Roger Pearson (Oxford University Press, 1990; new edition, 2006). There is a fascinating online exhibition "Voltaire's Candide" (2010) on the New York Public Library's website (candide.nypl.org).

Readers with knowledge of French should download the free iOS app "Candide, l'édition enrichie," a joint production of the Bibliothèque nationale de France and the Voltaire Foundation in Oxford. This contains the full text in French, with a range of annotations and other resources to provide context, and it allows you to listen to the text, read by the French actor Denis Podalydès. A recent collection of essays on *Candide*, showing a wide range of approaches, is *Les 250 ans de Candide: Lectures et relectures*, ed. Nicholas Cronk and Nathalie Ferrand (Louvain, Peeters, 2013), which contains an extensive bibliography of works in French.

The following books and articles in English will provide further angles of approach to the study of *Candide*:

Barber, W. H. *Voltaire: Candide*. London: Arnold, 1960 [excerpted in this Norton Critical Edition].

Bellhouse, Mary L. "Candide Shoots the Monkey Lovers: Representing Black Men in Eighteenth-Century French Visual Culture." *Political Theory* 34 (2006): 741–84.

Betts, C. J. "On the Beginning and Ending of *Candide*." *Modern Language Review* 80 (1985): 283–92.

———. "Exploring Narrative Structures in *Candide*." *Studies on Voltaire and the Eighteenth Century* 314 (1993): 1–131.

Bottiglia, William F. *Voltaire's Candide: Analysis of a Classic*. 2nd ed. *Studies on Voltaire and the Eighteenth Century*, 7A (1964).

Brady, Patrick. "Is *Candide* Really 'Rococo'?" *Esprit créateur* 7 (1967): 234–42.

Braun, Theodore E. D., Felicia Sturzer, and Martine Darmon Meyer. "Teaching *Candide*—A Debate." *The French Review* 61 (1988): 569–77.

Cronk, Nicholas. "Voltaire, Bakhtin, and the Language of Carnival." *French Studies Bulletin* 18 (1986): 4–7.

———. "Voltaire's *Candide*: Lessons of Enlightenment and the Search for Truth." *A History of Modern French Literature*. Ed. Christopher Prendergast. Princeton, NJ: Princeton University Press, 2017.

Dahany, Michael. "The Nature of Narrative Forms in *Candide*." *Studies on Voltaire and the Eighteenth Century* 114 (1973): 113–40.

Dalnekoff, Donna Isaacs. "The Meaning of Eldorado: Utopia and Satire in *Candide*." *Studies on Voltaire and the Eighteenth Century* 123 (1974): 41–59.

Dawson, Deidre. "In Search of the Real Pangloss: The Correspondence of Voltaire with the Duchess of Saxe-Gotha." *Yale French Studies* 71 (1986): 93–112.

Feder, Helena. "The Critical Relevance of the Critique of Rationalism: Postmodernism, Ecofeminism and Voltaire's *Candide*." *Women Studies* 31 (2002): 199–219.

Fletcher, D. "*Candide* and the Theme of the Happy Husbandman." *Studies on Voltaire and the Eighteenth Century* 161 (1976): 137–47.

Francis, R. A. "Prévost's *Cleveland* and Voltaire's *Candide*." *Studies on Voltaire and the Eighteenth Century* 208 (1982): 295–303.

Grobe, Edwin P. "Aspectual Parody in Voltaire's *Candide*." *Symposium* 2 (1967): 38–49.

Henry, Patrick. "The Metaphysical Puppets of *Candide*." *Romance Notes* 17 (1976): 166–69.

———. "Sacred and Profane Gardens in *Candide*." *Studies on Voltaire and the Eighteenth Century* 176 (1979): 133–52.

Howells, Robin. *Disabled Powers: A Reading of Voltaire's Contes*. Amsterdam: Rodopi, 1993. Chapter 4, "Candide as Carnival," 81–95.

Klute, Susan. "The Admirable Cunégonde." *Eighteenth-Century Women* 2 (2002): 95–108.

Langdon, David. "On the Meanings of the Conclusion of *Candide*." *Studies on Voltaire and the Eighteenth Century* 238 (1985): 397–432.

Langille, E. M. "La Place, Monbron, and the Origins of *Candide*." *French Studies* 66 (2012): 12–25

———. "*Le Roi des Bulgares*: Was Voltaire's Satire on Frederick the Great Just Too Opaque?" *An American Voltaire: Essays in Memory of J. Patrick Lee*. Ed. E. Joe Johnson and Byron R. Wells. Newcastle-upon-Tyne, UK: Cambridge Scholars Publishing, 2009. 240–52.

Leigh, Ralph. "From the *Inégalité* to *Candide*: Notes on a Desultory Dialogue between Rousseau and Voltaire (1755–1759)." *The Age of the Enlightenment: Studies Presented to Theodore Besterman*. Ed. W. H. Barber et al. Edinburgh: Oliver & Boyd, 1967. 66–92.

Mason, Haydn. *Candide: Optimism Demolished*. New York: Twayne, 1992.

Morrison, Ian R. "Leonardo Sciascia's *Candido* and Voltaire's *Candide*." *Modern Language Review* 97 (2002): 59–71.

Murray, Geoffrey. *Voltaire's Candide: The Protean Gardener, 1755–1762*. Geneva: Institut et Musée Voltaire, 1970. *Studies on Voltaire and the Eighteenth Century* 69.

Pearson, Roger. *The Fables of Reason: A Study of Voltaire's Contes Philosophiques*. Oxford: Oxford University Press, 1993. See in particular Chapter 8, "The Candid *Conte*: *Candide ou l'optimisme*," 110–36.

Racevskis, Karlis. "Candide's Garden Revisited, Again: The Post-Modern View of the Enlightenment." *Studies on Voltaire and the Eighteenth Century* 303 (1992): 307–10.

Scherr, Arthur. "Candide's Garden Revisited: Gender Equality in a Commoner's Paradise." *Eighteenth Century Life* 17.3 (November 1993): 40–59.

————. "*Candide*'s Pangloss: Voltaire's tragicomic hero." *Romance Notes* 47 (2006): 87–96.

Sherman, Carol. *Reading Voltaire's Contes: A Semiotics of Philosophical Narration*. Chapel Hill: North Carolina Studies in the Romance Languages and Literatures, 1985. Chapter 3, "*Candide*," 139–206.

Suderman, Elmer F. "*Candide, Rasselas* and Optimism." *Iowa English Yearbook* 11 (Fall 1966): 37–43.

Temmer, Mark J. "*Candide* and *Rasselas* Revisited." *Revue de littérature comparée* 56 (1982): 177–93.

Thacker, Christopher. "Son of *Candide*." *Studies on Voltaire and the Eighteenth Century* 58 (1967): 1515–30.

Tucker, Peter. *The Interpretation of a Classic. The Illustrated Editions of Candide*. Introduction by Giles Barber. Oxford, UK: The Previous Parrot Press, 1993.

Vilain, Robert. "Images of Optimism? German Illustrated Editions of Voltaire's *Candide* in the Context of the First World War." *Oxford German Studies* 37 (2008): 223–52.

Wade, Ira O. *Voltaire and Candide: A Study in the Fusion of History, Art and Philosophy*. Princeton, NJ: Princeton University Press, 1959.

Waldinger, Renée. ed. *Approaches to Teaching Voltaire's Candide*. New York: Modern Language Association of America, 1987.

Williams, David. *Voltaire: Candide*. London: Grant & Cutler, 1997.

Wolper, Roy S. "Candide, Gull in the Garden?" *Eighteenth-Century Studies* 3 (1969): 265–77. For the debate provoked by this article, see Lester G. Crocker, "Professor Wolper's Interpretation of *Candide*," and Roy S. Wolper, "Reply to Lester Crocker," *Eighteenth-Century Studies* 5 (1971): 145–56.

Wootton, David. "Unhappy Voltaire, or 'I shall never get over it as long as I live'." *History Workshop Journal* 50 (2000): 137–55.

Zagona, Helen G. *Flaubert's "Roman Philosophique" and the Voltairian Heritage*. Lanham, MD: University Press of America, 1985.